"A delicious dip into the shimmering dark urban underworld that, decades ago, Dashiell Hammett and Raymond Chandler mined to such great effect." —Amy Reiter, *Salon*

"Dazzling and densely plotted . . . Grand is a wizard at twisting a large cast into greater and greater knots. . . . *The Disappearing Body* will keep readers guessing until its last page."
—*The Boston Globe*

"A deeply ambitious, witty, disquieting reinvention of the noir thriller." —*Esquire*

"A circuitous noir takes on a corrupt post–Prohibition America where heroin takes the edge off and corpses up and vanish."
—*Details*

"Cleverly renovates a genre that has come to represent the sharpest, most anxious expression of American malaise."
—*The Village Voice*

"Grand . . . keep[s] us hooked with his zesty, over-the-top period prose . . . and lively array of mysteriously mutually involved suspicious characters. [The] brilliant plot is too . . . well, grand to give away. . . . Treat yourself to this one." —*Kirkus Reviews* (starred)

"Intricate . . . At the end of every loose string in *The Disappearing Body* is a delicious lesson in revenge or deceit."
—*The Portland Oregonian*

"A riveting story of urban corruption, scorching revenge and redemption." —Dylan Foley, *Milwaukee Journal Sentinel*

"A tough, raw, nerve-jangling adventure into the alternate underbelly of 1930s New York City. This isn't Martin Scorsese's New York; it's more like Weegee's. . . . A wild spectrum masterpiece." —*Ain't It Cool News*

"Intriguing, well-written . . . A great read if you like mysteries, mobsters and surprise twists." —*Hippo Press*

"Satirical noir at its mesmerizing best." —*Bookforum*

"At once an ambitious mystery, a political thriller and grotesquerie . . . Highly recommended." —*Publishers Weekly*

"David Grand is a stealth operator, a magician-architect in prose, building elegant, mysterious structures and then ducking through the astonished crowd as if he were not the one responsible. His surfaces are seamless, cool, and eerily funny, covering a Kafkaesque sadness underneath."
—Jonathan Lethem, author of *Motherless Brooklyn*

"Reading *The Disappearing Body* is a bit like watching a shootout between David Grand and the film noir thrillers of the thirties. In the end, only literature is left standing."
—Dale Peck, author of *Now It's Time to Say Goodbye*

"A brilliant and gripping portrayal of the colliding lives of scammers, schemers and dreamers in a city not unlike your own at a time when the fight for the soul of America was still raging. Grand writes like a demon."
—Thomas Kelly, author of *Payback* and *The Rackets*

"David Grand has made something new of noir here. *The Disappearing Body* is dark, antic, intricate, a novel of tough wit and brave poignancy, a moving meditation on the psychic burdens of corruption, war and loneliness. Plus it's got gangsters, molls, and dirty cops, which is more than you can say for most moving meditations."

—Sam Lipsyte, author of *Venus Drive* and *The Subject Steve*

"*The Disappearing Body* is an ambitious and entirely original novel with a labyrinthine narrative and a sweeping cast of characters; its beauty lies in its clear and clean prose that makes you feel as though you are hovering over the shoulders of the characters and at the same time watching them from above."

—Galaxy Craze, author of *By the Shore*

"*The Disappearing Body* channels the spirits of Dashiell Hammett and Nathanael West to create a 1930s American metropolis so atmospherically convincing that David Grand seems an old master using a young writer's word processor. But Grand is up to something all his own here; his work feels utterly contemporary and classic at once."

—Darin Strauss, author of *Chang & Eng*

"David Grand is a smart young writer blessed with a wild imagination, a rich, dark sense of humor, and an abundance of talent."

—Jessica Hagedorn, author of *Dogeaters* and *The Gangster of Love*

The Disappearing Body

ALSO BY DAVID GRAND

Louse

THE *Disappearing* BODY

A NOVEL

David Grand

A HARVEST BOOK · HARCOURT, INC.
ORLANDO AUSTIN NEW YORK SAN DIEGO TORONTO LONDON

www.HarcourtBooks.com

First published by Nan A. Talese, an imprint of Doubleday, a division of Random House

Library of Congress Cataloging-in-Publication Data
Grand, David, 1968–
The disappearing body: a novel/David Grand.
p. cm.
ISBN 0-15-602719-4
1. Drug traffic—Fiction. 2. Heroin habit—Fiction.
3. Anti-communist movements—Fiction. I. Title.
PS3557.R247D5 2003
813'.54—dc21 2003041721

Text set in Bulmer MT
Book design by Jennifer Ann Daddio
Title page illustration by Judy Lanfredi

Printed in the United States of America
First Harvest edition 2003

A C E G I K J H F D B

For Christine,

Sasha, and Nathanael

If a man is destined to drown
he will drown in a spoonful of water.

The Players

Victor Ribe—Ex-con, released after fifteen years of a 25-year prison term

Freddy Stillman—Munitions dispatcher at Fief Munitions

Evelyn—Freddy Stillman's ex-wife

Harry Shortz—Narcotics Bureau Commissioner, senatorial candidate, former WWI counterintelligence operative

Edward Kelly—Former state treasurer, Harry Shortz's father-in-law

Beverly Shortz—Harry Shortz's wife, Edward Kelly's daughter

Ira Dubrov and Pally Collins—Shortz's most trusted sergeants

Maurice Klempt—Shortz's lieutenant, murdered

Boris Lardner—Crooked pharmacist, murdered

Sidney Lardner—Boris's brother

Gloria Lime—Nightclub hostess

Janice Gould—Resident at the Beekman Hotel for Women

Johnny Mann and Jerzy Roth—Local crime bosses, owners of the Triple Mark nightclub; the *R* and the *M* in the REM Narcotics Syndicate

Elias Eliopoulos—Greek socialite, owner of American Allied Pharmaceuticals; the *E* in the REM Narcotics Syndicate

Lawrence Tines—Chief Investigator for the Department of Investigations

Reynolds and Shaw—Cops investigating a possible murder

Julius Fief—Owner of Fief Munitions

Max Waters and Henry Capp—Leaders of the Fief Munitions Workers Union

Paulie Sendak—Fief Munitions armory foreman, union member

The Players

Gerald Kravitz—Lawyer for the Fief Munitions Workers Union

Murray Crown—Owner of Crown Crackers, state witness, Mann and Roth associate

"Bubbles" Crown—Murray's bombshell wife

Faith Rapaport—Rising young reporter on the *Globe* metro desk

Sam Rapaport—Faith's dead father, legendary *Globe* columnist

Marty Volman—Editor of the *Globe* metro desk

Celeste Martin—Heiress, socialite, and real estate developer

Richard Martin—Celeste's taciturn brother

Noel Tersi—Real estate magnate, Celeste's longtime companion

Steven—Celeste's cook

Aleksandr and Nicol—Celeste's handymen

Byron Sands—Nicol's son

Dr. Joseph Gamburg—Employee of Leslie's Auction House

Dr. Jerome Brilovsky—Former owner of American Allied Pharmaceutical, former head of the communist Brigade

Arthur Brilovsky—Jerome Brilovsky's eldest son

Sheldon (Shelly) Price—Jerome Brilovsky's business partner and fellow traveler

Elaine (Price) Brilovsky—Shelly Price's daughter, Arthur Brilovsky's wife

Joshua Brilovsky—Elaine and Arthur's son

Professor Mikhail Tarkhov—Russian art historian, expert on the Soviet avant-garde

Katrina Lowenstein—Resident of Ten Lakes

Sylvia Lowenstein—Katrina's mother

Daniel Greely—Screenwriter and pulp novelist

Claude Fielding—Official at the Department of State, former WWI counterintelligence operative

Zelda—Harry Shortz's secretary

Shlomo Feldman—The heavy

Stu Zawolsky—The hit man

The Grizzled Men—The Grizzled Men

Benny Rudolph—The everywhereman

The Disappearing Body

Chapter 1

Early one frigid Thursday morning in mid-January 193–, sometime between the hours of four and five, a tired-looking prison guard holding a set of leg irons and handcuffs appeared outside Victor Ribe's cell. The guard, a burly man whose gray wool uniform tightly hugged at his shoulders and thighs, knocked his baton on the foot of Victor's bed and ordered him to get dressed. Victor, who didn't undress during the winter months, rolled back his tattered blanket and put on his boots and longcoat. The guard motioned with the baton to the cell operator, and Victor stepped up to the bars, his hands at his sides, palms extended outward. The roll and clank of the door echoed through the cell block; when the violent sound quieted, the guard motioned the baton at Victor as if he were tracing the shape of infinity in the air. "Out," he said, dropping the shackles and chains on the floor.

With his hands in plain sight, Victor took one large step out from his cell and with a practiced hand quickly arranged the cuffs and chains around his ankles and wrists; once they were set in place, the guard bent down and fastened the locks. He then stood before Victor, close to his face, so close that Victor couldn't look away from him.

"Is there any one thing in there you don't want to live without?" the guard asked quietly, almost intimately.

"Why?" Victor asked.

"Is there any one thing in there you wouldn't want to live without?" the guard repeated, this time with a sense of urgency. The guard continued to trace long figure eights with the point of his baton.

"Underneath the mattress," Victor said reluctantly, as quietly as the guard spoke to him. "Beneath the pillow, under the mattress."

The guard walked into Victor's cell and from underneath the mattress at the head of the bed, he removed an old photograph, whose paper had turned yellow and thin from touch. It was a picture taken in front of a cheap backdrop of a carousel, a picture of Victor, looking much younger and vital, and a young slender woman on his arm. They looked carefree, happy, unhindered. The guard respectfully placed the photo in the pocket of Victor's coat, and then circled around him.

"Walk," the guard ordered.

Victor Ribe, who was serving the fifteenth year of his twenty-five-year sentence, walked with the guard through the cell block, through damp rusting corridors. They walked outside, over a long narrow stretch of the yard's stiff frozen grass, which led them to the prison's gates, where waiting was a somber-looking sheriff's deputy and a paddy wagon with its engine running. Victor turned his head over his shoulder. "What's happening?" he asked.

"Eyes front," the guard ordered.

The sheriff's deputy opened the back of the paddy wagon and pulled out a crate. "Inside," he said to Victor. Victor stepped onto the wooden crate and then inside the windowless metal casing of the wagon. The guard said something to the deputy privately and then he looked up to Victor, raised his arm, and tipped his hat. Not knowing what to make of it, Victor squeezed his jaw tight and nodded his head, then took a seat on a bench that was bolted to the floor. The deputy slid the crate in by Victor's feet and then slammed the doors closed. The padlock banged shut, the compartment turned black, and then, with Victor's chains rattling all along the way, the sheriff's deputy drove him down bumpy roads for the better part of three hours.

When the sun had risen above the horizon, and the spectrum of color had dissipated white, through a small opening in a metal slat separating the driver's compartment from the back of the wagon, a thin stream of light crept down the arm of Victor's coat. As quietly as he could, Victor shuffled to the opening in the slat, cupped his large hands around his face, and squeezed his eye into the light. He could see through the small hole well enough to realize that they were driving through Long Meadow, the town in which Victor had grown up. He could see well enough to find that the streets were more crowded than he ever remembered them, that many of the buildings he best recalled from his childhood were no longer there, that the town appeared to have grown more dense with commerce; instead of tourist shops selling local crafts and figurines as there once were, in place of the small boutiques, were outlets selling guns and ammunition. As they approached the factory in which his father worked as a machinist, the sight of all this became a little more clear to him, as instead of the company name reading "Barkley & Sons," which used to manufacture bird figurines and bird feeders, it read "Fief Munitions." Limestone walls, as tall as the walls that had surrounded his prison cell, had been built around the factory, and the factory, which had been only on two square blocks, had expanded by several more.

As they reached the plant's entrance, Victor's long quiet morning ride was suddenly disrupted by what sounded through the thin metal walls of the paddy wagon like a battlefield of men on an offensive. The noise was converging all around him. As he tried to see where it was coming from, a large man with a shotgun slung over his shoulder backpedaled into the street. The deputy slammed on the brakes, and the next thing Victor knew he was lifting himself up off the floor and wedging his eye back into the opening in the slat. An angry mob of men carrying guns and truncheons were now crowding before them. Victor could feel the bodies bumping up against the wagon; he felt as though he could physically touch the anger in their riotous voices.

"What's happening?" Victor asked.

"They're filing into the plant," the deputy said quietly.

"What for?"

"Seems they're taking it over." Victor could see the deputy's thin smooth fingers nervously tapping at the steering wheel.

"Why?"

"There was an explosion inside one of the shops the day before yesterday. I guess they don't like the idea of their men getting blown up."

"There were men killed?"

The deputy's fingers continued tapping, slower and more deliberately than before. "Your father," he said as the congestion of bodies began to thin before them, "he was one of them. He and five other men."

A tightness took hold of Victor behind his eyes. "Is that why I'm with you?"

"All I know is that your father's dead and that I got a call to come get you late last night. That's all I know."

"Where are you taking me?"

"We'll be there soon enough."

The deputy shut the latch so that the small opening through which Victor was able to see was closed. Victor was once again in the pitch black of the wagon, alone with the news that his father was dead. He hadn't seen nor talked with his father in the fifteen years that he was imprisoned, not since the day he was sentenced for his crime.

When the paddy wagon cleared the crowd it picked up speed. Victor felt the wagon turn left and could feel in the clattering vibration of his seat the rapid monotonous drumming of piston fire. Tired of listening to the rattle of his chains, he pulled them into his body and tried to imagine where they were driving. If he was right, they were traveling north out of town up along the woods and meadows and creeks and streams of Palisades Parkway, right into the middle of the nature preserve that gave Long Meadow its name.

They motored straight ahead for about fifteen minutes. When

the wagon stopped, when the motor had been turned off, the deputy walked around back and opened the door. As if channeled through a kaleidoscope, a vermilion-colored light broke into the darkness off an ice-encrusted billboard on the side of the road. *Cardinals,* it read. *Cardinals in June.* Staggered at half-mile intervals up and down Palisades Parkway were billboards informing City tourists of what type of bird life they could expect to find in the Long Meadow Bird Sanctuary. With one of his hands resting on his holstered gun and the other carrying two large bundles wrapped in brown paper, the deputy motioned to Victor that he should stand up. "Hands," he said.

Victor, whose hands were tethered by chains to his ankle bracelets, moved his arms from his sides.

"Back to me," the deputy said as he stepped up and in.

"Do I know you?" Victor asked as he turned his back to the deputy.

"We went to school together," the deputy said as he placed the bundles on the floor. He removed a set of keys from his belt, and moving from one lock to the next, he set Victor free. "My mother worked alongside yours before . . ."

"Right," Victor said. "I remember now." The image of the deputy's face came into his mind as he stared at the wall of the wagon and he could suddenly see what he looked like when he was young.

"Get dressed," the deputy said. "I'll wait outside."

Victor opened the packages. Inside he found the set of clothes he had worn the day he was sentenced, as well as a beat-up scarf and coat. Standing exposed to the freezing wind rushing into the back of the paddy wagon, he removed his prison clothes and quickly redressed. When he had knotted his tie and tied his shoes, he removed the photo of himself and the woman from his prison longcoat and delicately slipped it into the breast pocket of his jacket. He then stepped out from the wagon onto a heavily wooded road.

"You'll be going with them," the deputy said to Victor as he pointed to a car parked across the road from where they stood. Two grizzled-looking men in heavy belted coats and fedoras, each of them with a cigarette sticking out the corner of his mouth, waved him over. They were a dark pair, unshaven, one distinguishable from the other mainly in that one looked happy and one didn't. Victor looked to the deputy for some assurance, but he said nothing more. Without looking at Victor again, he got back into the paddy wagon and drove away.

"Ride up here with me," the one with the sunnier disposition said to Victor as Victor walked toward the men. Victor did as he was told. He rode up front, and together the three men drove down the road.

"What's happening?" Victor asked again.

"You like to play cards?"

"Sure," he said. "Why?"

The man up front pulled cards out of his pocket as he drove and held them in the palm of his hand. "High-low," he said. Victor hesitantly grabbed a handful of cards from the top of the deck. He drew a nine of hearts. The man up front placed the cards in Victor's hand, then drew a one-eyed jack of clubs. He held the card up for Victor to see, for the man in the back to see, and smiled. "I think we're gonna get along just fine, you and me." The man scooped up the cards from Victor's hand and placed them back in his pocket.

"You're not the ones I'm talking to, are you?" Victor said.

The two grizzled men didn't say anything more. They drove down the wooded parkway in silence until Victor could see the broad-shoulder fenders of a black Ford sedan gleaming on the roadside. "Shut your eyes and keep still," the man in the back said to Victor.

"Why?"

"Do as I said."

Victor shut his eyes. He felt the man in the backseat shroud a smooth piece of fabric over his forehead and nose, and then it tightened. The man then placed a musty-smelling burlap sack over his head. As the sack touched Victor's shoulders, the car pulled over and came to a stop.

"Don't go anywhere," the man in the back said.

The front door opened and closed. The back door opened and stayed open, so the frigid air blew up into the sack, onto Victor's neck. He could hear footsteps approaching on loose dirt, the car wobbled, the door slammed shut, and then a calm, measured voice, damp and guttural and unhealthy-sounding, spoke to him from the backseat.

"You have any idea what you're doing here, Mr. Ribe?"

"No, I don't," he said, smelling his own dank breath as it hovered between him and the scratchy burlap of the sack.

"Did anyone tell you what happened to your father?"

"The sheriff. He told me."

"A real shame that is," the man said. "My condolences."

"What's this all about?"

The man in the backseat struck a match. Victor could hear the match spark. Then the smell of sulfur and burning tobacco. "Your father and I, we had a deal. I'm making good on my end of it."

"I don't understand."

"You will, in good time; but for now, I've got a proposition for you."

"Who are you?"

The man breathed a difficult breath that sounded like the thin, leafless branches of the birch trees whipping about in the cold wind outside.

"I'm listening," Victor said.

"If you agree to help me, when we're through with this, you'll walk down the road and attend your father's funeral as a free man."

"How's that work?"

"It just does."

Victor suddenly remembered which road he was on. He remembered the grove of cherry blossoms that bloomed in the springtime. He remembered walking barefoot with his childhood sweetheart, along one of the many brooks that fed the river. He remembered the plot by the field in which his mother was buried after she was taken by the Spanish flu. He could see in his mind the priest waiting for him at the foot of his father's grave. Considering that all his father's men were inside the plant, he thought that unless he walked down the road, the priest would more than likely be standing there alone. "What would I have to do?"

"Help me finish what your father started. Help me take care of the men who murdered Boris Lardner."

As when he'd heard the news about his father, it took a moment for this to sink in. Then the words came out like a stone skipping across water. "You mean, you don't think I killed him?"

"I know for a fact that you didn't."

"For a fact?" As Victor said this, a sadness came over his voice, a sadness that amounted to fifteen years of sadness. "And my father?"

"He knew it too."

"How?" Victor said, the sadness in his voice lingering.

"I've got evidence."

"Then what do you need me for? What did you need my father for?"

"To help me deliver the evidence."

"How do I know you're being straight with me?"

"You couldn't possibly know."

Victor was quiet. He listened to the man's labored breathing. He could see in his mind his father lying in his casket above the frozen earth, his hands folded over his chest in a way he would have never folded them over his chest in his lifetime. "Was it my father who caused the explosion at the plant?"

The man didn't say anything.

"Why won't you answer me?"

The man still didn't say anything.

Victor's head started to sweat from the warmth of his bad breath under the sack. "Where would I go from the funeral?" he said.

"The boys'll drive you to Fuller House, downtown. They've got it all set up for you. You stay there until you're needed."

Victor listened to the wind for a while longer. He listened to the wind and all he could see in his mind was himself sitting in his small damp cell, listening to the wind blowing and not being able to see the rustling trees beyond the prison walls. He could see in his mind the picture of himself and the woman in front of the backdrop of the carousel. He could see her as a young girl staring at him through her bedroom window as he stood on the street under a downpour of cold rain. He turned his head in the direction of the man behind him. "I'll need some money."

"Five hundred dollars has already been deposited under your name at First City Bank."

"Five hundred?"

"That's right."

"What's five hundred buy you these days?" Victor wondered out loud.

"In this case, peace of mind."

"Yeah," Victor said, not knowing what else to say. "All right," he said after another thoughtful pause, "I'll do whatever you want."

"We'll be in touch, Mr. Ribe," the man said abruptly. And with that said, the car door opened, the car wobbled, and Victor could hear the footsteps on the road's shoulder. After a few moments of sitting still, he heard the car engine turn over and the car pull away. He could then feel the two grizzled men retake their places.

"You can take that stuff off your head," the sourpuss in the backseat said.

Sunshine up front started the car, drove behind some nearby brush, and parked. "Get out. We'll be watching you from the woods. When you're through, walk back out to the road."

Victor dropped the blindfold and the sack onto the seat, opened the door, and stepped out. He looked back for a moment. "Go on," Sunshine said. He pointed up ahead to a clearing past a stand of trees. Victor walked into the woods and from the woods into the field. He could see the priest and the gravediggers standing in a small cemetery whose far border ran along the edge of the bird sanctuary. Victor walked to the gravesite and looked onto his father's casket, and looked over the frozen earth that extended as far as the precipice on the Palisades, and looked onto the icy current of the Westbend River at the bottom of the enormous bluffs, and he could see the immense grid of the City on the other side of the current, the island city that expanded into the distance like a continuation of the headstones in the graveyard, the island itself like an enormous tablet drifting into a gray industrial mist, eastward, as far as Victor could see.

GLOBE METRO REPORT, APRIL 23, 192-

RIBE GUILTY! SENTENCE IGNITES COURTROOM!

SAM RAPAPORT

Federal Court Building—After a 20-minute deliberation this morning, finishing what must have amounted to the shortest open-and-shut murder trial in City history, a jury pronounced Victor Ribe guilty for the brutal homicides of Alcohol and Narcotics Bureau Investigator Maurice Klempt and crooked pharmacist Boris Lardner.

The disoriented Ribe, suffering excruciating pains from heroin withdrawal, leaned against Public Defender Lenny Shapiro like a shaken rag doll as the verdict was read.

A palpable wave of relief broke through the gallery. The vindication released from the lungs of the victims' friends and families was enough to send a hot-air balloon to China.

The liberal Judge John Selby looked down onto Ribe from the bench and proceeded to pass sentence: 25 years to life on each count of murder, to be served concurrently at Farnsworth State Penitentiary in Farnsworth.

It came as no surprise to this reporter that the courtroom, denied a capital sentence, erupted into pandemonium.

Sid Lardner, brother of the murdered Boris Lardner, rushed Ribe and nearly got a piece of him with a bailiff's blackjack.

Loud protests were heard all around from ANB officials, including ANB Commissioner Harry Shortz, who, on record an opponent of capital sentences, broke face and shamed Judge Selby with some colorful language not fit to print.

The only ones not chanting for Ribe's life, it seemed, were his attorney, the judge, and Ribe's father, who upon hearing his son's sentence quietly stood up and walked out of the courtroom.

Farnsworth Penitentiary authorities, fearing for their own safety, quickly shackled Ribe and led him out to a waiting paddy wagon.

Over heckles and taunts, Judge Selby ordered bailiffs to clear the courtroom and then retreated into chambers.

On the courthouse steps, Sid Lardner swore vengeance, while arresting officers Sergeants Ira Dubrov and Pally Collins of the ANB expressed dismay. Commissioner Shortz made no comment.

Ribe's conviction for the murder of Lardner—Ribe's old war pal and personal heroin peddler—appeared to have largely rested on the testimony of Abraham (Shuffles) Levy, a convicted South End numbers runner.

Levy claimed to have witnessed a desperate Ribe quarreling with Lardner outside Schweitzer's Piano Shop on Proctor Street. The two men were apparently engaged in a heated fight over money.

The questionable Levy swore under oath that Ribe beat Lardner senseless, then mercilessly heaved him through the piano shop's window.

Making up for Levy's lack of credibility was testimony from several members of the Glory Be Temperance Alliance, who, while passing out pamphlets down the 700 block of Proctor Street, in front of Lovey's Juice Joint, heard the sound of shattering glass.

Although none of the Glory Be members heard or saw Ribe's argument with Lardner, they claimed that when they reached Schweitzer's Piano Shop, they found Ribe standing over the deceased's body, looting his pockets. They then watched him flee toward the Shrine Street el platform.

According to two witnesses waiting for the train, when Vice Unit Investigator Klempt attempted to arrest Ribe, Ribe resisted, and a struggle ensued.

They testified that while lying prone on his back, Ribe kicked Klempt in the chest and knocked him into the path of the oncoming train.

PD Shapiro, who insists Ribe was unfit for trial, plans to appeal.

Chapter 2

As a town on the cusp of a metropolis, Long Meadow had always been known for being tenaciously small-minded and big-willed. For more than sixty years the residents of the town consistently refused offers of incorporation by the City. At the height of the Industrial Revolution they saw from their shore of the Westbend River the city plume with dust and smoke; they witnessed the lush green fields and farms, the gentle slopes and textures of the island's upper peninsula, uprooted and paved over with cobblestone and brick; limestone and brownstone, granite and marble, were mined from nearby quarries and up rose modest and then not-so-modest buildings that reached skyward. The empty spaces that remained were soon fitted with steel girders and concrete blocks, and higher and higher the conic water towers stood fixed atop their structures. As space closed in, as the value of the City's property increased, as the shipping lanes of the river became more dense with traffic, the property along the Westbend's edge was increasingly in demand. For many years, without success, businessmen and bankers from the City tried to buy their way onto the docks and into the real estate offices of Long Meadow. However, the docks, all the land along the Palisades, and a good deal of the real estate downtown was owned by the Barkley family, and the Barkley men and women, devoted to the ideals of such thinkers as Fourier and Thoreau, were both zealous and stubborn when their land was in question. They were avid bird lovers and watchers, and from time immemorial in the family's memory, they were the protectors of the meadows, the virgin forest, and all the wildlife that ran along their shore. As the City continued its century-long expansion, Long Meadow became a haven for a variety of birds traveling the route of their spring and autumn migrations. City dwellers would escape the crush of overcrowded streets and ride the Barkley ferries from the City's North End to witness the spectacle; they would come in droves to watch from Promontory Peak the skies darken and teem with meadowlarks and thrushes, grackles and cardinals, warblers and blue jays, herons and egrets, ducks and geese.

At the turn of the century, Theodore Barkley and his sons, encouraged by a prestigious group of ornithologists, converted a failed ironworks on Main Street and began manufacturing small metal bird figurines and bird feeders. They sold their trinkets and feeders and Audubon prints from a shop at the edge of the docks. They soon fitted the ironworks to manufacture field glasses and telescopes. They opened a carriage stable and employed the townspeople of Long Meadow to guide tours along Palisades Parkway. Excited by the success of their ventures, Theodore Barkley and his sons borrowed money against the worth of their land and began financing restaurants and inns, craft shops and greenhouses and family farms, and refurbished several schoolhouses whose emphasis was to educate its students as naturalists.

For more than twenty-five years, the modest trade generated by the Barkleys' ventures brought in most of the town's revenue. But then something unforeseen happened. Perhaps the winds changed course, perhaps the multitude of visitors lying about in the tall grasses of the meadows made the landscape appear threatening; maybe, as the open spaces in the city had once dwindled to people, the open space among the birds fighting for a small piece of land in Long Meadow became too spare; whatever the reason might have been, almost all the species of birds that visited the fields, over just a few years, mysteriously stopped darkening the skies over the scenic parkway in the spring and autumn, and instead, to the utter devastation of Theodore Barkley's sensibility, started to nest in the

City, atop the roofs and terraces of the office and apartment buildings, where the birds swept down from the skies to open piles of rubbish, to discarded human refuse.

When the birds dwindled from the skies over Long Meadow, the tourists stopped visiting as they once had. They stopped strolling through the business district, stopped buying the small figurines and feeders manufactured at the plant, the field binoculars, the Audubon prints. Eventually, lines of empty carriages lined the street and the guides were left to watch their horses' tails sway and swat away at flies circling their hindquarters. The Barkleys, to their dismay, had overextended themselves, and for the first time in over eight generations, their land was in peril of being taken from them by the bank, and the town of Long Meadow was made nearly destitute.

When the Barkleys and the town were near ruin, they were approached by Julius Fief, owner of Fief Munitions, whose struggling munitions plant had recently been awarded a grant from the Public Works Project Board to stockpile munitions for military training exercises. Fief, who had profited nicely during the Great War, maintained his offices in the midtown section of the City and was now barely making ends meet manufacturing light arms and ammunition fifty miles up the river in the small town of Broadbent. With the promise of government money in his pocket and potential future subsidies, his intention was to move his manufacturing base to the City, closer to his headquarters—and he was seeking out a location to accommodate his needs. In the City itself he was unable to find a suitable lot of manufacturing space and docking slips; in Long Meadow, however, he found everything he could possibly hope for—two miles of vacant shore, a workable plant, and a failing town in need of work.

Unlike others who had come before him, Fief, knowing Theodore Barkley's reputation, proposed to the Barkley family and the Long Meadow town council that if he was able to manufacture his munitions in their town, with the exception of a half mile of shoreline, he would set aside a small percentage of the company's profits to maintain the meadows and fields of the Palisades, and he would put in writing that Long Meadow residents for the duration of a thirty-year lease would be offered jobs before workers outside the municipality. In return, Long Meadow would agree to fund whatever Fief's government grant didn't pay for to retrofit the Barkley & Sons plant, build the docks, and finance whatever other construction was needed to deliver their munitions.

Although Theodore Barkley had profound reservations about doing business with a munitions company, he could see that the town council was in favor of it and that his voice in this matter held precious little weight. With so few jobs available, with men and women so desperate to work, Theodore Barkley reasoned that as long as the people had the Palisades preserved for their recreation and spiritual revitalization, perhaps their occupation didn't matter so much. With his reservations noted in the council's chambers, Theodore Barkley agreed to Fief's terms. After securing a loan for the construction, over a period of a year, the town expanded; it refitted and retooled the plant; docks were built for heavy freighters; private service roads to the docks and to the train station were laid for trucks delivering heavy weapons and artillery; tall limestone walls topped with wrought-iron spears were built around the plant; and soon enough armed guards, stationed in turrets, thuggishly looked over what used to be the quaint business district of Long Meadow.

GLOBE METRO REPORT, NOVEMBER 25, 191-

Harry Shortz Appointed State Alcohol and Narcotics Bureau Commissioner

SAM RAPAPORT

Civic Center—Senator Thomas O'Connell announced today that the State Narcotics Bureau will be widening its authority to include Prohibition laws passed last month, which threaten to lock down our saloons and dry out our liquor cabinets. Heading the State Alcohol and Narcotics Bureau—the new name officially given to the bureau this afternoon—will be former counterintelligence field operative Harry Shortz.

Shortz, a big lumbering man with a large *basso profundo* voice and a chest the size of a cement mixer, was enthusiastically introduced by Senator O'Connell "as the only man fit for the job. Come January when Prohibition officially goes into effect, I can think of no one better suited to command the transition."

Before today's appointment, the 29-year-old Shortz, who hails from the working-class smelt-stacked mining town of Portsmith, was unknown in state political circles. Unless, of course, you take into account that he is the son-in-law of State Treasurer Edward Kelly.

Mr. Kelly, a wealthy financier, who has boasted that he is largely responsible for Senator O'Connell's election success, said today from his office at the Treasury that Mr. Shortz won the new position of Alcohol and Narcotics Bureau Commissioner on his own merits.

Mr. Kelly, who also happened to serve as Mr. Shortz's commanding officer during the war, claimed, as

Senator O'Connell did, that Shortz, hands down, was "the only man fit for the job."

Mr. Kelly added that "there is no one out there tougher than Harry, no one more persistent and fair-minded, no one more cunning and intelligent, no one with greater moral conviction. The fact of the matter is that the man didn't want the job. It was only his stubborn obeisance to the call of public service that made him agree to take it. And I'll tell you something else," the plain-talking Mr. Kelly sparked, "the people will be better off with a man who hasn't had his hands in the pockets of every hoodlum and mobster and machine politician out there. Mark my word."

Mr. Kelly was no doubt referring to former Narcotics Bureau Commissioner Chester Debs, who ascended through the ranks of the City's South End machine. Mr. Debs was ousted from this position in disgrace last month after State Department of Investigations Officer Lawrence Tines arrested Mr. Debs on charges of extorting owners of opium dens throughout the City for a cut of their profits. Mr. Debs is currently serving a six-month sentence upstate at Farnsworth.

Mr. Shortz announced today that his first order of business was to conduct a thorough investigation into Mr. Debs' underhanded activities and give the bureau an overhaul. "No heads will be spared," Mr. Shortz promised.

The newly appointed commissioner has his work cut out for him. However, the confident and sober Shortz appeared to be unimpressed by the skeptics today. In response to rumors that South End mobsters were already stockpiling liquor by the barrel to be sold in underground clubs, Mr. Shortz alluded to his most famous exploit during the war, when he gained entrance to Kaiser Wilhelm's inner circle while posing as an Austrian official. "If I was able to infiltrate the Kaiser's castle," he said, "I think I can knock down a few doors just below street level."

Chapter 3

Shortly before daybreak, while Victor Ribe was en route from Farnsworth to Long Meadow in the back of the paddy wagon, six officers from the State Department of Investigations boarded a Barkley ferry on the City's North End Docks and started out across the icy waters of the Westbend. After halting midstream for tugs and freighters to pass, the ferry continued on to the Long Meadow Docks, where the officers, driving three to a car, sped off the gangplank in their black Ford sedans.

They roared up the winding road to Palisades Parkway and traveled north atop the bluffs for a few miles until they hit a grass path that descended back toward the river. The cars barreled down the path toward a fishing shack a hundred yards from the shoreline. Armed with shotguns and flashlights, the six men climbed out of their cars, walked in file to the shack's brittle wooden door, and kicked it in.

Bright shafts of light swept the dark room until they all converged on a cot draped with a patchwork quilt. One of the officers bent down, lifted the quilt, and dragged out from under the cot a tarnished brass footlocker marked *MW.* The other officers gathered around and shined their flashlights onto the footlocker as the officer on his knees opened it up and pulled out eight sticks of dynamite wrapped in a two-day-old issue of the *Globe.*

The bent officer replaced the bundle of explosives as he had found them and shut them away, and as the others filed out of the shack behind him, he gingerly carried the footlocker to one of the cars. Together, the men drove back along the Palisades in the direction of town as the sun crept up over the City's skyscrapers.

When they reached downtown Long Meadow, the cars split up, each driving to a different but similar-looking clapboard house just off Main Street. All the men removed their revolvers from their shoulder holsters as they pounded on the doors.

Max Waters and Henry Capp, the leaders of the Long Meadow Munitions Workers Union, answered the loud knocks dressed in pajamas. When they opened their doors, they were wrestled down, shackled, and dragged from their homes as their wives and children screamed after them. They were both ferried to Delacort Prison, located on a small island in the harbor, where they were placed in separate cells and brought up on charges of sabotage and manslaughter.

Back in Long Meadow, minutes after Waters and Capp were arrested, word spread, and a mob of union men, fresh out of bed, armed with guns and truncheons, converged on the plant. Upon hearing the news, the guards opened the plant's doors and allowed the men to enter. They filed into the shops, the armory, and the offices. Once inside, the leaders of the mob manned the office phones and called the newspapers and the radio stations. They told the press that if Waters and Capp weren't released by the end of the day, they would destroy the plant and take up arms against anyone who tried to stop them. They then called Narcotics Bureau Commissioner Harry Shortz.

Harry Shortz received the call about the Long Meadow Munitions Workers Union while he was at the Hanover Hotel checking in on Murray Crown, owner of Crown Crackers and distribution man for the REM narcotics syndicate. As part of an agreement with the Narcotics Bureau and the State Attorney General, Crown was to testify against the leaders of the syndicate at a grand jury hearing the following morning. Harry wanted to get a look at Crown before he went on. He didn't like what he saw. Crown was a sad puffy mess. He looked as though he was hopped up on laudanum.

When the phone rang, Sergeant Pally Collins answered the call and tried to hand it over to Harry, who was sitting on the edge of the room's bed, observing the disconsolate cigar-smoking Crown play out a hand of solitaire. "It's for you, Harry," Pally said.

"Who is it?" he asked, still studying Crown's beleaguered face.

"Zelda."

"What does she want?"

"He wants to know what you want," Pally Collins said into the receiver. ". . . You, she wants you."

"I know she wants me. What does she want?"

"Do you mind?" Crown protested weakly with a wet soporific glaze in his eyes.

"Tell Zelda I'll call her back from the lobby," Harry said, watching Crown flip a card with the vigor of a lightbulb about to go on the fritz.

"He'll call you right back," Pally said into the phone. ". . . Yeah, I'll tell him."

"Tell me what?"

"It's urgent."

"Ten minutes."

"Ten minutes, he says," Pally said into the receiver and then hung up the phone.

"Why don't you take him with you," Crown mumbled, still focused on the cards. "He grates on my nerves, this one."

"What nerves?" Harry said to himself. He turned to Pally. "Where's the washroom?"

"Right back there," Pally said.

Harry gestured to Pally to go out into the hall, then went into the bathroom.

"If you need anything . . ." Pally said as he bent over Murray Crown, his lips close to Crown's ear.

"If I need anything . . ." Crown said to his cards.

"If you need a tooth pulled or . . ."

"Maybe a little bridgework done?"

"How about I call Bubbles for a little entertainment?"

"How about I take the Fifth?"

"You're losing again, Murray."

Murray turned around so that a shock of gray hair limply hanging over his forehead rested an inch from Pally's nose. "Proctor Street," Murray whispered with cigar breath. "We'll see who loses what when I tell what I know about Proctor Street in the morning."

"That's not a very smart move right there, that one you just made."

Murray turned back to his cards. "I know what I'm doing," Murray continued, whispering. "I know what I know."

"I thought I told you to go into the hall," Harry said to Pally as he stepped out of the bathroom.

"I'll be in the hall," Pally said to Murray, his voice turning cold.

Harry waited until Pally was gone. "I'll be by early tomorrow morning to take you to the courthouse," he said.

"I so look forward to it," Crown said, his voice as tart and juiceless as a squeezed lemon.

"Try to cheer up, Murray."

Harry started out.

"Hey, Mr. Commissioner . . ."

"What is it?"

"If anything happens to me . . ."

"Nothing's going to happen to you, Murray."

". . . tell Bubbles I love her."

"Nothing's going to happen. You have my word," Harry said as he walked into the hall and shut the door behind him.

Sitting on two folding chairs next to the door were Pally Collins and his partner, Sergeant Ira Dubrov. Pally and Ira were both heavyset men with fat cheeks. They wore spit-shined oxfords and waist-tight pinstripe suits. They talked through their upper teeth with a heavy South End accent that made them sound like they had midget fists permanently implanted in their cheeks. They were big men, like Harry, with big voices, big hands, big chests; unlike Harry, they were brash, not too attractive, and spirited like a couple of juvenile delinquents. To soften their coarse looks and rough demeanor—as part of a futile attempt on Harry's part to make them appear above the fray (an attempt made after the papers started referring to Dubrov and Collins as Shortz's goon squad)—Ira kept a meticulously groomed pencil-line mustache and Pally habitually wore a vibrant hothouse carnation in his lapel. Neither item seemed to fit. On the two of them, they looked like props from a bad Gilded Age costume drama and gave them the appearance of the very element they were trying to rid the City of. Regardless, Ira and Pally were cunning and resourceful, and because of that, for the many years they'd worked for Harry, they'd been his interpreters of the City's underbelly, his eyes and ears, his most trusted men, whose influence on the bureau was probably equal or greater to that of Harry's.

"Has he been moping like this the whole time he's been in there?" Harry asked.

"Yeah," Ira said. "Moping. Playing solitaire. Game after game after game after game. All through the fucking night sometimes. We offered to play a little gentleman's poker with him . . ."

". . . but he won't shut the fuck up," Pally said. "So fucking dark, this guy. Every five minutes he's wondering out loud why he just doesn't off himself. He keeps saying, '*Who do you think you bums are? You think you're so goddamn invincible you can keep Johnny and Jerzy from getting to me?*' Forget it, I'd rather sit out here with Ira and pitch pennies."

"He's scared," Harry said.

"He's a nuisance," Ira said. "Unpleasant. I don't know how that wife of his puts up with him. How'd a beautiful woman like that ever get herself interested in a bum like him?"

"You seen the jewelry he's bought her?" Pally said out the corner of his mouth. "She lights up brighter than New Year's Eve."

"On a stormy night," Harry said.

"What have you got against Bubbles, Harry?"

"Nothing. I've got nothing against Bubbles, Ira."

"It don't get much better than that. Really."

Harry smiled at the sight of Ira's gorilla face rapt in thought about Bubbles Crown. "Anyway," Harry said, "I want to know what you two think is the best way to get him to the courthouse tomorrow morning, without making a spectacle of things."

"I say we call Klein to work out the details," Ira said.

"Yeah, Klein," Pally said. "He's got a good head for that."

"That's 'cause his head is so fucking big," Ira laughed. "Have you ever seen such a big head outside of the fucking freak show?"

Harry shook his head in mock frustration. "Who's making the call?"

"Me," Ira said. "I'm making the call. I can't stand looking at this wall for another minute."

When Harry and Ira reached the lobby of the Hanover, the concierge approached Ira and told him he had a phone call. Ira excused himself with his hands on his jacket's lapels as he walked away from Harry and followed the concierge to a phone at the front desk.

"Yeah, Dubrov here," Ira said when the concierge had walked away.

"It might interest you to know, Sergeant Dubrov," a raspy voice said on the other end of the line, "that Victor Ribe is out of prison."

"Who is this?"

"He'll be up at Jack's Basement Tavern . . ."

"Where?" Ira asked as he hastily got out a pad and pen.

"Jack's Basement Tavern, four P.M., fifty-six West Eighty-third Street."

The phone clicked off. Ira stood with the receiver to his ear for a moment, the comic lines of his fat face smoothed over some as he looked around the lobby to see if he was being watched. He felt like he was being watched. He kept looking around until he noticed Harry looking at him from his phone booth. Ira then turned his head back to the phone and tapped at the line for the operator to get in touch with Klein.

When Harry called his secretary and learned what had happened over in Long Meadow, and that he had been asked by the union to act as arbiter between them and the Department of Investigations, Harry immediately called Chief Investigator Lawrence Tines at his office in the Civic Center.

"He's over at Delacourt, Mr. Commissioner," Tines's secretary told him.

"Can I reach him there?"

"I'll call him for you. Hold the line."

The secretary came back on a few minutes later. "What would you like to tell the chief, Mr. Commissioner?"

"Tell him that the Long Meadow Munitions Workers Union has seized Fief's plant."

Harry heard the secretary convey the message.

"He's aware of that, Mr. Commissioner."

"Tell him that they've asked me to arbitrate and that I'm on my way over there right after I get off the phone."

The secretary conveyed the message. "Go ahead," she said.

"Tell him that I'd like to bring them some news to calm them down and get them out of the plant safely."

"Anything else?"

"Tell him that if he could arrange to have Waters and Capp arraigned by the end of the morning and released on bail with the promise of a further investigation, I think I can get them out of there safely."

The message was conveyed.

"He says they'll be out within the hour, Mr. Commissioner."

"He does?" Harry sounded puzzled.

"Yeah, he says he's already sent them over to the courthouse."

"Did they confess?"

The question was asked.

"No, they haven't."

"Anyway . . . tell him, thanks."

The message was conveyed.

"He says, you're welcome."

Harry hung up the phone and walked out of the phone booth, still wondering why that had been so easy.

"Why do you look so stunned?" Ira asked as Harry walked toward him from the phone booth.

"I'll explain everything later," Harry said. "What did Klein say?"

"He said he'll put his big head to work on it."

"Who called you down here?"

"It was the wife," Ira said. "Pally told her she could reach me here."

"How is Claudia?" Harry asked, his head still on Tines.

"Fine, just fine. Riding my back like a jockey with a mallet. I should have married a broad with smaller fists."

"Maybe next time around," Harry said as he drifted away from Ira toward the door.

Indicting Jerzy Roth, Elias Eliopoulos, and Johnny Mann, the three principals who made up the REM narcotics syndicate, was Harry Shortz's last order of unfinished business before he completed his final term as State Narcotics Bureau Commissioner. The syndicate had been a thorn in Harry's side for as long as he had held his office. No matter what the bureau did, they could never get enough evidence on the syndicate to make arrests. Otherwise, Harry's record was impeccable. Over the course of his tenure as Alcohol and Narcotics Bureau Commissioner—the longest served by any commissioner since the position was created—Harry miraculously managed to enforce the widely unpopular Prohibition laws without becoming unpopular himself; in fact, well after Prohibition's repeal as head of the renamed Narcotics Bureau, he was still thriving, holding a level of respectability unrivaled by almost any other public official, law enforcement or otherwise. He had proved himself to be a man of the people, of the little guy, the down-and-out guy; and well into the Depression, when task forces were uprooting the state's corrupt political machinery and sending its undesirables into retirement in droves, this meant something. It meant that Harry Shortz was flourishing. He had played it straight, and he had played it smart. He did it by not driving the little people into the ground. During Prohibition, he overlooked the small quiet gin joints and ragtag juice bars, and like an understated superhero from some kid's comic book, made his name by picking fights in public with the larger-than-life South End gangsters who ran the big speakeasies, the gambling parlors, the dope dens, numbers rackets, and brothels; he took on the neighborhood thugs who were committing murders by the dozens, extorting thousands by the week, rolling over ordinary people by the minute to keep themselves in business. With Ira and Pally's help, Harry Shortz soon inspired the same kind of fear and awe in the gangsters as the gangsters did in the City streets. The bureau busted up nightclubs, confiscated liquor, raided dope dens, exposed beat cops and ordinance men and crooked politicians with their pants down and their pockets outturned.

Harry Shortz had not only avoided unpopularity in what was supposed to be an impossible arrangement, but had become so well liked in the Depression years that for the upcoming fall election he was nominated by the state's Liberal Party to be their senatorial candidate. Building on his reputation and a long-held and well-known class bias, the very night he accepted his nomination, he started forging a social reform platform complete with coming-of-age stories about growing up alongside subsistence-wage miners in his hometown of Portsmith. Ostensibly, Harry's interest in the everyday plight of the working man and woman made it as far as the shores of Long Meadow.

When Harry left the Hanover, his driver taxied him to the North End Docks, where they caught a Barkley ferry. As soon as they were off, he walked upstairs to the ferry's passenger landing for some fresh air and found himself blinded by a sudden fireworks display of bursting flashbulbs. He was surrounded by reporters. With his hands shielding his squinted eyes, he bellowed over the raucousness as if he were announcing a boxing match.

"Ladies and gentlemen!" he cried. "Please!"

He dropped his arms and peered out onto the quieting deck, his controlled gaze looking into the eyes of the reporters. He plainly said to all of them, "The Long Meadow Munitions Workers Union has asked me to act as arbiter between themselves and the Department of Investigations in the matter of Max Waters and Henry Capp. Seeing that I'm here, obviously I've accepted their invitation to do so. If I said anything other than that at present, I'd be showing bad faith. So, since I'm not here to talk to you people, at least not yet, why don't you let me enjoy the rest of the ride across the river."

Harry had started to turn around and head for the lower deck, back to his car, when a reporter from the *Herald* called out, "How about taking a few questions about the syndicate, Mr. Commissioner?"

Harry turned back. "What do you want to know, Spike?"

"I want to know how you plan on breaking it up when half a dozen of its insiders have turned up dead since Crown's arrest while the rest of them have gone on the lam."

"Last I heard, dead men don't cause too many problems."

"What about the others who'll end up back in the City once the heat's off?"

"Who says the heat's gonna be turned off?"

"Winter don't last forever."

"I don't follow that. You people follow that?"

"Winter . . . the heat . . ."

"Cute, Spike," Harry said. "Real cute."

"Have you figured out how Crown was linked to Eliopoulos and American Allied Pharmaceutical?" another reporter broke in.

"Yes."

"How?"

Harry looked around the room for another question.

"Will you at least say when you expect to make arrests, for crying out loud?" Caruthers of the *Times* asked.

"After Crown has testified."

"It's good timing for you, isn't it, Mr. Commissioner?"

"It's good overall, Mr. Caruthers."

"That's not what I meant."

"I know what you meant, Mr. Caruthers."

"Do you think the Munitions Workers Union feels you're sympathetic to their cause?" a woman's voice called out from behind the pack of men. Harry couldn't find the woman's face. He just smiled out onto the crowd and held the smile. "I'll see you all after I've met with the union."

"Hang on, Mr. Commissioner . . ."

"Where do you think you're . . ."

"Just one more . . ."

Harry raised his hand as if he were directing traffic on the street, then turned away from the reporters and went back down the stairs to his car. He took a seat behind his driver and stared out the window, across the water, to the undulating machinery crowding the Long Meadow Docks.

A few minutes later, Faith Rapaport, a reporter on the city desk at the *Globe,* gently rapped on Harry's window. When Harry rolled the window down, she said, "They do think you're sympathetic to their cause, don't they?"

"I thought it was you asking that question, Miss Rapaport."

"Will you tell me the answer?"

"I already said I'm not talking. Not until I've talked with them."

"Fair enough," Faith said.

"Let me alone for the time being?"

"Sure," Faith said. "I'll just sit in my car, if that's all right with you."

"Whatever you like."

Faith smiled at Harry and opened the back passenger door of the car right next to Harry's.

"So that's how it is," Harry said.

"That's how it is."

Faith sat down and closed the door of her Hupmobile, then rolled down the window. "It's awfully cold," Faith said.

Harry's eyes slowly turned in their sockets toward Faith.

"Can't even talk about the weather?"

"Yeah, Miss Rapaport—it's cold, it's damn cold."

"You know, Mr. Commissioner . . ."

"You grew up in the newspaper business, isn't that right, Miss Rapaport?"

"That's right."

"Your father got around, Sam did."

"He was known for that."

"He always knew how to twist the knife into the right part of the body when he had you in front of the world. He could make it hurt pretty bad when he got in there nice and good."

"Dear old Dad, he did that to you?" Faith said with a wry smile.

"Yeah," Harry said, smiling back at Faith as he rolled up his window, "he sure did."

GLOBE METRO REPORT, OCTOBER 14, 192-

Undercover Operators

SAM RAPAPORT

South End—Long-sought-after low-life flimflammers Marla Darden and Frank Diggs were arrested on assault charges late last night shortly after police happened by them and found them dragging a half-dressed unconscious man out of the Sullivan Arms Hotel on Proctor Street.

When asked what in G-d's name they were doing, they dropped the man in the gutter and ran for it.

Police immediately caught up with them and took them into custody.

While police recorded statements from Darden and Diggs, Freddy Stillman, a midtown munitions dispatcher, awoke to the sight of his embarrassed wife inside a hospital room at St. Agatha Ann's, suddenly wishing he had more than just a grenade-sized lump on his head.

According to police, Mr. Stillman and Miss Darden became acquainted in the back room of Lovey's Smoke Shop, where the doorman said they left arm in arm, a little more than mellow, and a little more than just taken with each other.

Mr. Stillman escorted the sloppy Miss Darden to the Sullivan Arms Hotel, where they paid 25 cents for an hour's occupancy.

Following a few steps behind them was Mr. Diggs.

When Cecil Taylor, the desk clerk at the Sullivan Arms, saw Mr. Diggs walk after the couple, he went onto the street in search of a copper.

According to Mr. Taylor, he recognized Mr. Diggs from a previous incident, and had no intention of "cleaning up after his mess this time."

With no cops to be found, Mr. Taylor went into his office for his gun and made his way upstairs.

But it was too late. By the time

he opened the door to the room, Mr. Diggs had already clobbered the half-naked Stillman with a sack full of marbles and was in the middle of removing Stillman's wedding band.

Needless to say, Diggs was taken by surprise at the sight of the gun, and pled with Mr. Taylor to take a piece of the action.

Mr. Taylor, who said, "I run an upright establishment," would have no part of it. He ordered Diggs and Darden to get the H— out and take their mark with them.

Seductress and brute lifted Stillman over their shoulders and dragged him down the stairs to the street, where, fate would have it, an officer was standing by.

Mr. Stillman was admitted to the hospital with a severe concussion.

Marla Darden and Frank Diggs will be arraigned this afternoon.

Chapter 4

"Third Precinct? . . . The trouble? There's been a murder. . . . The Beekman Hotel for Women. . . . I said the Beekman Hotel for Women. . . . The ninth floor, south side, middle apartment. . . . No, I don't have a room number. . . . No, I'm not at the murder scene. . . . From my office window. . . . Across the air shaft from the Fief Building. . . . Yes, I'm an employee. . . . Why do you need my . . . Yeah, all right, fine. Stillman. Freddy Stillman. . . . Midtown nine eight seven, extension three. . . . Good. . . . Good. . . . Thank you."

Freddy Stillman nervously hung up the phone and removed a cigarette from his jacket pocket. He struck a match and drew the fire to his lips. When he could feel the calming rush fill his lungs and the front of his head, he removed a pair of binoculars from the top drawer of his desk and edged the barrels into a small crack of light between the drawn blind and the window jamb. While standing there waiting for the police to arrive, Freddy listened to the clamor of voices outside his office, to the bustle of feet restlessly trying to find their proper places. Peering one-eyed through a short binocular tube he looked into the apartment window across the narrow air shaft, into the cold eyes of a young man with a thin smile and a crooked nose. The young man with the thin smile and the crooked nose was a painting set in a gold-leafed grand baroque frame, hung above a modest bureau covered with a mirror, perfume bottles, cosmetics, and a pearl-handled hairbrush. Waves of yellow and hues of reddish brown shaped the contours of the young man's jaw, the curve of his hair, the ball of his fist planted under his chin. The strokes of the painting were broad and soft, so that when magnified, the features of the young man nearly blurred into obscurity, every feature, that is, except his eyes. His eyes were cold and sharp and thin, like his smile. Freddy, paying especially close attention to this figure, suddenly felt as though he knew this man, or at least a man resembling this man. A man from his past, perhaps. Or perhaps a man he occasionally saw on the street.

Looking at the painting and the items on the bureau, Freddy remained still, until two uniformed police arrived in the woman's apartment and entered the foreground. Both were tall and square in the shoulders, nearly identical, uncannily so. They were police, with broad chests and wide chins; clean-shaven; dark, short-cropped hair; thick long coats wrapped around the butts of their guns and billy-club handles. They searched the apartment briefly . . . jotted a few notes in their books, looked up and admired the painting of the young man above the bureau. When it appeared that they had finished looking around, they turned to the air shaft and drew their long triangular noses to the window, fogging small holes. Freddy could feel them looking at him, looking directly at him, but he wasn't sure if they could see him. Taken by surprise at this, he stood paralyzed, with the hollow of his eye firmly pressed against the binocular eyepiece, wondering if he was being seen. One of the officers tried to open the window, then the other, and then they both walked out of sight. When Freddy thought the officers had gone, he went back to his desk and returned his binoculars to the top drawer, looking at them cautiously before he shut them away. He rubbed his already extinguished cigarette into his ashtray and picked up the phone again.

"South End three nine eight. . . . Thank you. . . . Evelyn? . . . Yeah, it's me. . . . I just wanted to see how you and the baby were. . . . C'mon, just tell me you're all right and I'll get off the phone. . . . I just wanted to hear something good about the world is all. . . . No, I'm all right. . . . I'm fine. . . . I'm telling you, I'm fine. . . . I know I shouldn't be calling. . . . I just . . . I know. . . . I won't, I promise. . . . C'mon, Evelyn, I just wanted to know the baby was doing okay, all right? . . . That's all I wanted to know, Evey. . . . See, that wasn't so hard, right? . . . I won't. . . . I said I wouldn't. . . . I will. . . . Yeah. . . . Yeah. . . . So long."

Freddy hung up the phone.

When Freddy hung up the phone, an old supply clerk, whose name Freddy could never remember, opened Freddy's door without knocking. "They're in, Freddy," the clerk said self-importantly as he made his way over to Freddy's desk. The clerk's face was sallow and craggy, the rims of his eyes purpled and yellowed. "There in for you. I know you were out, but now they're in. You've been waiting patiently. I appreciate that. I really do." The clerk placed a brown cardboard box next to the ashtray on Freddy's green blotter. A card was taped to the top of the box by its corners. It read:

FIEF MUNITIONS

Freddy Stillman, *Dispatcher*
Midtown 987, Ext. 3

We hold the monopoly on domestic tranquillity!

The slogan at the bottom of the card bubbled out of the mouth of the company's logo—a square-jawed infantryman with a red-white-and-blue twinkle in his eye.

"Thank you," Freddy said, stroking the box absentmindedly with his hand.

"You're welcome," the clerk said. The clerk turned on his heel and, leaving Freddy's office door open, slowly walked in a straight line over the display floor, through moving huddles of preoccupied technicians who were preparing to merchandise a floating mobile of their newest torpedoes. Freddy watched the nameless clerk drift across the marble floor past dollies full of torpedo casings and spools of high-tension wire, through the middle of an evenly displayed colonnade of marble mannequin infantrymen perched on marble pedestals—gunmetal grenades on their hips, mortars at their feet, belts of ammunition strapped to their chests. Freddy, who was now standing in the doorway of his office, watched the clerk until he disappeared into a doorway on the other side of the floor.

The morning light was beginning to angle through the plates of the ninth floor's glass-ceilinged rotunda, starkly illuminating the infantrymen's helmets and shoulders, faces and chests, all in all accentuating their predatory gestures. Watching the light wash over the figures, the floor, the pillars, Freddy momentarily felt some semblance of calm, which was abruptly interrupted when he noticed his supervisor, George Ludlow, striding determinedly across the display floor with the two officers who had responded to Freddy's call.

George Ludlow, an officious man with a square head, developing girth, and an unusually unreadable face, looked unusually nervous. He expressed some discomfort on the sides of his mouth, barely legible creases, very slight, very slim. Nevertheless, this barely perceptible change to George Ludlow's unclassifiable face was clearly apparent to the technicians, who, quieted by his altered appearance, as well as the officers' presence, froze into a messy tableau of silent gawking onlookers. "These officers are here to see you," George said to Freddy as he reached the door to his office. At this proximity, Freddy could see he wasn't only nervous, he was angry. He peered his head around Freddy's shoulder in order to see into his office. Once satisfied that there was nothing out of the ordinary about it, he stepped back and allowed the two officers to approach. The two officers approached, and with the aid of George, ushered themselves in. George Ludlow, without saying a word, without making eye contact, firmly shut the door behind him and marched away, audibly. With the door securely closed—with George's angry footsteps no longer audible—the muted voices and noises coming from the display room resumed, and one of the officers walked around Freddy's desk to the closed blind, reached out, and snapped it open.

"Mr. Stillman," he said, pointing across the way, "you were the one who called?"

Freddy's eyes wandered across the air shaft to the apartment.

"Yeah," Freddy said carefully. "It was me."

The two officers sat on the two chairs opposite Freddy's desk. Now that they were before him, Freddy couldn't see any resemblance between the two men. They were as different-looking as a cactus and a pear. They were the same height and build, similar coloring, but one's face was broader than the other's, and one's skin was smooth while the other's was blotchy and whiskered.

"I presume you'll want to be as helpful as possible?" the one marked Reynolds said—the prickly one.

"Of course I'll want to be as helpful as possible."

"Of course you will. The helpful are always easiest to understand."

"I wouldn't know anything about that," Freddy said, not liking Reynolds from the start.

"What is it you were calling about, Mr. Stillman?" the other officer interrupted. He was marked Shaw.

"I'm sorry?"

"What was it you were calling about?"

"The woman."

Reynolds smiled and raised his eyebrows at Freddy meaningfully.

"The woman?" Freddy said again. "Across the way?"

"They're all women across the way," Reynolds said. "It's a hotel for women."

Freddy nodded in agreement, then waited.

"What about the woman?" Shaw asked.

"Like I said to the operator when I called for you, the woman's been murdered."

"What brought you to that conclusion?"

"When I arrived at work this morning, I sat down at my desk here, and when I looked up, I saw her being strangled, right over there, right behind that window."

Reynolds shifted his weight in his seat. "Who? Who was doing the strangling?"

"I don't know."

"You said you saw her being strangled."

"I did. But I couldn't see who was strangling her."

"Big short fat thin?"

"I don't know."

"Then what do you know? What did you see?"

"I saw a large pair of hands. Hands and arms, the sleeves of an overcoat, the rim of a hat edging out from behind the curtain, and the woman."

"And that's it?"

"Yeah, that's it."

"Well, you say you saw a woman strangled over there, but there's no woman strangled over there," Reynolds said. "There's no dead body, no sign of struggle, no sign that the room was forcibly entered."

"How's that possible?"

"Maybe you're seeing things? Maybe you were daydreaming?"

"It wasn't no dream," Freddy said, adamantly shaking his head.

Reynolds snickered a little. "Well, there's still the little problem that there ain't no body over there."

"Maybe he took it with him," Freddy offered.

"Yeah, walked right out onto Central Boulevard with it, right over his shoulder in the middle of rush hour." Reynolds snickered some more.

"He always like this?" Freddy asked, turning to Shaw.

"How about a description, Mr. Stillman?" Shaw asked in return.

"Of the woman?"

"Yes, of the woman."

Freddy sat up in his seat a little. "She was, what? Maybe in her early twenties? She had a slim waist . . . I remember she had a slim waist because her waist reminded me of her neck. She had a slim waist, long auburn hair, a full round face, and . . . and that's all that comes to mind."

"Anything else?"

"She liked to get made up," Freddy recalled instantly. "Made up with cosmetics, that kind of thing. She was a smart dresser."

The officers exchanged glances and let a moment of silence pass before them.

"Now," Reynolds said, beaming a little, "do you know the woman who lives over there, Mr. Stillman? Miss . . . what's the name the concierge gave us?" he asked Shaw.

"Gould," Shaw said, looking down at his notebook. "Janice Gould," he said, looking back up at Freddy.

"No," Freddy said, pointing at the window. "Not beyond, no."

"You're sure about that?"

"Yeah, I'm sure," Freddy said, suddenly not sounding so sure.

"The way you describe her, it sounds like you know this Janice Gould pretty well."

Freddy didn't say anything. He cast his eyes down at his hands, to the desk's blotter, where he noticed for the first time that his fingers were perspiring and that he was leaving dewy fingerprints on the blotter's thin green felt.

"Does she keep her curtains open often, Mr. Stillman?" Reynolds asked.

Freddy could feel his face turn hot. "Yes, fine," he said as he wiped his hands on his slacks. "I see what you're getting at and . . . yes, fine."

"Can I take that for a 'yes'?"

"Yes. I said yes. She keeps her curtains open. But, I'd only seen her once or twice before. She hadn't been living there long."

"What was she wearing today?"

"A robe," Freddy said reluctantly.

"Did the robe have a color?"

"Powder blue." Freddy now smiled awkwardly. "Powder blue. The sash was pink."

"So then," Shaw said, "she was a thin woman with a round face, long auburn hair, a long neck, slim waist. She was wearing a powder-blue robe and liked to get made up."

"Yes," Freddy said.

"And she was strangled by a large pair of hands," Reynolds said with his hand covering his nose as he let out a few more snickers.

"Yes."

"Good enough," Shaw said, looking to his partner.

"Yeah, very nice," Reynolds said with a lascivious grin. He looked across the air shaft. "A very nice spot you have here, Mr. Stillman."

Freddy didn't say anything. He didn't move. He just sat there feeling the heat emanating from his body.

"We'll get some more information about Miss Gould from the Beekman's concierge," Shaw said to his partner. "See if we can't track her down."

"Yeah," Reynolds said as he looked Freddy over one last time. "That's a fine idea."

The two officers rose from their seats. They both looked down at the box of cards on top of Freddy's desk.

"You mind?" Shaw asked.

Freddy opened the box for them with an unsteady hand. "Have as many as you like."

Shaw took one and Reynolds took one.

"Have one of mine. We'll be in touch." Shaw placed his card on Freddy's desk.

With that said, Freddy followed Officers Shaw and Reynolds to the door and watched them walk out onto the display floor. As they crossed under the rotunda, the large room became frozen and silent again. The officers walked as solidly as the marble infantrymen might have. When they cleared the display room, all discerning eyes turned on Freddy and looked him over with some suspicion. Freddy briefly returned their stares and then retreated back into his office, shut the door, and drew the blind to his window. He removed some paperwork from his filing cabinet and sat at his desk, looking over dispatch forms, thinking of his neighbor dressed in her powder-blue robe as she stood at the bureau, in front of her vanity, under the painting of the young man leering down at her with his severe eyes and smile, and he tried to work.

Chapter 5

When Harry Shortz returned to his office, his secretary was on the phone saying, "The Commissioner's out of the office. . . . That's right. . . . That's right. . . . If you don't like it, buddy . . ." The secretary sounded a short laugh with something sharp in it. "All right, have it your way if you're gonna be like that." She slapped the phone down, then turned to Harry. "The phone's been ringing all morning. Everyone wants to know what you were doing over in Long Meadow." The phone started ringing again. She looked at it like she wanted to throw it out the window.

"Unless it's Tines or Crown's lawyer, I'm not here."

Zelda, a thin, energetic woman who moved like a sparrow, tried handing Harry a stack of messages.

"You hold on to those for now."

The phone started ringing again. Zelda steered her lips to the side of her face and stared at the phone defiantly.

"Answer the phone, Zelda."

Zelda lifted the receiver and placed her hand over its mouthpiece. "The missus is inside."

Harry walked into his office to find his wife, Beverly, standing in front of a mirror on the wall, touching up her face. She was dressed in a plaid wool skirt and a pale blue silk blouse with a wide collar, open at the neck, just enough so that the dimple in her throat was exposed. By all accounts around town, in the gossip columns, in the fashion pages, by all authorities who judged with whom one should be seen, Beverly Shortz was an elegant woman, regal in spirit, always tastefully dressed, witty, vivacious, independent, modern, and in her middle age still a woman who could turn the heads of young men. When Harry saw her standing there, he was compelled to touch her.

"I thought I would stop in and say hello on my way home," she said, smiling at him in the mirror.

"On your way home from where?" Harry walked over to Beverly and took hold of her by the waist, brushed her hair away with his nose, and kissed her neck. He kept holding her.

"Dad and I had breakfast this morning."

"How'd that go?"

"About as well as a breakfast with my father goes."

"Feeling a little overwrought?"

"I should: we mostly talked about you."

"Not sure how I should take that."

"I sometimes think it's as if he birthed you himself."

"I'm pretty sure it was dear ol' Mom that spit me out into the world."

"Anyway, he told me to tell you that he wants to arrange a dinner party over at the house to kick off the money grubbing."

"His words?"

"No," she said, smiling, "mine."

"Tell him I'll be happy to oblige."

"I'll let him know," Beverly said as she pried Harry's fingers from her waist and walked behind him. She took Harry's coat off and carried it over to a closet opposite his desk. "And where were you?" she asked as she leaned against the closet door.

"Long Meadow."

"What brought you out there?"

"A little man with a bad complexion."

"So now you're consorting with trolls?"

"Paulie Sendak—armory foreman of the Long Meadow Munitions Workers Union. A little man with a bad complexion. A troll of sorts, I suppose. He had the mind to give me a call to settle a dispute the union has with Tines."

"What's the problem?"

"Well, according to Tines, some dynamite found in some fishing shack somewhere along the river belongs to two of the leaders of the union. According to the union, the dynamite was planted in the fishing shack by the owner of the munitions factory."

"Oh, right," Beverly said, her eyes studying her manicure. "That explosion the other day."

"Right," Harry said, his attention drawn to Beverly's hands. "That."

"So you actually had a talk with Tines?"

"I did."

"And you made everything right for the union?"

"As right as I could. . . . And then I went to Long Meadow to put the little man with the bad complexion at ease. Him and all his armed men."

"Why were they armed?"

"They had taken over the plant."

Beverly looked up from her nails and stared at Harry crossly. "I wish you wouldn't tell me these things."

"Better from me than from the papers."

"Did you get them to put down their weapons?"

"I did."

"Without incident?"

"Without incident."

"Good." Beverly, no longer looking cross, but relieved, walked over to Harry, sat him down on a sofa, and then took a seat on his lap. "I ran into Hope Drummond on our way out of the restaurant this morning," she said, her tone more light now.

"How is the old broad?" Harry asked with a genuine lack of interest.

"As young as ever. . . . I can't remember, Harry. Did I tell you that the Martins are holding a private auction at their country estate Saturday afternoon?"

"No, you didn't. What's it all about?"

"You'll never guess."

"I'm sure I won't."

"Soviet art," she said, accentuating both words slowly and carefully, as though she had said "The Queen of England." "Of the revolutionary period, no less."

"Is that right?"

"Can you imagine? Celeste Martin and Noel Tersi? They're as much communists as Herbert Hoover is." Beverly laughed. "Can you see the two of them trying to pass themselves off as lumpen proletariat? Of the people? Of any people? Please. They've always been eccentric, I'll give them that much. Celeste, in particular, has always gone out of her way to be outrageous. Ever since she and my mother were girls at school."

"I'm sure if Noel Tersi is behind it, there's some money to be made."

"Along with the artwork they've apparently imported some renowned Russian art historian," Beverly continued, obviously preoccupied with the subject, "to give a lecture before the auction—Tarovski, or something like that. Anyway, Hope said that they're boasting that they've invited some of the more prominent members of the American Communist Party, including," and she paused, holding for a punchline, "Jerome Brilovsky."

"Dr. Brilovsky? The former head of the Brigade?"

"That's right."

"I haven't heard that name in a long time."

"It's as though they're daring everyone to be there. I find it peculiar, don't you?"

"I take it we weren't invited? Is that why this is suddenly interesting to you?"

"No, we were invited. We received the invitation in the mail a few weeks ago. I just didn't think there was any point to telling you. I thought it would upset you."

"Why in the world . . ."

"And I wouldn't bring it up now if Hope hadn't reminded me about it this morning. I said to her, 'Do they really expect my husband, in his position, with a senatorial election only months away, to be made a greater target for Lawrence Tines than he already is?' "

"Is that what you were thinking?"

"To be as leftward-thinking as he is already, and then to be in the company of Dr. Jerome Brilovsky?"

"I see."

"I said, 'It was partly Harry's doing that helped put him in jail for killing that poor young woman. You've got to be kidding,' I said."

"It wasn't my doing, Beverly. And you know I'd have no objection being in the same room with anyone, including Dr. Brilovsky."

"Yes, I know."

"Then why did you refuse the invitation?"

"Because I feel uncomfortable around a man like Dr. Brilovsky and his ilk."

"But now that you know Hope is going . . . ?"

"She's set on it. As is everyone else. It's suddenly the thing to do. According to Hope, anyone who knows anything about modern art will just have to be there. 'The Soviets being the forerunners of the avant-garde, how could they miss it?' Hope said to me. I don't know, darling. It kind of feels like gangrene is setting in."

"With envy?"

"What could you possibly mean?" Beverly flashed Harry a surrendering smile as if to say she knew exactly what he meant. "What bothers me most about all this," she continued, as she played with a button on his shirt, speaking like a pouty little girl, "—and tell me if I'm being hysterical—is that in the name of art they're luring in all these good-intentioned people, who'll end up paying for a painting—some of whose proceeds will probably end up in Stalin's brutish hands. Don't you think so, dear?"

"It's more likely the money will fall into Tersi's old decrepit hands."

"But possible?"

"Anything is possible."

"Good. At least I'll have something to say tonight when I'm at the theater."

"You're going to the theater tonight?"

"Yes, don't you remember? Agnes Carlyle is taking me to see the opening of *Prometheus Bound.*"

"How appropriate."

" 'Harry said it's highly likely,' I'll say," Beverly said, paying no mind to Harry.

"I'm sorry."

"Tonight at the theater."

"Right."

"I'll say, 'Harry said it's highly likely.' "

"That's not what I said."

"In any case, I might be able to deter at least a few reasonable people from going."

"Why don't we just go, if you're feeling left out."

"I've already declined the invitation, Harry."

"Not to mention you've probably been talking like this with all your friends ever since you received the invitation."

"I would look like a fool and a hypocrite if we went now."

"Such troubles you have. You and all that blue blood of yours must be boiling."

"You love every drop of it."

"If I could only help myself."

"In any case, Harry, I'll blather on a bit and try to raise a few eyebrows," she said as she self-consciously raised her own arched eyebrows and smoothed them over with her finger.

Harry gave Beverly a hug and a gentle kiss on the mouth. He helped her off his lap and picked up her fur coat from the other end of the sofa. He draped it over her shoulders and walked her to the door.

"Off I go into the cold cold cold."

"I'll see you tonight, dear."

"Yes, tonight, in the sack, I'll be there."

When Harry shut the door behind Beverly, he took a seat at his desk and sat before several framed photographs, one of Beverly, himself, and their two sons, Eric and Harry, Jr., who were eleven and nine. There was a photo of Harry's parents taken at their family home, which stood on a small plot of land in Portsmith, where his mother and father, two Belgian émigrés, worked for the mining company most of their lives. Beside this image, in a considerably more elaborate setting, on the grounds of their country estate, was a photo of Harry's in-laws, Clarissa and Edward Kelly. Hanging on the walls were small trophies and plaques from rescue missions and temperance groups honoring his service, along with photos of him standing beside several Presidents.

Harry noticed sitting on top of a stack of papers in his in-box a manila envelope he hadn't seen when he had come in that morning. He reached over for it. It was marked *Commissioner Shortz,* no return address. As he was about to open it, Zelda knocked on his door and stuck her head in. "There's a Mr. Gerald Kravitz from the Long Meadow Munitions Workers Union to see you. He says he has an appointment."

"Send him in," Harry said. He placed the envelope off to the side and stood up to meet Mr. Kravitz. "How do you do, Mr. Kravitz?"

"Fine, thanks."

"Take off your coat and have a seat."

Gerald Kravitz, a fast-talking man with a febrile glow in his cheeks, doubled as a machinist and one of the union's lawyers. He removed his coat and hung it and his hat on a rack beside the door. He then took a seat in front of Harry and opened his briefcase.

"Any word on Waters and Capp?" Harry asked.

"It all went smoothly, thanks to you."

"Have they set a date for the hearing?"

"Three weeks."

"Not a lot of time."

"It's time enough if Chief Investigator Tines is cooperative."

"I certainly hope he is."

"It'll be rough, I think."

"Why's that?"

"Tines has it out for them for certain youthful indiscretions."

"What did they do?"

"Wrote some hotheaded remarks on some hotheaded subjects in *The Masses* a long time ago."

Mr. Kravitz opened his briefcase and handed Harry a few articles that Waters and Capp had written.

Harry read. "They sound pretty hostile."

"It was twenty years ago."

"Still," Harry said, "it doesn't help matters."

"No," Kravitz said, "it doesn't."

"Not with Tines feeling as he does about sympathizers."

"And you? How do you feel?"

"It's simply beside the point."

"I'm relieved to hear that."

"So, Mr. Kravitz," Harry said, leaning forward in his seat a little, "the reason I asked Mr. Sendak to send you over here this morning is because I'd like to know why someone other than Waters and Capp would have a motive to cause an explosion at the plant."

Mr. Kravitz reached into his briefcase, pulled out some papers, and handed them to Harry. "I think the answer to that question is somewhere between the lines of this agreement Fief has with Long Meadow."

"How so?" Harry asked as he placed the papers before him.

"Simply put? Fief wants to open up the shop to workers outside of Long Meadow. He wants to drive wages down. Claims with the current closed-door policy, he's not competitive any longer."

"Is there any truth in it?"

"I suppose so."

"He never expected the union to be so strong?"

"Of course he did. That was the nature of the agreement. It was a three-way partnership between Fief, Long Meadow, and the government. Fief, at the time, was sinking. The government threw him a bone to stay afloat. Long Meadow paid for most of the factory's construction in return for job security and bargaining power. So for Julius Fief, it was a ripe deal. Now that the company's strong and it looks like things are starting to heat up around the world and there's a chance he might hit a few more boom years, he's itching to muscle us out."

"So, what's this got to do with the explosion at the plant?"

"If a court says the union is too hostile for him to conduct his business, he gets to slip out of that agreement. An indictment for sabotage and manslaughter helps his case an awful lot. Starting to get the picture?"

"Yeah, sure," Harry said, giving his chin a rub.

"And Tines?" Gerald Kravitz said, nearly spitting Tines's name. "He wants to see working stiffs with their heads in the rubbish heap. It ain't communism he's fighting, it's regular bums like us he's after. Us and the government that gave Fief the development money that helped create us."

Harry, who was still gripping his chin, smiled at Kravitz with some amusement. "But tell me this," Harry said. "Why doesn't Fief just offer you a settlement?"

"Because he'd lose the plant and everything in it. It goes to us to cover our debts. He can't afford that."

"So, he's stuck with you."

"And vice versa. And he's going to be stuck with plenty more, because if I know my boys, they're going to vote to shut down the plant starting tonight. We've got annual contract negotiations coming up right around the time the trial starts—coincidentally—and, regardless of how it looks, we're not gonna let Fief think he can fuck with us without feeling a little hurt himself."

"That is a little coincidental, isn't it?" Harry agreed.

"Very." Kravitz nodded his head quickly and gave his nose a tug.

"But if you go on strike, aren't your men concerned that it'll look like another hostile act to add to the list of hostile acts? Don't you think you may be playing right into Fief's hand?"

"Frankly, they're too angry to think like that. The union's stubborn, Mr. Commissioner, and they don't like Fief. And I can't say I blame them. But I do see your point. But you have to see the union's. When it comes time to negotiate the new contract, we have to show Fief that our backs are made of steel. If we bow down to his and Tines's intimidation, we're as good as lost."

"You realize, however, if you go on strike it's going to make it almost impossible for me to influence Tines to give Waters and Capp a fair shot."

"No offense, Mr. Commissioner, but you and I both know that nothin' you say to Tines is gonna get him to clear those two. The only thing we're hoping for is to get through to you so you can help us put up what at least looks like a reasonable fight."

"And what do Waters and Capp say about all this?"

"I'm sure they're scared, but they won't keep the men back."

"And the men won't hold off for the sake of Waters and Capp?"

Gerald Kravitz curled his lips down and shook his head.

"You mean to say they'll just sacrifice them?"

"Like helpless little lambs."

"Then why all the hullabaloo this morning?"

"War cries. We use what we've got."

Harry leaned his large heft back into his seat and shrugged his shoulders. "I'll do whatever I can," he said without much enthusiasm.

"That's all we ask, Mr. Commissioner. Thank you for seeing me."

Gerald Kravitz closed his briefcase and collected his coat and hat. "Good day," he said to Harry and shook his hand.

When Gerald Kravitz stepped out of Harry's office, Harry reached back over to the envelope he had set aside and opened it.

If you don't want the public to know about Sylvia and Katrina Lowenstein, drop out of the Senate race by Saturday afternoon. If you aren't careful, more than just your career will be at stake.

Along with the note was a carbon of a deed to a piece of property transferred to Harry's name a few months earlier, a ring, and a photograph of an old country house set against an empty field on one side and an apple orchard on the other. Harry sat there, blisteringly numb, studying the photo.

"Zelda!" Harry growled loudly at the door, the sound of his own voice unsettling him. He could hear Zelda jump.

"What is it?" she asked when she opened the door.

"Who sent this?" Harry said holding up the envelope.

"That? It came by messenger while you were over in Long Meadow."

"Who sent it?"

"Hold on a second." Zelda quickly walked to her desk and returned.

"Who?"

"It says here . . . Lowenstein. Katrina Lowenstein."

Harry was speechless.

"There was no return address," Zelda said after a moment. "Just the name."

"All right," Harry said, his tone quieting.

"Everything okay, Mr. Commissioner?" Zelda's face was blanched.

"Yeah, everything's peachy," Harry said pensively. "Just peachy."

"You startled me," Zelda said in a wounded voice as she pulled the door closed.

Harry sat there in a stupor for a while, unable to figure out how it all added up. He tried to put it all together for a few minutes, and then, in a rage, gathered the papers with the photograph and walked over to the closet in which Beverly had hung his coat. Inside the closet, behind the clothes, was a small safe. Harry dialed the combination and opened the door, placed the package inside, and shut it away. He removed his coat from the hanger, put it on, and walked back to his desk and picked up the ring. It was gold, nesting a large amethyst. He held the amethyst up to the light, and while looking at it he simultaneously felt a sense of longing and anger. He charged out of his office and told Zelda that he would be gone for the better part of the afternoon.

Chapter 6

Celeste Martin, who would be hosting the auction of Soviet art at her country estate on Saturday, was currently upstairs in the roomy attic of 319 West Eighty-third Street, rummaging through a trunk in search of a box of old photographs. Other than being well known as an aging society matron who had slummed through the better part of the last decade with the heavy-drinking Oak Street set, Celeste Martin was best known as the real estate baroness of Gravesend Avenue. Celebrated by some, reviled by others, awe-inspiring to all, Celeste had become a City icon when, after the war, she cavalierly demolished three blocks of historic homes—from the corner of Eighty-third and Langore Square to Eighty-third and Gravesend Avenue—bequeathed to her in her father's will. Only two homes—319 and 322—were spared. 319 was her mother's place of birth, and 322 her father's place of death, as well as the home in which Celeste grew up, and the house in which she now resided with her brother, Richard, and her elderly companion, the successful property developer Noel Tersi.

With Noel Tersi's guidance, Celeste consulted the visionary architect Raymond Montgomery to create in the grand neo-Gothic style a row of idiosyncratic buildings, twenty-three stories high, that would run to the gates of her mother's and father's homes and be crowned with gargoyles cast in the image of Celeste's Croatian handyman, Aleksandr. The son of a master builder, and a master builder by training himself, Aleksandr was, by all accounts, the inspiration for this awesome undertaking. According to the papers, early one Sunday morning, on her way home from an exhausting night on the town, Celeste Martin was overwhelmed by a vision. She saw from the back of her car what she thought was the face of an Orthodox Christian icon framed within the stained-glass doorway of the Langore Square Orthodox Church. When she realized that the sunken eyes, sagging jaw, gaunt cheeks, and thin pert lips of this beatifically sorrowful face belonged to her handyman, and that the child in his arms wasn't baby Jesus, but Aleksandr's young daughter, she felt the overwhelming presence of God. As Aleksandr stood there forlornly in his humble and hapless pose, looking so lost and fragile as he did, he appeared to Celeste as an immigrant-saint whose image, she believed, should be preserved on a landmark that would stand the test of time.

On a whim of the highest order, Celeste commanded her driver to halt, then jumped from the car onto the street and rushed Aleksandr away from his wife and children and urged him to immediately begin the work of re-creating himself in the form of a sculpture. She did this with such great passion she had turned crimson. "This, for the sake of your own posterity," she argued breathlessly. "And for all like you to come. And because I will pay you handsomely. Handsomely."

The molds for what would eventually become very somber-looking grotesques were cast by Aleksandr's father in Split, Croatia, in the shadow of the two-thousand-year-old palace of the Roman emperor Diocletian. They arrived in hundreds of crates insulated with hay and were stored away inside a South End warehouse until the finishing touches were being put on Celeste's buildings. Raymond Montgomery looked on with Celeste as the figures were anchored onto the eaves of the roofs, and when the work was finally completed, Aleksandrs in the hundreds stood fixed over all of West Eighty-third Street, looking down with arms outstretched as if each and every one of him were contemplating suicide.

. . .

The Disappearing Body

When Celeste found the box of photographs she had been looking for, she shut the trunk and carefully made her way out of the attic and down the stairs, then crossed the street to her home. Celeste's townhouse was a five-story brownstone whose bottom-floor windows were draped with ivory-colored curtains that hadn't been opened in twenty years, not since the day Celeste's father, Benjamin Martin, passed in his sleep on the divan opposite his easel, where he had been painting his last bouquet of lilacs. This darkened room had been his parlor, the room to which Celeste, as a young girl, had run with large bundles of flowers picked from the bushes in the backyard each spring. She would arrange the bouquets in immense urns her father had had shipped from Egyptian tombs. In memory of her late father, the parlor was kept as a shrine, exactly as it was the day Benjamin Martin died. The half-painted bouquet of flowers on its easel, the pigments dried on their palette, the smock he had worn draped at the foot of the divan.

When Celeste closed the front door, she quietly walked around a mahogany stairwell into the dining room, where hanging above the dining room's mantel was a portrait of Benjamin and Rosemary Martin. Hovering before their venerable eyes were ribbons of cigar smoke that funneled into the fixtures of the chandelier; they wrapped around the individual crystals on their way up toward the yellowed ceiling. "Don't let me disturb you," Celeste said to Noel Tersi, Dr. Joseph Gamburg, and her brother, Richard, who were sitting at the table discussing the final arrangements for Saturday's event. She placed the box before Richard and whispered in his ear, "I found it, darling. But I'm afraid it's locked. I'll try to find the key." Richard nodded at his sister, then returned his attention to Noel, who, sitting opposite him, was pointing his cigar at Dr. Gamburg, a curator for Leslie's Auction House. Dr. Gamburg, a middle-aged man, modestly dressed, with a full head of black hair and hardly a line on his face, stared intently into the deep crevices that made up Noel Tersi's mouth.

Richard Martin watched Noel and the doctor engage in conversation, but had his mind elsewhere. He was the eldest of this group at the age of seventy-three, was in ailing health, and had little interest in art or the society that formed the art world. In his day, he had run from the family business to escape the expectations cast upon him by his father. A shy but adventurous man, he traveled to distant countries with the ambition to write books about all things he found exotic. But, in the end, he never wrote one. Instead, he spent many years living as a vagabond until his father died, at which time he returned to his sister to help settle the estate. Today, as on many days in the decades since his return, he sat in his chair without commenting on Noel Tersi's business matters.

"What did Director Tines want exactly?" Dr. Gamburg nearly yelled as he moved his chair closer to Noel Tersi.

"What?"

"What did Director Tines want?!!!"

Noel Tersi was hard of hearing, more so than he liked to admit. He spoke very loudly in a clipped, sometimes incoherent syntax that at the moment left a very consternated look on Dr. Gamburg's face. "He has some concerns."

"Concerns?!"

"About the nature of the show. Concerns about the show."

"Why does he feel it's his place to . . . !!!"

"He doesn't like Tarkhov. He has a past."

"A past?! We all have . . ."

"It's nothing but numbskullery. He's a young curmudgeon is what Tines is. A gen-U-ine ass on a crusade."

"Noel, what exactly did he want?"

"What's that?"

"I said, what did he want us to do for him?!"

"Details. Records. Nonsense."

"Wha . . . ?!" Dr. Gamburg shook his head as though he were confused. He looked tired from talking so loud.

"Records. He'll want records of what's sold. To whom and so on."

"That's unlawful."

"Hmm?"

"That's unlawful!"

"It was a request," Noel said quietly, his eyes widening as he took a puff of his cigar. "He made a polite request."

"What did you tell him?!"

"Before or after he threatened to send some men out to the estate?"

"So that's how it is."

"What's that?"

"I said, so that's how it is!!!"

"Yeah," Noel said as he ashed his cigar and planted it in the corner of his mouth.

"Noel, I don't need to tell you that I've gone out of my way to get very important people interested in this show! There are very important moneyed people interested in attending Saturday's auction, and they're not going to come if they think a gaggle of G-men are snooping into their business!"

"And you've done a smashing damn good job of it too."

"Did you hear me?!"

"Hmm?"

"The point is, I don't think these people . . . !" Dr. Gamburg took a breath. "I don't think these . . ." Dr. Gamburg looked over to Richard for some help. Richard had his eyes shut. He had fallen asleep in his chair.

"Listen," Noel Tersi said severely. "Don't you concern yourself. Let's just pretend I didn't say anything at all if it makes you feel any better."

"Surely you understand that I have to think of the reputation of Leslie's and its clients in all of this! I can't . . . I can't just pretend that . . . We can't afford a scandal of this nature!!!"

"Are you so sure?" Noel said slyly, now leaning in toward Dr. Gamburg.

"What are you getting at?"

"Hmm?"

"I said, WHAT ARE YOU GETTING AT?!!!"

"Don't you see how this might work to our advantage?"

"No!" Dr. Gamburg said with a little bit of "yes" starting to form on his face.

Noel Tersi smiled, his yellow teeth glistening in the dim light of the room. "The more to-do made over this? The more to-do . . ." Noel made circles with one of his fingers.

Dr. Gamburg sat back in his chair and studied Noel's eyes. They were full of delight and mischief. "Noel?!" he said, leaning back over the table, "Out of curiosity . . ."

"Hmm?"

"Out of curiosity! Do you know who it was that happened to tip off Tines about the show?!!!"

Noel continued smiling.

"So that's how it is."

"Hmm?"

Dr. Gamburg didn't repeat himself this time. He just started mulling it all over in his head.

"Look," Noel said in a way suggesting he wasn't sure if he'd gotten through to Dr. Gamburg, "you let me worry about who's going to be upset about what, all right? You just be a good kid and run on up to the estate and keep this bit of gossip to yourself if you think that's what's best. But if you ask this old dog, I'd be . . ." Noel Tersi started manically flapping his fingers together as if his hand were the head of a rabid puppet.

"You sly old bug," Dr. Gamburg said.

"What's that?"

"I said, I'll keep it under the rug for the time being, if that's all right with you!"

"Suit yourself." Noel shrugged his shoulders and took another puff on his cigar. "But can't expect something like this to stay hush-hush."

"I suppose not!"

"That's a good kid."

Dr. Gamburg laughed a light knowing laugh. "I think I'll run up to the estate to get everything ready for the professor and leave you to . . . !" Dr. Gamburg started flapping his fingers together as Noel had done.

"That's the right idea."

"Yeah," Dr. Gamburg said, nodding. "All right."

Just as Dr. Gamburg came to this, Celeste entered the dining room and gently shook Richard awake. "I'm back with it, Richard," she said. She turned to Noel. "Isn't that wonderful, Noel?!!"

"Yes, darling, it is," Noel said as he stood up. "Dr. Gamburg, why don't I show you on your way."

"Yes, I'm anxious to get a start! It was a pleasure seeing you again, Celeste! Richard!"

"No need to yell at us, dear," Celeste said cordially.

"I'm sorry, I just . . ." Dr. Gamburg said, flustered. "I just . . ."

"We'll see you on Saturday," Celeste said in a whisper. "I do look forward to it. Everyone I've talked with is. Did you know the Department of Investigations has taken an interest?" Celeste asked innocently.

"Very good to hear it," Dr. Gamburg said, shaking his head in wonder.

"It's all very exciting, isn't it?"

Dr. Gamburg turned the shake of his head into a nod and waved an awkward goodbye as he followed Noel into the hall.

"This is what took me so long," Celeste said to Richard when the noise from the men's heavy footsteps ceased. She held up the key to the box. "I couldn't for the life of me remember where I had put it. Finally, I realized it was hanging on a hook in the upstairs hallway. It must have been there since you returned . . . gathering dust."

Richard smiled at Celeste as she opened the lock. With the lock undone, she gently pulled open the lid and removed a package of photographs, the first of which was a picture of Celeste and Richard standing on a hillock in the park the year Richard returned home. Behind them were passersby, clearly defined figures wearing dark suits and hats.

Chapter 7

Arthur Brilovsky just happened to be walking through the park the day Celeste and Richard met the photographer for their picture. He was in a great rush and never even saw the pair when he passed them on the little hill, not even for a moment. Something catastrophic had just occurred and his blood was rushing through him so hard the veins in his temples were visibly pulsating. He was formulating words there, a long speech for his father, full of explanations, a course of action, thoughts that were making it hard for him to think clearly. But there was absolutely no indication of Arthur's crisis depicted in the photograph. Captured as he was, he looked like an average man of average height and build; his face was slightly out of focus, just enough so one could easily misconstrue his torment for euphoria—especially since he had raised his arms into the air, bathing them with sunlight. Casting such a pose, he seemed to be making an appeal for mercy to the cloudless sky and to the newly burgeoned magnolia blossoms that swagged into the upper right-hand corner of the camera's frame. It was a portrait of a spiritual awakening, one at which Celeste and Richard marveled when they first saw the image.

Arthur Brilovsky was twenty-two years old in this photo, a doctor in training, and the son of Dr. Jerome Brilovsky, a respected physician, entrepreneur, and political radical. The Brilovskys were well-educated Russian Jewish émigrés who, while living in St. Petersburg, had been vocal against the czar and his army, and had supported the eradication of his regime. In return for such outspoken beliefs, Arthur's father survived two assassination attempts and painfully grieved the undignified and cowardly murder of his brother, Lev, who was shot between the eyes while eating a piece of bread with honey at his dining-room table. Dr. Jerome Brilovsky vowed, in return for this assault, to destroy the aristocracy of his former country. He fled to America, to the City, where he opened a medical practice on Elsworth Street and made a success of American Allied, a pharmaceutical company located on the Southside Docks. Here the Brilovskys amassed a considerable fortune, and with it began funding the most formidable opposition against the czar, the notorious Brigade, which was the largest American organization to contribute funds toward revolutionary activities.

A week before Celeste and Richard's photographer captured Arthur striding through the park, a young, elegant woman of about nineteen entered Dr. Brilovsky's office and was greeted by Arthur at the front desk. The young woman wore a yellow silk dress that hugged at her hips and shoulders. Her face was powdered so that her brown eyes glistened in the late-afternoon light shining through the office window. She had a severe haircut that sharply hooked under her jaw and fanned out in front of her face when she leaned over the desk to shake hands with Arthur. Arthur, who was reading a speech his father was to deliver to members of the Brigade that evening, placed the paper down, stood up, and shook the woman's hand. She shook firmly, didn't smile; she looked around the office and listened at the open doors of the examination rooms. There was no one in the office at the time. The nurse had already gone home. Arthur's brothers had gone to join his father.

"I was told that you perform abortions," the woman said bluntly. Her voice was deep and unemotional, but so determined Arthur imagined her practicing this statement in front of a mirror at home.

"I'm afraid you've been misinformed," Arthur said to her plainly.

"Shelly Price says abortions are performed here," the woman persisted.

"Shelly Price told you this. . . . How is it that you know him?"

"He's my father. I'm his daughter, Elaine."

Arthur considered her for a moment, looking at her more closely, at the brunette wisps of hair that curled onto her cheek. They stuck to the dampened powder on her face.

"I see," he said.

It was true that Arthur's father did occasionally perform abortions, with which Arthur had assisted him on more than several occasions, and Arthur, in fact, had performed a number on his own. As for Shelly Price, he was a new business associate of his father's, whom Arthur had met only a few times over lunch but whom he liked very much.

"Your father told you to come here?"

"He insisted that I come here."

Arthur allowed this answer the silence it deserved. And in the interim of this silence the strength Arthur felt in Elaine Price's handshake appeared to drain from her body and her voice. She and the yellow dress slowly wilted into the hard chair before the desk. "He insisted that I come," she repeated softly. She drew her knees together and tightened her lips, clutched hard at a black beaded bag she was carrying. She looked at Arthur, then looked out the window. "I would like you to perform the procedure on me as soon as you can fit me in, please," she said, looking back at him.

Arthur didn't ask any questions. He simply looked into her intense brown eyes and showed her he was capable of attending to her needs. He sat down, reached across the scattered surface of the desk, pushed aside his father's speech, and began to flip through the appointment book. He wrote her name and told her to come back the following week first thing in the morning.

. . .

That evening inside the American Allied warehouse, Dr. Jerome Brilovsky, a stout and formidable man with a pile of red kinked hair addressed Shelly Price and over a hundred members of the Brigade with news that American Allied Pharmaceutical had profited well beyond expectation and would be the largest American contributor to Russia's provisional government. Because of this auspicious moment, he was proud to announce that Kerensky had requested a meeting with him and that he would be traveling to Russia at the end of the month to discuss what more the Brigade could do to quicken the pace of the revolution and ease the famine that faced the people of Russia.

When he was through with his speech, when everyone was properly won over by the news, everyone ate. Dr. Brilovsky sat at the head of the table that night. On his right was Shelly Price, on his left, Arthur, who, to Arthur's great surprise, was sitting opposite Elaine. Elaine, who hadn't realized Arthur was the son of Dr. Jerome Brilovsky, couldn't look across the table; nor could she look at her father, who was engaged in conversation with the doctor. Arthur did his best to ignore Elaine and kept his mind focused on his father's conversation. Together, Dr. Brilovsky and Shelly Price privately discussed the ongoing needs of the local unions and the Southside Docks dockworker strike planned for the following week and moved on to talk of what they should present to Kerensky in Petrograd. Shelly Price, one of the largest partners in American Allied next to Dr. Brilovsky, suggested that they offer to continue their financial support, but that they start approaching American industrialists who wanted to open new markets overseas.

Arthur listened to their conversation, listened for mention that Shelly Price had sent his daughter into the clinic that afternoon. However, there was none. The only indication that Mr. Price was aware of his daughter's presence at all was when he cast his eyes on her in the middle of a sentence or in the middle of a drink and his brow furrowed, his thoughts drifted, and his overall expression became tinged with a certain flare of the nose that made him look like he was smelling something unpleasant.

Only when a number of members of the Southside Docks local arrived at the head of the table to discuss some concerns with Shelly and Jerome about the strike did Arthur approach Elaine and ask if she would like to go outside with him for some fresh air. She agreed with a withdrawn nod of the head and walked in front of Arthur up the aisle, through the smoke and clamoring voices. When they exited the meeting hall and shut the door behind them, the voices quieted, and they could hear a small electrical buzz from the nearby manufacturing plants and the brays of horses coming from the milk wagon stables. A greenish tint cast from a half-moon coated the debris of an ironworks across the way. An occasional breeze whistled through the twirling canals of metal scraps and carried the scent of manure and oil. A burly man dressed in overalls pushing a wheelbarrel full of something dark and viscous passed before them.

Arthur took his jacket off and laid it on the front steps of the warehouse. He sat down first and invited Elaine to sit beside him. Elaine, a little apprehensive at first, crouched down next to him, so that Arthur could smell her sweat and the cigar smoke that mingled with the perfume in her hair. Her shoulder pressed against his a little, which gave Arthur a fluttering sensation in his groin. At that moment, he had nearly forgotten their awkward meeting earlier that afternoon, that she was pregnant and distraught. There was a crude and brazen part of him that felt like taking her hand and resting her palm in his lap. That is, until her eyes turned on him.

"He isn't a bad man," Elaine tried to explain.

"No," Arthur said, knowing she was speaking of her father.

"What I did was wrong, very wrong," she said. Elaine was more casual now, talking as though she were talking to God more than to Arthur. "He isn't even a man of such restrictive scruples," she continued. "He's simply practical. He doesn't want me to be alone with the child, and he couldn't live knowing I'd be with the man who got me pregnant."

"Are you in love with him?" Arthur asked innocently. "With the man?"

"He's deeply in love with me."

"Are you in love with him?" Arthur repeated.

"He's a dear man. He's gentle and sweet, but . . . a little helpless. And . . . I don't really know. But I do know that Father's right." She nodded her head quickly. "He is right."

"Yes, I'm sure he is."

Arthur and Elaine sat on the stoop for some time. When Elaine finally allowed herself to cry, without looking at him, she took Arthur's open hand and pulled it onto the soft flesh of her belly, and wept.

The morning Elaine Price was to have her abortion, the two grizzled men—the very ones who collected Victor Ribe off the side of the road in Long Meadow at the start of this story—sat at a picnic table in the park. They had just bought from a young buck-toothed boy with a lame leg the very first deck of playing cards they would use for an ongoing game of gin. On this day in the park, the score had yet to move beyond zero to zero—there was no winner or loser, no black book filled with numbers. Both men were feeling very optimistic. On this day, they sat under two maple trees whose leafless limbs crossed perfectly over a wading pool for birds. Yellow warblers migrating north for the summer bathed and warbled and plucked at seedlings and worms under uncut grass sprouting from the cracks of the pool's cement. The birds darted after galloping dogs fleeting across a great open lawn. Flying just inches from the undulating canine spines, the birds brought smiles to the unshaven faces of the two grizzled men. They had just returned from a job well done. Posing as members of the Southside Docks local, they carried a handful of scabs across a picket line, and, in the process, knocked together a few heads, got a couple of good knocks back, and incited a small riot. One of the recruited scabs was sent to the hospital with a broken leg, another was knocked into a coma, a third lost three teeth, and a fourth, an innocent striker trying to save his scab cousin, was killed from stab wounds. In their estimation, it was a morning well spent. The two grizzled men were well paid. Even though it was morning, and a little too early for both of them, the men broke into a local speakeasy, filled two pints of beer, took a bagful of peanuts, and went to the park.

It was at about the same time that the two grizzled men settled down at the picnic table that Dr. Brilovsky arrived at the office. Arthur was already there, bustling about, preparing the operating room, while a dark-haired Russian woman dressed in a short black dress and clutching a silver cross in her hand sat on a hard chair in the waiting room, bouncing her foot nervously against the sharp edge of her high-heeled shoe. As Arthur took in the sight of this woman's tightened face, the phone rang, and the woman began bouncing her foot even harder, so hard that her heel cracked right off the bottom of her shoe. His father, who was paying no attention to any of this, answered the phone. "Allo. . . . Yes, it's me. . . . Sheldon. . . . Sheldon. . . . Don't worry, I'll be right there." Jerome Brilovsky hung up the phone. Without a word, without consulting his son or his appointment book, he hurriedly ran out of the office and onto an approaching streetcar.

Arthur remained behind. He was standing by an open office window that looked out onto a terra-cotta building with busts of men wearing conquistador helmets. He noticed Elaine standing in the shade under the awning of the entryway with a tall lanky man in a suit who was carrying a large bundle of white roses. "Please, Victor, I want to go in alone. Let me go, and try to understand," Arthur heard Elaine say. The man was speechless. "We mustn't have bad feelings for each other. Not ever. Do you promise?" The man remained still. Elaine took hold of his free hand, squeezed her face into his chest, and then abruptly walked away from him toward Dr.

Brilovsky's office. As the tall man watched Elaine walk away from him, he smelled the flowers, then turned and handed them to the doorman standing in one of the building's double-arched doorways behind him.

Victor Ribe, young and uncorrupted, walked down the block toward the entrance of the park, away from Elaine Price, his one true love. Waving his hands about and talking to himself, he walked through couples and groups of workmen congregating on the street corners. He walked without seeing them. When he reached the park's entrance, he walked onto a path of freshly cut grass, on either side of which were purple tulips cupping up to the sky. The sight of their thick, fresh green stems and their delicate plum petals reminded him of the flowers he had just dropped into the hands of the doorman. With this thought in mind, he diverted off the path into the rows of bulbs. He stepped on each and every tulip along his way. He crushed their delicate petals so that when he lifted his heavy feet, the secretion of tulip water impressed itself onto the soles of his shoes. What remained was the scrawny, frizzled meat of the flower, its purple veins bleeding onto the recently defrosted soil that had just turned the perfect temperature for the blossoms to reach their pinnacles, and bloom.

Women of all ages shamed Victor with harsh stares and shouts. "Have you no shame?" He could see in his mind the doctor spreading Elaine's legs, spreading her apart and reaching inside her in search of the small delicate piece of himself that he had left with her. He was still young and sensitive enough to feel a deep connection to the sanctity of the future. The future hadn't yet come for him when he would be forced to stick bayonets through the chests of men until all that was left was gushing holes draining into ditches, when he would need to stick needles into his arm to infuse his heart with forgetfulness.

Victor walked to the open field, where he climbed onto a large boulder and stood on its broken edge. He looked down and across to the two grizzled men who were now playing cards, onto the warblers chasing the dogs, onto the photographer who had just arrived and was preparing his tripod and occasionally pulling out his pocket watch. But Victor saw nothing. It was only a matter of minutes until Richard and Celeste would arrive, wearing their finest clothes. And it was only a matter of some more time passing until Arthur Brilovsky would come walking blindly through the field, stepping into the picture and becoming the tip to what might have been a perfect equilateral triangle—Victor, the two grizzled men, and Arthur—Richard and Celeste Martin somewhere in the middle. As the grizzled men played gin, as the socialites became immortalized, as Victor sunned himself and calmed himself on the rock, Arthur would remain panicked, panicking and praying, preparing speeches in his head for his father, digging away at drying blood from under his fingernails, preparing to drag the doctor from the jailhouse to explain to him a very grave error he had just made.

GLOBE METRO REPORT, DECEMBER 17, 191-

Brigade Offices Raided, American Allied Sold to Greek-Born Socialite

SAM RAPAPORT

Southside Docks—This afternoon, with a court order in hand and a team of investigators at his side, Department of Investigations Officer Lawrence Tines raided the Southside Docks offices of the Brigade, the well-known revolutionary communist apparatus that has long been suspected of lending its moral and financial support to the Soviets. At the time of the raid, the Brigade offices—located in the American Allied Pharmaceutical warehouse—were being dismantled by its members.

Officer Tines was issued a court order this morning to seize all Brigade files after newly appointed Alcohol and Narcotics Bureau Commissioner Harry Shortz—on behalf of his own interests, as well as Tines's—testified before Judge John Deaver that an investigation into the business practices of American Allied Pharmaceutical would be jeopardized if the Brigade, in its move, destroyed documentation linked to American Allied's trade in raw opium.

The ANB has reason to believe that American Allied was leaking opiate derivatives onto the black market, including heroin and laudanum.

Tines's raid comes a little over a year and a half after Dr. Jerome Brilovsky, leader of the Brigade, was sentenced to seven years' imprisonment at Delacort Prison for performing an illegal abortion on the wife of a former Russian diplomat, which resulted in the woman's untimely demise.

Because of the careful scrutiny given to the Brigade and American Allied by law enforcement officials, after Dr. Brilovsky's arrest his family and the members of the Brigade agreed last month to liquidate their assets and reinvest them overseas.

Upon hearing the news that American Allied was up for sale, Elias Eliopoulos, Greek-born socialite and owner of the Southside Docks property, bought American Allied Pharmaceutical from its controlling partners.

According to unconfirmed reports, Dr. Brilovsky's son, Arthur, his wife, Elaine—daughter of one of the Brigade's high-level backers—and their infant son left last week for Petrograd with a substantial percentage of the money advanced by Mr. Eliopoulos.

Chapter 8

Be at Jack's Basement Tavern at 4 P.M., 56 West Eighty-third Street

The note was waiting for Victor in his room when the two grizzled men dropped him off at Fuller House. No larger than his cell at Farnsworth, it was a small dark room that consisted of a chair and a bed and a narrow window lined with bars that looked out onto an old mariners' cemetery. The note was waiting on his pillow. He stuffed it into the pocket of his coat and walked downstairs into Fuller House's basement. He had noticed a sign on his way in: *Resurrect Your Spirit and You Shall Find Your Way*. What he found was an old faltering priest holding mass to an audience of three disheveled men in dirty coveralls. As he was about to turn and leave, the priest caught Victor's eye and with a wave of his arm beckoned him forward to take communion with the others. Victor hesitated at first, but then stepped down past the pews and bowed down to the mottled hem of the priest's robes. Victor lifted his chin, opened his mouth, received the wafer and the blessing, and as the wafer dissolved in his mouth, he could see in his mind the towering stone wall outside his prison cell thinning and becoming translucent, revealing the trees on the other side.

When Victor was through with his prayer, two nicely dressed men who had walked downstairs while Victor kneeled before the altar trailed after him upstairs through Fuller House's old brown varnished lobby onto Pearlmutter Lane. They walked down the block in the shadow of the downtown skyline, through a passage of the City that smelled like the viscera of the sea. They weaved in and out of the stand-still crowd of the Pearlmutter Fish Market, where they passed gutting tables and buckets of fish guts and heavily bundled mongers slapping freshly gutted fish onto carts full of ice. Victor walked with his nose buried in his scarf, feeling the thwacking blows in his temples of fish hitting ice, until he reached the coffee shop on the corner. He and the two men took seats at the counter, at which point Victor reached into his pocket and laid out the photograph he had kept of himself and the woman in front of the carousel. With some pocket money given to him by the two grizzled men, he bought a coffee and a roll and just stared down at the woman, occasionally brushing bread crumbs off her hair as they fell from his lips.

When he was through with his breakfast, Victor walked down toward the river, near the warehouse district by the Southside Docks, where he watched freighters drift up- and downstream. He followed with his eyes the wakes of the boats as he caught glimpses of them through the alleyways between black smoke-stained brick warehouses and manufacturing plants, through piles of scrap and garbage and barbed wire. After all the years he was in jail, not since he worked the docks after the war had the M. J. Morris Paperclip Company fixed its fencing. Victor squeezed through the old rusted tear to the river's edge and strolled along a narrow truck transport that ran from docking slip to docking slip. From this road, he could see unobstructed the mouth of the harbor, and from the harbor, the ocean, and where the harbor's fresh water met salt, the fine curve of the horizon. As he looked onto this scene, his two shadows, who inconspicuously stood on the road a few hundred feet away, looked with him. Another hundred or so feet beyond them, Victor noticed another person trying to look equally inconspicuous, a woman not exactly dressed for the docks, looking very much out of place. The woman and the men all looked onto the horizon with equal contemplation, and watching them watch this, Victor turned away from his entourage and continued his way uptown.

He casually strolled along the river, looking up at the erect skyline over his shoulder. As he marveled at the needles and clock towers, the gilded spires and domes built during the boom years in which he was imprisoned, he turned back into the City's streets, through the crowded throng of the financial district, stopping occasionally to glance inside the cavernous and ornate lobbies of the office buildings, at the massive expanses of concrete and steel rising above him. As he looked at the faces of the well-heeled men and women that passed before him, however, it seemed to Victor as though these buildings that were vibrant and astonishing to him were already ancient artifacts to those people passing by, as if the inspiration, the optimism, that had prompted these buildings' construction, had faded long ago.

Victor couldn't exactly put his finger on it, but he somehow felt more comfortable among these somber hardened faces, these melancholy mopers, more comfortable than he remembered feeling all those years ago when he walked about the City's streets after the war. It was as if the world had gone through a transformation that made it fit more easily into Victor's pocket. These people had lost something. Their eyes had surpassed yearning for whatever it was that was gone. They were focused on what they had, and weren't looking back.

When Victor reached Adams Square in the heart of the Jewish quarter, he knocked on the door of a townhouse that had once been well kept, but now had fallen into some disrepair. An elderly man dressed in a worn brown wool suit, as unkempt as the house, answered the door. Victor, who had thought about this moment for as many years as he was jailed, wasn't sure what to say.

"What do you have to say for yourself?" the man asked in a heavy Yiddish accent. It was obvious from his tone that he didn't recognize Victor.

"Mr. Price, it's Victor Ribe."

"Victor Ribe . . . Is that possible it is Victor Ribe?"

All Victor could think to do was to reach into his pocket and pull out the photograph he had kept of himself and Sheldon Price's daughter. He handed the picture to Mr. Price. The old man removed a pair of glasses from his vest pocket and put them on. He looked over Victor's outmoded clothes, his work-worn hands, and when he saw the photo, the old man became transfixed. "Victor," he said again, this time as though he were saying the name of a ghost. The man looked over Victor's face, and at the moment he comprehended that it was indeed Victor Ribe who stood before him, a troubled look came over his face, making Mr. Price look much older than he initially appeared. Holding on to Victor's photo, he stepped away from the door, and as if he felt it was something that must be done for some reason greater than himself, he made room for Victor to pass.

The house was unclean and dusty; books and newspapers were piled indiscriminately in corners, on tables, chairs; spoiled dishes on top of the papers and books made for an unpleasant odor. The old man led Victor into the living room and made a place for him to sit on the couch. He then sat on a chair he obviously sat in often, and started tapping his fingers on the chair's arms as he continued looking at the image of Victor and his daughter. "I assume you've come to find out where they are?" he said ponderously.

"Yes."

"I see." The old man continued tapping and staring at the picture. "If a man such as yourself came looking for your daughter and grandchild after all these years," Mr. Price mused, "what would you say to him, Victor?"

"I would be reluctant to say anything, sir."

"Yes," Mr. Price said, still looking at the picture. Now a sadness came over his hollow face and for a moment he seemed to disappear from the room and the conversation. "It's unfortunate . . ." he said from his distance, "it's unfortunate what some men become when they lose the people they most cherish in life." Mr. Price lifted his head from the photo and looked around the room, at the disarray in which he and Victor sat. "Isn't it, Victor?"

"Yes, sir," Victor said. "Yes, it is."

"There is nothing that can replace their absence."

"No, there isn't."

The old man's eyes suddenly focused inside the ashen fireplace opposite his chair. Victor watched Sheldon Price once again disappear from the conversation and remembered how when Mr. Price was a young man he could stand before a crowd of workingmen and have them scream out for the heads of their bosses.

"If I tell you where to go, you must promise that you'll be gentlemanly," Mr. Price said after some time.

"I promise," Victor said, his spirit rising.

"If I hear you've caused any problems, I'll be sure to make a big headache for you. Don't be deceived by all this," he said, pointing to his house, to himself, to the disarray. "You have known me since you're a child and you know that until I'm dead I still have it in me to cause a good deal of unpleasantness."

"I assure you, I have no intention of making any trouble."

The old man reached for a pen from a table and ripped a piece of paper from a book. "You go here. You wait in the lobby. You wait and watch, and then you see. This is the way, is that understood?"

"Yes, I understand," Victor said quietly.

"Like yourself, they've only recently returned to the City. I would wait a little time before you present yourself, to give them some time to reacquaint themselves with their surroundings."

"I agree."

"Now go show yourself to the door and be on your way."

Victor got up from the couch. He delicately took the piece of paper and the photo from the old man's hand, and without saying anything more, he walked back onto the street, relieved that Mr. Price had been helpful. As he started walking uptown again, he was followed by the two men and the woman, who he could see were shivering in the cold. They all rode the subway to midtown together and exited on the east side, where, after walking a block from the subway station, Victor entered the lobby of the Ansonia Hotel and took a seat. The two men entered the hotel's lobby right behind Victor and went to the hotel restaurant. The woman went across the avenue to a coffee shop and took a table by the window. The hotel's elevator doors opened and closed, the revolving door to the street swung around and around, the phone rang and the concierge said names of women and men, and Victor waited impatiently, his chest tight from anticipation, with every entry and exit, with every word spoken.

Victor had been waiting nearly an hour when a woman in her later thirties, accompanied by a boy no more than twenty, walked out of the elevator. When he saw her profile, when he saw the boy's fair skin and taller-than-average height, and, especially, the length of his face, and the way he walked, Victor knew it was them. The woman and the boy walked through the lobby and right by him as if he were invisible. Victor, the two men, and the mysterious woman followed the woman and the boy uptown through the crowded streets.

Victor watched her move and was reminded of how she had moved with him through the fields of Long Meadow so many years ago. Victor couldn't believe that the moment was real; he could feel his heart rate triple; he could feel his pulse beating behind his ears, in his palms, inside the balls of his feet. He couldn't imagine that she would still be so beautiful to him, and he couldn't have ever imagined that the boy would be as he was, as tall and as fair as he was, as handsome and fit. He followed them as far as the entrance of Zeligman's Department Store on Thirty-eighth Street, and not wanting to risk being noticed by them just yet, he watched them disappear behind the doors.

Chapter 9

Freddy Stillman anxiously idled away the rest of the morning approving shipments of grenade fuses and detonators, rifle barrels and cocking levers, scrolling each order into a cylindrical container, and sending each container through the pneumatic tube beside his desk to the shipping foreman on the third floor. The shipping foreman telephoned in the orders to the manufacturing plant's armory in Long Meadow, where the arms and munitions were inspected, crated, loaded onto barges, planes, trains, all bound for military installations across the country, all over the world.

Just after noon, when Freddy heard the technicians break for lunch and clear the display area, he put on his coat and homburg, scarf and gloves, and walked out of his office. The floor was empty and quiet. The nearly completed mobile of torpedoes hung from the very center of the rotunda and circled and undulated about like a pinwheel of fish chasing each other's tails. Freddy rode the elevator into the lobby and swung through the revolving doors into the dense pack of pedestrian traffic on Central Boulevard.

It was the most frigid day of winter thus far, a day so crisp one wouldn't know how to remember spring. The chill passed through the heaviest wool and fur, into the innermost warmth of the body. It was a freeze that chafed the most hardened bedrock of exposed skin. For some weeks now, a steady gust of this debilitating weather had blown down from the north. The winds leveled against the backs and chests of men and women who trudged their way to work and home, along the dozen-mile stretches of the City's boulevards. It ran through the brightest hours of the day, through the bluest of cobalt skies; it howled about the office towers and made the gleam of afternoon light refract off the City's detritus. Palls of colorful dust became a fog of airborne fool's gold. Yet, the weather being what it was, hawkers still took to the streets, vagabonds stood in lines for brackish soup and hard bread, jackhammers pulverized earth, steel was welded and stacked, pipe was hauled and laid. Trains and trolleys ran round the clock, and into the earliest hours of the morning, freighters and liners drifted through the icy narrows of the harbor to their docks. The theaters and taverns remained full, and the nightclubs and dope dens were respectively as electric and down as ever. If at this time, so many years ago, people had been able to look onto the City from space, they would have confirmed all the feelings they had that they lived at the center of the universe. If they could only have seen the site from just outside the atmosphere, as the earth turned on its axis away from the sun, they would have seen the City appear as a bright heavenly body embedded into the land, where everything around it—all the darkness and the cloud cover—swirled in its gravity, in a perpetual vortex of motion.

With one hand holding down his hat, his other gripping the collar of his coat, Freddy leaned into the wind and ventured toward the flapping awning of the Beekman Hotel for Women, through whose lobby windows he briefly glanced, and seeing nothing but the concierge at her desk, he continued his way downtown with the throng. He passed a row of failed haberdasheries and shops selling ladies' finery, then trailed behind a phalanx of trundling clothes racks along Thirty-ninth Street. As the garment workers pushed the racks through the entryway of Zeligman's Department Store, Freddy stopped and lit a cigarette, and watched the anonymous bundled faces of the lunch crowds pass. After carefully looking down the block from which he had just come, he walked into Zeligman's lobby, through the elevator banks, through the menswear section, and exited the rear lobby onto Thirty-eighth Street. He crossed over onto the south side and walked past the street-level boutiques of the exclusive Gable Hotel, keenly aware of his moving image obscurely reflecting back at him from plate-glass windows. He passed over Central Boulevard and walked to the edge of the city, near the bank of the Eastbend River, where he turned the corner and entered Grimes's Delicatessen, a narrow storefront with a few tables in the back. The deli was empty, except for a man Freddy only knew as Feldman.

Feldman, the fat, clean-shaven sort with sweet liquored breath and a triple chin, was sitting at a table in the back corner. His short belt-warmer tie pressed up against the edge of the table, so much so that when he tried to stand up to shake Freddy's hand, all the table's condiments shook and the pickle jar nearly fell over.

"Good to see you," Feldman said as he took hold of Freddy's hand.

Freddy nodded his head and sat down. He didn't remove his coat or hat. He turned his chair so that he faced Feldman, so that from behind he couldn't be seen. A waitress wearing a white apron and a dress patterned with oversized petunias approached the table and asked Freddy what she could get him. Freddy, without looking up, ordered a pastrami sandwich and a beer.

"I wasn't sure you'd come after not calling me this morning," Feldman said when the waitress had walked away.

"I only came to say I shouldn't be here. You shouldn't try to contact me anymore."

"What's gotten into you?"

"What can I say? . . . I don't trust you. I don't trust any of this."

"I hate to break it to you, but this isn't about trust anymore, Freddy. And I think you know that."

"I'm not going ahead with this thing," Freddy said in a quiet voice.

"Is this about money? You want that I should go back and ask them for more money?"

"No."

"Then what the hell's this about?"

"Look . . ." Freddy said.

"You look," Feldman said harshly. "You've done everything right so far. You made the call and you told your story. It's done. I watched the police come and go. Anyone who matters knows they came and went. All you've got left to do now is a few secretarial duties."

Freddy shook his head.

At the sight of this, Feldman tightened his face and then relaxed it. Freddy expected the anger to come then, but instead, to Freddy's surprise, Feldman said, "Look, it's your prerogative. But I do feel obligated to say," Feldman continued, leaning over the table as much as he could, "there isn't anything smart about what you're doing, see. Believe me, if you weigh this against the stew of bad decisions you've made in your life up to now, I think the more you reflect on this, those won't seem so bad."

Feldman chewed on his tongue for a second. "Well, if you're not of the mind to do yourself a favor, why don't you at least think about Janice, and the spot this puts her in."

"What are you saying, Feldman?"

"I think you know what I'm saying, Freddy. I think you know exactly what I'm saying."

"You wouldn't hurt Janice. I know you wouldn't."

"Are you so sure? Thanks to you she's as good as dead as far as the cops are concerned."

"No," Freddy said as he nervously tapped his finger on the table. "You're not using Janice to get to me again. Not again."

Feldman chewed on his tongue some more. "You know I can't do nothing to stop what you're starting here, right?"

"Just do me a favor and tell your people I'm through with them."

Feldman looked a little sorry for Freddy. The sorry look on the sad-sack Feldman's face made Freddy think, made him feel, as though with these last words he was signing a contract he couldn't get out of. Freddy's eyes shuffled about and his breath became shallow as he thought about what he was doing.

Freddy stood up abruptly to leave.

"Don't do that," Feldman said amiably, taking hold of Freddy's arm, the empathetic expression on his face now a bygone. He pushed the table away a little and stood up. "I'll go. You stay." He winked. "I've already eaten. You enjoy yourself while you still have the chance."

Freddy, feeling a chill run through him, sat back down while Feldman, continuing to appear amiable, straightened his tie so that it laid flat over his bloated midsection, then started patting at the breast pocket of his jacket. He reached into the fold of the pocket with his thumb and index finger and pulled out a small manila envelope the size of his hand. "Just in case you have a change of heart," Feldman said, "you'll find what we're looking for in here." Feldman placed the envelope before Freddy, put on his oversized coat and hat, and wished him a nice afternoon. Feldman sauntered down the narrow lane of Grimes's, his bulging sides brushing up against the wall and the deli counter, and walked out onto the street. As the door closed, the waitress slid Freddy's pastrami sandwich onto the table and placed his beer next to the packet.

"Can I get you anything else?"

"No," Freddy said, not looking up, looking at the envelope before him—a plain manila envelope, as plain as could be. The waitress walked away and Freddy slipped the envelope into his coat pocket.

When Freddy returned to the ninth floor of the Fief Building, he was relieved to find that the display floor was still empty. He went into his office, locked the door, hung up his hat and coat, and removed the envelope given to him by Feldman. He placed it on his desk, on his blotter, and from the same drawer that held his binoculars, he removed an orange Bakelite letter opener, which he used to slice open the seal. With the mouth of the envelope opened, he slipped out three folded pieces of paper. On them was an extensive list of components to build grenades, mortars, armor-piercing bombs, and recoilless rifles. There were gun barrels and locking rings; equilibrators and recoil sleighs; firing shafts and breech blocks; lead balls; strikers; primers; base plugs; springs; triggers; grips. They were all items Freddy oversaw, and given an hour or so on any given afternoon, he could conceivably dispatch the order without anyone taking notice.

Freddy placed the pieces of paper back into the manila envelope, which went back into his coat pocket. The clamor of voices and shuffling feet on the display floor had returned. Freddy could feel the noises shrouding his skin, enveloping it in what felt like a thin sheet of plastic. As the noises escalated in pitch, Freddy's head began to ache. It was a familiar ache. It was an ache, like a creaking floorboard, that constantly bent its way through his chest and stomach and head. As the ache continued, there was a knock on his office door; whoever it was tried to enter, but found the door locked.

"Hang on a minute," Freddy groused. He took a few steps to the door and unlatched it. In walked Harvey Brace, a soft-spoken clerk who felt the need to regularly remind his colleagues that he was living with only one functioning lung—as a result of living through a mustard gas attack.

Not a second after Harvey's body was fully inside Freddy's office and he had closed the door behind him did the phone ring. Harvey sheepishly looked at the phone. "It's George," Harvey said.

Freddy looked at Harvey queerly, then looked at the phone with the same look. He lifted the receiver to his ear. "Yes?"

"Stillman?"

"Yes."

"Is Harvey there?"

"He's right beside me."

"Good. Listen. In light of what happened this morning, in light of what I've heard, Stillman, I think it would be best if you had some time to yourself today. To think. Think of what all this is about. Think about how you're to conduct yourself in this office from now on."

"I'm sorry, George?"

"Harvey there will take over your paperwork for the time being."

"I don't understand, George."

"There's nothing to understand, Stillman. You're taking the afternoon off while Harvey keeps you up to speed."

"I . . ."

"You don't want to push this, Freddy. You don't want to know what I'm thinking. You do what I tell you to do."

George hung up.

Freddy slowly hung up the receiver and looked at Harvey. "Did he say anything to you?"

Harvey Brace shook his head. "Only to come in here and finish up your paperwork. . . . He's in a foul mood." Harvey quietly walked around Freddy to the window and leaned back against the sill.

"What's he so cranky about?"

"The thing over at the plant this morning. It's gumming up the works."

"What happened?"

"Two union leaders were arrested for sabotage."

"Sabotage?"

"The Department of Investigations says the explosion was a setup by the union."

"You don't say."

"That's what they say."

"Will they strike?"

"Well, they took over the plant and threatened to destroy it after their men were arrested."

"Are they still inside?"

"Yeah, but they cooled down and went back to work."

"So they still might strike then."

"They haven't said as much, but I think that's what George thinks." Harvey shrugged his shoulders and looked around Freddy's office. "I'll be careful with your things, Freddy. I'll keep it all in order."

"That's fine, Harvey. I'm sure you will."

"I'll go see if you've got any new orders in your box." Before Harvey turned to go, he opened the blind. "I don't see so good in this light," he said, and then walked around Freddy and onto the display floor.

Freddy meanwhile didn't move. He was flustered by what he saw. Across the air shaft, Janice Gould's apartment was empty. The painting of the young man was gone, the bureau and all that was on top of it was gone, the navy-blue curtains that had once hung in the window were gone. The apartment was empty. He had no idea what this could mean, if it meant anything, but whatever it did mean didn't settle well in his stomach.

Freddy placed his briefcase on top of his desk, opened it up, and put in it the binoculars he kept in his desk drawer, as well as a few other personal belongings—among them an old broken pocket watch that was his father's, a brooch that was his mother's, and a tiepin Evelyn had bought for him for their tenth anniversary. He neatly slid all these things away into a sleeve within his briefcase, shut the lid, and locked them away.

Harvey returned with a stack of papers and placed them on Freddy's desk. "Like I said, I'll keep everything in order."

"Thanks." Freddy put on his coat and hat, wrapped himself up in his scarf. "See you," he said to Harvey.

And with his briefcase in hand he walked out onto the display floor. He didn't look around to see if anyone was looking. He could hear the lull in the conversations, in the work, but he didn't care. He walked to the elevator and rode down to the lobby. He pulled the collar of his overcoat up, pulled his hat down so it fit snugly onto his head, and walked back out into the bustle of Central Boulevard.

A dark cloud of bobbing hats uniformly drifted over the shaded sidewalk, through strips of ineffectual winter sunlight breaking eastward across the City's narrow streets. Freddy crowded into the flow of bodies and, with each step, braced himself against the gusts of strong headwinds. The gales channeling through the canyon of buildings had grown even stronger since he was outside, and with the increased wind, the cold grew more bitter. As he fought his way down toward a warm yellow glow emanating from the island's southern tip, he felt as though he were part of a massive funeral procession prematurely mourning the loss of his own life. He kept feeling as though he were about to be blown off his feet and flung into the air. He kept imagining himself effortlessly hovering just above street level, going unnoticed.

Hunched and frozen, Freddy walked for almost an hour. By the time he reached the run-down townhouses of the Franklin Field section of South End, his pale face had turned blistering red and his windblown tears had left a thin crust of salt running down his cheeks like a wayward meander. He had walked thirty-three blocks in all when he entered Cuccio's Bakery on Dunleavy Street.

Mrs. Cuccio, a dark grandmotherly woman, stood behind the counter. Upon seeing Freddy, she made a face. "This is the last time, mister," she said. "No more after this, I swear it." She crossed herself as she looked up to the relief of crosses laid into the tin ceiling of her shop. Freddy removed his wallet from his pocket and placed a dollar bill on the counter. Mrs. Cuccio reached out reluctantly and took the money. "The last time," she said less emphatically, and then turned away. She pulled down a pink box from a shelf and filled it with some miniature éclairs, an assortment of cookies, a charlotte russe. She bound the box with twine and put on her coat, and while Freddy watched from the store window, she walked outside into the wind and across the quiet tree-lined street, where she rang the bell of the apartment building on the first floor. A few moments passed, the front door of the apartment building opened, and there, standing in the foyer, Freddy could see Evelyn's long narrow face and brunette curls; he could see her cheeks turn rosy the second they met the cold air, and he watched as she smiled warmly at the sight of Mrs. Cuccio's pink box. He looked on as Mrs. Cuccio delivered Freddy's gift and his message. She told Evelyn that she had been thinking of her and the baby, and thought she might like to have some sweets in the house. Evelyn thanked her, gently touched the top of Mrs. Cuccio's hand with her hand, and then slipped into the darkness of the hallway.

Before Mrs. Cuccio could walk back to the shop, Freddy opened the door and walked down Dunleavy Street, back to Central Boulevard, where he rejoined the crush of bodies and walked uptown with the cold needling wind now to his back.

Chapter 10

Byron Sands, a handsome young black man dressed in a brand-new suit and coat, leaned over the steering column of his truck as the seven-story passenger ship, the *Bethlehem,* majestically inched its way through the glistening ice and chop of the harbor toward South End Pier #17. He watched as the ship's enormous hawsers descended from holes in the bow and the stern into the small hands of men ready to set them on their bollards. When the ship was secured, the gangplank lowered and hundreds of well-heeled men and women bundled in fur and overcoats lazily perambulated down to the landing. As the first passengers reached the parking lot, Byron stepped out of the truck with a sign reading "Professor Tarkhov." Dozens of passengers and porters passed, and then, out of a small crowd, a short stocky middle-aged man with a thick graying beard and wireless spectacles approached him with four ghostly-white porters in tow, pushing a number of large wooden crates and some luggage.

"I am Tarkhov," the man announced to Byron in a heavy Russian accent. His eyes were tired and bloodshot and looked a little wary. "And exactly who are you?" The question came out like an accusation.

"Me?" Byron lowered the sign to his waist, looking a little confused.

"Who sent you, please?" the professor asked sternly, his eyes squinting as he looked up into Byron's thin dark face.

Taken aback by Tarkhov's gruffness, Byron hesitated before answering. "Mr. Tersi, sir."

Tarkhov coldly stared at Byron for a moment longer.

"Mr. Tersi," Byron repeated more convincingly, "he told me to come collect you and drive you to the estate."

Byron could see the young porters talking to each other as they looked over his getup, at his spit-shined shoes and his leather gloves.

"Dr. Gamburg is waiting for you up there, sir," Byron said, as if he were trying to coax a child into a bath. He lowered his head a little, turned his back on the porters, then said into Tarkhov's ear, "I ain't here to steal nothin' from you, sir, if that's what you're thinking. I just come to give you a ride."

Tarkhov, continuing to look uncertain, turned his head from Byron to the porters. "Please, gentlemen, in the truck there. Very very gently."

"Yes, sir," the lead porter said with a smug smile on his face for Byron. The men began loading the truck under the professor's supervision, and once they were done, Tarkhov clumsily climbed onto the bed and meticulously made sure each crate and piece of luggage was stable and properly tied down.

"Thank you, gentlemen," he said when they were through. He then climbed into the passenger seat of the truck and slammed the door.

Byron, who had been leaning against the side of the truck while the porters worked, reached into his pocket and pulled out a few coins. With a smug smile that matched the one the porter had given him earlier, he held the money up in the air on the palm of his glove and waited. The lead porter walked up to him, and with a scowl grabbed the coins from Byron's hand. Without thanking him, the lead porter turned with the others back to the ship.

"We must drive very slowly," Tarkhov said to Byron as Byron joined the professor in the cab of the truck.

"Yes, sir."

"Very slowly and carefully," Tarkhov said with the same seriousness he had greeted Byron. "It is my life," he said. "My family's life," he emphasized, "in the back of your truck. Do you understand?"

"I'll get you and everything there safe and sound," Byron promised. He pulled out the choke and turned the engine over.

"Good," Tarkhov said, looking around him, around the docks, as if he were looking for someone. "It's been such a long journey with many worries," he said aloud, talking to himself. "From Leningrad to Moscow to Leningrad to Helsinki, across the Baltic, the bad weather in the North Atlantic, gathering paintings in London . . . I tell you . . ."

Byron didn't say anything. He just listened to the professor's murmurings as he backed the truck up, shifted gears, and slowly drove off down the road in the direction of the South End thruway.

When Byron Sands and Professor Tarkhov reached the Martin estate outside the sleepy town of Rainskill Falls, Dr. Gamburg was waiting at the top of the private road leading to the house. A half-dozen art handlers from Leslie's stood beside him with handcarts.

"Professor Tarkhov," Dr. Gamburg said eagerly as Tarkhov stepped down from the cab of the truck. "Joseph Gamburg."

"Yes, very pleased to make your acquaintance," Tarkhov said unconvincingly as he took the professor's hand. He looked beyond Dr. Gamburg's face to the immensity of the Martins' Tudor mansion.

"I hope you had a pleasant drive."

"Yes, pleasant."

"I'm afraid I had a few things to attend to here—otherwise I would have met you myself."

"It's quite all right," Tarkhov said. "The passing countryside was very good company."

Dr. Gamburg waved the group of art handlers over to the back of the truck and then turned to Byron, who was now standing beside Tarkhov. "Byron, will you please take the professor's luggage to his room and then come join us in the gallery. We could use your help."

Byron nodded and then walked to the back of the truck.

"This is quite an impressive home," Tarkhov said as he followed Dr. Gamburg up a short staircase to the front door.

"It isn't a palace," Gamburg said wryly, "but I would venture to say that the Russian royalty would have been more than comfortable in such a home with so much unused space."

Tarkhov grimaced a little. "Indeed."

"Yes, well," Gamburg muttered, "the important thing is that some of that unused space is at our disposal for the time being."

Tarkhov nodded slightly as they entered the foyer and slowly walked down a long hallway. The hall was carpeted with an Oriental rug that stretched the length of the corridor, on whose walls were hanging a number of portraits of men and women dressed in Puritan robes. There were several Revolutionary War and Union Army officers of various ranks as well as judges, clergymen, businessmen. Interspersed between the portraits were naturalistic landscape paintings of the Westbend River Valley spanning several hundred years of its settlement, and including such figures as trappers and Indians, African slaves and their masters. The forests became noticeably more and more denuded and splintered and stacked into cabins and cords of firewood as the succession of paintings went on. The professor glanced at the artwork with curiosity, but didn't let his eyes wander too far from Dr. Gamburg.

"Out of all the painters to come out of the Postimpressionist movements," Dr. Gamburg said as the handlers slowly pushed by them with the artwork, "I can't tell you enough how moved I am by the work of Rodhinsky."

"You have seen some of Rodhinsky's work?"

"Only a few of his very early paintings."

"I see."

"But the few paintings that I have seen lead me to believe that his images truly reflect the modern Russian era."

"Yes, he was, well, he *was* a visionary."

"Did you know him?"

"Yes, of course, I knew him." Tarkhov's serious demeanor seemed to fade. "Yes, he was a man who was very difficult not to know. He had a very boisterous way about him, to say the least. What's interesting is that this unbridled personality he was famous for, almost all throughout his career, was so completely contained when he was painting. As a man, he was a bard, a folk hero, an *enfant terrible;* as a painter, he was an intellectual, an emotional intellectual, yes, but still, a calculating mind, a calculated imagination."

"But when I've looked at his work, I remember feeling a good deal of emotion behind it. It's abstract, but it has feeling."

"Yes, yes, of course it does. Especially the later paintings that I have brought with me, the ones most directly meditating on his preoccupations with death and futility."

"Is it really true that he died the way everyone says he did?"

"That is the legend, yes. Whether it is true or not, no one can say with absolute certainty, but you can see how he died, in his work, this image, most literally in the very last painting he made."

"*The Disappearing Body*?"

"You are familiar with this painting?"

"I've only heard rumors. Do you mean to say that you have it with you?"

"Yes."

"How—if you don't mind me asking—did you manage to get your hands on it? I thought the painting had mysteriously vanished after Rodhinsky's death."

"It had."

"Then how . . ."

Tarkhov smiled and shook his head. "There are certain things that are best not asked or answered in a situation such as this."

"The collector prefers to remain anonymous—I completely understand. But please, you must show it to me immediately."

"Yes, of course."

Dr. Gamburg eagerly led Professor Tarkhov to the end of the hall and into the gallery, where Byron and the handlers were beginning to open the crates. The gallery was set in what had once been a reception hall, with high vaulted ceilings and polished parquet floors. A series of windows ran the length of the room and looked out onto a sculpture garden bordered by a semicircular stand of maples. Running through the center of the hall was a standing partition on which the paintings would be hung, and set at the top of the partition were curved brass fixtures that would light each image. The professor walked over to a crate marked EP 001.

"Byron, please . . ." Dr. Gamburg said as he waved Byron over. "Bring over those tools and open this one over here."

Byron walked over with a hammer and chisel. With a few motions, he managed to open the crate, and from two slats, he pulled out Rodhinsky's large painting. With the help of a handler, he hung it on the partition. The other handlers stopped what they were doing and gathered around.

"If you notice," the professor said with his arm outstretched, "this painting reconnects completely to the corporeal form, a form Rodhinsky so determinedly moved away from in his youth. It is the most realistic of paintings Rodhinsky ever did. It is more like Caravaggio than Rodhinsky. It is a simple but carefully rendered portrait of himself, something so bare of pretense and bare of artifice that, given the circumstances of his death, you shudder to think how much he labored over the inevitability of his death, how there in each one of those labored strokes was his fate, complete and realized. Evgeny Rodhinsky standing over a pickax wedged between the floorboards, there in the privacy of his own studio, but, but, you notice here, in the stained glass of the window, in miniature, the very Rodhinsky-like forms—overshadowed by the brutal realism of the portrait. Here is the only thing that links the painting to him—to his past endeavors, to his revolutionary style—there, looming in the windows like a requiem. It is very moving and thought-provoking, especially if it is true that he was found with that masonry tool driven through his heart and the police only minutes away from his flat."

"Why'd he go and do it?" Byron asked.

"Yes, why?" Tarkhov said, looking at Byron's eyes fixed on the painting. "Because he felt he had lost his place in the world, I would imagine."

Byron walked closer to the painting, to look at the pained expression on Rodhinsky's face.

"But even if this isn't what happened . . ." Dr. Gamburg said.

"Does it matter? It is what people believe."

Dr. Gamburg stared in awe at Professor Tarkhov. "This is very exciting."

"Yes, yes it is," the professor said, grimacing once again.

"I think it will make a great impression."

"You and the owner of these paintings will profit nicely, I am sure," the professor said to himself.

"I'm sorry?" Dr. Gamburg said.

"It will be a very enlightening event."

"Let's hope so," Dr. Gamburg said. "I am very pleased."

"The collector thought you would be." Professor Tarkhov placed his hand on the doctor's shoulder and smiled. "And now, Dr. Gamburg, if you don't mind, now that I have shown you the Rodhinsky and I have seen this beautiful gallery, I believe I'm ready to rest awhile. My body is so tired I can hardly feel it."

"I'll show you to your room," Dr. Gamburg said as he walked the professor out of the opposite end of the gallery. The two men walked through a smoking room to a staircase and continued on upstairs to the guest bedroom. "Sleep as long as you like," Dr. Gamburg said jovially. "You should be well rested for what's to come." And with that, Dr. Gamburg turned and walked back down the stairs.

Professor Tarkhov retired to his room and shut the door. The room was as spacious as every other room in the house. It consisted of a large four-posted bed, throw rugs, a Colonial-style armoire, and a writing table. On top of the writing table was a stack of paper, a pen, a telephone, a pitcher of water, a glass, and a tray with some cucumber sandwiches and chocolates. Before the table was a window with lace curtains that looked out onto the sculpture garden and the stand of woods. It was all tasteful and comfortable. As much as the professor's senses were pleased by his surroundings, he couldn't allow himself to enjoy them for a moment.

The professor removed his coat and laid it on the bed, then sat down at the desk. He touched one of the crustless sandwiches with his fingers and then turned to pick up the phone. He reached into his jacket pocket and pulled out a piece of paper. "Midtown nine five eight, please, the Ansonia Hotel."

The professor listened to the phone ring several times.

"Room three oh nine, please."

He waited again, more ringing.

"Arthur Brilovsky, please. . . . Yes, I have arrived safely and will meet you as planned. . . . No, I don't believe you should look forward to seeing me," the professor said harshly and hung up the phone. He reached for the cucumber sandwich, sniffed at it, and dropped it back down onto the tray in disgust.

Chapter 11

Harry Shortz watched leafless trees flicker past the window from inside the northbound train to Ten Lakes, trying to recall the features of Sylvia Lowenstein's face. He was still distraught about the blackmail letter, and was starting to see his entire future unravel like a Chinese yo-yo thrown clear off its stick. The timing of the threat couldn't have made it appear more like he was being set up for a big fall; one, he felt, he probably had little chance of avoiding. He would be ruined and disgraced, and he couldn't even conjecture how Beverly and his children would take the news. Not to mention his father-in-law.

The truth of the matter was that Harry had buried the memories of Sylvia and Katrina Lowenstein inside him for so long now that when he read their names in the blackmail letter, the idea of their existence felt as though it had emerged from the shadows of a long-forgotten dream. With the exception of one man who had stumbled upon his secret, a man long since dead, Harry had managed to keep his relationship to Sylvia and Katrina concealed from the world. He had never confessed to anyone—not in nineteen years, not to his closet confidants—that in the early years of his marriage to Beverly, he had had an ongoing affair with a young Hungarian prostitute; he had solicited her at a bar one night shortly after returning home from the war. It was strictly business to begin with, but, in time, Harry fell for her, and didn't like the idea of sharing. Using his wife's family money and connections, he bought Sylvia Lowenstein a fresh start, pulled her out of the brothel in which she worked and lived, set her up in a room in the West End, and helped her find a secretarial job at an ad agency. He then unwittingly helped get her pregnant. When she refused to give up the child and showed no signs of letting Harry off the hook, Harry, full of shame and regret, exchanged Sylvia's silence and some distance for money and a country house in a mountain resort town an hour northwest of the City.

Harry wasn't entirely sure what he would find when he reached Ten Lakes, but after receiving the note, he knew he couldn't sit still in his office for the rest of the day without trying to look Sylvia Lowenstein in the eye and ask her what in the world she was at and who exactly she had talked to.

When the train pulled into the Ten Lakes station, the ground had turned to snow, and the winds outside had picked up considerably, so that the icy powder that had blanketed the gable roofs of the clapboard houses and storefronts along Main Street spiraled into the air like desert dust devils. Inside the train station, a few cab drivers sat on benches near the exit, quietly reading the newspaper. Harry pulled his hat down over his forehead a little and pulled his scarf up over his chin, then walked over to them. An older man with an unlit cigar clenched between his teeth looked up from his paper first and caught Harry's eye.

"You available?" Harry asked.

"Where you headed?"

"Pine Valley. Overlook Road. I need a ride there and back."

"Sure thing." The man stood up, buttoned his coat, and pulled the flaps of a beaver hat over his ears. Harry followed the man out to a rusting gray Packard and slid into the backseat. They drove out of town onto a two-lane road that swung around Abilene Lake. Through the clearings in the trees along the shore, Harry watched snow from the beaches gently brush over the lake's frozen surface, as if an invisible broom were sweeping it along. The two men drove quietly, over a short hillside pass and into a valley. They drove past a few homes and a roadside coffee shop and then along a meadow that extended into a marsh.

"It's coming up on the left," Harry said. They approached a two-story house in need of paint and a new roof. Smoke rose from one of the chimneys into the air and trailed out over the meadow and hovered over the snow like swamp fog.

"Oh, that old place," the driver said. "I don't recall exactly what month, but the woman who lived there passed on just last year. Heart attack, I think. Something to do with her heart, anyway."

"What the hell . . ." Harry thought he said to himself.

"I'm sorry."

"Are you sure you're talking about the woman who lived there in that house?"

"Yeah, I'm sure. I drove a few men from town out to the funeral. They buried her up the road a little way, under a couple of sycamores on the top of the hill, by the overlook. I remember the daughter . . . she stayed behind in the house until just recently, but then she left town. Funny thing, I can't for the life of me remember their names."

"Lowenstein?" Harry said. "Sylvia and Katrina?"

"That's right. Sylvia and Katrina Lowenstein." The man pulled the car up in front of the house and looked it over a little. "The daughter, Katrina, I remember well. She was pretty broken up over it. A real beauty, that one. Like her mother. But I don't think it was easy for her being her mother's daughter."

"Why's that?"

"I can't say the mother was all that well liked by the women around here, if you know what I mean. She was quite a beautiful woman, and, well, let's just say she did all right for herself."

"I see," Harry said, still feeling unnerved by the news. "I tell you what . . . why don't you go back up the road to that coffee shop and come back and get me in say twenty minutes or so." Harry reached into his pocket and pulled out his money clip. He offered the man a couple of singles. "Treat yourself to whatever you like."

"It'd be nice to get out of the cold," the man said, looking at the large sum of money. He took Harry's two dollars. "I'll be back."

"All right," Harry said.

He watched the man turn the car around and head back down the road. Then he stood outside looking at the house, at the peeling paint, the loose shutters and screens, the broken railing on the front porch. He remembered how when he brought Sylvia out here to look at the house all those years ago, the flower beds were full of daffodils and the small apple orchard in the meadow was in blossom.

Harry walked up the steps to the front porch. He opened the screen door and knocked several times. A sullen-looking man, unshaven and unkempt, appeared in the window beside the door. He wore a tattered navy sweater and baggy tan trousers.

"What can I do for you?" The man appeared to Harry as though he were only half alive. He looked weary.

"I'm looking for Katrina Lowenstein."

The man stepped away from the window and opened the door. "As far as I know, she hasn't been living here for some time."

"You happen to know where she is?"

"No, I'm just renting the place for the winter. What's this about?"

"My name's Carl Reese. I work for Reliance Bank. My bank has the mortgage on this house, and the owner's in default. I've come by to assess the property. You mind if I come in and take a quick look around?"

"No," he said, shaking his head. "My day's already ruined. I might as well officially declare it so." The man stepped away from the door and made room for Harry to enter.

The two of them were standing in the kitchen, a large country kitchen with a wood-burning stove and a maple table, on top of which was a portable typewriter, a stack of paper, and a few packs of cigarettes.

"Miss Lowenstein seems to have a good deal of unfinished business," the man said as he reached for a cigarette. He offered Harry one as an afterthought.

"No, thank you," Harry said.

"I've been without electricity for the past two nights." The man lit his cigarette and blew the smoke over his shoulder. "I spent the better part of the morning trying to track down the power company. I didn't realize a power company could be so elusive. But now, with you here, everything's starting to make a little more sense."

"I'm sorry to hear you've been so inconvenienced."

The man turned his back on Harry and walked to the sink. "Can I get you anything to drink?"

"No, thank you."

The man reached for a teacup from above the sink and placed the cup down on the stove. He poured hot water from a steaming teakettle and squeezed in a wedge of lemon that sat on a chipped ceramic plate.

"I realize it doesn't look like much, but it calms my nerves."

"I didn't get your name," Harry said.

"Daniel. Daniel Greely."

Harry removed a pen and a small notebook from an inside pocket resting against his gun. "A writer?" Harry asked, pointing to the typewriter and the large stack of paper.

"Yes." Daniel Greely looked over to the typewriter and the stack of paper and blanched at the site of Harry writing as he spoke. "What are you writing?"

"I just wrote down your name, that's all."

"For what purpose?"

"For future reference, in case I need to ask you any more questions about Miss Lowenstein. It's urgent that we get in touch with her before we foreclose on her mortgage."

"I'd prefer it if you kept me out of this." The lines in Daniel Greely's face darkened a little.

"I'll only call on you if it's absolutely necessary, Mr. Greely."

Greely took a sip of hot water and lemon and tilted his head, as if he were staring at the gun resting under Harry's arm, under his coat.

"What do you write?" Harry asked.

"This and that." Greely's head turned upright again. "Novels mostly."

"Anything I might have heard of?"

"I doubt it. It's mostly pulp."

"You'd be surprised. I travel a lot. Do a lot of reading on the train."

"I don't like to talk about it much, if that's all right with you."

"That's quite all right."

Daniel Greely wiped his nose with his sleeve. "Please," Daniel Greely said to Harry as he placed his teacup down, his hand shaking a little, "look around as much as you like. I'll be back in a minute."

Harry watched the peculiar man walk away into the living room. He heard a door squeak open and slam shut. When the house felt still, Harry removed his gun, placed it in his outer pocket, and discreetly turned over a page in the stack on the table. ". . . *if I bludgeon you with an ax handle don't you dare frown, for the lemon wedges I insert in your smiles and the rinds with which I wedge open your eyes will not for a minute insinuate that I feel anything sour for you but that I am only as cruel as any man who would intentionally eviscerate you alive with a peeling knife for the sake of grim decadence. . . .*"

Harry, who felt as though he were somehow being watched through the walls by this man, continued the charade of being the banker. As he looked over the kitchen, he wrote on his pad: *Jasper wood-burning stove, kitchen table, small china cabinet, china, ice-*

box. When he walked into the living room, Daniel Greely reappeared through the cellar door and walked behind the sofa.

"It's a little unseasonable and out of the way to be here for the winter," Harry said pleasantly once he saw him. "Does it ever get to you?" Harry wrote on his pad: *sofa, armchair, writing table, throw rug, fixtures (3).* The house was still furnished with the furniture Harry had bought for Sylvia when she first moved in. However, the sofa and the chairs were now stained and worn.

"I enjoy it for what it is," Daniel responded. "The cold weather doesn't bother me in the least."

"Are you up from the City?"

"No. I've come from out west. I was out west, doing some work for the movie studios."

"I see," Harry said as he walked over to the mantel and picked up a photograph of Sylvia, older but still youthful, her dark Hungarian eyes warm and full of mischief. On her arm was who could only have been Katrina. She was nearly the exact image of Sylvia, though she was taller and slightly bigger-boned than her mother, yet still slim and feminine. As he handled the picture, something occurred to Harry.

"Can you tell me, Mr. Greely, who's handling this property?"

"Yeah," he said. "I made the arrangements with Donello and Sons. Forty-seven Main Street, I think."

"Should I ask for anyone in particular?"

"Frank Donello."

"Very good." Harry wrote down the name and address. He then poked his head into the den and wrote down the few items in there: *radio, sofa, dining table.* "I'm just going to take a look upstairs and then I'll be on my way."

"I'll be in the kitchen working," Greely said.

Harry walked up the staircase to the second floor. There were two bedrooms and a bathroom. In one of the bedrooms was an empty easel, and scattered about the easel, tubes of paint and a palette. He was drawn to a desk beside the easel and began to flip through a stack of papers. When he got to the bottom, he found a scrap of paper with the name Benny Rudolph written on it, and beside it a phone number. It took Harry a minute to recall where he had known the name, for it had been so long since he had thought of it, but when he remembered it, he remembered that Pally and Ira had collared Rudolph for running an extortion racket for the syndicate; Rudolph would beat the owners of City pharmacies silly until they would agree to sell the syndicate's dope over the counter.

Harry was baffled. He was further baffled when he found paper-clipped to the scrap of paper an old, worn photo of himself with Sylvia, one they had taken together while on a short trip out of town. A dark black line separated the two figures, and both were smudged with paint. Harry picked up the piece of paper and the photo and stuck it into his jacket. He looked through the papers more carefully now, but when he was through riffling the pile, he had found nothing else that seemed significant to him. He wondered what business Katrina would have with Rudolph. He wondered what they had in common, how it was that he knew about her.

Downstairs, Greely was back in the kitchen, sitting in front of his typewriter, typing with a lemon wedge glistening from between his lips. He spit the mangled lemon wedge onto the table when he saw Harry and kept typing. "All through?" he asked over the sound of the clacking key punches.

"Yes," Harry said calmly as he placed the pad in his pocket. "Thank you for letting me in. It was a great help."

"Think nothing of it," Greely said, stopping his typing for a moment.

Harry looked out the window and saw that his driver had returned. As he was about to say goodbye and walk out of the house, he turned back to Greely. "I nearly forgot the cellar," he said.

"Nearly forgot the cellar," Greely said to the typewriter.

"I'll only be a minute," Harry said, looking to Greely for some response. But Greely just sat like a stone, his dark eyes watering from the tartness of the lemon.

Harry went to the cellar door, turned on the light, and walked downstairs, from where, through the floorboards, he was able to hear the forceful clacking of Daniel Greely's typing. It was a dirt-floor cellar lined with cords of firewood. There were some metal washtubs, an old rusted lawn mower, and a pile of mouse traps. Near the wall closest to the road, a boat tarp hanging on metal hooks descended from a beam to the floor. As Harry started walking over to the tarp, Greely suddenly stopped his typing again. Harry could hear the hollow thud of the typewriter case close; he heard the latch click shut; he heard Greely walk to the living room, back to the kitchen, and then the front door opened and the screen door crisply slammed against its jamb like a frozen branch snapping in a windstorm. With the door open, a slight breeze of frigid air descended into the cellar through the floorboards and the tarp began to sway and creak on its hooks. Harry, feeling uneasy, removed his gun from his holster, cautiously approached the tarp, reached out to it, and swept it aside, to find, lining the wall, about fifty boxes with Murray Crown's face on them. Crown Saltcrisp Crackers.

Crown Crackers was Murray Crown's legitimate enterprise and was located on the Southside Docks a few doors down from American Allied Pharmaceutical. Aside from manufacturing morphine that went to hospitals, pharmacies, and doctors' offices, Allied supplied Johnny Mann and Jerzy Roth with the heroin, laudanum, and smoking opium that made its way to the gangsters' statewide network of crooked pharmacies. Crown's fleet of trucks made the deliveries.

Harry, who on a number of occasions had posed for the press next to a large stack of confiscated Crown Crackers boxes, knew full well what to expect. He opened one of the boxes before him and found it full of ready-to-sell heroin packets. He raised the butt of his gun to his head and started pacing. He paced back and forth, now understanding why the deed to the property had been transferred into his name.

Harry put his gun back into his holster and walked upstairs.

The kitchen table had been cleared and the screen door was knocking against the house in the wind. Harry walked outside and shut the door behind him. He could see Daniel Greely's footprints tracking out into the snowy marsh.

"You all set?" the driver asked when Harry climbed into the backseat of the car.

"Yeah," Harry said as though he had just gotten knocked in the head by a two-by-four.

"Peculiar that that man walked off in that direction with a typewriter and a heavy bag."

Harry didn't say anything. He was in no mood to make small talk.

"Must know someone on the other side of the ridge."

Harry stayed mute.

"Where would you like to go?" the driver asked.

"Back to town. To Donello and Sons on Main Street."

"Sure thing." The driver pulled out of the driveway and drove away from the house. As they drove along the meadow, and as the house quickly receded into the distance, a gust of wind blew and the snow whirled, extinguishing the house's facade from view.

"I thought you might like a nice hot cup of coffee," the driver said to Harry, as he handed back a thermos. "I filled up, so help yourself. The cup's clean."

"Thanks." Harry held on to the warm thermos in his lap, but he didn't do anything with it. All he could think of was how he was being set up, how it was possible that Katrina would know Benny Rudolph, how this was looking even worse for him than he initially thought.

"I got to talking to Peggy in the coffee shop while I was waiting for you," the old man said with his eyes on the road. "She told me it's about three months that Katrina left Ten Lakes."

"She have anything else to say?"

"Just that a couple of really big fellas came out and picked her up in a nice car. They stopped by the coffee shop on their way over to the house. They sat in a booth and bickered over some game of cards or something. She said she remembered the day so well because she had such a bad flu and she had to close up early. . . . What else did she say? Just that she thought Sylvia got it bad around here and didn't really deserve to be treated so poorly. That's all."

"So, three months ago then."

"That's right."

When the two men returned to downtown Ten Lakes, the driver dropped Harry off in front of Donello and Sons Realty, and Harry handed the man back the thermos, paid him, and said goodbye. The Donello and Sons office was a small rustic storefront advertising seasonal rentals and lakeside homes. When Harry stepped through the door, a cluster of bells hanging on the door handle rang out, and a small corpulent man in his fifties, wearing a navy jacket and dark trousers, approached Harry with a forced smile.

"How do you do?"

"Just fine, thanks. Would you happen to be Frank Donello?"

"Yes, that's me. What can I do for you?"

"Well, I just came out from the Lowenstein house, and the man renting told me that you were handling the property. Is that so?"

"Yes." Frank Donello suddenly lost his smile and looked a little confused. He took notice of Harry's well-tailored suit and expensive hat. "You're not actually interested in that place, are you?"

"No," Harry said, now smiling himself. "No. I'm trying to locate Katrina Lowenstein about an urgent matter and was wondering if you might have an address for her."

"Oh, I see," the man said. "Sure, sure, I have it. I've been mailing the checks to her once a month. Let me just get it for you." Frank Donello walked to his desk and pulled an index card from a box. He wrote the address on a piece of paper and then returned to Harry.

"Here you are," he said, holding the paper at his side. "What's this urgent matter all about, if you don't mind my asking?"

Harry, having no patience for this, held his hand out for the address.

"Do I know you from somewhere, mister?" Mr. Donello asked.

"I don't think so," Harry said.

"You look awfully familiar. You come up from the City?"

"Yes."

"My wife and I spend a lot of time down in the City in the winter, with her sister."

Harry shook his head.

"Come to think of it, you look an awful lot like . . ."

Mr. Donello reluctantly raised his arm as he was about to say Harry's name. Just as he was about to say it, Harry took hold of the paper. "Thank you, Mr. Donello," Harry said, cutting him off.

Frank Donello was taken aback. "Yes," he said. "You're welcome."

"Have a nice day, Mr. Donello." Harry left the office and once outside read the address Frank Donello had written: *The Beekman Hotel for Women. 470 Central Boulevard. Room 9F.* He placed the address in his pocket and headed down to the train station. He trudged through the snow, sinking into it, feeling his legs buckling beneath him, feeling as though he were made of something less than flesh, something more like clay or putty. Harry couldn't help but feel all the matter that made him what he was decomposing, rapidly, from whatever it was that made him a man in the first place into whatever it was that made someone a little less of a man.

Chapter 12

After Freddy Stillman left Cuccio's Bakery, he aimlessly walked the streets for a while. When he could no longer bear walking against the arctic gales and the feeling of the cold biting into his fingers and toes, he made the long descent underground into the Central Boulevard subway station, where, hovering above the platform, was a tile mosaic of nondescript bodies packed ten rows deep, waiting calmly, staring blankly. Freddy pressed himself into the narrow gap between the rush-hour crowd in the picture and the rush-hour crowd on the platform. He walked as far into the station as he could until the inert bodies before him weighed so heavily against his back, shoulders, and chest that all he could do was stop, stare blankly, and wait calmly.

When the train arrived, as if through a sieve, the platform filled the cars, the bodies moving like small Japanese women constricted within the confines of a kimono. Freddy slipped his hand through a cracked leather strap and while swaying against the same bodies he had pressed against on the platform, he contemplated the grip the leather strap had on his bare wrist. A ring of taut pink flesh. It reminded him of the blood pumping from his heart and through his legs. It reminded him of what the body looked like when the blood became still, when the blood leaked out, when a body was emptied of all blood and rigored in the sun. In the slate-gray window, he watched faces morbidly reflect back at him, without detail, without feeling. He being the dimmest of all. He was without eyes or mouth, hunched over, his image trailing against the steel arteries running parallel to the train's path. He could suddenly see the image he had been keeping in his thoughts when he was talking to the police, the image of the hands in the window choking Janice across the air shaft. He imagined the powder-blue robe with the undone sash, the small arc of flesh around Janice's belly, a lock of swaying auburn hair dangling in front of her nose. And then, he suddenly saw himself in those same hands, his throat in those hands across the air shaft.

When the doors opened at the Eighty-fifth Street station, he squeezed his way through the crowd and stepped onto the platform, his body barely in motion as it moved up the stairs, his thoughts as still as the stark moon that followed him along the edge of the park. The moonlight dispersed into ambiance, into the dying afternoon light, and disappeared when he entered Jack's Basement Tavern on Eighty-third Street.

During Prohibition, Jack's had been known as the Porter Club, a high-end speakeasy with gaming tables built into the walls and a pristine rosewood bar with brass fixtures, crystal cupboards, stained glass, and a number of safes built into the floor. Nowadays, the bar was just a bar, somewhat dilapidated, and the gaming tables that used to pull out of the wall had been replaced by wood tables with several years' worth of initials carved into their thick shellac.

"You're in early," Jack said to Freddy as he wiped down the counter with a wet rag. Jack, a solid man with a wounded face, had run the Porter Club in its day, and now he owned the place. He set the rag down, turned over a green-tinted glass, and poured Freddy a double bourbon.

"I'm not talking today," Freddy said as he took his whiskey from the counter and nodded to a pruned old couple he was acquainted with at the end of the bar.

"To each his own," Jack rebutted. "To each his own."

Jack leaned toward Freddy, and Freddy, out of politeness, leaned over the bar to meet Jack halfway.

"They let Victor out," Jack whispered. "He's sitting right there."

"Is that right?" Freddy said, clearly astonished.

"See for yourself."

Freddy followed the direction of Jack's finger and discovered the back of Victor Ribe's head sulking in the corner of the room. Freddy would have recognized the back of his old war buddy's head anywhere in the world. His soft brown fleecy hair always stood up in tufts as though it had been whipped into a lather. Freddy, looking at the back of Victor's head the entire time, walked away from the bar to the opposite end of the empty sipping room to one of the booths in the back, back by the bathrooms, where it smelled like cedar shavings and stale beer. He wasn't ready to say hello just yet.

"What do you say, Freddy?"

Freddy turned his head to the familiar voice and found Gloria Lime walking out of the ladies' room, her strong dimples and frail-looking pale green eyes gleaming in the yellow light of the tavern.

"Gloria? How is it that . . ."

"You mind if I . . ." Gloria lifted her drink off the table next to Freddy's and leaned toward him.

Freddy paused for a moment and then shook his head. He was taken off guard. "No, not at all. Of course not."

Gloria pushed Freddy's things over, slipped her full figure over the worn leather seat of the booth, and got cozy. She took Freddy's free hand and pulled it close to her. "Did you see Victor?" she whispered.

"Yeah, I saw him."

"I didn't say anything to him. I couldn't bring myself to. I mean, what it really is, Freddy, is that he gives me a good scare."

"You know anything about it? How it is he . . . ?"

"Paroled . . . I heard him talking to Jack."

"I see." Freddy patted Gloria's hand and let go. "It figures, I guess. It's been a long time." He took a drink from his glass, watching Gloria nod her head. He felt simultaneously attracted to and repulsed by her.

"Yeah, it's been a long time," Gloria mused, turning her head back. She looked at Victor and turned back to Freddy. "All I can say is that he's awful lucky they didn't put him in the chair." Gloria was raising her voice a little, and Freddy was starting to feel annoyed. "Awful lucky."

"Tell me," Freddy said, obviously wanting to change the subject, "you still in the same place?"

"Yeah." Gloria daintily gripped her straw with her fingers and took a sip from her drink. "I'm still living in the same place, still at the club. I can't really say all that much has changed since we last saw each other."

"But everything's good with you?" Freddy's tone, to his surprise, sounded tender.

"Can't really complain," she said, taking pause at the sound of Freddy's voice. "You know how it is, Freddy: some things get complicated, some things, well, some things just don't."

"Yeah," Freddy said, feeling all the confusion of his life at once.

"How about yourself?"

"You know me. Things could always be a little better."

"You seen Evelyn?"

"No." Freddy turned his glass in his hand.

"I heard she got married, had a baby."

Freddy continued turning the glass in his hand. He didn't want to be talking about this with Gloria. Not with Gloria.

"You're still torn up over that, aren't you?"

"Not so much anymore," Freddy lied. From a reflection inside his glass, Freddy could see a sadness come over Gloria's face. "I got other things on my mind," he said.

"Is that right?"

Freddy looked up from his glass and into the whorl of blond hair hanging on Gloria's shoulder. He hated her. He hated every inch of her. "I was down at the club a few times not so long ago."

"Is that right?"

"For whatever reason, I didn't catch you there."

Gloria leaned a little in Freddy's direction. "You should've just looked me up."

"I guess I should have," Freddy said, looking down at the table now, into the cracks between Gloria's fingers. It was always like this between him and Gloria. No matter where they stood in a room, no matter how hard they tried to not be attracted to each other, they were drawn together.

Gloria lifted her hand and took hold of Freddy's chin. "To tell the truth, I've missed you like mad."

Freddy nearly smiled. With her hand still holding him, he found himself saying, "I've missed you, too," without really meaning it. And then Freddy immediately felt guilty for saying this. And then as guilty as he felt, as unexpected as it was to have run into Gloria Lime, Freddy unexpectedly felt something lift inside him, as if a small parachute had opened in his chest. "I wanted to call, but . . . I mean, it's funny running into you like this."

"Listen," Gloria said, her eyes studying Freddy's face, "why don't you take me out tomorrow night. There's a new picture I want to see playing down at the Castaway. We'll have a bite, take in the picture."

"I can't . . . I shouldn't . . . make any promises, Glory. But I'll give you a call. What do you say?"

"I say you're like the old Freddy I know is what I say." Gloria's face changed, her mood turned downcast, and she started to get up from her seat.

"Wait a minute, Glory," Freddy said. "Hold on." He reached for her hand and gripped it tightly, as if it were keeping him from falling off a cliff. "What time?"

Gloria looked at Freddy's hand, gently took hold of it, and placed it back on the table. Her face lit up again. "I'll meet you at the coffee shop by the theater at seven."

"Good. I'll see you there."

"It's the least you could do."

Freddy tried to smile kindly at Gloria, but wasn't sure if he succeeded. Gloria downed the rest of her drink, bundled up, and said goodbye.

Holding the double doors open for Gloria on her way out were a couple of large men Freddy had never seen before. One wore a thin mustache while the other wore a vibrant red carnation in the buttonhole of his coat. They both gave Gloria's stockinged calves a nice long look as she pushed up the stairs and stepped out into the smoky cold with her face buried in her collar. With some obvious satisfaction expressed in upside-down smiles on their brows and lips, the two heavies let the doors go and swaggered over to the bar with their chests barreling out their coats.

As the men ordered drinks, Freddy started reworking the conversation he had had with Feldman earlier in the day, and he started to fear that this drink he was currently nursing was going to be his last. That was unacceptable to him. He wanted to be good and plastered when his time came. He wanted to be good and plastered in the comfort of his home. And he decided right then that he wanted to get to work on that right away.

As Freddy was about to stand up and make his exit, however, Victor turned around and stared across the sipping room in Freddy's direction. Victor's long jaw and sunken eyes might have looked menacing to some, but to Freddy, Victor simply looked tired. He looked as sad as a clarinet with a splintered reed and dry, cracked finger pads, older and weathered and beaten-down. Long in the legs, chest, and forearms, Victor rose from his seat and walked to Freddy's booth. The two men at the bar turned their heads and watched, eyes trailing, as Victor moved across the room.

"You mind if I sit down, Freddy?" Victor asked, pointing at the seat.

"No," Freddy said with an edge in his voice.

As Victor sat, his hair arched forward a little over his eyes. He combed it back with his fingers and then looked Freddy over. "Listen," he said, a reluctance in his voice, "regardless of what's happened, you and I know each other, right?"

"If I recall correctly," Freddy said, more welcoming, "you saved my life at least once or twice. . . . It's good to see you're out."

"Thanks."

"I heard you were paroled."

"Who would have thought," Victor said, cracking the slightest of smiles. He started scratching at his thumb and slowly turned his head to the bar, to the two men, who both drew their glasses to their lips at the same time.

"I'm sorry I was never up to visit you," Freddy said, "but Evelyn, she didn't like the idea. She didn't like it at all, and, well, I wasn't good at arguing with her about it."

"How is she, Evelyn?"

"I don't really know, to tell you the truth," Freddy said.

"What happened?"

"She broke things off last year, moved downtown."

"I'm sorry to hear it."

"Don't be. She's happy. She remarried and had a baby."

"The two of you always seemed happy together," Victor managed.

Freddy shrugged his shoulders. "I got what I deserved," he said mournfully.

"Anyway, Evelyn was right to be bothered about you coming to see me. I wasn't good to the two of you when I'd get strung out. You had good reason to stay away."

"It wasn't like that."

"Maybe you've just forgotten."

"Maybe I have," Freddy mused. "But, look, whatever it was then, it's bygones now."

"If that's the way you want it."

"Yeah, that's the way I want it." Freddy finished off his drink, and as he looked over at the two men at the bar looking him over, his strong thirst started growing stronger. "Where you staying?"

"Downtown at Fuller House. Until I can get on my feet."

"What brings you up here?"

Victor looked over his shoulder, then back at Freddy. "You ever seen these two before?"

"No, never. Why?"

"I just got a bad feeling."

"Yeah," Freddy said, "I know what you mean." Freddy looked at his empty glass, looked at the two up at the bar, at Victor. "What do you say we walk over to my place. I've got a full bottle. We can have a few drinks and catch up."

"Yeah," he said, "why don't we."

Freddy and Victor stood up, put their coats on, and started walking out. However, before they got to the front door, the two men at the bar stepped in front of them.

"Victor Ribe," the one with the mustache stated. Before Victor could answer, the two men walked on either side of him, and the one with the carnation in his buttonhole gently eased Freddy back toward the sipping room with a hand on his chest. Once he had placed Freddy a good distance away, the man with the carnation quickly plucked the flower from the buttonhole of his coat and placed it on the bar. If Victor even tried to struggle as the two men took him by the arms, it was invisible. He was overpowered by the two giants. They easily dragged him out of Jack's, up the stairs, and onto the street.

"Who are they?" Freddy asked Jack when the door closed.

Jack's hard face looked indifferent. "Narcotics."

"What you think they'll do to him?" Freddy asked, suddenly feeling relieved it wasn't him.

Jack didn't bother to answer.

Freddy walked over to the window but couldn't see anything. "Should I try to get a cop?"

"They are the cops."

Freddy stood by anxiously, waiting for a sign that it was over.

After a few minutes, the big men walked back down the stairs rubbing their hands over their knuckles and straightening out their coats. When they entered the bar, the carnation man stuck his flower back into his buttonhole while the other dropped a few coins into Jack's fist. The two of them were breathing heavily on their way out, and even though they looked calm and untouched, they were both wide-eyed and shaking a little.

Freddy started following them out.

"Freddy," Jack said.

Freddy turned around.

"Take one of these." Jack threw Freddy a rag from behind the bar.

"Thanks."

Freddy walked up to the street, into the haze of early-winter twilight, where he found Victor's legs sprawled out from behind a huddle of trash cans.

GLOBE METRO REPORT, MAY 23, 192-

VICTOR RIBE SPEAKS HIS PIECE

A SAM RAPAPORT EXCLUSIVE

Farnsworth—One month into serving his sentence of 25 years to life at Farnsworth Penitentiary, Victor Ribe, who was convicted in April for the double homicide of Alcohol and Narcotics Bureau Investigator Maurice Klempt and dope peddler Boris Lardner, looked none too worse for wear. When he finally got his chance to speak his piece, his eyes were clear, his speech lucid, his attention focused. He was in the pink.

This was far from the case last month when Ribe's attorney, Lenny Shapiro, refused to let Ribe testify. And who could blame the counselor? The strung-out Ribe, suffering from a cold-turkey dope withdrawal, couldn't speak a word of sense. Today, however, he seemed full of it.

According to Victor Ribe, the bloody events that took place underneath the shadow of the el on the corner of Proctor and Shrine streets started when Victor's eyes just happened to wander up to the tracks above. At that very moment he looked up, he found flying through the sky, in his white lab coat, his old war buddy and personal druggist, Boris Lardner.

Ribe at first didn't believe what he saw. He'd been waiting for Lardner, in bad need of a fix. For a second Victor thought the whole thing was a hallucination that would go away with a rub of the temples.

No dice. Victor blinked his eyes a few times, but Boris Lardner's flying body didn't disappear. It continued plummeting through the air, spiraling toward Victor in an arc until it sailed over his head and crashed into the plate-glass window of Schweitzer's Piano Shop.

Splinters of glass stuck out of Boris's body. Growing puddles of blood shimmered in the light breaking through the train tracks.

Victor walked into the piano store through the busted window and bent over his old friend's jittering body. Clutched in Lardner's fist was a brown leather wallet.

"This one," Lardner painfully exhaled with one bloody eye focused on the wallet. "Find this one."

Victor nearly had to pry open Boris's fingers in order to take the wallet from his hand. Then he began searching through Boris's pockets for his fix.

"Where did you put it?" Ribe shouted.

But Victor hadn't noticed that Boris was no longer breathing to answer. Nor did Victor notice that a group of women from the Glory Be Temperance Alliance, who had been demonstrating outside a row of speakeasies just down the block, had gathered round and were watching him. Their mouths gaped open as Victor's bloody hands rummaged through Boris's pockets.

"Where did you put it?" Victor continued aloud. "Where did you put it?"

Everything he found in Boris's pockets—a set of keys, an empty vial, a silver flask—he stuck into his pockets until his shabby tweed coat was stained with streaks of blood.

After Victor had searched Boris's last pocket, he finally looked up to notice the gaping mouths of the temperance women. There was a long silence as Victor's large puffy eyes beheld all the faces. And then all of a sudden, one of the women at the window pointed a finger at Victor and screamed, "Murderer!"

She happened to have a whistle around her neck and started blowing it. All the women had whistles around their necks. And as the first one blew into her whistle, the rest whistled along with her.

An alarm of whistles rang through the piano store and up and down the block. Some drunks staggered out of the speakeasies to see what was to be seen. Victor could feel the posse of curiosity-seekers bounding toward him. He looked at Boris Lardner's lifeless body and then jumped through the broken window straight at the ladies.

He ran right through them. He ran down the middle of the street, under the train platform. He could see the shadow of the downtown express curving around the bend in the near distance. He frantically ran to the staircase leading to the embankment, cursing his dead friend.

"Where did you put it?" he kept saying aloud. "Where did you put it?"

When he reached the top of the stairs, Ribe stopped running and took off his jacket. He folded it over his arms so the blood was concealed from view and then he slowly walked into the small crowd waiting for the train.

He removed from his pocket the wallet Lardner had been clutching and looked through its contents. He found a few dollars and an old photograph of a broad, bulky, earnest-faced man with a flapper on his arm.

As he looked at the photo a little more closely, he realized that the earnest-looking man presently walking toward him, about two steps away, was the man in the picture.

"What did you do with it?" Victor said to the man. "What did you do to him?"

As the man reached under his coat, he said something to Victor, but Victor didn't hear him. The train was nearly at the station. When Victor didn't respond to whatever it was the man was saying, the man pulled out a pistol and leaned forward to hit Victor in the temple with its butt.

Victor blindly fell back and knocked his head against a steel grate. When his vision cleared, he saw the man bending over his body, the gun pointing at his face. Thinking the man was going to shoot him, Victor lifted his knees and kicked him in the chest, sending him reeling backward.

Victor leaned up on his elbow and helplessly watched the man fall back onto the tracks as the train pulled into the station.

All the people on the platform began to shrill as the conductor slammed on the brakes, but to no avail. The man's head was severed clean. It fell through an opening in the tracks, and because it had so much momentum from the train, it spun out of control and bounced all the way down Proctor Street until it landed at the door of Lovey's Smoke Shop, known to the locals as Lovey's Juice Joint.

Victor was off again. He ran down the stairs, down the middle of the street, once again through the pack of temperance women. This time he ran into a dusty alley and didn't stop running until he reached Boris Lardner's apartment on the other side of town.

Victor nearly knocked down the door before he could slip the key into the lock. He went straight into the back room, to a small metal box, from which he took a large vial of morphine.

He sat himself down at Boris's desk and shot himself full. He fell over on top of a photo of himself and

Boris standing in front of a brothel just days before they were shipped to the front.

The next thing Victor knew, he woke up in jail facing a couple of sweating Chinese who'd just been hauled in from an opium den. It turned out he was in a downtown cell awaiting his arraignment for the double homicide of Boris Lardner and ANB Investigator Maurice Klempt.

Chapter 13

Harry Shortz returned to the Central Boulevard station as the sun was going down. With deafening gusts of wind to his face, he walked in lockstep with the rush-hour crowd down Central Boulevard to the Beekman Hotel for Women.

The hotel's lobby was serenely quiet. All Harry could hear was the trickle of water emanating from around the replicated feet of a *Venus de Milo* standing over a small marble fountain in the waiting area. He removed his hat, patted down his hair, and walked around the circular fountain to the concierge—a young woman, thin, with a long neck and straight black hair that wound into a cylindrical bun on the crown of her head. She sat poised like a blue-eyed hieroglyph, her head positioned in half-profile. She wore horn-rimmed glasses on a silver chain and a charcoal-gray sweater set, and had a tidy compact bust that hovered over the hotel's directory. When Harry reached her, she slowly turned her head and lifted it, and when she had lifted her chin so that the skin of her throat had stretched out from the cover of her blouse, she removed her glasses and batted her lashes.

"Would you please ring Katrina Lowenstein's room and tell her that she has a visitor."

"Lowenstein?" The young woman skimmed through the directory's names with her finger. "I'm afraid not," she said, shaking her head. "No one's registered under that name."

Harry removed the piece of paper with Katrina's address on it.

"I was told she was in room nine F," he said, showing the piece of paper to the woman.

A look that was subtly indistinguishable between suspicion and intrigue came over the woman's face. "No," she said, trying to remember, "I'm almost positive that wasn't her name." She quickly glanced back down at the directory. She shook her head again. "No, nine F was Janice Gould." She turned the directory around so that Harry could see the name next to the room number. "And a good thing, too," she added, "that is, if Miss Lowenstein is anyone you care about."

"Why's that?"

"Miss Gould was reported murdered early this morning."

"I'm sorry?"

"Apparently a man in the building next door witnessed her being strangled from his office window, but . . ."

"But . . ."

"But when the police arrived, they couldn't corroborate the report because Miss Gould was nowhere to be found."

Harry looked noticeably affected. The taut flesh on his face appeared to lose hold of its musculature.

"Are you all right?" the concierge asked.

Harry's mind disappeared for a moment and then returned. "Would you happen to know the names of the officers who were assigned to the case?" Harry took out his badge and identification to show the woman who he was.

"No," she said. She carefully looked at Harry's badge and ID, appearing less suspicious and more curious about what was happening. "Harry Shortz? The Harry Shortz running for the Senate?"

Harry nodded his head.

The woman smiled and looked Harry over a little more as she spoke. "I'm afraid I don't remember the officers' names, but I'm pretty certain they were from the Third Precinct."

"Did you talk to them?"

"Yes, briefly. They seemed to think the whole thing was some kind of a put-on."

"I don't understand."

"Neither did they exactly. They suggested there was something a little off about the man who called them over. . . . If you like I can leave word for them to get in touch with you if they should come around again."

"That won't be necessary," Harry said, ruminating. "However, it would be helpful if you could give me the key to nine F, so that I can make my own report."

"Yes, all right," she said. "But I'm afraid there won't be much to look at."

"Why's that?"

The concierge removed a key from a wooden box below the desk and pointed Harry in the direction of the elevator. "The odd thing about it was," she said as they walked, "Miss Gould left word with the front desk early this morning that she would be moving out immediately and that she had hired a moving company to take care of her belongings. The movers arrived sometime in the late morning, shortly after the officers came."

The concierge placed her hand on the sleeve of Harry's coat and turned to the elevator operator. "Ninth floor," she said and turned back to Harry, leaving her hand on his sleeve. Harry glanced out the corner of his eye to the burgundy polish on the woman's nails; it nearly vanished into the dark wool of his overcoat.

"You wouldn't happen to know the name of the moving company, would you?" Harry asked, still looking at the young woman's hand.

The concierge slowly ran her fingers down the length of Harry's coat sleeve. "I can check at the desk if you like, before you leave," she said with a little flirtation in her voice.

"Thank you. You're very kind." Harry, feeling his heart rate quicken, looked away from the concierge to the black wand above the door and watched as it turned clockwise toward number 9.

The elevator swayed and bucked as it came to a stop. The elevator operator pulled open the gate and pushed open the door, and Harry and the concierge walked down the hall, over a navy carpet with a tangle of yellow-and-green vines along the borders. When they reached 9F the concierge produced the room key from a small waist pocket in her sweater and opened the door. The two of them walked inside, into an open and empty apartment. Harry immediately started looking through cupboards and closets and drawers, not sure what he was looking for.

The woman silently followed Harry around and watched him scrutinize the few mundane objects remaining—a crushed lightbulb, a few loose scraps of paper, a stretched pair of silk stockings laid out on the floor inside the bathroom. When she saw Harry making for the open Murphy bed in the bedroom, she walked ahead of him and took a seat. She hitched up her skirt a little, crossed her legs, and watched as Harry ran his fingers under the edges of the bed's mattress, which smelled strongly of too-sweet perfume.

Harry occasionally glanced up at the woman as he examined the seams of the mattress to see if by any chance anything could have been slipped inside. The sight of the woman sitting on the dirty mattress suddenly made Harry feel sick. As he reached the part of the bed she was sitting on, the concierge stood up and walked to the window. Harry's eyes followed her, and as they did, out of the corner of his eye, he noticed a man moving about, outside, through the window, across the air shaft.

Harry politely stepped around the concierge and walked over to the window, where he saw a thin balding man with a lopsided face sitting at his desk, sorting through a pile of papers.

"It was the man in that office who made the report?" Harry asked.

"That would be my guess," the woman said.

Harry looked at the concierge and then looked across the air shaft. As he looked at the man, a vertiginous feeling overcame

Harry, as if the Beekman Hotel had been rapidly submerged into the earth. "What building are we looking at?"

"The Fief Building."

Harry's heart started to feel as if it were engorged with blood; he felt a shock break through his body. "I've seen all I need to see," he said.

The concierge looked at Harry with concern and followed him out of the room, down the hall to the elevator. Harry wondered why he hadn't realized it before. If he had been walking from downtown and not uptown, it would have occurred to him sooner where he was. He rang for the elevator. As he watched the moving wand above the elevator's doors, Harry suddenly felt a sense of loneliness that he had never felt before, the feeling of being trapped in the middle of an unsolvable paradox.

"The stairs, where are the stairs?" Harry asked the concierge with a sense of urgency in his voice.

"Right there," she said, pointing a few doors down from the elevator. "But the elevator will be here in just a minute, Mr. Commissioner."

Without another word, Harry left the concierge waiting at the elevator and made his way down the stairs with a red panic on his face. In his haste, he sent a shock through three women as they entered the stairwell on the third floor. Without apologies, he continued on his way down to the lobby, and through the lobby onto the street. He walked the short distance to the Fief Building, entered its lobby, and after looking at the directory, rode the elevator to the ninth floor. When he reached the ninth floor, he walked along the curve of the display floor, along the edge of the rotunda, and turned down a corridor leading to Julius Fief's office.

Harry removed his badge and ID from his coat pocket and said to Julius Fief's secretary as he approached her, "Please tell Mr. Fief that Harry Shortz is here to see him on official business."

"I'm afraid he's not in, Mr. Shortz."

Harry leaned his hefty torso over the desk. "Let him know I'm here."

The secretary, visibly intimidated by Harry, stood up from her chair and stepped back a few steps. "As I said, he's not in."

Harry walked passed the secretary's desk and entered Julius Fief's office. All along the floor were various Fief products mounted on pedestals. On the walls, ammunition, assorted by size, as if itemized like a taxonomy of cocoons, hung suspended from metal prongs. Frames, in assorted sizes, held photographs of battle scenes, of barbwired trenches, gas masks, exploding mortars, soldiers marching onto battlefields, into rivers and streams; wounded marchers marched passed roadside carnage, mass graves, fields blurred with white crosses; liberation marchers; celebratory marchers; marchers on ships; ancient marchers, intricate etchings of thumb-sized, palm-sized marchers, marching onto Troy.

As Fief's secretary said, Julius Fief wasn't in.

Harry turned around and walked past Fief's secretary in a silent rage. He made his way around the rotunda, back to the elevator bank. He rode the elevator to the lobby and started back downtown to his office through the dense crowds spilling into the street and fighting for a place on the sidewalk like scared zoo animals afraid to run free from their cages.

Chapter 14

When Gloria Lime returned home from Jack's Basement Tavern, Boris Lardner's brother, Sidney, a disheveled man wearing a couple days' growth on his face and a loosened coffee-stained tie, stood in her apartment doorway reading *The Kaiser's Cat: A War Memoir,* by Harry Shortz.

"I seen that book in the store window the other day," Gloria said when she walked up and saw what Sidney was reading. "Is it true the Kaiser used to look for advice from his cat?"

"If he'd only talked to his cat, Shortz wouldn't be the man that he is today, and Hitler would probably be some second-rate stooge somewheres."

"I don't get it," Gloria said. "Is it true or isn't it true?"

"It's true, it's just that the cat ain't the cat. The Cat was Harry Shortz."

"Harry Shortz was the cat?"

"The Cat, Glory. The Cat. The sneaky Cat who *shnooked* the Kaiser."

"What? Shortz is all of a sudden a confidence man?"

"Yeah, a confidence man, a spy, whatever you want to call him."

"The Cat?"

Sidney nodded by jutting his chin into his chest and raising his hands a little.

"I get it—*the Cat.* . . . I still don't understand what he's got to do with Hitler."

"Never mind."

Gloria opened her door and let Sidney Lardner follow her in. Sidney took a seat on Gloria's sofa. Gloria lived in a small two-room apartment upstairs from her sister and brother-in-law's candy store. She always had an ample supply of chocolate-covered cherries in a bowl when she knew Sidney was going to be by. Sidney liked to snack. He had a belly.

"Help yourself to the chocolates, Sid. I'll only be a minute."

Sidney stuffed a whole cherry in his mouth and wiped his fingers on his pants. "You see, this is the way it is," he said as Gloria went into the other room and got undressed. "They never mention the invisible men. They only talk about the ones who had honorable duties and didn't get killed. They never talk about the shameless orders. Those things they say once, then hide forever."

"What are you going on about?" Gloria said from behind the half-open door.

"I said this book is nothing but a bunch of lies is what I said. To make a hero out of the bum, so he comes off good. So when he's running for the Senate, he makes a big splash."

Gloria came out in a black Chinatown robe with gold dragons running down the sleeves. She took a seat on the chair opposite Sidney, lit a cigarette, and crossed her legs.

"Over there, overseas, they accept invisible men," Sidney continued, chewing. "The next-door neighbor's an invisible man. The milkman's an invisible. Groups of people are invisible crowds."

"Sidney, what are you talking about?"

"I'm saying they're used to it. They're used to everybody not appearing to be what they are. People speaking out of two sides of their mouth. People saying they're going to do something for you and then getting you arrested or kidnapped or killed. I mean, people's people, but they're used to people being like that over there."

"C'mon, Sidney—the point."

"That is the point. Over here . . . over here it's the same story, but we *think* it's a different story, see. Over here we think we can say anything we want, but the truth of the matter is . . . the truth of the matter is that a guy like Harry Shortz—war hero—big shot—can come along and turn you into something you don't want to be. I mean, my brother, and don't get me wrong . . . my brother was a little mixed up, but Harry Shortz, *Herr* Commissioner, helped make him into a bigger puzzle than he already was."

Gloria Lime raised her eyebrows as if to say, Tell me something I haven't already heard a million times. "I don't want to hear it tonight, Sidney. I know the story. I don't want to hear it. Not tonight. Really!"

"Yeah yeah," Sidney said pathetically, waving her off with his hand. "But like I say, he wouldn't have been so mixed up if it weren't for Shortz. He wouldn't have never gotten mixed up with the likes of Roth and Mann if he weren't forced into that. If he weren't forced into being one of Shortz's seeing-eye dogs, he wouldn't have done that."

"You can't prove that, Sidney, and you know you can't."

"I can't prove it, but I knew my brother. He was mixed up, but he had smarts."

"C'mon, Sidney, even if I can't get you to shut up, it's been too long already to be going on about this. And besides, you know I don't believe a word that comes out of your mouth. You don't see what's in front of your face. Forget what's invisible."

"No, you listen here. My brother wasn't the kind of man they made him out to be in the papers."

"How do you know? How do you know what anybody really is?"

"I knew my brother. And he wasn't no third-rate stooge that'd turn on the likes of Mann and Roth, even with the likes of Harry Shortz breathing down his neck. He wasn't that stupid. Ever since we were kids, he knew what was what."

"You known me since we were kids, right? You think you know me?"

Sidney paused and looked into Gloria's face through the cigarette smoke. "I like to think so, Glory."

"Suppose I said I got strong feelings for the communists? Suppose I said that?"

"You got feelings for communists, Glory?" Sidney said with his voice pitched high on "communists."

"I'm not saying I do or don't, Sidney. I'm saying, suppose. Then what? Then that might make me what? What would that make me in that crooked mind of yours, Sidney?"

Sidney didn't say anything. He just looked at Gloria with his sad eyes. Sidney did have sad eyes, big bovine eyes.

"Jesus Christ, Sidney! You're the most ridiculous . . ." Gloria Lime snuffed her cigarette out and walked to the kitchen. She poured a drink from a bottle on top of the icebox and then walked back into the living room.

"Look," she said, standing before Sidney with her drink in hand, "you want to know what happened, or what?"

"Yeah, I want to know what happened," Sidney said. "What do you think I'm here for? But Glory . . . Glory, you ain't no communist, are you?"

"No, Sidney, I ain't a communist. I'm Gloria Lime. I live on Bauer Street above my sister's candy store and I haven't had a date in over six months. That's who I am, Sidney, I'm a lonely girl living above a lot of chocolate-covered cherries, all right?"

"You ain't had a date in six months?" Sidney said, as if he were heartbroken.

"No, I ain't had a date in six months. And you can drop it now, thank you."

"I'll take you somewheres, Glory."

"Sidney! You heard me."

"Yeah, all right."

"So anyways . . . Where was I?"

"You weren't anywhere yet."

"I was down at Fuller House this morning is where I was when I saw Victor coming down the stoop."

"Did he see you?"

"No, he didn't see me. I stood in the doorway where you told me to stand and I kept my distance. . . . But I wasn't the only one following him. He had a couple of big lugs after him too. I think he seen the two of them."

"Who were they?"

"How am I supposed to know? Big dopey-looking guys in suits. They had anvils for heads. I never seen 'em before."

"Did they see you?"

"I don't know, Sid. I know for pretty certain that I ain't invisible like the rest of the nobodies in your head. But what I did was—they followed him, so I followed them."

"So where'd you all go?"

"It's all here," Gloria said as she reached for her purse. She took out a piece of paper with all the stops written on it.

Sidney looked over the list.

"He went over to Jack's?"

"Yeah, the two of us."

"You let him see you?"

"Yeah, I let him see me. I was freezing my behind off the way this crazy bum was walking around like a zombie in the bitter cold. . . . Besides, Jack knows me there. Everybody knows me there. It's not like it was anything suspicious that I'd show up for an afternoon drink."

"What happened to the guys who were following him?"

"I don't know what happened to them. They disappeared all of a sudden. But then these two new dopes came in as I was leaving to meet you."

"What they look like?"

"Cops. They were Narcotics. I seen 'em up at the club."

"You catch their names?"

"No."

"They talk to him?"

"I don't know. Like I said, I was on my way out."

"Did you talk to him?"

"No, I didn't talk to him. But I did run into Freddy Stillman." Gloria uncrossed her legs, recrossed them, then smiled. "Freddy I talked to."

"What did Victor do?"

Gloria rolled her eyes. "Nothing. He just sat there. That's all he did all day. He wandered. He talked. He wandered. He sat. End of story."

Sidney sat with his legs open and his hands on his thighs, shaking his head. "That's it? That's all you can tell me?"

"What . . . you're disappointed?"

"I just don't know what to make of it. The old man, the cops, the woman, and the kid?" Sidney squeezed his nose with his fingers.

"I don't know what you expected, Sid. The poor slob just got out. He's got a lot of catching up to do. You'll figure it all out, I'm sure. In the meanwhile, put the money on the table and scoot. I want to get some rest before I go to work."

"All right," Sidney said, reaching into his pocket. "All right. Take the money. Go ahead." Sidney reluctantly spread some cash out on the table.

"If you don't like parting with your doubloons, Sidney, I don't know why you didn't just do it yourself."

"I got my reasons." Sidney stood up, still looking at his money. "What did Freddy have to say?"

"Nothing worth mentioning."

"He didn't say nothing about nothing? You said you talked."

"He's taking me out tomorrow night, if you really want to know."

"I figured."

"Dinner and a movie at the Castaway."

"Fancy that."

"It was *my* idea."

"So then, you still have it for him after all this time?"

"It's none of your business, Sid."

"Even with that ex-wife of his on his mind? Even after all the trouble you caused him with his ex-wife? Breaking up his marriage the way you did?"

"What's it to you?"

"I'm just lookin' out."

"You're just jealous is more like it."

"I can't be jealous?"

"C'mon, already." Gloria laughed. "You and me, Sid? Get it out of your head already. You'll live longer. Besides, I could never fit in there with all the invisible men running around."

"Fine, all right, you go ahead and laugh, Glory." Sidney's eyes began to swell a little. "But one of these days . . . one of these days you'll come to your senses." Sid nearly started to choke up.

"Oh, Sid," Gloria said more compassionately. "Really, you gotta get it out of your head, honey. You're tormenting yourself. With me. With Boris . . ." Gloria stopped speaking and looked at Sidney with some concern. "It just doesn't have to be that way."

"I am what I am," Sidney said. "I can't help feeling what I feel." He turned away from Gloria and walked to the door. "I'll talk to you soon, Glory."

"All right, Sidney. Good night."

Gloria went to the door and watched him walk down the dimly lit stairs until he was out of sight. When she shut the door, she reclined on the couch, popped the last chocolate-covered cherry in her mouth, and then counted her money.

When Sidney stepped out in front of the darkened window of the candy store beneath Gloria's apartment, he walked down the quiet tree-lined block of Bauer Street to the corner, where he took a seat at the counter of Ledig's Coffee Shop. Right as he sat down, a thick man with doltish features stood up from a nearby table and sat down next to him.

The man was well-dressed and well-manicured, his hair

combed back with a healthy serving of brilliantine that made it look like he was wearing black leather on his head.

He placed an envelope on top of the counter and smiled at Sidney. Sidney, seeing the man smiling at him, swiveled around on his stool to see if there was someone behind him, then looked back at the man. "You the one who called and told me Ribe was out of jail?" Sid asked.

"That's me," the man said in a strikingly damp guttural voice. "Benny Rudolph."

Sid shook his hand. "You don't sound so well," Sid said.

"Yeah, I've heard that before."

"You said you had something interesting to tell me, about Boris's murder."

"I surely do," Benny Rudolph said, his eyes keen, studying Sidney's face as though he were sizing him up. "But first things first. You like doughnuts? The doughnuts are good. You want a doughnut?"

Sidney's eyes narrowed.

"I'm getting you a doughnut and some coffee. I think you need a doughnut and a little coffee before we get started. Miss . . ." Benny waved down to the end of the counter by the cash register. An old waitress with a stacked head of hair and a cranky look on her face walked over. "Give us a few chocolate doughnuts. . . . Coffee?" he asked Sid.

Sid nodded.

"And two coffees."

"Who are you?" Sid asked as the waitress stuck her pen in her hair and walked away.

"Don't concern yourself with that," Benny Rudolph said, smiling.

"Why shouldn't I if I'm going to trust whatever it is you have to say to me?"

"Because what I've got to say to you doesn't require anything from you other than that you listen and look and use a little common sense, that's why. You knowing who I am would only get in the way of that. Understood?"

The waitress walked over with the doughnuts and coffee. Sidney grimaced at her as he attempted a smile. He ripped one of the doughnuts in half and started eating.

"Today's kind of a big day, Sid," Benny said, smiling again, this smile a bit of a revelry. "It's the kind of day that all of a sudden makes everything you believe, all the truth that you've held close to your heart, change into something you don't recognize." Benny started talking with his hands, as if he was polishing a car. "It's kind of like a rose ain't a rose after all, it's kind of like all the furniture getting rearranged in your apartment and you can't find your favorite pillow to rest your head on."

"Quit the routine and get to the point, will you?"

"Tell me," Benny said more seriously, "what would you do if I could prove to you that Victor Ribe didn't kill your brother? But that it was Harry Shortz who was behind the whole thing?"

"Shortz?" Sid said. He fingered the book he had in his hand. "What makes you think that?"

"You mean you never had that feeling over the years? Knowing what you know about Shortz?" The man nodded his chin at the book and took a bite of his doughnut.

"The thought hadn't really crossed my mind. I mean, I always figured he had something to do with it, but not like that."

"Then what makes you so interested in him? What makes it so I should bring it up and there you are walking in here with that book in your hands?"

"Coincidence?" Sid said. "Because I got an interest?"

"Yeah," Benny said with a grunt, "if that's the way you want it."

Sid dunked his doughnut into his coffee and took a soft spongy bite. "Maybe I do, maybe I don't."

"Let's say you don't."

"All right," Sid said hesitantly, "let's say."

"What would you do, is the question, if I could make you believe it? Given that you don't know me from Adam."

"I don't know," Sid said, after thinking about it for a few seconds. "At this point it's all hypothetical."

"You'd be interested in justice, right?"

"If you can prove it to me, sure."

"You think you got the gall to do what's right when it comes time?"

"You bet I do."

Benny smiled a toothy grin. "That's what I wanted to hear from you, Sid."

"All right, so let's see you do your part."

"Tomorrow afternoon, where will you be?"

"In my shoe repair shop, in the lobby of the Prescot."

"All right, just be sure to be there."

"Who are you? You a cop?"

Benny Rudolph laughed. "That's a good one."

"What do you really want from me?" Sid asked. "If it's money you're looking for, I don't have any to give."

"Like I was saying, I'm just interested in setting things straight."

"Well, I'll tell you one thing: I ain't no pushover."

"Far be it from me to think that, my friend. . . . Just be in your shop tomorrow afternoon. You'll have everything you need to know and then some."

Sid looked Benny Rudolph over one more time. "I'll be there," Sid said. "I'll be there all day."

"And if you're not? Don't you worry," Benny said, "I'll find you." It sounded almost like a threat.

Benny Rudolph put on his hat and pushed his large heft up off the edge of the counter. He tucked his envelope under his arm, and then with a wink shot at Sidney, he stuffed the rest of his doughnut in his mouth and made his exit.

Sid collected himself and paid for the check. He ambled back down the quiet empty street to the candy store, where he stood in front of a heart-shaped display of red hots. He stared up to Gloria's still lace curtains, hoping to see her silhouette, and wondered what harm would be done if he rang for her. He wanted to spend some more time with her. He wanted to just sit in the same room with her, watch her lounge on her couch in her robe, and get her mad at him all over again. If a rose wasn't a rose anymore, Sidney couldn't even start to count the ways he loved Gloria Lime.

Chapter 15

"You want me to take you to the hospital?" Freddy asked Victor when he found him on the street outside Jack's, beside the trash cans. The two men who had dragged Victor out of the tavern had driven his face into a brick wall and busted his nose. His nostrils, his cheeks, his lips, his hair, the collar of his coat, his scarf steamed with blood; the soft flesh under his eyes was beginning to swell and turn black.

"No," Victor said to Freddy as he tried to sit up, "I'll be all right."

"If you say so." Freddy lifted Victor up by his shoulders, leaned him up against the wall, and while crouching down beside him delicately dabbed at Victor's face with the wet rag Jack had thrown at him on his way out. When Freddy had sopped up as much of the blood as he could off Victor's neck, cheeks, and mouth, he wrung out the rag and handed it to Victor. Victor tilted his head back and pressed the bloody rag to his nose.

Freddy Stillman lived a few blocks down Eighty-third Street on the corner of Gravesend Avenue in the first floor apartment of Celeste Martin's mother's home. As Freddy and Victor approached 319 West Eighty-third a soft shaft of yellow haze flooded out of the attic's dormer window onto the darkest part of the street. When they reached the gate bordering the property, the light was suddenly extinguished and Victor stood standing in the dark. "Jack said they were Narcotics, the ones who did this to you," Freddy said as he stood against the outside gate.

"I'm not certain, but I think they might have been the ones who arrested me."

"How'd they know where to find you?"

"I don't know." Victor looked over Freddy's head as he spoke, to the end of the block, across the darkened river. The icy water reflected the lights of the Long Meadow Palisades on the opposite shore. As Victor continued to look out onto the embankment of his old home, Freddy walked up the stairs and was nearly knocked back down as the door swung open and Celeste Martin stepped out, her back landing squarely against Freddy's chest. When she turned around, she greeted Freddy with a startled smile.

"Oh my! You took me by surprise, Freddy." Celeste fluttered her eyelashes. "I was just up in the attic, lost, yes, quite lost." Clutched in her arms was a stack of letters bound by twine. "I only meant to be there for a moment to put something away in one of Mommy's old footlockers when I came across these old letters Daddy had written to Richard while he was away traveling." Celeste smiled again into Freddy's face, which in the flickering light of the porch's lamp looked rubbery and tired. Celeste spoke in the manner one would expect from a grand princess. Her voice lilted and her pronunciation and elocution were exact. Although she was a woman of sixty-three, her voice was eerily sweet and youthful as a schoolgirl's.

"I'm sorry, Miss Martin," Freddy said, "I didn't mean to startle you."

"I'll be all right, Freddy. Really." Celeste, recomposed, looked down the darkened stoop to Victor. "And who have we there?" she asked. "You haven't had anyone over for ages, Freddy." Before Freddy could answer, Celeste walked down the stoop and stood in front of Victor. She briefly looked at his shadow, reached out for the cuff of his coat, and dragged him into the light. As Celeste pulled Victor up, Freddy could hear in the distance the heavy engine-thrum of a passing barge and through it her exclamation. "Oh my!" Celeste cried out again, with the same startled manner with which she had greeted Freddy.

"You remember Victor Ribe, don't you, Miss Martin?" Freddy said, trying to put her at ease.

"Victor?"

"Victor Ribe. He used to spend time with me and Evelyn some years ago."

"Oh yes. Yes, I do, as a matter of fact." Celeste turned back to Victor. "Hello, Victor."

"Hello, Miss Martin."

"What happened to you, if you don't mind my asking?" Celeste held on to Victor's cuff, looking intently at the large bump that had formed on the bridge of his nose, at the frozen encrusted blood layered on the collar of his coat, on the rims of his ears.

"It's nothing," Victor said. "I had a bad fall on a patch of ice." He good-naturedly allowed his arm to rest in Celeste's soft grip.

"Please, Miss Martin," Freddy said, "if you'll allow me, I'll take him to my apartment and clean him up."

"No," Celeste said immediately. "No." Celeste's eyes were emphatically lit. "Why don't we let Steven have a look at him. He's very good at tending to such things." She stood up as straight as she could to look into Victor's swollen eyes. "Will you agree to that, dear?"

Victor turned his head to Freddy. Freddy didn't indicate one way or the other how he felt. He knew that it was Celeste's nature to intervene and that if she weren't allowed to, she would be insulted. It was with this same generosity of spirit, in fact, that she had offered Freddy, at that time a stranger on a park bench, newly married, without a job, just back from war, the bottom-floor apartment in her mother's old home.

"Come then." Celeste took Victor's hand, tucked it under her arm, and walked him into the street. Freddy followed them to the entrance of Celeste's home.

When Celeste opened the front door, a cacophony of bickering voices and the heavy smell of chicken soup came from a room beyond a mahogany stairwell. Celeste led Victor around the stairs and off to the kitchen, where Aleksandr, the handyman already mentioned, Nicol, another handyman of Haitian origin with a thick graying mustache, and Steven, the cook from Hong Kong, sat around the kitchen table in front of empty plates speaking a pidgin English so unique in the English-speaking world it could be presumed only those participating at that table understood it. The men abruptly ceased their conversation and sat dumbfounded by the sight of the broken man, bloodstained and swollen, arm in arm with Miss Martin.

Steven, Aleksandr, and Nicol eventually rose to their feet, took Victor by the arms, and sat him down at the head of the table. Steven cautiously removed the bloody rag from Victor's hand and threw it in the garbage can beside a countertop covered with chicken fat and greens. Nicol and Aleksandr, in turn, gently removed Victor's coat and set it off to the side.

"Steven, will you be so kind as to get some ice from the service porch and see if you can't clean this man up a little. He's had a very bad fall."

"Yes, all right," Steven said in his choppy accent. Steven, who was only a year younger than Celeste, and who was thin and blotchy, had large sagging cheeks and a pious frown. As he waved in recognition of Celeste's request, his cheeks jiggled a little with understanding. Then he was off to the service porch with an ice pick in hand.

"And Steven?"

"Yes, Miss Martin." Steven turned back to Celeste.

"When you're through with him, make sure he and Freddy here get a nice hot plate of food."

"Yes, all right." He turned away.

"And Steven?" she said, this time saying "Steven" as though his name were an idea suddenly occurring to her.

"What is it?" he said with his back to her.

"Give Victor one of Mr. Tersi's old suits. And an old coat and hat." Celeste turned to Victor. "I have a very good eye for these things. I can tell any one will do. Do you hear that, Steven? Any one will do."

Steven just nodded his head this time and waved his free hand over his ear as he walked to the service porch.

Freddy, who had been standing in the doorway during all this, was now waved into the kitchen by Celeste, to an empty chair between Nicol and Aleksandr, who welcomed Freddy with clear familiarity, moving their chairs off to either side to make room. Both these men were his upstairs neighbors across the street. Nicol and his family occupied the second floor and Aleksandr and his family occupied the third. They were both looking at Victor in stony silence, heads cocked slightly, not exactly sure what to make of him. Victor stared back down the table through the swollen narrow slits of his eyes.

"Are you two boys free on Saturday?" Celeste asked rhetorically. "If you're free on Saturday, you're invited to the country estate for a party. Would you like to come? If you'd like to come, I think you two would be a fine addition to the guest list."

"I'm not . . ." Freddy began.

"No need to make up your mind now, dears. If you'd like to come, just come up with Nicol and Aleksandr. They'll be leaving sometime tomorrow evening. You come with them and spend the night."

"Thank you, Miss Martin," Freddy said. "We'll do our best to make it."

"I do hope so."

Victor smiled at Celeste as she stepped away with her letters and left the men to themselves and the kitchen's sounds of simmering soup and hissing gas.

. . .

After Steven returned from the service porch with the ice, everyone in Celeste Martin's kitchen remained perfectly quiet while he swabbed away the flecks of dry blood that stubbornly clung to Victor's lips and stubbled chin. He twisted two fistfuls of ice into thin white dish towels and dropped them into Victor's hands. Victor gripped the ice and leaned his head toward Steven. "Thank you," he said, nodding a little, his pupils slowly tracing his thick lids. "It's nothing," Steven said quickly, waving the rust-colored swabs in Victor's face, lifting his chin with quick thrusts. Victor pressed the two cold bundles to his narrowed eyes, resting them on either side of his nose, with his eyes covered and his head leaning back. Nicol and Aleksandr each let out a long, audible breath and relaxed their faces. Although they were otherwise irrepressible in each other's company, they had been noticeably, silently nervous and apprehensive in front of Victor. Now that his eyes were hidden, however, the two appeared more relaxed. Steven, meanwhile, threw the bloody swabs into the trash can, then lathered up at the tap. "Chicken soup coming," he said, scrubbing with strong and orderly strokes. "Chicken soup," he said again, giving the words some song.

"What is this party Miss Martin has planned out at the estate?" Freddy asked.

"It's not a party, really," Nicol said.

"They're having exhibit, an auction," Aleksandr followed.

"A Russian professor," Nicol said. "He arrived in the port this afternoon with the paintings."

"We've just finished building gallery in country house for him—Tarkhov is his name, I think—to hang his paintings," Aleksandr said proudly. "Not *his* paintings . . . I mean paintings he carries with him. Rodhinsky, a painter who died some years ago, these are his paintings."

"Yes, Tarkhov," Nicol affirmed.

"A Russian?" Freddy asked.

"Yes, a Russian. And this Rodhinsky—famous Russian painter, he was."

"Aleksandr," Nicol said, pointing his thumb at Aleksandr, "he once met him."

"Yes, when I was boy. He visited Split on his way back to Russia from Italy and stayed short time in church my father was working on, to learn a thing or two about masonry."

"And that's not the half of it," Nicol said, still gesturing with his thumb, prompting Aleksandr to continue.

"Yes, well . . . he was very nice man, always pouring me glasses of wine. Several years after the revolution, on the eve he was to be arrested for some kind of inane remark he made to high communist official, he used pickax my father had given him as gift to kill himself."

"How?"

"Believe it or not, by falling, with all his weight, onto point of ax." Aleksandr spread his arms out and tilted his body forward. "He placed pickax between two floorboards and fell forward. The point of the ax, it went right through his chest, into his heart."

"I don't believe it," Freddy said, seeing the image of the man falling toward the tip of the tool, thinking of what kind of impulse would drive a man to do such a vicious thing to his body.

"It's true," Nicol said.

"Yes, it's true," Aleksandr said. A smile came over his face. "And today, they say they keep that very pickax in Kremlin vault in Moscow."

"Why did he do it?"

"To make a statement of some sort, I would guess. What it was, I don't know. All I know is that my father—without shame, at the expense of this poor man—takes great pride in the fact that it was his ax."

Freddy pictured himself standing over the ax, looking down at it, thinking of the point piercing his sternum.

"A very strange legacy for an old man to have, I know," Aleksandr said, "but such are the yearnings of old men." Aleksandr shrugged his shoulders.

"Here we are," Steven said as he brought over the first two bowls of soup and placed them in front of Freddy and Victor. "Go ahead," he said to Victor. "You sip on the soup. It take your mind off pain." Victor tilted his head down and placed the packets of ice in his lap, then gripped the large spoon before him and delicately dipped it into the steam. As Steven continued serving, Freddy's eyes followed the mist of his soup up to the wall before him. A picture of a single yellow pear and a greenish hand reaching for the pear reminded him of the morose painting of the man across the air shaft of his office, the one that had hung above Janice Gould's bureau. As he was about to open his mouth and take his first spoonful of soup, he suddenly lost his appetite.

Freddy and Victor walked into the light at the top of the brownstone steps and through the front door of 319 West Eighty-third. Victor was now wearing an old coat of Mr. Tersi's, a thick wool herringbone with a fur lining, and he was carrying over his arm one of Mr. Tersi's suits and hats. Freddy locked the door behind them and then led Victor through a narrow hallway to the back of the house, through another locked door, and into a large room furnished with Federal-era furniture.

When Evelyn moved out and took the furniture to her new apartment, Celeste had taken pity on Freddy and ordered Nicol and Aleksandr to move a sofa, a table and chairs, a desk, a love seat, and a few end tables from the attic. The room looked like an old woman's parlor. Included in Miss Martin's charity was a gift of a teakettle, a tea cozy, a set of old teacups, and, on the walls, nearly indecipherable watercolors of the open land and stand of woods in Rainskill Falls on which now rested the Martins' country estate.

Off through a set of French doors with stained-glass panels was Freddy's bedroom. Both the bedroom and the main room were tidy and looked hardly lived in. The only place in the entire apartment that did look lived in was a small area near the back window, where standing on a tripod was a sleek metal telescope. Beside it were a few dirty plates, a bottle of bourbon with a teacup slung over the bottle's neck, and an ashtray mounded with the nubs of cigarettes.

Freddy threw his coat and briefcase over the arm of the sofa. He walked into the bedroom, picked up the bottle of bourbon from the floor, and placed it on the table. He pulled a clean ashtray from a drawer and another teacup off the desk, then filled the cups to the rim. Victor took hold of his drink and sipped off its edge.

"Can I ask you something, Victor?"

"What is it?"

"Just something I was thinking about while we were across the street."

"What is it?"

"You remember the time when we were stranded out in the French countryside during the war?"

"Yeah, sure, I remember."

Victor remembered the very simple woman and the very simple child and the small barn in which he, Freddy, and Boris had spent the night. He remembered Freddy's face when he saw the woman and the child in the vegetable garden, limp and crooked, the blood from their slit throats filling the crevices of moist tilled earth. Freddy caught sight of the soldier that did this, and when he chased him down, he unloaded his side arm into the man's face.

"You think he would have been grateful that I spared him a lifetime of bad memories?" Freddy asked.

"I don't know," Victor said as he recalled the stricken faces of the men that he had disposed of in the trenches.

"He was the first, the first one I'd seen up close before I killed him."

"You killed a lot of men," Victor said tiredly. "We all did."

"The funny thing is, I never really saw his face before I did away with it . . . he fell face first into the mud when he was trying to run away."

"He deserved what he got, Freddy."

"Maybe so, but I'll tell you, he's the one I dream about most." Freddy looked away from Victor to one of the muddy watercolor paintings of the Martins' country property. "It was the smell of the woman's and the girl's blood that made it stick to me, I think. The fact that when we buried them, I could actually smell the blood after coming out of the trenches, away from the stench of all that rotting flesh." Freddy shook his head as he lit another cigarette. "It's strange, since Evelyn left, I see her face like I see that soldier's. It's not so horrific as that, but it's just everywhere. Everywhere I look, I see her, as if she were some kind of apparition."

Victor didn't know what to say. He just stared at Freddy in such a way that his spirit seemed to momentarily vacate his body. He recalled the emptiness he had felt while in his cell, the longing he had to be touched by another person, the memories he had made sacred of him and Elaine Price riding the ferries between the City and Long Meadow when they were young.

"I know it's on the early side," Freddy said, "but I think maybe you should get some rest."

Victor nodded his head. "It's been a long day."

"You want to stay the night?"

"You don't mind?"

"Come on, I'll take you downstairs."

Freddy put out his cigarette and walked down the hall leading to the kitchen. Victor rose from his seat and followed Freddy. As they walked down the hall, Freddy looked to Victor like a thin pool of a man flattened against the wall, nearly folding in on himself.

Freddy opened the door next to the stove, turned on a light, and walked down some stone steps into the cellar. The cellar was a large, low-lying space that expanded across the foundation of the house. Strewn about half the floor were pipes and hardware, some gardening implements leaning against columns, and a few broken-down brass bed frames. The other half of the floor contained a potbelly furnace, a large metal bin filled with coal, a table, and a chair. On top of the table was a shortwave radio with a wire running out its back, inching up the wall and out a small hole in the windowpane. Beside the table was a canvas cot, a bulky pillow, and a heavy gray wool blanket. With all its clutter it was a clean, dry room filled with the deep and constant sucking noise of the furnace.

Freddy took a seat before the shortwave radio and flipped on a switch, to listen in, to listen to something on the outside for a minute. A soft brush of static burst out and then was invisibly consumed by the furnace fire. An occasional detached voice rose above the hush as Victor, without removing Noel Tersi's coat, laid himself out on the cot and stared up to the thick beams of the ceiling, listening to the words as they whispered into his ears. ". . . tug at the stern . . ." static ". . . long journey, long indeed . . ." static "nice to be . . ." static "nice to be . . ." Freddy watched Victor's swollen eyes shut and watched his breathing ease. He watched him until Victor was deeply asleep, then pulled the blanket over his legs and up to his chest.

Chapter 16

After his visit to the Fief Building, Harry Shortz started back downtown to the office, briskly, but after a few blocks, the brisk pace turned into a stroll and the stroll came to a halt. He had stopped dead in his tracks, in the middle of the rush-hour crowd, his feet feeling like they were rooted to the sidewalk. Every part of himself that made his body move felt like it was stuck. The bodies behind and approaching detoured around him and bounced off his rigid arms as though they were limbs of a tree jutting up from the bottom of a river. He stood solid like this in the frigid headwind until his cheeks and nose had become numb with pain, when suddenly from behind, a man as large as Harry accidentally knocked into him and spun him around. Harry's feet started moving again, and now that he was facing uptown, away from the office and in the direction of home, he decided home felt like the right place to be.

Harry and Beverly Shortz lived in a three-story East End townhouse on Sixty-third between Grand and Shrine. The house was dark when Harry arrived home. Beverly was at the theater and the boys were having dinner at the Kellys'. The darkness suited his mood, so he kept it that way. He hung his coat and hat in the foyer closet and went straight for the liquor cabinet in the front parlor. He splashed a little seltzer into a tumbler and added a very long shot of scotch.

"I didn't know you went in for the drink, Harry," Harry heard from behind him. The bottle of scotch slipped from Harry's hand and fell onto the floor as Harry reached for his gun.

"Why'd you go and do that, Harry?"

"Who's there?" Harry asked harshly as he thrust his gun into the darkness over by an armchair in the corner, over by the front window.

"It's Claude."

"Jesus Christ," Harry said as he placed the gun back into his holster and picked up the bottle from the floor.

Claude Fielding and Harry had served together in counterintelligence during the war. Claude now had a high-level position at the Department of State. Beverly was friendly with Claude's wife. Claude's kids were the same age as Harry's. The two men weren't close, but knew each other well enough.

"What the hell's the idea?" Harry asked as he was about to turn on a light.

"Don't turn on the light, Harry."

"Why not?"

"Let's go into the back of the house, away from the street, and I'll tell you why not. And if you got anything left in that bottle, why don't you pour me one while you're at it."

Harry grumbled a little as he watched Claude's dark figure stand up from the chair and move over to the doorway. His hand still shaking from the fright, Harry finished pouring the scotch for himself and poured one for Claude with what was left in the bottle. Harry walked over to the door and led his old friend into the back of his house, into the library; he placed the drinks down on a small desk and drew closed the heavy velvet curtains hanging in the window.

"All right," Harry said as he turned on the light, "start talking."

Claude Fielding was a thin rail of a man with a bald egg-shaped head and a mouth the size of a garage door. He had a baritone voice that fit with his oversized Adam's apple. He was carrying an attaché and looked jaundiced in the dim light of the library.

"I'm sorry I startled you," Claude said.

"What's with the snooping around?"

"I've got some sensitive news."

"What's it all about?"

"Why don't you sit down and start on that drink."

Harry was trying to sound like all was well with the world, but wasn't doing such a good job of it. His voice sounded a little wounded. Harry handed Claude Fielding one of the glasses, and the two men sat across from each other surrounded by the books lining the walls.

"It's like this," Claude said with a solemn expression on his face. "You're in a good deal of trouble and I'd like to see you avoid it if I can."

"How do you figure I'm in trouble?" Harry asked, suddenly feeling unsure if he could trust Claude.

Claude opened up his case and looked at Harry squarely. "This part of the conversation is between us, Harry. If you ever say I said anything to you, I'll deny it."

"If you're not willing to stand up for what you have to say, Claude, then why are you telling me anything at all?"

"Because I don't like the idea of you getting broadsided like this and I don't think you deserve to go through the rest of your life not knowing why it's being done and who's doing it. But I'm not willing to give up my life for it, either, all right?"

Harry didn't say anything. He just stared at Claude, thinking him a coward.

"We have an understanding?" Claude said.

"Yeah," Harry said, "I get it."

"Okay, then." Claude slipped out a photo and handed it to Harry. "You recognize this man?"

"Yeah," Harry said. "I met him for the first time this morning, over in Long Meadow."

"Paulie Sendak," Claude said, "armory foreman, the man who called your office to get you out there this morning."

"That's right," Harry said, looking over the picture of the small rotund man with the pockmarked face.

"He was also the one who incited the men to take over the plant." Claude pulled another photograph out from his attaché and handed Harry another photo. "He's taking orders from this man."

"Who's this?" Harry asked.

"You don't recognize him?"

"No."

"His name is Benny Rudolph. He's a former private investigator. Worked both sides of the law."

Harry looked at the picture more closely, momentarily thinking of his trip up to Ten Lakes and the boxes filled with heroin in the basement of the Lowenstein house. "I don't know the face, but I know the name," Harry said. "Two of my men sent him away a long time ago on extortion charges."

"Well, currently he's unofficially doing some dirty work for Tines."

Harry blinked hard a few times. "What's Tines's hand in this?"

"On Tines's orders, Rudolph got Sendak to start the hullabaloo this morning, and gave him the order to call you in. He also got Sendak to plant the dynamite in Waters and Capp's fishing shack."

"What's Sendak's role in all this?"

"To help Tines bust up the union."

"His own union?"

"He's getting paid, Harry."

"You mean to tell me that Tines is going that far outside the law to bust up this union?"

"It depends on how you look at it."

"What do you mean?"

"Try to get this, Harry: if the union is strong enough to cease the production of munitions whenever they damn well feel like it, what happens if we find ourselves getting caught up in a war? What if the munitions plants fall the way the steel plants did just last year? You got a lot of people asking those kinds of questions right now."

"Is this you talking, Claude?"

"No, but it's the talk I've been listening to. The idea of a munitions workers union acting as they please is making people nervous, and those people have given Tines the authority to do as he pleases."

"You mean people in the Department of State."

Claude's Adam's apple made a long swooping motion.

"What else?" Harry asked with more than a little bluster in his voice.

Claude, picking up on Harry's tone, said, "Remember, Harry, I'm here as a friend."

"What else?" Harry persisted with the same bluster. "What's Long Meadow got to do with me?"

Claude's egg-shaped head formed some lines in it that made it look like it was going to crack open. "The way I understand it, Tines is responsible for relocating Fief somewhere outside of Long Meadow and it seems no one wants to take a chance that you and your labor platform are going to stand in the way of that."

"So Tines is sending this thug Rudolph after me, to scare me out of the race?"

"That's the gist of it, yeah."

Harry gripped his glass so tightly it should have broken. "And how exactly do your colleagues at the Department of State figure I stand in the way?"

"Some people figure on you winning. You're a popular man, Harry. An honest man. A man who does what he says he's going to do. They don't like the idea of it. Not one bit. They have it in their heads that your allegiance is with the worker and not with the country."

"What makes them think that the average worker's allegiance isn't to their country? They're the ones building the fucking place. What makes these people think that labor would want what they've built torn from their hands?"

Claude didn't bother answering.

"And what do these people figure I should do? That's what you're really here for, isn't it, Claude? To tell me what to do."

"I'm not here to tell you what to do, Harry. I'm just here to tell you that if you're not careful you're in for a fall, and as far as I can tell from how Tines is going about it, it's going to be steep."

Harry scratched at his face and started pulling at his ear. "All he'll be doing is challenging an honest cop if he tries."

"Anything questionable in your past," Claude said with emphasis, "anything unseemly-looking in the present, he's going to use to destroy you." Claude looked into Harry's eyes with what appeared to be genuine apology, and shook his head. "All that's going to help is if you take a bow and step off the stage."

"I'm not buying."

"I think you should think about it," Claude said, standing up. He reached out and picked up the pictures of Sendak and Rudolph that Harry had set on the table. "You of all people, Harry, shouldn't be so naive as to think that the good can't fall as hard as the bad."

Harry shook his head with disgust. "You believe in this, Claude?"

"Would I be here telling you this if I did?"

"Then why don't you help me?"

"I'm not that kind of a man, Harry, and you know it." Claude started walking away from Harry. "I should be going."

"I'll show you out."

"I can find my way."

"I'll show you the way," Harry said.

Chapter 17

While Victor slept downstairs in the cellar, Freddy sat up in bed, drinking and smoking cigarettes. From the drawer of his night table, he took out a pad and a pen, and an old newspaper clipping he had found in the *Globe* a few months ago, a Miss Lonelyhearts column that he had already read a few dozen times.

Dear Miss Lonelyhearts,

A year ago a steel girder clipped me in the back on a job and left me crippled so bad I can't get out of bed no more. I got no insurance and no money, and to add insult to my injury, after the accident, my wife left me because she said I was an ungrateful loudmouth and a goodfornuthin. When my wife left, an old lady in my building looked after me, but she died last week of a bad heart, god rest her soul. She cooked me all my meals and cleaned up after me and let me stay with her cat when she was out doing the shopping. I been calling my wife every day since the old lady died, but my wife, she says I deserved what I got and that she don't want nothing to do with me no more and that she don't have an ounce of pity left for a poor slob like me when she's gotta wait in lines at the soup kitchen for her next meal. I get so sad and angry for being messed up like this, and without being able to take care of myself, the only thing I got left to do is make some peace and say goodbye. I know my wife, she reads your column every day, and

I just wanted to let her know that I got no more hope for this world and it's time for me to check out. Please don't let me down Miss Lonelyhearts. Please print this letter, because by the time you get it, I ain't going to be around no more, and I want to make sure my wife knows that I love her regardless of her cold heart.

Yours truly,
Hopeless and Full of Remorse

Freddy placed the clipping back into the drawer of his night table and then for the better part of the night, as he drank his way down to the bottom of his bottle, he labored over a short letter to Evelyn.

Dear Evelyn,

There's no point in telling you how miserable I've been without you. I know you know this and I wish I were better at hiding it from you. But as we both know, my misery is my own burden and your devotion to me for all those years I treated you so badly could never have remedied my flaws. I have many regrets for treating you like I did over the years, and I just wanted you to know how grateful I am to you for putting up with me for as long as you did. That, and I also wanted to say how truly sorry I am. With all this time between us, with all this time I've had to myself to think about what's been eating at me, I only now realize how sick my heart is.

Other than to apologize for all the pain and trouble I caused you over the years, I'm writing to you now because I think I found a way out of this misery once and for all. The details aren't important. What's important is that if you receive this letter, you should know that I'm now at peace with myself. Although you may not like that this comes from me, enclosed is an insurance policy that makes you and the baby the beneficiaries. If all works out as I think it will, you'll have a nice start for the baby's future. Please take it and use it. It's the only thing I've done in so many years that I feel proud of. I love you always, and urge you not to be sad for me anymore.

Everlasting love,
Freddy

Finished with his letter, Freddy reached under his bed for a Sterling Company hatbox in which he kept the insurance policy he had taken out for Evelyn and the baby a few months earlier. He removed the folded papers from the box, then tucked them inside an envelope, which he addressed to Evelyn on Dunleavy Street. Freddy placed the envelope on his night table, then laid his head onto his pillows. He was drunk, drunk enough to sleep, but he was kept awake, not thinking of Evelyn any longer, but thinking about the woman who lived across the air shaft in the Beekman Hotel for Women.

He had lied to the police. Freddy had known Janice Gould. He had met her three months ago. He had been standing on the curb outside the Fief Building smoking a cigarette, looking uptown in the direction of the park, where he could still see emanating from the tops of the trees an orange autumn glow that filled the sky just before dusk. From behind, Freddy heard, *"Say, honey, would you be a doll and give me a hand with this thing."* It took him a moment to realize he was "honey" and was being spoken to, but then he slowly turned around and found a young woman standing beside a bureau, waving him over. *"The doorman just stepped out for his dinner. If I don't get this thing inside, I'll be sitting on top of it, directing traffic."* She was just like Freddy described her to the police—young, a full round face, long neck, slim waist, long auburn hair, made-up, beautiful, gorgeous. *"You do this for me,"* she said, *"I got enough on me to take you out for a nice stiff drink. Whatta you say?"* Freddy said, "If you put it that way." *"I took you for a drinking man,"* she said. When Freddy found his feet had turned heavy at the sight of her, at the prospect of her, she placed a hand on her hip and said, *"Whatta you waiting for?"* The orange autumn light shrouded the woman's long auburn hair, making it look like it was about to catch fire. Freddy casually walked over to her and hugged the heavy, cumbersome piece of furniture around its girth and, struggling to keep it upright, followed Janice into the lobby. He set the bureau next to two plaid valises and the painting of a young man with a thin smile and a crooked nose. "Your boyfriend?" Freddy joked. *"No, silly, that there's my father. In his youth."* She looked cross. "I didn't mean to make light of it." *"My mother, she painted it before she died. What do you think?"* "Nice," Freddy said. *"You don't think much of it, do you?"* "I think it's real fine." *"That's all right, honey, I know what it is. I just like to keep him around to remind me of my happy homelife, see."* "If you say so." *"You thought I was mad at you for a second, didn't you? . . . No, don't answer that. Answer this—where we going for that drink I promised you?"*

The two of them walked around the block to the Hotel Trouville and sat at the bar. *"Fancy,"* she said, looking over her shoulders, sizing up the place. *"You come here often?"* "No," Freddy said. "Never been here before in my life." *"Then what the hell are we doing here?"* "Since you were buying, I thought we'd give it a shot." *"One drink and then we're out of this joint. Then you're taking me someplace nice and cheap so we can poison ourselves right."* Freddy looked at her as if she was a religion of her own making. *"What? You don't have plans, do you?"* "No," Freddy said. *"I didn't think so."* They each had a highball at the Trouville, then took a cab uptown to Jack's. *"Now, this is more like it,"* she said. *"This one's on you, sweetheart."*

The dour-looking men in Jack's, Jack included, jealously watched Freddy get drunk with the woman in the back corner of the sipping room. After their fifth round, she was sitting beside him in the booth, nuzzling her reddened nose into his neck. *"The thing is,"* she said quietly, *"is that my husband, he couldn't take an inch of me. To expect him to take the whole nine hundred miles, forget it."* "So you picked up and left him." *"Four times I left him already. In two years.*" She held up four fingers. *"Four times he's sent a flatfoot after me, and four times he's gotten down on his knees and begged, I mean begged, me to go back to him."* "And you went back four times." *"Four times. But no more, buster, I said to him this time. Nothin' doin'. You can send out the entire landed army and I ain't coming back to you this time, I told him. That's final."* "Good," Freddy said. *"I bet you think it's good."* "Why do you say that?" *"I'll show you, I'll show you."*

She showed him. Freddy woke up the following morning with Janice Gould's soft mane of auburn hair swept across his chest. He could hardly move his legs, they were so wrenched out of shape. *"One thing I learned from my poor deceased mother,"* she said with her cheek burrowed into Freddy's chest hair, *"is that no heartache's worth going to the grave for, boyo."* "Your mother, she had a bad heart?" *"No, honey, she had a first-rate heart. Her heart was so first-rate, she pined away for one galoot for so long, it was like she was beatin' it for both of them. And when she was done with the whole wrestling match, she managed to cut her life right in half like a thin piece of paper."* Freddy gave her a sad grin as she lifted herself off him. *"Don't you worry, kid,"* she said with some determination when she saw Freddy's face, *"I don't got my mother's heart. Mine don't beat for no one but me."*

For the next several weeks, Freddy woke up in the mornings, worn out and hungover, with his arm lying across the soft pouch of Janice's belly, his face pressing against her tangerine-sized breasts, and he would listen to her talk. How she liked to talk. *"What do you think, Freddy, you think my tits are too small for me to make the burlesque houses? They gotta cry out for them! Cry, I tell you."* "You got me crying for them, don't you?" *"Yeah, but you, you're a pushover. I'm saying, if you was to have seen me for the first time on the stage with this chest, would it take your breath away?"* "Like I said . . ." *"I know what you said, but, think, I gotta take their breath right out of their lungs so they can feel it right here,"* she said, taking hold of her naked groin as she stood up from the bed in front of Freddy. *"Don't you get it, bub, I want to knock them right in their seats and have 'em scream for me like none of 'em can live without me."* "They're good enough," Freddy urged as Janice turned them away from him. "They're the best I can recall." *"No joke?"* "No joke." *"Oh, Freddy,"* she cooed, looking back at him, her waist in a half twist, *"I didn't think you had it in you."* "What's that?" *"You can lie real good."* "I'm not lying." *"That's what makes it so good."* Freddy looked at her a little stupefied. *"It's going to be the legs they'll be screaming for. I got knockout legs,"* she said slapping herself on the behind and running her hand down the back of her thigh, her ass presenting itself to Freddy like a split peach. Freddy crawled to the edge of the bed on all fours and rested his nose in the crack of Janice's ass. "Thank God," he said. *"What's that, honey?"* "I said, 'Thank God.' " *"That's exactly what I want them to say."*

After a few weeks of auditions, Janice Gould told Freddy that she had settled for a job as a hatcheck girl downtown at the Triple Mark, hoping she would be able to work her way into the burlesque shows. The Triple Mark was well known for its burlesque, for its knife juggler and dancing Pekinese, for Verushka, the buxom baton twirler, who, to a lengthy drumroll, could simultaneously balance jugs full of red table wine between her scantily covered breasts. "You know what goes on in there, don't you?" Freddy said to Janice timidly when she told him about the job. *"You getting protective over me, Freddy?"* "I'm not sure I'd know how." *"Who are you kidding, Tarzan? You got enough ape in you to uproot a banana plantation. You're a regular beast. . . . Jesus Christ, come give Janey some smooch."* As much as the Triple Mark was known for its burlesque it was equally known for pleasuring its clientele in its upstairs rooms: gangsters, cops, politicians, businessmen, and then, of course, regular John Q. Citizens, overmarried, and eager and drunk enough to blow a week's wages on a showgirl. Freddy had done just that on more than a few occasions while still married to Evelyn.

It was when Janice took the job that she started to slip away a little. She worked late into the night, stopped sleeping at Freddy's, and started staying in her room at the Beekman. From across the air shaft, in the late mornings, Freddy would find Janice standing in her open robe, half naked in front of her window, staring at Freddy in his suit, working his job, and Freddy would stare back at her, wishing at times he were that young again.

It was a Thursday night at Jack's that Freddy met Feldman for the first time. Feldman worked for Mann and Roth at the Triple Mark. He had come in Janice's place. *"She wanted me to come down and tell you myself, so that you shouldn't worry."* "Worry about what?" *"The thing with the husband. You know about the thing with the husband, right?"* "Sure I do." *"Well, Janice, she spotted a familiar face outside the Beekman earlier, some shamus."* "Is she all right?" *"She's just fine. Johnny Mann himself is looking after her. And when he's not looking after her, I'll be looking after her."* "She and Johnny Mann . . . ?" *"He's just looking out for the kid,"* Feldman said. *"He's taken a shine to her. He thinks she's got talent, not to mention some real balls. Turns out he knew her mother."* "Where from?" *"I think she did a little work for him a long time ago."* "You don't say." *"That's what I heard."*

Freddy liked Feldman. He was awkward, the way big fat men are awkward; self-deprecating, the way fat men are self-deprecating. What's more, for a while Freddy sort of liked the idea of spending time with one of Mann and Roth's men. *"If I weren't so big and tubby,"* Feldman said to Freddy when Freddy asked Feldman how he had fallen in with Mann and Roth, *"I'm not sure I would have ever fallen in with them at all. I'm sort of a conversation piece, like I'm some monument to the organization, their very own Taj Mahal."* The right corner of Feldman's mouth slowly rose until his cheek was pinched into a nice round pink ball of flesh. *"They took one look at me and started laughing. They keep me around for laughs. Send over the heavy, they say about me. The heavy'll get the job done. Let's see what their heavy can do with our heavy. We got the heavy of all heavies. Feldman, he's the heaviest in the business. Got a problem with one of the girls? Send in the heavy to talk some girl-talk. The girls feel comfortable with the heavy talking girl-talk. . . . They got a million lines for me. What can I say? My mother, she fed me well. And I like to eat. I like to eat a lot."*

Over the next couple of weeks, Feldman, who said he liked Freddy's company, started to drop by Jack's and sit with Freddy in the back booths of the sipping room. They got around to talking about Freddy's life, the little that there was of it, and eventually they got onto the subject of Freddy's line of work, about the kind of munitions he dispatched for Fief, about how the paperwork went in, who checked it over, how the calls were made to the factory, who oversaw the shipments at the docks in Long Meadow. Then one night, Feldman had news about a new nightclub Johnny Mann and Jerzy Roth were going to open in Tangiers. *"They got some hoity-toity resort there or some such thing. Lots of money rolling in. And people with lots of money, hell, they don't know what fun is until people like Johnny and Jerzy teach them a little something about fun. I mean, a for instance, look at this Eliopoulos character, the Baron, he calls himself, he comes up to the Triple Mark five nights a week with the cream of the crop on his arm; he got himself a private room upstairs; he got himself his own table. These high society types, they get tears of boredom running out their eyes. In the circles they circle around in? Who could blame them? Johnny and Jerzy, they figure, why not have a monopoly on that boredom, export a little excitement. All that's left to be done is greasing the right palms over there with the right currency and we're in."*

"I'm going with Johnny to Tangiers," Janice told Freddy the next time they were together in Freddy's bed. *"He says he'll let me make a go of it as a dancer if I go with him. I told him straight, I wasn't gonna be his moll. Either you let me dance or I'll grab me some royal heinie, I told him. He got the message. You happy for me, Freddy?"*

"I'm happy for you," Freddy said with disappointment in his voice.

"That's all right, hon, I'll miss you too. But I won't miss that private dick trailing after me. I'm just hoping I can skip town before that husband of mine catches up with me."

It was right around that time that Feldman appeared at Jack's after Freddy got off work and told Freddy that he had been talking to Johnny and Jerzy about him. *"They sounded very inspired,"* Feldman said. "I got a job fit for a numbskull, Feldman. What could be so inspiring?" *"To be honest, Freddy, they were more inspired by the possibility of what you could do for them."* That's when Feldman revealed himself. *"It's like this, see. Johnny and Jerzy, they want to do business over in Tangiers, but like I said, they got some politicians getting in their way, and well . . ."* Freddy could see it coming like a meteor about to fall from the sky. *"You get us what we want and you have no more financial worries for the rest of your days, my friend."*

Freddy didn't know what to say, but he liked the idea of it. He liked the idea of not having to work, of spending more of his days sitting in Jack's, mulling over his life, drinking, having enough money and time to drink himself to death if he liked. He liked the idea an awful lot, but said he would need to think it over. Feldman told him to take his time, but not too much time, because they didn't have time. Feldman gave him a day.

At the end of that day, Freddy found Janice Gould on his doorstep, her lip bloodied and her clothes half torn apart. Freddy took her in and sat her down. "Who did that to you?" *"He came out of nowhere,"* she said angrily, shaking her head violently. *"Can you believe it? He jumped me from behind, that lousy no-good coward. He jumped from behind, 'cause he knew I'd give him a fight."* She started to cry. Freddy went into the bathroom and brought back a damp washcloth. *"Right down the subway steps he pushed me,"* she said as Freddy delicately dabbed the wet cloth to her face. *"I bet he would have killed me right then and there if someone hadn't held him back."* "What happened to him?" *"He broke loose and ran off."*

Freddy put her into a hot bath. *"I don't want to go back out there alone, Freddy,"* she said to Freddy, who sat beside her on the toilet lid. "You'll stay here tonight." *"No offense, Freddy, you lift a heavy piece of furniture like a pro, but I think I'd feel more comfortable if you gave Feldman a call."* "You'll be safe here, Janice." *"Lesson one in etiquette, Freddy,"* she said, aggravated, *"when your girlfriend gets thrown down a flight of stairs by her husband, you don't argue with nothing that she has to say, understood?"* Twenty minutes later, Feldman was sitting inside Freddy's apartment, and together, Freddy and Feldman drank while Janice lounged on a love seat and cried every now and then.

It was at that moment, when the two of them were in Freddy's apartment together, that Freddy realized for the first time that there was something wrong with the whole setup. *"I want to shake him once and for all,"* Janice said. *"I'll do anything to get him out of my life, anything short of killing him. . . . No, I take that back. I'd kill him. I'd have him killed." "If that's what you want, Janice . . ."* Feldman said. It was the way Feldman said those six words that got Freddy to see what he needed to see. Feldman was suddenly acting. He was saying these words and the words that followed as if he had recently rehearsed them. It was the way he unconsciously looked over to Janice for reassurance. Freddy realized Janice had made him rehearse. He could see the two of them rehearsing. Or was it that they didn't have time to rehearse? And then he wondered if it wasn't Feldman who was carrying Janice through this routine. Freddy started recalling how it was he'd met Janice, how easily she'd become part of his life, how seamlessly Feldman had found his way into his confidence, and then he knew that they were both there to ask something more of him.

Feldman brought up the idea. *"I got an idea,"* he said convincingly. *"What is it, Feldman?"* Janice said flatly. *"Instead of getting rid of your husband, why don't we just get rid of you." "Real cute, big guy." "Not for good, not for real, no, no, we fake it. So the shamus buys it. What do you care, kid, you take on a stage name after that. You make up the whole thing from top to bottom, a part of the act." "Say,"* Janice said, clunking through her lines, *"that—ain't—such—a—bad—idea,—Feldman." "After we make the report, we send you ahead to Tangiers."* Janice turned to Freddy. *"What do you think, Freddy?"* Freddy couldn't believe how bad this was being executed before him, and he wanted to say so, but Feldman outweighed him by about two hundred pounds and he was carrying a gun. All he could think of to say was, "If that's how you want it, sweetheart." Janice took hold of the idea like it was the best thing she'd heard since she was born. *"In fact,"* Feldman said, *"we can do it the same day Freddy makes out that order for Johnny." "What—a—great—idea,—Feldman. What—a—great—i-de-a."*

Chapter 18

When Freddy finally drifted off to sleep, behind locked doors, in almost complete darkness, a few dozen men, using flashlights, were crating up the American Allied Pharmaceutical plant on the Southside Docks. Benny Rudolph was upstairs inside Elias Eliopoulos's office. He sat behind Eliopoulos's Louis XIV period desk, smoking one of his cigars and drinking brandy from one of his snifters. Through a crack in a venetian blind, he looked out onto the loading docks where Eliopoulos, with the help of a jade-capped cane, clumsily climbed into the backseat of his limousine. His chauffeur shut him in, got behind the wheel, and drove the car off in the direction of the Crown Cracker plant. As Benny watched the car drive away toward the opposite end of the docks, the phone on Eliopoulos's desk started ringing. Benny swiveled around in his chair and picked up the receiver.

"Yeah?" he said in his broken voice.

Uptown in the basement of the Triple Mark nightclub, the two grizzled men were standing over Johnny Mann and Jerzy Roth. Both Mann and Roth were knocked out, tightly bound to chairs, gagged, and blindfolded. Standing with the two grizzled men was Feldman, who was leaking sweat down his forehead and from around his collar, under his arms. He alone had carried Johnny and Jerzy from Johnny's office on the second floor down the back stairs to the basement. The grizzled man with the sunnier disposition was the one calling. He said to Benny, "They're out cold. But they should be opening their eyes any minute now."

"They make the call to Dubrov and Collins before you put them out?" Benny asked as he swiveled back around in the chair to look out the window. A man and a woman sandwiched by two of Rudolph's men were walking toward him down the narrow gravel path leading from Crown Crackers to American Allied's front entrance.

"Yeah, it's all taken care of."

"What about their men?"

"We got Feldman here. The others we took care of."

"Good. Tell Feldman what he's got in store for him in the morning. Tell him he better make a good show of it."

"I think he'll get the picture, boss."

"Make sure he gets it good."

As Benny hung up the phone, there was a knock on the door. The door creaked open and a man with a long chin leaned his head inside. "I've got 'em for you, boss."

"Send them in and wait in the hall," Benny said from behind the desk. The man and the woman Benny had seen walking toward the warehouse just a moment earlier walked into Elias Eliopoulos's dark office. "You disappointed me, Katrina," Benny said as he looked at the man.

"It weren't Daniel's idea, Benny," Katrina Lowenstein said as she saw how Benny was looking over Daniel Greely. She shook her auburn hair out from underneath the hood of her coat and let the coat fall off her arms as she sat down on a small leather couch opposite Benny. "I put him up to it."

"I have no doubts." Benny ticked his tongue as he shook his head between Katrina and Greely.

"I mean, c'mon, Benny, what you expect?" Katrina went on, her tone flippant, her legs crossed, her slit skirt showing off her lean smooth thighs. "You left a small fortune in dope down in the cellar of my house. Daniel's got a good picture to make, and, well, I figured . . ."

"Yeah," Benny said. "You figured wrong, kid."

"For what I been through, for what I've done," Katrina snipped without losing her poise, "I figured I deserved to get a decent start, is what I figured."

"You've got quite a flair for the drama, don't you. . . . You write a drama, Greely? With a role for the hard-nosed young dame with a lust for trouble?"

"It's a comedy," the disheveled Greely said, shrugging his shoulders. "With a murder mystery . . . a sort of comedy of errors, sort of."

"And what's she play?"

"She plays the killer."

"The killer, hey?" With a nicely manicured finger, Benny tugged on some flesh from under his eye, and he looked at Katrina.

"Who are you kidding, Benny? You ain't mad. I can tell you ain't mad at me." Katrina stood up and walked over to Eliopoulos's desk and sat on it. "I can tell you got a soft spot for me and Greely. So why don't you just let us be on our way, huh? Think of it as a little extra something. I deserve a little extra something, don't you think? I got you what you needed. I delivered Stillman, delivered a dead Janice Gould, kept an eye on Feldman . . ."

"It wasn't like I had to twist your arm to get you to do any of these things, sister."

"Sure," Katrina conceded, "it was for a good cause and you and me we'll have our revenge on Harry Shortz, but . . ."

". . . if memory serves me, you got yourself a handsome stack of cash . . ."

". . . but poor Greely here, he's in love with me and he had to live with the idea of me and that sad Stillman together in the sack. Don't Greely get his fair share for having to put up with that? He's got a strong mind and a sensitive heart," Katrina said, pointing to Greely. "He can't stand the idea of me with another man."

"He better get used to it," Benny said, looking over to Greely.

"From what I can see, and I've seen my fair share, it won't be the last time."

"So you're going to let us go?" Katrina said, looking over to Greely with a smile.

Benny was silent for a moment. "No," he said. "I can't do that."

Katrina slipped off the desk and walked back to the couch and fell onto her coat. Greely walked over and took a seat beside her. "What are you going to do with us?" Greely asked.

"What did you expect to do with the dope?" Benny asked Katrina.

"We were going to sell it."

"To who?" Benny asked Greely.

"We were going to parcel it out," Greely said. "On our way out west."

"Feldman," Katrina said, "he was going to come with us."

"Was he?"

"He had the list of the syndicate's pharmacies. We were going to split the money three ways from the sales."

Benny nodded silently, then started tapping his finger. "Give Mr. Greely a kiss and say goodbye," Benny said to Katrina.

Katrina looked at Greely and then looked at Benny. "What are you going to do to him?"

"Say your goodbyes, Mr. Greely. Go walk out that door and go show the man on the other side where to find your truck."

Greely gnawed on his lip as Benny told him what to do. He then turned to Katrina and looked into her eyes. Katrina started to say something, but Greely planted his lips on hers and then got up from his seat and walked out of the room.

"What's on your mind, Benny?" Katrina asked as if she still couldn't grasp the severity of the situation.

"I don't like being deceived," Benny coughed.

"It wasn't personal," Katrina sighed. "Why do you make it sound like I was doing it to get at you?"

Benny took out a handkerchief from his jacket pocket, spit out a little blood, and stuffed the handkerchief back into his pocket. "You knew the dope had to be in the house. You knew we transferred the property into Shortz's name. You knew . . ."

"I knew you had more than enough on him to get whatever it is you need from him," Katrina said, holding firm. "Knowing what little I know, Benny, I can see that. All you gotta do is replace those boxes with more boxes and that's the end of it, and let us go about our lives, Greely and me."

Benny was quiet.

"I know you don't have it in you to get rid of us, Benny. You'd be forlorned for the rest of your life for killing us, full of regrets and nightmares."

Benny continued his silence. He leaned over his desk and rested his chin in his hands.

"Besides, you can't kill me twice, Benny. You can't just kill me as Janice Gould and then go kill me as Katrina Lowenstein. Someone will figure it out."

"Don't you know when to shut up?" Benny said to Katrina.

"What's so important about having Janice Gould dead anyhow?"

Benny stretched out his face. "My client, he wanted a dead seductress."

"I ain't anonymous," Katrina said.

"You're right. Around these parts, you're Janice Gould. If you turned up dead, you'd be Janice Gould."

"What about Greely?"

"What about him?"

Katrina's boldness started to relent a little. She wouldn't let herself look scared, but she was starting to look angered. She was starting to think unpleasant thoughts, and in her rage was wagging her finger at Benny.

Benny stood up and walked over to the door. The man with the long chin was standing by. "Go do it like I said," Benny said. "Make sure you juice her up good."

"Yeah, all right, boss."

Benny turned back to Katrina, "Go with him. He'll take good care of you."

"Where's he taking me?"

"It was nice knowing you, kid."

"Where's he taking me?"

"You'll find out when you get there."

Benny grabbed hold of Katrina Lowenstein, and with a firm grip on her shoulders he walked her into the dark hall and pushed her at the man with the long chin. As she was about to say something more to him, he shut the door and sat back down at Elias Eliopoulos's desk.

GLOBE METRO REPORT, MAY 17, 192-

ACE *GLOBE* REPORTER SAM RAPAPORT FOUND DEAD

MARTY VOLMAN

West End—It is with great sorrow that we report the passing of one of our own. Sam Rapaport, whose inimitable voice filled the pages of the *Globe*'s Metro Report with vitriol and wit for more than 25 years, is dead at the age of 48. He was found this afternoon inside his West 34th Street apartment with a mortal gunshot wound to the head.

Mr. Rapaport is survived by his 15-year-old daughter, Faith, who found her father at his desk, pistol in hand, empty bottle of bootleg whiskey at his feet, and in the typewriter a suicide note, which shall remain private.

According to police, the cause of Mr. Rapaport's death is still under investigation, but all evidence, they say, points to suicide.

Sam Rapaport, whose contributions to the *Globe* can hardly be weighed in newsprint, will be sorely missed in these pages, and his shoes will most certainly never be filled. He reported what he saw, lived what he reported, and stood up for the truth in all its disguises. Sam Rapaport was the real McCoy, a legend in his own right.

Memorial services will be held at the Blue Room tomorrow evening at 6 p.m. Open to the public.

Chapter 19

Some hours after the American Allied Pharmaceutical plant had been packed up and loaded onto trucks in the cargo bay, Faith Rapaport was in bed, asleep. She had been at the the Globe Building until two in the morning, finishing up a two-part story: an interview with Max Waters and Henry Capp about their alleged role in the bombing, and coverage of a meeting held by the Munitions Workers Union inside the basement of the St. Francis Cathedral in Long Meadow. As Gerald Kravitz had anticipated, the union voted to walk out on Monday morning if Fief didn't meet their contract demands.

Faith was so fast asleep she didn't remember picking up the phone. But the receiver was in her hand, nestled into a soft pink pillow, and she was speaking to a man with a distinctly damp, guttural voice.

"Is this Faith Rapaport?"

"Who wants to know?"

"I'm calling East End nine four four. Is this East End nine four four? Faith Rapaport. I'm calling Faith Rapaport."

Faith dozed off.

"Is this Faith Rapaport, Sammy Rapaport's little girl?"

"What time is it?"

"Four, four-thirty in the morning."

"Sam's dead. Dead a long time."

"Yeah, no kidding. That's what I'm calling about."

"Anyone tell you you got a funny voice, mister? Sounds like

someone's got your little apple caught between their teeth. It sounds like it's leaking."

"Aren't you cute."

"Yes, yes I am."

Faith dozed off again.

"Are you there?"

Faith let out a grunt.

"You own a car, Miss Rapaport?"

"This is about my car?"

"No, it ain't about your car. It's about you getting into your car and taking a drive. Like I said, it's about your father. It's about your father and it's about the fact that the grand jury hearing you're supposed to cover today ain't going to be taking place."

"My father? My father's dead."

"We've already been through this."

"Right. What's this about the hearing?"

"Now listen, girlie . . ."

"Girlie, is it?"

"Now listen here. If you want to know what happened to your father, if you want to know why Murray Crown ain't going to make it to testify in court this morning . . ."

"Murray Crown . . . my father . . . in court this morning?"

"If you want to know why Murray Crown ain't going to make it to court today, if you want to know what Murray Crown's got to do with your father, you listen up. Don't start thinking about nothing, don't doze off, or you're gonna lose your chance."

"Who is this?"

"You just listen, don't think no more, and wake yourself up. Open those soft misty eyes of yours and pull yourself together."

"What do you know?"

"Your father, he weren't no suicide, is what I know."

Faith was silent again, but this time she was awake, her eyes now open, staring into the darkness of her bedroom, into the part of the darkness that appears to writhe with life when you look at it with open eyes for a moment too long. "Who is this?" Faith asked again.

"Southside Docks. Crown Crackers plant. Under the sign by the thruway, you'll find a garage. The lock's undone. Go on upstairs and take a quick look around."

"What am I supposed to be looking for?"

"A key. On his desk, there's a key."

"What kind of key?"

"You'll know it when you see it. Like I said, don't you start thinking about this. You think for more than a few minutes, your time is up. You got less than an hour before the coppers get there. Get the key."

The phone clicked and the voice disappeared. As soon as Faith hung up, the phone rang again.

"Yeah," she said, "what is it?"

"I'd recommend that you pull out whatever stories your father wrote on Victor Ribe's murder trial."

"Whose murder trial?"

"Victor Ribe's. R-I-B-E. Ribe, Victor."

"What's Victor Ribe, R-I-B-E, got to do with this?"

The man hung up again.

Faith pulled off the heavy blanket covering her body and groped around in the dark and yanked down on the cord to the lamp on her night table. The burning filament in the lamp's bulb filled the darkness of the early morning as if someone had smothered wet plaster over everything. Without thinking too much about what she was doing, about what she would do when she got there, she started scavenging about through the clutter of her small room in search of a bra and her shoes. She threw on a sweater and a pair of wool pants she had draped over a chair piled with clothes, brushed out her black curls, laced up her boots, put on a heavy coat and olive fedora, then popped a Lucky into her mouth on the way out.

She usually wouldn't act on a tip like this unless it came from one of her regular sources. She didn't mind getting her nose dirty. She liked to snoop, she liked even more to snoop into places she didn't belong. This started early on, and ceaselessly got her into trouble with Marty Volman, her editor, who had played father protector to Faith ever since Sam's death. Faith at the tender age of fifteen dropped out of school and became Volman's protégée, and, right away, proved herself her father's daughter: she was a natural at getting herself into the thick of dirty business. Her first big break came at age seventeen, when a story she wrote helped the police send Gorgeous Ziggy Lipskin to Farnsworth for murder. Pretending that she was a lovesick puppy wanting to catch Gorgeous Zig's eye, she followed Lipskin door to door as he made the rounds through his protection racket. At 55 Bankhead Street, inside a South End jewelry store, Lipskin let a few rounds run from his gat and Faith saw where he threw the gun. For that, she got page one, and was then kicked to a desk for six months to work over copy. For being reckless.

A trip to Murray Crown's private warehouse entrance in the middle of the night had Marty Volman's disapproval built into it as loud as a sign reading High Voltage, but Faith didn't care, not when it touched such a dark, unanswered part of herself. Over the years since her father's suicide, no one had so much as brought up Sam's death, aside from the times when people recognized her as her father's daughter and recalled with admiration what a beast of a reporter he had been. Otherwise, her father's case was closed, and when it was open it was hardly even questioned. The police came and went. The medical examiner's men took the body. Sam Rapaport was figured to have taken a bad turn and let himself have it.

Faith, of course, never wanted to believe that her father would leave her to fend for herself the way he did. He was hard-drinking, foul-mouthed, bullheaded, moody, full of strong opinions, but he was equally sweet and tender and full of love for Faith. So when she came home from school that day and found him shot through the mouth with his gun, she couldn't believe that anything in the world could have gotten so bad for him that, if given the choice, he would choose to leave her. He had left her all alone in the world, no family—that is, no family other than a bunch of aging rummy reporters down at the *Globe.* Her mother lived life hard and ran out on her and Sammy not too long after Faith was born. She was her father's daughter through and through, grew up in smoke-filled rooms, bars, backroom speakeasies, in the offices of politicians and councilmen, in the backyards of union leaders, socialists, mobsters, murderers, mayors. But there it was, a note written in her father's scrawl, begging her forgiveness, saying that she had everything she needed in life, and that even though her mother had run off, once he'd gone, she'd make do with her good wits, good looks, that she had what it took to make a living; everything that he had given her—he wrote in his brief note—though not pretty, would serve her well.

Faith rode the elevator downstairs to the dingy lobby of her apartment building, then drove her Hupmobile into the artificial crepuscular glow of Central Boulevard; passed shining window displays, brightly lit lobbies and mezzanines; she ran red lights, the whole time rubbing away at her eyes and at snowflakes of frost on the inside of her windshield.

When she entered the far reaches of South End and started driving over rough-and-tumble cobblestone, the dim blue light that lit the rest of the City was suddenly extinguished and Faith could smell coming through her closed windows the smell of barge sludge and ocean brine. She drove under the Westbend thruway that ran parallel to the Southside Docks. When she cleared the underpass, she came face to face with the thick brick facade of the Crown Crackers plant, which was covered with a three-story Crown Crackers ad, a painting of Murray Crown ("The King of Crackers"), smiling and crunching into a handful of his famous Saltcrisp Crackers. The cracker pieces exploded around Crown's tall shock of gray hair, making his head look like the tip of a lit sparkler.

All Faith knew about Murray Crown was what everyone knew about Murray Crown. She knew that he owned Crown Crackers. She, like everyone else, knew his face from his picture on the boxes of his saltines. Like everyone else, she knew he was married to a bottle-blond bombshell named Genie, who went by Bubbles, and who stood a whole foot taller than Crown when dressed in heels. She knew that Crown had long been thought to be orchestrating his fleet of cracker trucks to ship illegal contraband—alcohol to underground nightclubs during Prohibition days, narcotics to crooked pharmacies. Until now, only Crown's drivers had been indicted. They would routinely serve a light sentence, then get out and go back to work. She knew that Crown made it no secret that he was pals with Johnny Mann and Jerzy Roth. They all had grown up on the Southside together in the same tenement buildings. She knew that although they were never seen in public together, it was only too obvious that Crown was connected to Elias Eliopoulos, whose American Allied plant shared the same slips. She knew that Crown had agreed to turn evidence on Mann, Roth, and American Allied for a reduced sentence. She was to cover the hearing that very morning, but now, she knew, the story was about to take a turn.

Faith parked her car underneath the mural of Murray Crown's exploding head and, with a flashlight in hand, walked out onto the gravel road that ran alongside the thruway. As the nearby piers creaked against the river's current, she traced the beam of light over the lines of mortar on the side of the building until she found a metal door painted over to make it look like part of the brick facade. The door was slightly ajar, as the man on the phone said it would be. Faith swung the door out onto the road and found a metal cord dangling overhead. She pulled on it, and a garage lamp lit up, shining a parabola of light onto the roof of a black sedan. Faith walked inside and closed the door behind her and started toward the door leading into the building. The garage was just large enough for the car, small enough that Faith had to sidestep her way in around the fenders. When she reached the door at the car's front end, she pushed it in and found, leading up a steep staircase, small splatters of drying blood, little droplets, every few feet or so. She stepped into the empty spaces between each splatter and, using her flashlight to light the way, walked up three flights, passing a number of unmarked doors, all padlocked. When she reached the top landing, she came to another door, this one made of steel, a thick bolt wedged into its jamb. She placed her ear against the cold steel of the door, and when she couldn't hear anything on the other side, she unlatched the lock. A loud thwack echoed through the darkness of the stairwell and she found herself inside a storage room filled with filing cabinets and stacked on top of them Crown Crackers boxes adorned with the same image as the one on the outside of the building. Everywhere her flashlight roamed was the explosion of cracker crumbs, Crown's gaping eyes, his shock of hair standing on end, the white of his teeth crackling with excitement. It was almost as if Faith could hear the handfuls of crackers being simultaneously crunched.

The trail of blood continued on to another latched door. She grabbed hold of the bolt and pushed, again the heavy thwack sounding through the stairwell. As the door swung open with its own momentum, Faith found sprawled out in front of her, partially lit up by a desk lamp, a man, a gun in his hand, his face, his gun, his hand, all submerged inside a puddle of blood that seemed to Faith to still be flowing out of the man's mouth and out of a crater in the back of his head. The image of her father immediately entered her thoughts and she could see Sam clearly, flung back onto the floor from the impact of the blast, his eyes stark and wide, staring up to the white plaster ceiling sprayed with his blood.

Faith tremulously stepped into the room, an office with glass windows, an observation platform, that looked down onto the plant floor, an open room that immediately made her feel vulnerable. She could hear in her thoughts again the funny, sickly-sounding voice of the man who called her that morning. The voice was so tangible, she could feel the man's presence, almost as if he were beside her, somewhere in the shadows. Faith walked around the growing pool of blood and saw on a rolltop desk in the corner of the room a note that read,

> *Dear Genie,*
>
> *Please don't think any less of me for opting out of this thing, but I couldn't take the pressure. I couldn't take living in fear like that anymore. I can't tell you how sorry I am about this. I thought it would be best for all involved, except me, of course. But why kid anyone? I had it coming.*
>
> *See you on the other side, baby.*
>
> *Eternal love,*
> *Murray*

Beside the note was a key. Faith pressed down on the key's head with the finger of her glove and dragged it off the desk until it fell into her hand. ITB684, it read on the head. She put the key in her pocket, and with the key in her pocket the smell of fresh blood started to register in her stomach and she recalled the moment again when she first saw her father, how she gagged and vomited into the pool of his blood at her feet. Suddenly feeling herself wanting to retch, she covered her nose and mouth, stepped back around Murray Crown's mutilated body, and made her way back downstairs, latching the doors shut as she departed. She thought about the key she had taken from the desk. She thought about the bloody crater in the back of Murray Crown's head. She continued to recall the image of her father's dead body. *See you on the other side, baby,* is all she could think to herself. *See you on the other side.*

Faith turned off the light to the garage. She pushed the garage door out toward the road. When she stepped out onto the gravel, she could see the sun rising on the other side of the thruway, and she could see out the corner of her eye a car down the road that hadn't been there before. She pretended not to see it. She tried to act as if she belonged there. She walked to her car and got in. She turned over the engine, her hands visibly shaking for the first time that morning. As she drove away, she looked into her rearview mirror and could see a man, a large man with slick black hair, too far away to make out completely, sitting in his car, watching her.

Chapter 20

Harry Shortz was awake at a quarter to five in the morning when his phone started ringing. He was sitting in the dark at the time, in an armchair beside his bed, watching Beverly sleep, looking at her arm outstretched over a pillow, her hand resting on the depression of space in the mattress that Harry's body normally occupied at this time of night. Her hand remained so still, it was as if she were dreaming that the pillow Harry had put in his place when he got out of bed was still him, and that she was holding on to his large sturdy frame. When the phone loudly rang out in the darkness, she didn't stir, her breathing remained easy; all that moved was one of her fingers. One finger curled into her fist, and Harry, looking at how her finger slowly dragged on the sheet, suddenly remembered the way Sylvia Lowenstein used to lie naked in hotel beds pretending that she was asleep when Harry left, so she wouldn't have to say goodbye to him.

"Yes," Harry whispered into the phone.

"After today, you'll be nothing more than a ghost of the man you once were."

"Who is this?"

The man didn't answer.

"Rudolph?" Harry continued cautiously, whispering. "If it is, I want to talk."

There was a long silence again.

The man on the other end of the phone loudly cleared his throat and then coughed a bad cough.

Harry looked over at Beverly. "What is it that you want from me?"

"Ask Dubrov what happened to his hand."

"What?"

"Ask your sergeant what happened to his hand."

Harry now was silent.

"And ask yourself why it is you've never been able to corner the syndicate after all these years."

Harry continued listening.

"Ask yourself these things, and then maybe we'll talk."

"What did you do with the girl?"

The phone went dead. Harry hung it up and continued staring at Beverly's darkened figure. Just as Harry was about to get up to walk down the hall and look in on his sons, the phone started ringing again.

"Yeah?" he said when he picked up the receiver, still whispering.

"I'm sorry to bother you at this time of night, sir. . . ." It was one of the men standing watch over Crown. His voice was tentative.

"What is it?" Harry asked, his voice sounding equally as tentative.

"As I said, I'm sorry to bother you this time of night, but Crown's disappeared."

"What do you mean, Crown's disappeared?"

"We just checked in on him, about twenty minutes ago. The window of his room was open and he wasn't there."

"But you're on the fourteenth floor," Harry said angrily, his full voice now filling the bedroom.

"I know, sir."

"Where could he have gone?"

"We don't know."

Harry faltered for a second. "Start checking the rooms on that floor."

"We've already checked all the rooms on this floor, but nothing, sir."

"Then get started on the rest of the hotel."

"We've already started on that."

"All right . . ." Harry said, trying to think clearly. "Well, get on the phone and get more people over there," he ordered. "Get someone to Crown's house, get someone to check the docks. . . . And while you're at it, send someone up to visit Mann and Roth. See what they have to say."

"Yes, sir."

"I'll be right over."

"Yes, sir."

Harry hung up. He was livid.

"Harry?" Beverly said, still half asleep. "Is everything all right?"

Harry looked into Beverly's half-open eyes and felt a profound sadness come over him. "Everything's just fine, sweetheart. Go back to sleep." Harry got up from his chair and started getting dressed.

"Would you like me to make you some coffee?"

"No, dear. Please, just go back to sleep. I'll give you a call later."

He gave Beverly a long kiss on her forehead.

"Mmmm," Beverly said.

"I love you."

"Mmmm," Beverly said again and fell off back to sleep.

When Harry arrived at the Hanover, an officer in a rumpled tweed coat, wearing a thick mustache, looking exhausted, stood in the doorway waiting for him.

"You find him?" Harry asked as he charged toward him.

The man shook his head. "Sorry, sir."

"You make those calls?"

"Everyone's out looking."

"Were you both awake?"

"Awake, sitting by the door. Swear to God."

"And you didn't hear a goddamn thing?"

"Nothing. He was as quiet as could be."

"You checked the room before he bedded down?"

"We checked it and double-checked it. I'm telling you, sir, we did it by the book. Everything. He must have just crawled out on the ledge and found an open window somewhere."

"All right," Harry said as he entered Crown's room with the officer following him. The bed looked like it had been slept in. There was a half-finished game of solitaire on the table, along with a half-finished bottle of bourbon, a half-full ashtray, and a pair of slippers, one on top of the other, sitting under the table. The closet was full of his clothes, the bathroom full of his toiletries, and on the couch was his coat. The window was still slightly ajar and the freezing wind was blowing in hard against the curtains.

"If he went out on his own, why wouldn't he have taken the coat?"

The officer tried to explain it: "Maybe he was afraid it would blow him around in the wind?"

Harry looked at the ledge outside the window. It was large enough for someone to walk down without too much trouble. As Harry turned from the window, he noticed the light from the ceiling fixture reflect off something. He looked around until he noticed something metal lying on the floor just peeking out from under the dust ruffle on the bed. Harry bent down and grabbed it, lifting it gingerly—a straight razor slightly streaked with blood. "He shave tonight?" Harry asked, holding the razor up in front of the officer's face.

"That I don't know."

The floors were carpeted, a forest green. Harry looked closely and noticed a few dark spots leading to the window. He removed a handkerchief from his pocket, stuck a bit of it in his mouth, then rubbed the wet cloth into the carpeting where it was discolored. As he lifted the handkerchief the phone started ringing. The officer went to the phone to answer it. Harry sat there, crouching, looking at a rosy blemish on his handkerchief. He folded the straight razor closed, wrapped the handkerchief around it, and put it in his coat pocket.

The officer walked back over from the phone. "Crown's car is missing from the garage he'd parked in when he came over here."

Harry nodded, trying to calm himself. "What time were Ira and Pally supposed to relieve you?" he asked, his voice restrained.

"At five-thirty."

"Have they been here?"

"Pally was here just a few minutes before you got here . . . ten minutes ago, about."

"What about Ira?"

"Pally said something about him having a fight with his wife. Something about punching his fist through a window. Said he sent him over to the hospital to get stitched up."

Harry could feel his stomach tightening as he thought about what the man on the phone had said to him. "Where's Pally now?"

"He offered to go down to Crown's plant."

Harry nodded and walked over to the window again and looked at the latch. The lever that hooked into the latch was cut clean through.

Harry started to feel suffocated and blind. *After today, you'll be nothing more than a ghost of the man you once were* was all he could hear in his thoughts. He sat down at Murray Crown's unfinished game of solitaire and started playing out the remainder of his hand.

"What next?" the officer asked.

Harry's head remained still as his eyes slowly looked over to his man.

"I'll go and see what kind of progress we're making with the search," the officer said. He turned away from Harry and left him to Crown's cards.

The phone rang just as Harry lost Crown's hand at solitaire.

"Yeah," Harry said as he lifted the receiver.

"Harry, is that you?" It was Pally.

"Yeah, it's me."

"Bad news. . . . He shot himself in the mouth inside his office."

"Seems he was playing a losing hand, after all," Harry muttered.

"What's that?"

"Nothing. . . . Anything else?"

"Yeah," Pally said as if Crown's being dead wasn't the real bad news.

"What?"

"Just so it don't take you unexpected, you should know Tines showed up just as I did. He's got all his goons down here looking around."

Harry stayed quiet, took in the news, thinking of his conversation with Claude Fielding last night.

"Said he got a call," Pally said. "Said he was tipped off by someone."

"And?"

"He says he's taking over the case."

Harry started gathering the rows of cards on the table and piling them together.

"Did you hear me, Harry?"

"Yeah, I heard you. Let him go ahead with it."

"What?"

"You heard me."

"But Harry . . ."

"And you don't say a word to him, you hear me?"

Pally was quiet now.

"You just keep to yourself until I get down there. Understood?"

Harry could hear Pally's feet pacing. "Yeah, sure," Pally said.

Harry looked out the window onto the brick walls of the nearby buildings brightening with light. "Where's Ira?" he asked as he started flipping cards over.

"What's that?"

"I said, Where's Ira? I was told he wasn't with you. Where is he?"

"He and Claudia, they had a bad fight last night."

Harry was quiet again, listening intently to Pally's voice.

"You know Ira, how he gets," Pally said as though he were listening intently to his own voice. "He punched his hand clean through a window. I drove him over to the hospital to get it stitched up. It's a real mess."

"I'll bet it is."

"Anyway, Harry," Pally persevered, "you should get down here right away."

"I'll be there shortly."

Harry hung up the phone and set the cards down.

Harry left the Hanover after giving his officers the news. He told them that they should report to the Department of Investigations when they were through calling off the search. He got into his car and made his way down Central Boulevard as a pale golden light cut eastbound across the streets and flickered into the dark shell of his sedan. When he reached the Southside Docks, he cut through the frozen gravel road running alongside the warehouses, his tires and the roadway making like thousands of teeth grinding their way down to raw nerves. Harry passed the painted ad of Murray Crown crunching into the handful of exploding Saltcrisp Crackers, passed the fleet of Crown Crackers trucks parked in the loading zones, and drove up to the plant's entrance. A couple of department men were standing guard. Beside them stood Pally Collins.

"Let's take a walk," Pally said when he greeted Harry.

"Where?"

"Over there," he said, pointing down the service road to the American Allied plant.

"What is it?"

Pally didn't say anything.

"I don't like the sound of that look you're giving me, Pally."

"I'm afraid you won't like the looks of it either."

As far as Harry could tell, Pally was his usual self, but there was suddenly something not quite right about him, something Harry couldn't put his finger on. He wasn't nervous or jumpy, he was just the opposite. He was too collected for all of what was happening.

"Where's Tines?" Harry asked as he walked alongside Pally.

"He just left. Said he'd be in touch with you."

Harry shook his head. The feeling of the setup was about as subtle as the bullet that had exploded out of Murray Crown's skull that morning.

"What do you suppose happened, Pal?" Harry asked as their feet crunched over the gravel.

"According to Crown's note, he couldn't take the heat."

"So, you think Crown did it on his own, then?"

"Guys have done themselves in for a lot less than what Crown had to face up to."

"Yeah, but why come all the way down here to do it? Why not just kill himself inside the Hanover?"

"I don't know."

"Don't you think it would have been more comfortable that way? He could have just thrown himself out that window. Did you ever think of that? Why would he go to all that trouble to get back to the plant?"

"Maybe he had some unfinished business? I don't know,

Harry," Pally said with an almost beatific calm, "maybe somebody pulled him out of that room."

"Like who?"

"Mann and Roth, say."

"All right, let's say it was Mann and Roth."

"Let's say."

"How'd they find out where Crown was?"

"They might have followed one of us over to the Hanover."

"Maybe."

"If not them," Pally said, "who are you thinking did it?"

Harry didn't answer Pally. After a few silent steps through the gravel, Harry said, "Claudia, she go with Ira to the hospital this morning to get his hand patched up?"

"No, I dropped him there on our way to the Hanover. He didn't want to go, but I insisted. He was bleeding pretty bad."

"What were they fighting about that Ira got so upset?"

"He wouldn't say."

"He wouldn't say, huh?"

"Something about money, I think. Something about Ira going down to the track a little too often."

Harry nodded his head. "What time you pick him up?"

"Around four-thirty."

"What time he put his hand through the window?"

Pally stopped walking and turned to Harry. "What is it that you got to say to me, Harry?" Pally said, now showing his nerves. His calm was starting to come undone in his eyes; they were squinting as if he'd walked out into the sun after being inside a dark movie house.

Harry stopped and stepped into Pally's space, and although he didn't want to have it out with Pally right then and there, he couldn't help himself. "How long have you and Ira been on the syndicate's payroll?"

Pally blinked hard a few times and stepped back from Harry, laughing. "What the hell are you talking about?"

"Does Claudia know that she's going to have to testify for Ira?"

"About what?" Pally's eyes shot open as if he wanted to hit Harry.

Harry pulled the straight razor out of his pocket and held it with his handkerchief. "You two didn't expect Crown to go to bed with this under his pillow, did you?"

Pally looked at the razor, then looked at Harry. He looked confused. Harry didn't know if he looked confused because he didn't know what he was talking about or because he didn't know how it was Harry could have found the razor.

"What's this all about?" Pally asked. "You're losing your mind, Harry."

"I had to wonder if you two were capable of being that careless, but . . . why not? It was dark. You needed to get out before the boys heard you. Maybe it was worth it for some reason to take the risk of leaving this behind."

"I don't know what you're talking about, Harry," Pally said, still postured as if he wanted to throw a punch at Harry, "but if you're saying what I think you're saying, I got nothing more to say to you, Harry. Nothing. At least nothing that I might regret saying later."

Pally, looking at Harry in disbelief, backpedaled away from Harry, back in the direction of Crown's plant.

"Did you know that Benny Rudolph was in town?"

Pally stopped for a second and doubled back. "You really are losing your mind, Harry, you know that, don't you?"

"What did you and Ira do to him to get him so angry?"

Pally shook his head as if he wanted to say something conciliatory, as if he was about to confess something, but he couldn't bring himself to do it.

"What did you do to him?"

"Nothing. Not a goddamn thing."

"All right," Harry said, looking down the road. "I'll give you an hour to make up your mind. You come talk to me," Harry said, his hand banging on his chest, "or you'll be trying to explain to Tines why it is that the window in Crown's room had been tampered with, why it is this straight razor was found under Crown's bed, why it is that Ira needed to go to the hospital to get stitched up. Don't you get it? . . . No, I know you get it. That's why you're so damn . . . You're smarting from your idiocy."

Pally stood there and took it, his face hard as a rock.

"Go find Ira and bring him to me."

Pally continued shaking his head, gritting his teeth. "You think you've got a case against us, you try to make it," he said.

"I will."

"Then you better get started."

Pally turned away from Harry and made his way back in the direction of Crown's warehouse. Harry watched him go. When Pally was far enough away, Harry continued walking to the front end of the American Allied plant, wondering what it was that could have brought Ira and Pally to this, wondering if by turning on them, or not turning on them, he would be playing into Tines's hands. As Harry turned onto the front lot of the American Allied plant, he stopped in disbelief. "How the hell did he manage this?"

Harry Shortz stood in front of an empty parking lot and by empty slips. No trucks. No freighters. No workers. The doors and the loading docks were all open, the sound of the wind violently echoing through the empty building. The whole facility had been stripped bare. American Allied Pharmaceutical was no longer there. No machinery. No lab equipment. No furniture. Not one flask or Bunsen burner. It was swept clean. Everything gone.

Chapter 21

Victor woke up early that morning. As a lavender light luminesced the dusty cellar window, he removed his bloodied suit and put on the clothes Steven had rummaged out of Mr. Tersi's closet. He left his own clothes neatly folded on the cot and quietly walked upstairs to the bathroom. He used the toilet, gently splashed some water on his face, carefully dabbed at his bruises with a musty towel. His face looked worse than it had last night, but, all in all, in Mr. Tersi's nicely tailored clothes his condition somehow didn't appear so dire.

Victor found Freddy asleep, the bottle of bourbon on his night table drained, the ashtray full of cigarette butts. Victor didn't want to wake Freddy, so he wrote him a note and placed it on the kitchen table. He then bundled up into Mr. Tersi's thick fur-lined herringbone coat, put on his new hat, and stepped out into the brisk cold.

Standing at the curb in front of 319 West Eighty-third were two men Victor hadn't seen before. One of them flashed him a badge. "Department of Investigations," the man said. "We've got a few questions about your father." Both men had baby faces. One tried to cover his boyish features with a thick desperado mustache, but it wasn't doing him any good.

"What about him?" Victor asked.

"About the incident over in Long Meadow the other day."

"I don't know how I can be helpful to you. I haven't seen my father for fifteen years, since I got sent upstate."

"Did you have any kind of correspondence?"

"No."

"Do the names Max Waters and Henry Capp mean anything to you?"

"Yeah, sure. They worked with my father at Barkley & Sons. They all grew up together. I went to grade school with their kids."

"Did you know your father ever to have connections to the Communist Party?"

"Not exactly."

"What do you mean, not exactly?"

"I mean just that. When I was growing up I was close with Shelly Price's daughter, Elaine. Shelly Price was—"

"—one of the former leaders of the Brigade?"

"Yeah, my father and Mr. Price, they got to know each other, sort of. Enough so that my dad went to a few meetings. But it was nothing more than that so far as I know."

"Would it surprise you to know that your father went to more than just a few meetings, like you said? That he went to more than a couple dozen?"

"I can't say I know my father well enough to say it would, but my father was a freethinking man."

"Would it surprise you to learn that up until the day he was killed, your father was an active member in the Communist Party?"

"Look, I hadn't talked with the man in fifteen years. I suppose nothing you say about my father could surprise me."

"Then it wouldn't surprise you to learn that your father intentionally sabotaged the Fief Munitions plant in Long Meadow the other day? To ignite a conflict between the Long Meadow Munitions Workers Union and Julius Fief?"

"Why would he do that?"

"Apparently your father was as disgruntled as he was freethinking, Mr. Ribe. A rabble-rouser. . . ." The baby-faced man doing the talking leaned into the car, opened the glove compartment, pulled out a few pieces of paper, and started reading. His voice, which suited his face, was full of adolescent-sounding invective. "Comrades, rise up! . . . The means of production can be OURS! . . . Stop thinking like menial servants, like indentured laborers, like field fodder, and ACT as men of ACTION would!" The man angrily slapped the piece of paper with the back of his hand. "Do you know who wrote these words, Mr. Ribe?"

"That would be my father?"

"Yeah, your father, who led a group of men with families to their destruction."

"If you say so."

The man took a breath. "Look, I know you haven't had any contact with your father in the past fifteen years, but do you think you might recognize his handwriting if you saw it?"

"Probably."

"Does this look like your father wrote this?"

The officer handed Victor a letter dated the day of the explosion. It read,

Dear Victor,

What I do today, I do for more than just us. If for some reason something goes wrong, please know that I'm sorry I doubted you, son, and I'm sorry I didn't fight for you as hard as I've fought for my men in all these years you've been imprisoned. Your mother wouldn't approve of what I'm about to do, I know, but she would at least have understood the bull stubbornness that fortifies my spirit to do what I feel I must do.

Love,
Dad

"The handwriting looks like my father's, but I can't say it sounds like him much."

"Men change in fifteen years."

"Some do."

"I expect that your father is the sort that did."

"So?"

"So, you haven't anything to say about the fact that your father managed to kill himself and five of his men on a matter of principle?"

"I don't believe he meant to kill anyone. I'm not sure I believe that he even did it."

"You will."

"If you say so."

"I do." The man climbed into the passenger seat, slammed the door shut, and rolled down the window. "Don't leave town," the man said. "We'll need you to testify."

Victor turned away from the detectives and started walking. The moment the detectives' car drove past him, another car pulled up alongside Victor, and Victor could see it was the two men who had shadowed him the day before.

"Where we going?" Victor asked as he got in the backseat.

"Where would you like to go?"

"The Ansonia Hotel."

"We'll drive you there."

"I figured as much."

The driver pulled the car away from the curb.

"You need to be somewhere at one," the man in the passenger seat said.

"All right."

"So whatever you got planned, just keep it in mind at half past noon, you're going for a ride."

"All right by me."

"That's what we figured."

The two men drove Victor down to the Ansonia and parked the car. They all got out. Victor went inside the lobby and the two men went into the Ansonia's restaurant and took a table from which they could keep an eye on Victor. And as Victor had done the day before, he sat in the Ansonia's lobby and waited for Elaine and the boy to walk through the elevator doors.

. . .

An hour or so after Victor had left, Freddy woke up, hungover. Outside his bedroom window a heavy bank of storm clouds moved toward him in the far distance over the rooftops. He watched it move for a while and then got out of bed and went into the kitchen to make some coffee. On the kitchen table, he found Victor's note. *Freddy*, it read, *Thanks for taking care of me last night. I didn't want to wake you. Needed to be somewhere. I'll stop by again when I can. Victor.* Freddy put up a pot of water to boil, lit a cigarette, and went to the bathroom to use the toilet. As he was about to sit down, he heard a few quiet knocks on his door. Thinking it was Aleksandr or Nicol asking him if he had any trash to go out, he walked to the door and opened it, to find, standing in the threshold, a big man, a man a little bigger than big, wearing a trench coat, his face toughened like a boxer's. This overwhelming figure pushed his way in and shut the door. Before Freddy could speak, the man grabbed him by his nightshirt and threw him down onto the couch, knocking his cigarette onto the floor.

"Where were you?" the man asked harshly.

"I'm sorry?" Freddy responded. "Who . . ." he said, trying to think clearly.

"I waited for you all night."

"I'm sorry," Freddy repeated. "Do I . . ."

The man took a small step toward Freddy and bent forward a little so that the two of them were face to face.

"I want the other half of my money. I was told you would deliver it at the club, midnight."

Freddy looked puzzled. "I couldn't have . . ."

"Is it midnight? Are we at the club? Or are we right here, right now?"

"Please," Freddy said. "Get to the point, to the point."

"Don't play dumb. What did you expect when you didn't show up? That I'd disappear without a word?"

Freddy could see a drop of angry sweat begin to form between the man's eyes. It was about to drop right off his nose into Freddy's gaping mouth.

"Look," Freddy said. "You've obviously got me mixed up with someone else."

"Freddy Stillman. Three-nineteen West Eighty-third Street, first floor. Two hundred bucks."

"You've got to be kidding. I don't have that kind of money."

"No?" The man stood up erect and reached into his pocket for a pair of leather gloves. "Then why would you make a deal to pay me that kind of money?"

"I couldn't even begin to tell you, because I didn't make the deal. What was the deal?"

"It seems pretty simple to me. Half up front, the other half when the job was done, twelve midnight at the Triple Mark. That was the agreement. Can it be any simpler?" The man smiled as though aggravated. With his gloves now on his fists, he pulled Freddy off the couch and stood him up.

"Was it Feldman? Was it Feldman who put you up to this?"

"I don't know no Feldman."

"Listen," Freddy said calmly, as calmly as he could. He tried to find an image of Evelyn in his mind, but he couldn't. "Wait," he said. "Just wait."

"No, I don't think so."

And then it came to him. He suddenly was able to see her sitting in her bathrobe at the kitchen table drinking a cup of coffee, no smile on her face, no anger on her face, just Evelyn, waking up, her hair resting on her shoulders, her eyes tired, the morning light on her fingers. "Okay," he said.

The man shook his head—he was plainly disgusted. He cocked his fist back, turned Freddy so that his back was facing the hall, and then unleashed a punch right on Freddy's jaw that sent him backpedaling into the kitchen, where he banged into a cupboard, whose wood buckled in on itself. Dizzied from the blow, Freddy sat there, wedged into the cupboard, on the edge of falling unconscious, seeing Evelyn that much more clearly at the kitchen table, until the man pulled him up and sent him back down the hall with another roundhouse delivered this time to the side of his head.

Freddy toppled over the coffee table in the living room and landed on his side. When he looked up, the man was standing over him with his foot resting heavily on Freddy's knee. The man bent down, took hold of Freddy's ankle, and asked him again, "Do you have my two hundred bucks?"

Freddy took a deep breath and shut his eyes so he wouldn't have to watch. "No," he said.

"That's a shame," the man said matter-of-factly.

"You mean you're just gonna break my fucking leg," Freddy said as he realized what the man intended to do. He could feel the pressure of the man's foot on his knee increase.

"What? You want it to be an arm and a leg?"

"No," Freddy said, not wanting to explain what he wanted. "But just let me be clear here," he continued, "that's all you're gonna do? All you're gonna do is break my leg?"

"What do you expect? You expect that I should kill you? If I kill you, how the hell am I gonna collect my money?"

Freddy, feeling the pressure increase that much more on his knee, shook his head. "I've got twenty-five bucks, twenty-five and some change."

"You got it here?" The man started lifting Freddy's ankle so that the joints in both his knee and ankle started to stretch and distend.

"Yeah," Freddy grunted. "In the kitchen, in the kitchen above the stove, in a coffee tin."

The man let go of Freddy's ankle and stepped off his knee. He then lifted him up by the nightshirt collar. "Show me."

Freddy stumbled down the hall ahead of the man to the kitchen. "Just tell me," he said, not looking back, "what's this all about?"

"You tell me. You're the one who hired me."

"To do what?"

"Just shut the fuck up and get the money. Show me that money before I wrestle you back down to the ground and break your leg off for good." The man pushed Freddy between the shoulder blades.

Freddy plunged forward and slammed up against the stove, knocking the pot of boiling water onto the floor.

"And don't be reaching into anything."

From a cabinet above the burners, Freddy removed a coffee tin and handed it to the man. The man lifted the lid and pulled out a bunch of crumpled bills, which he stuffed into one of the pockets of his coat. He then reached out for Freddy's throat and gripped it with his large hand. "Don't say anything," he said, his teeth gritted. Freddy shook his head cooperatively. "Just look at me." Freddy looked at him, at his face, in his eyes. "I'll be waiting for you at the club tonight, ten o'clock. You get that?" Freddy nodded again. "You talk to anyone about this, I'll turn you inside out. You get that?" Freddy nodded again. "All right then. Go find my money."

"And if I don't?"

"I'll break a new bone in your body every day until you do."

"Great," Freddy said.

And with that, the man let go of Freddy's throat, turned his back on him, and exited the apartment. When he was gone, Freddy sank to the floor and cradled his face in his arms, trying to figure out what had just happened. He lifted himself off the floor and stumbled over to the mirror in the bathroom to find himself in one piece, the side of his face already swollen from the blows. He gently washed up, got dressed, and, still dizzied, started his day as though nothing out of the ordinary had happened at all.

Chapter 22

Faith Rapaport arrived at the Globe Building a little after eight, after a long bath and a pot of coffee. She half expected the police to be waiting for her, but the offices were quiet. It was post-deadline for the late morning edition, and most of the reporters on the city desk were already out on their beats. Those who weren't sat around reading the paper, their feet up on their desks beside their typewriters, waiting for nine o'clock to roll around so they could start making calls. Marty Volman was the only one waiting for her. He stood in the threshold of his door, looking over his staff as if they were a pile of open books he regularly thumbed through. Although he was getting old, liver-splotched, round, bald, his boyish eyes looked like they could burn a hole right through human flesh. When Marty saw Faith walking toward her desk, he waved her over to his office. He was collected on the outside, but as Faith made her way over she could tell from the way he was fumbling with his shirt collar that there was some sort of groundswell about to rise up to the surface.

"The Long Meadow pieces were good, real good, Faith," Marty said as she crossed the threshold of the door. "The interview had real bite."

"Where'd you stick it?"

"Page one, just like I said I would."

"I've heard that line from you before, Marty."

"Well, this time it happened to turn out that way."

"Good thing," Faith said less enthusiastically than she thought she should. She looked over Marty's shoulder, out the window onto a blue mist lightly floating down the corridor of midtown buildings. Beyond it, she could see a tall bank of storm clouds collecting over the far side of the river. "What have you got for me?"

Marty was trying to look reserved, but it was apparent that he was agitated. "I just got a big tip about a corpse."

Faith felt an involuntary twinge inside her belly, as if there were a baby in there, kicking. Already knowing what the answer would be, she asked the question anyway: "Who's the corpse?"

"Murray Crown."

"That is big," Faith said with all feeling hiding behind her clenched jaw.

"Very big," Marty said, thrown by Faith's seeming lack of interest.

Faith felt the twinge again, this time more violently. "Who called it in?"

"It was anonymous."

"What did anonymous say?"

"He said, 'Murray Crown's dead, shot, in his office, at his plant.' He said, 'It's not what it looks like,' is what he said."

"What's that supposed to mean?"

"It means 'It's not what it looks like.' What do I know? It's a tip. A big tip. And it's yours, your story."

"I guess I won't be going to the courthouse today," she said, her voice now fading into an almost inaudible whisper.

"That's one way to look at it," Marty said. His confusion indented itself on his forehead.

Faith stared at Marty Volman for a long time and could feel her left ear getting hot. She could feel it turning crimson. It was burning.

"If I didn't know it was you, cupcake, I'd almost say you look a little broken up about Crown getting it."

Faith stepped into Marty's office and shut the door. "Marty . . ."

"What is it, honey?"

Faith took a seat next to Marty's desk. "You take this call yourself?"

"Yeah."

"The guy sound like he busted a gasket?"

"Come to think of it, yeah. How'd you know?"

"He called me first," she said, reaching for a Lucky in the hip pocket of her pants.

"And?"

She lit her cigarette. "I've already been there. I got there before the cops did."

"Do I want to know about this?"

"I don't know, do you?"

Marty started tapping his fingers on the edge of his desk. "Start talking," he said.

"Look, Marty, I didn't know he was dead when I went."

"Then why'd you go down there?"

Faith removed from her pocket the key she had taken from the desk. "For this." Faith pointed to the key with her nose and handed it to Marty.

"Goes to a safety deposit box would be my bet," Marty said, handling the key as if he were holding the tail of a dead mouse.

"That's what I figured."

Marty handed the key back to Faith. "I wouldn't have gone," Faith said, rubbing her finger over the key's teeth. "It's just . . ."

"Just what?"

"He had a good line. He got me hooked."

"On what?"

"Pop."

"What's this got to do with that no-good son of a bitch?"

"He called up looking for Sammy Rapaport's little girl. He said that Pop didn't shoot himself. That if I went down to Crown's plant . . ." The words starting spilling out of Faith's mouth. "He said that if I wanted to know why Crown wouldn't be testifying in court today, if I wanted to understand how it is that Pop ended up dead the way he did, I should go down to Crown's plant, find this key, and have a look around."

"You lost me, kid. What's the connection?"

"All I know is that when I walked into Crown's office and saw him lying there, it was the same setup. Gun in hand. Note to the next of kin saying goodbye and good luck."

Marty puckered his lips and pondered this for a few seconds. "It's a pretty universal setup," he said thoughtfully.

"Yeah, true, but why? Why would someone want me in that room, with the corpse like that?"

"I don't know. It's curious, I'll give you that." Marty reached his hand out toward Faith. "Give me one of those," he said, pointing to her hip pocket.

Faith squeezed out a cigarette and handed it to Marty.

"Putting this thing with your father aside for a second," he said as he lit the cigarette, "though I still don't put it past that bastard to put a gun to his head, mind you—what I want to know is how Crown got over to his plant in the first place. Narcotics was supposed to have him under wraps."

"Obviously they didn't have him wrapped up too tight."

"Shortz is going to have a lot to answer for. I'd like to see the look on his face when he tries to explain how his favorite kicked dog finally kicked it. If you ask me, this might just undo him, right out of the race. . . . I want you down there as soon as they announce a press conference."

"All right, Marty, but that's a little beside the point right now," Faith said, holding the key up for Marty to see.

The sight of the key made Marty pout. "I'm still not sure I want to know about this."

"If you want to be fair about it, the door was open, Marty. I just walked in."

"Still, it doesn't look good."

Marty gave Faith one of his looks.

"Look, if it makes you feel any better, as far as I'm concerned, you don't know a thing, all right?"

"Let's try to keep it that way."

Faith looked at Marty obsequiously, and then looked at the key.

"I won't even ask if you're planning on turning it in."

"I was thinking, maybe I'd take a look at what's inside first? Just a little peek? I can always turn it in after that, after I get my look, right?"

"I don't know," Marty said. "It's tempting, I'll give you that." Marty tamped out the cigarette. "But I just don't like it. I don't like any of it."

"Since when do you get scared off by the possibility of a good story?" Faith said, trying to win him over.

"Since it's obvious that you're becoming even more reckless than your old man, and because I do know about that thing in your hand, and I don't want to get locked up."

"But what if Pop didn't shoot himself? What if whoever did this to Crown did the same to Pop?"

"What if it was Crown who did this to Crown? . . . And we both know your pop was capable of anything, including putting a gun to his head." Marty was wagging his finger at Faith now.

"Then we'll let them both rest in peace if nothing comes of any of this."

"Somehow I don't think you or either of them are capable of that. I'm sure you'll all be giving each other hell all over damnation."

"Look, Marty . . ."

"I don't think you should be chasing this one, Faith. Really . . ." Marty's brows drifted together like the colliding storm clouds out in the distance. "It feels like some of your father's worst unfinished business."

"Speaking of which, what do you know about Sammy's take on Victor Ribe's murder trial?"

"Why do you ask?"

"Anonymous. He said I should look into it."

Marty looked perturbed all over again. "All I know is that all the people involved were about as lowlife as you would expect from a story your father pursued and that he stuck his neck out for Ribe."

"Why?"

Marty raised his lower lip then relaxed it.

"Are the clips downstairs?"

"You got me."

"I'm going to go take a look." Faith stood up and looked at Marty, thinking she should tell him that someone saw her leave Crown's garage, but then she thought better of it.

Marty shook his head at Faith. "I hate to say it, cupcake, but you're on your own with this one."

"I don't buy that for a minute," Faith said.

"Well, look, whatever you're going to do, I don't want you missing the commissioner's press conference."

"I have no intention of missing it."

"In that case, you be sure to act dumb, you understand?"

"Don't worry, I'll mind myself," Faith said as she stood up and walked to the door. She watched as Marty shook his head some more and reached for the bottle of seltzer sitting on the corner of his desk. "If I should only live long enough," she could hear Marty say on her way out.

Faith walked out onto the press floor. The typewriters were picking up rhythm now, clerks were delivering messages and paperwork, talk was fast on the phones, cigarette smoke choked the air. It made Faith want to smoke more. She lit another Lucky, rode the elevator down to the archives, and went to the Samuel R. Rapaport files. Her father had filed so many stories over the years about bootleggers, bookies, speakeasies, opium dens, pimps, whores, about all the scumbags everyone loved to read about, that he had gotten a memorial filing cabinet that in the top drawer held an urn filled with his ashes. The file cabinet, which had a cheap brass plaque with Sammy's vitals, was Samuel R. Rapaport's mausoleum.

Faith found exactly what she was looking for right under R. RIBE, VICTOR. Transcripts, notes, stories, testimony, depositions . . . She grabbed the file, took it back to her desk, and started reading.

Chapter 23

All along his walk to work, Freddy was still in a daze from his beating. The storm clouds suddenly turned the sky gray, and the wind that had been blowing so hard for weeks had suddenly stopped, and snow flurries began falling. As the flurries clung to Freddy's coat and eyelashes, time seemed to slow down considerably and the people before him appeared to walk less diligently. The air had thickened and had become more vaporous; billows of smoke blew from mouths and noses and mixed with the steam rising from manhole covers. Up and down the boulevard, people emerged from the subway stations with their heads hung low and their eyes looking down at their feet, at the crystalline paths of sidewalk that began to glisten like quartz. The damp, lingering cold felt good on Freddy's face, but with it came a sharp chill that kept seizing his body and rattling it so badly he had to tightly cradle his chest with his arms until he stopped shaking.

When Freddy approached the Fief Building, the cops that had questioned him in his office the day before unexpectedly swung through the revolving doors onto the street and greeted him. The gruff one with the prickly face took hold of Freddy's chin and looked over his swelling head and face. "Look at this, Shaw," he said, turning Freddy's head to his partner. "Looks like someone planted one right where he thinks." The officer turned Freddy's face back to him. "You do think, don't you, Mr. Stillman?"

Freddy sneered into the officer's dark eyes for a second and tried to pull his head away, but the man's large gloved fingers held tight, pinching the cleft in Freddy's chin together. Freddy thought of Victor standing before Miss Martin last night. "I took a fall on my way over," Freddy said with some difficulty, his jaw stiff and uncooperative in the cop's hand. "On a patch of ice."

"He says he took a fall," the cop said as he let go of Freddy's chin.

"Is that what happened, Mr. Stillman?" Shaw asked. "You took a fall?"

"Yeah," Freddy said as he massaged his jaw.

"Tough break."

"It's nothing," Freddy insisted.

"Well, I tell you what: Reynolds, he'll get you some ice for your head when we get downtown."

"Yeah," Reynolds laughed. "No lack of ice where we're going."

"Where're we going?" Freddy asked.

"We think we found your neighbor," Shaw said mildly as he turned away from Freddy and started walking to the patrol car parked at the curb.

"Found her where?" Freddy said to Shaw's back. He tried not to sound alarmed, but he was alarmed. "Found her where?" Freddy asked Reynolds when Shaw didn't answer him.

"You all right?" Reynolds asked. "You seem a little jumpy." Reynolds turned to Shaw. "Don't he seem a little jumpy?"

"We'd like you to come down and answer a few questions," Shaw said as he opened the driver's door of the patrol car.

"I should go up and let my supervisor know where I'll be."

"He already knows," Reynolds said, stepping in front of Freddy as Freddy tried to move toward the building's revolving door. Freddy stopped short and looked over to Shaw.

"How about it, Mr. Stillman?"

"It doesn't seem like I have a choice."

"That's because you don't."

Reynolds pointed to the curb. "Go ahead and get in the back."

Freddy did as he was told. He got into the backseat of the car and shut the door. Reynolds took a seat beside him. Shaw made a U-turn and drove down Central Boulevard in the direction of downtown. It was snowing more heavily now, but the traffic was lighter than usual. People with waxen gazes huddled together in doorways, under awnings, as they stood waiting for streetcars. Doormen scattered salt on the sidewalks as though they were feeding pigeons in the park. Every few blocks, Shaw worked the manual windshield wiper and brushed away the frost collecting on the glass with his glove. Freddy sat with his face to the car window, looking at the snow reflecting off the passing midtown office tower windows.

"Looks like we're in for a big storm," Reynolds said, looking at Freddy. "I don't know about you, Mr. Stillman, but I kind of enjoy it when the city freezes over a little. People don't struggle as much in the cold. When it's as gray and ugly out as it is on a day like today, I've noticed that most men lose their will; tend to give up on lofty ideas that don't suit them. It's pretty debilitating, this kind of weather. When you can feel the crunch of snow under your feet, it kind of makes you realize how fragile every step is, doesn't it?" Reynolds leaned over to Freddy so that Freddy could feel Reynolds's weight beside him. "My partner, for instance, he tends to shut down in this weather. Isn't that right, Shaw?"

Shaw grunted softly.

"He gets very bearlike. Stops shaving, stops ironing his uniform, doesn't talk as much. It's like he's hibernating, waiting for some warm weather to thaw him out and give him some fight. . . . I, on the other hand? I don't know what it is, but I thrive in this weather. It doesn't seem to hypnotize me like it does most people. It has just the countereffect on me—it invigorates me, actually. Makes me more keen and aware, gives me, uh, insight into all those people who are walking around in their trances."

Freddy turned and found Reynolds smiling at him probingly.

The big cop slowly eased himself back over onto his side of the car and slipped a cigarette into his smug grin. Freddy looked Reynolds over some with a touch of malice in the bent corners of his eyes, then turned back to his window. With the tone set for their trip downtown, Reynolds kept his mouth shut for the rest of the ride and just blew smoke. The three men drove in silence as the City's buildings and neighborhoods on either side of them increased and decreased in scale. The mass of congested architecture gave the flat topography of the island the texture of a manmade mountain pass, cut straight through with sheer brawn and determination equivalent to blasts of dynamite.

When they reached the horseshoe of white granite buildings that made up the City Civic Center, Shaw parked the car in front of police headquarters. They all got out, stepped into the accumulating snow, and walked down a flight of stairs leading to the basement, to the City Morgue.

"When you say you found her," Freddy said nervously, "where did you find her?"

"Down in the boiler room of the Beekman," Reynolds said.

"In the boiler room?"

Reynolds opened the door to the morgue and immediately the sweet smell of formaldehyde filled all their lungs.

"Who did you identify her as?"

"Janice Gould . . . Name still doesn't ring a bell?"

"No," Freddy said, sticking to his story, feeling his story about to shatter into pieces. "No, it doesn't."

"She was a hatcheck girl up at the Triple Mark. Very pretty. Like you said, 'Thin neck, slim waist.' " Reynolds continued to smile as though someone were pinching his cheek.

"We're still trying to contact next of kin," Shaw said.

They walked down a long hallway, where men in white lab coats crisscrossed back and forth from one frosted-glass doorway to another. "She was nicely folded up in that powder-blue robe you described to us yesterday," Reynolds continued, "and stuffed into the coal bin by the furnace. Hog-tied. Not exactly the nicest place to be put to rest, is it?"

"It's horrible," Freddy said, thinking of Janice's delicate, pliant features covered in coal dust.

"Ain't it though?" Reynolds said.

The thought of someone disgracing such a beautiful girl that way, the thought of Reynolds talking about her like she was a broken piece of luggage, tightened Freddy's chest and filled his throat full of hot air. He felt like a radiator about to burst open.

"It just so happens that the coal man made his delivery last night. Funny enough, it wasn't the first time he found a body in a coal bin. Seems that it's a popular place to dispose of bodies, in a coal bin. Kind of funny, don't you think so, Mr. Stillman?"

"No," Freddy barked as though the release valve in his throat had been opened all the way up. "And it ain't a funny thing to make light of."

"Is that so?" Reynolds started to laugh.

Freddy had become truly incensed. He stopped walking and turned to Reynolds. "What's so funny?"

"There's just something about you, something funny. I don't know exactly how to say it, Mr. Stillman, but you're a stitch and a half." Reynolds wasn't making light now. He looked serious and angry himself. His large body became erect and his broad chest threateningly stuck out of his coat.

But Freddy didn't avert his eyes from Reynolds's face.

"Enough of that," Shaw said. "Let's go, Mr. Stillman."

"Keep moving, you worm," Reynolds said under his breath.

Freddy turned away from Reynolds and continued walking, feeling those words sink into him through the unsettling silence of the morgue's white-tiled walls. Freddy imagined himself in jail, locked away, feeling as miserable as he had been, and he couldn't stand the thought of it, not for a second. When they reached the middle of the hall, they turned a corner, at which point Shaw told

Freddy to stay put. The two cops walked over to a door labeled *Medical Examiner's Office* and stood in the doorway talking to someone Freddy couldn't see. They occasionally shot glances over their shoulders at Freddy, either checking on him or making reference to him. Freddy couldn't tell which, but it made him even more nervous.

Freddy remained where he was, standing next to the doorway of a small lecture hall. The room was full of unusually still, quiet students, all of whom sat with a tangible sense of anticipation in their eyes as they looked in Freddy's direction. Directly across the way was a long narrow dissection lab in which eight bodies were laid out on metal slabs, their heads wrapped in cheesecloth. Three men in lab coats sat on stools at various sections of the bodies, and with an assortment of sharp instruments cut, plucked, and scraped away their skin as they intermittently sipped on coffee and ate cinnamon buns. Freddy could vaguely hear them joking about one of the dead men, in particular, who had played professional ball and had had a horrendous slump over the past few years. "If you ask me, we're better off he's here with us," one of the men said, the one working on his body. He reached between the ballplayer's legs, took hold of the scrotum with his bare hand, and lifted it up for the others to see. "I've been wanting to do this for I can't tell you how long," the man said, laughing. The other men laughed along. They sipped their coffee and bit into their buns and laughed some more.

A man wearing a lab coat and red bow tie wheeled one of the bodies in the dissection room past Freddy and into the lecture hall. The cadaver was a tall lean woman with particularly wide hips. It had already had its skin and fascia removed and was ready for its final cuts. With its braided musculature exposed, the specimen looked like a large floppy rubber toy, which the students immediately started sketching when it was rolled into the room. Freddy couldn't take his eyes off the corpse. He'd seen bodies blown apart, bones shattered, skulls split open, dismembered feet still in their boots, but he'd never seen a body so meticulously preserved and cared for, never one made to look so benign and anonymous and inhuman.

Just as the professor started his presentation, Shaw and Reynolds returned from the Medical Examiner's Office followed by a short, bald man with a beard.

"This way," Shaw said.

Freddy hesitated as he waited to see what the professor would do with the cadaver.

"Let's go," Shaw said. Freddy followed them. They walked back around to the main hall, and as the lab man continued on down the hall, Freddy and the officers entered a small dark room with a large plate-glass window looking into an examination room. The exam room was empty and was lit by a single bulb screwed into a socket by the door. "We just want to be sure this was the woman you saw yesterday," Shaw said.

"Is this necessary?" Freddy asked.

"Yeah, it's necessary," Reynolds said bluntly. Reynolds's eyes had not stopped squinting since their last exchange.

A few uncomfortable moments passed and then the man with whom they had just walked down the hall wheeled a gurney into the examination room. On the gurney was a body—toes, breasts, nose, head contoured by a white sheet. The man set the gurney in the center of the room and turned on a pair of overhead lamps. The lamps shined onto the white sheet, which cast the stark light onto the faces of the three men in the observation room. As the man pinched the edge of the sheet with his fingers, Freddy suddenly felt both aroused and sickened. He could feel his palms dampen as the man slowly pulled the sheet off the woman's head. He pulled it down so it revealed Janice Gould's face and her neck and the upper part of her chest. Her thick auburn hair, which Freddy had so many times wrapped around his knuckles, was carefully tucked underneath her head, under the nape of her neck. Her chin, which angled up toward the ceiling, was tilted in the direction of Freddy and the officers. Even in the bright light, there was a blue tint to her skin, and even with the discoloration, Freddy could see the very distinct marks on her neck from the murderer's hands.

"Is that her?" Reynolds asked.

Freddy took a second to answer him. He was transfixed by Janice's face, by how even in her death, she was so radiant, she seemed so alive. The image he had kept in his mind, the fantasy that he had only imagined the day before, suddenly recurred in his thoughts, and he couldn't get over the fact that what he reported to Shaw and Reynolds was now real.

"Yeah, that's her," he said, trying to maintain his composure.

Shaw leaned over to a small hole in the glass. "Thank you. That'll be it."

The man slowly pulled the sheet back over the woman's face and then rolled her out of the room. Then Shaw turned on a light in the observation room. "Have a seat, Mr. Stillman," Shaw said to Freddy. There was a small table and two chairs. Freddy sat on the edge of the chair's wooden seat, Shaw sat back in the other. Reynolds stayed on his feet, hovering over Freddy's shoulder. "Now, Mr. Stillman," Shaw continued, "my partner and I have a curious problem."

"What's that?" Freddy asked.

"Well, yesterday, after we got the call from the Beekman's super about the body, we went back to Janice Gould's apartment. When we got there and took a closer look at things, we found this piece of paper brushed under the curtains." Shaw removed a small piece of paper from a pocket in his shirt and placed it on the table. It was torn in half and read:

319 West
Triple Ma
Midn

Freddy wasn't sure what to say, so he just looked at the paper and then pushed it back at Shaw.

"It's not exactly much to go on, I realize," Shaw said, "but . . . Mr. Stillman, can you tell me your home address, if you wouldn't mind."

"Three-nineteen West Eighty-third Street," Freddy said.

"You see how that's a little interesting to us?"

Freddy's composure cracked. "Are you implying that I had something to do with this?"

"Maybe so, Mr. Stillman," Shaw continued. "There are lots of buildings with a three-nineteen West address in this city. Maybe she knew someone at such an address. Maybe that piece of paper had been sitting there from before she moved in. There are a good number of possibilities how such a coincidence can come about. But you gotta understand—in our line of work, it's rare to have those kinds of coincidences. Usually, these things are what they appear to be."

"I don't know what to tell you," Freddy said. He didn't know what to tell him. He didn't know what to say, so he thought he should continue saying as little as possible.

"Well, my partner and I, we went up to the Triple Mark last night, just on the outside chance that something might explain the other part of this piece of paper. And at midnight, we were struck by another small funny thing. . . . At midnight, who walks in other than Stu Zawolsky. That name ring a bell, Mr. Stillman?"

"No, no, it doesn't."

"Stu Zawolsky, he's a contract killer. Stu Zawolsky came into the Triple Mark alone last night and he sat at the bar drinking vodka, kind of with a look on his face that he was waiting for someone, if you know what I mean. He kept leaning his head over to the door at everyone who's walking into the joint. You see where I'm going with this?"

"I see where you're going with this, yeah. But I don't see how this Stu Zawolsky being at the Triple Mark tells you too much. The joint ain't exactly known for its sophisticated clientele."

"True, true," Shaw said. "Only, the two of us stayed up pretty late and kept an eye on him. When we got tired, we called in for a little help. Well, this morning, when we got into work, what did we find?"

Freddy could feel his eyes widening. He had to fight himself to keep from jumping out of his seat.

"We found a message saying that first thing in the morning Stu Zawolsky took a ride over to three-nineteen West Eighty-third Street. He stayed for ten minutes and then got back in his car and drove home. Now, Mr. Stillman, let me ask you again: Are you acquainted with Stu Zawolsky?"

"No, I don't know Stu Zawolsky."

"Then Stu Zawolsky didn't come visit you this morning at your home?"

"No, I don't know anyone by the name of Stu Zawolsky."

"Did you have any guests this morning, Mr. Stillman?"

Freddy shook his head. "No," he said quietly.

"Well . . . will you tell me again what happened to your face?"

"I already told you," Freddy said, his thoughts drifting back a few minutes to the sight of Janice's neck. He could feel the hot air rising up in his throat again. "I took a bad fall," he blew. "Now, you tell me this: Are you two arresting me for being clumsy?" He looked up at Reynolds.

Reynolds smiled that stupid smile of his. "Not just yet, Stillman. Only because if you're in the kind of fix that we think you're in," Reynolds said knowingly, "we want to see what the outcome's gonna be."

"Well then," Freddy said, feeling relieved, thinking that if the outcome was as bad as all that, that was fine with him. "I think I should go."

Freddy got up from the table and carefully walked past Shaw and Reynolds. He walked out into the hall. The smell of formaldehyde was noxious and his nerves were so tight and twisted that he felt like he was going to be sick. He passed the dissection lab and could see, inside the lecture hall, the professor pulling the woman's abdomen apart with his hands and reaching inside it. Freddy's pace quickened. He ran through the hall, past the lab technicians, and out onto the street, where his feet slipped out from under him on the thin sheet of snow on the sidewalk. He fell facedown in it.

When Freddy's fat acquaintance Feldman saw Freddy drop to the ground outside the morgue, he nonchalantly stepped from behind a parked patrol car and approached Freddy. He walked quickly, his footsteps in sync with Freddy's spastic breaths, timing his approach so well that he lifted Freddy off the ground by his collar just as Freddy had finished wiping the snow from his face.

"Don't speak," Feldman said. "Just walk."

"What is this?" Freddy said, his voice tight from his coat collar constricting his breath.

"Like I said, don't speak." Feldman jabbed Freddy in the back with something blunt.

Freddy turned and looked at him.

"Gun," Feldman said. "Walk," Feldman said. "We need to talk," Feldman said. "Serious," Feldman said. "Very serious."

As Freddy and Feldman walked away from the Civic Center, the winds that had lulled at the start of the storm started to pick up again and the falling snow became more and more like fists of ice. Cars appeared to be moving more sluggishly. Men and women walking into the arctic gales shielded their eyes with their hands.

"Into the alley," Feldman said after a short walk to Bowdler Lane in South End. He pushed Freddy from between the shoulder blades and Freddy plunged forward into a narrow alley, under a skyward erection of fire escapes. Chiseled in stone over the alley doorways were "Bromberg Hosiery," "Knights of Columbus," "Shineburg's Kosher Wine," "Max Fishburg's Deli."

"Through that door," Feldman said, pointing to Fishburg's. Freddy walked through a door propped open by a chair and could immediately smell pastrami and corned beef. He walked through a narrow corridor, through the kitchen. He passed a sink full of blood and a chopping block covered in cow tongues, and he entered into a back room, red velvet, with three tables covered with checkered tablecloths. The room was empty of people. One table was set. "Sit down," Feldman said.

Freddy didn't see a gun, but Feldman kept reaching into his pocket to move something around. "What's this all about?" Freddy asked.

"I'll get to that," Feldman said. "Heshey! Where are you?"

"How'd you know I'd be at the morgue?"

Feldman looked at Freddy as if he were stupid. "Your arrogance astounds me, Freddy. But your lack of judgment astounds me even more. . . . Heshey!!!"

A waiter dressed in an overly starched white shirt and a red velvet jacket turned a corner. He said something to Feldman in what sounded to Freddy like German. The waiter jotted down a list of items on his order pad as they spoke, and as they continued to speak the waiter stopped writing for a while, as if he were digressing, and he kept pointing up to a set of photographs on the wall, signed photographs of actors, in costume, mid-scene, onstage, in a play. When the waiter kept pointing with his pad to the pictures, Freddy noticed that the same actor was consistently in each of the pictures, dressed in a different costume, playing a different portly character in each role. The more Freddy studied the pictures, the more he saw that the man in those pictures was the man who he knew as Feldman. Freddy started to stand, to take a closer look at one of the photographs.

"Did I say to stand up?" Feldman said as he waved the waiter away.

The waiter walked off, back into the kitchen.

"That's you," Freddy said. He read the signature. *Shlomo Feldman,* it was signed. "That is you, isn't it?"

"Yes."

"Shlomo Feldman."

"That's right."

"You're an actor?"

"It's sort of a sideline. Something to take my mind off shmucks like yourself." Feldman grabbed hold of his fat face and ran his hand from his forehead down to his chin, and held on to his jaw.

Heshey the waiter returned with a bowl of chicken soup and a plate of thick slices of brisket soaked in gravy. He was followed by one of the cooks, who was carrying two bowls, two plates, and a ladle. Feldman ushered them away and started serving himself and Freddy. "Eat," Feldman said to Freddy. "You need your strength with what I've got to tell you."

"What happened to Janice?" Freddy asked.

"We'll get to that. You just keep your trap busy with the brisket."

"It's a little early for brisket."

"Shut up and eat it."

"What happened to Janice?" Freddy asked again, not touching the brisket.

"From what I hear, you set her up for a hit."

Suddenly the arrogant and stupid comment made sense to Freddy. "You know I had nothing to do with that."

"That's not what the cops think, now is it?" Feldman glared at Freddy for a second and then took a healthy bite of his meat.

"She didn't have that coming to her," Freddy said. "What happened?"

"What do you think happened?" Feldman said with his mouth full. He swallowed. "If you had just done what you were supposed to do, she would still be alive. But no, you had to be weak and question . . ." Feldman shook his head.

"Was it you who . . ." Freddy's head started to ping right between his eyes.

"Was it me who did what?" Feldman's eyes squinted. "Me? Was I the one who went back on my word? You, Freddy Stillman, were supposed to file some paperwork yesterday, and you didn't do it. What did I say to you yesterday?" Feldman ran his hand over his face again. "What did I say, Freddy? I said there wasn't anything smart about what you were doing. God couldn't have made it more clear. I said there would be consequences. These are the consequences." Feldman stuffed another healthy piece of brisket into his mouth and washed it down with big spoonfuls of soup.

"You really mean to tell me that if I had filed the paperwork by yesterday afternoon, Janice would be alive?"

Feldman nodded his head. His mouth was too full to speak.

"And now I'm being set up for her murder?"

Feldman once again nodded his head as he swallowed. "Not just set up, Freddy," Feldman said, a little out of breath. "You're already a condemned man as far as those cops are concerned. But that's not what this is really about. See, you're already going to do time for Janice's murder. That's already in the books. That's just for fucking with us. That's for thinking you could weasel your way out. But, like I said, that's not what this is really about."

"Then what is this about?"

"This is about us putting our foot down is what this is about, see? This is about you going back to that office of yours and filling out that paperwork the second I let you walk out that door with your fucking balls attached to your cock is what this is about. And if that isn't clear enough for you, if that doesn't penetrate that mongoose brain of yours, let me tell you how serious we are about you going back to your office and filling out that paperwork."

Feldman lifted his napkin from his lap and wiped his saucy chin.

"Now that you understand to what lengths we will go, Freddy, keep in mind that the next time you and I see each other, it's going to be to visit your ex-wife on a fucking meat hook, understand?"

Freddy, without thinking, stood up from his seat and started around the table to Feldman. Feldman, with astonishing, almost invisible deftness, had his napkin back on the table and his hand in and out of his pocket and a revolver trained on Freddy before he managed more than two steps.

"No no no," Feldman said. "Sit down," he ordered. The revolver wiggled in Feldman's hand like a wet fish. "Down, I said!"

Freddy flopped back down in his seat.

"Eat your brisket," Feldman said, shaking the gun in Freddy's direction a little more.

Freddy stared at Feldman and didn't move.

"Eat your goddamn brisket if you know what's good for you!" he said angrily.

Freddy sat defiantly.

"Suit yourself. You don't know what you're missing." Feldman placed the gun back in his pocket. "Now, all you need to do," he said, "is walk back out into that alleyway, return to your office, fill out the paperwork, then you call this number and tell them it's done." Feldman reached into his pocket, the one in which he kept his gun, and he pulled out a piece of paper with a phone number on it. "You tell them that the order's been dispatched."

"What about the money?"

"What nerve." Feldman shook his head again. "I'm afraid it's too late for that, pal. Besides, what the fuck do you think you'll be buying out of Farnsworth?" Feldman waved his hand at Freddy as if he were shooing away a fly. "Now get away from me. Away. I wash my hands of you now. . . . Heshey!!!"

The waiter entered from the kitchen with a platter of herring and turkey legs. "Clear away his place," Feldman ordered, "and SHOW HIM OUT!" Heshey laid out the platter in front of Freddy and then removed Freddy's bowl and plate. He handed the bowl and plate to a lackey who followed behind him.

"Oh, and one last thing, Freddy," Feldman said with a grin full of shredded meat wedged between his teeth, "unless you want to show up at Farnsworth in a wheelchair, I'd find a way to pay Zawolsky the rest of his money. He ain't one to cross." Feldman's chins started to jiggle as he motioned for Heshey to take him on his way.

Heshey walked Freddy through the kitchen, back past the chopping block full of cow tongues, the sink full of blood, through the door leading into the alleyway. All Freddy could think of was that he had to keep Evelyn safe.

Freddy walked into the snow, toward the street, where he was met by two large men. Freddy had never seen them before but they looked at him as though they knew who he was. Vaguely preparing himself for another beating, Freddy studied the two men's faces: they both looked similarly grizzled, but one seemed distinctly happier, the other mopey. The one with the sunny disposition looked at Freddy and tipped a little snow off his hat as Freddy walked by. The other looked over him cold and hard. They then ventured into the alleyway, under the fire escapes, and Freddy watched them enter the doorway from which he had just come. He didn't know what to make of it. He didn't care to make anything of it at all.

Chapter 24

When the two grizzled men reached the open door of Max Fishburg's Deli, they walked into the kitchen, where the waiter and the cooks were preparing a platter of stuffed cabbage and kishka. When they saw the two grizzled men with their guns drawn in one hand, their index fingers over their lips, shushing them to be quiet, the restaurant staff stopped what they were doing and anxiously inched their way to the alley door. "Out," the more severe man said to them. Very quietly, the waiter and his staff turned away and quickly walked through the short hall to the alleyway. The two armed men relaxed visibly with the staff gone, and showed themselves into the dining room, where they found Feldman clutching a herring in one hand and a turkey leg in the other. His mouth was full and he was masticating like a cow chewing its cud. But as soon as he saw the two men, Feldman's mouth stopped chewing; his whole body froze—he didn't blink. The grizzled man with the severe countenance walked behind Feldman and slid the gun out of Feldman's pocket and dug it into his back. "Don't stop chewing," the sunny one said. "I don't want you choking. Not just yet."

Feldman started chewing again, slowly. With the herring and the turkey leg still raised off the plate, he chewed until he was able to swallow. Then he blinked, quivered slightly, and nervously dropped the fish and fowl onto his plate and wiped his hands. "I thought Benny was coming for me?" The zeppelin of bluster Feldman had excoriated Freddy with suddenly popped into a cloud of humility. "Why are you here?"

"Everything work out with Stillman?" the sunny one asked.

"Yeah."

"He bought it that the girl was a corpse?"

"Yeah."

"You expect he'll do what he's supposed to do?"

"He's scared witless. He's still got a big soft spot for that ex-wife of his."

"Good," Sunshine said, smiling. He glanced up to the pictures of Feldman on the wall and continued smiling. "You should have kept to acting, Feldman."

"Not enough . . ."

"Yeah," the grizzled man said, "acting's a thin world, Feldman, I know. You already gave us the speech the other day. A real thin world, skinny. And when you're gone, when you've taken your final bow, there'll be a hundred thousand fat men standing in line to take your place."

"Where's Benny?"

"He's up at the club waiting on us, so get your coat on."

"What's he doing up at the club?"

"Get your coat on, Feldman, before I let this bum bring you into the kitchen and have him show you what he can do with a carving knife."

"No need to get morbid."

"I'm sorry, Feldman," Sunshine said, mocking Feldman. "It's just been a morbid day. . . . Will you get your fucking coat on!"

Just west of Central Boulevard on the corner of Forty-seventh and Lemark Avenue was the snow-dusted chrome facade of the Triple Mark. The elegant hotel–dinner theater looked oddly misplaced in the run-down company of boarded-up theaters, taxi dance halls, grind houses, and sideshows; it looked as though it should have been planted five blocks east, right under the hot electric signs of the Central Boulevard theater district.

"Let's go," Sunshine said to Feldman as the car came to a halt.

"Aren't you gonna tell me what's going on before you send me in there?"

"What's the point? You're goin' anyway."

"Move your fat ass, Feldman," the moper said, knocking Feldman in the back of the head with the muzzle of his gun.

The three men got out of the car and walked in through the stage entrance on Lemark Avenue. They made their way around aquamarine musicians' boxes decorated with sparkling treble clefs, through an oasis of artificial palm trees, and up a narrow winding staircase marked with a big sign that read PRIVATE. When they reached a landing that looked over the empty dinner theater, the moper knocked on the door. A buzzer sounded, and the grizzled men pushed their way into Johnny Mann's office. It was dimly lit by sconces, a fire in the fireplace, and a green glass lamp on the desk. The soft light glowed onto the walls and ceiling in such a way that their ornate patterns of filigree appeared to become animate, like a waving bed of sea moss. Johnny Mann and Jerzy Roth, who had spent the night bound and gagged to chairs in the basement, had been moved into Mann's office. Mann, a diminutive figure in a dark double-breasted suit with a powder-blue handkerchief in his breast pocket, sat in a high-backed leather chair at his desk before a ledger. He had short slick black hair and butterscotch eyes, and was in need of a shave. His hands were bound behind his back and his mouth was gagged. He didn't look happy. If his eyes could talk, they would have been spitting invective at Feldman.

Jerzy Roth, a large, muscular man with a wide face, dressed in an unseasonably colorful lightweight suit, sat across from Johnny Mann on a couch near the fireplace. He too was bound and gagged. He too didn't look happy. He too looked like he wanted to make sausage out of Feldman. Benny Rudolph sat on the couch with Jerzy and watched as a bearded man wearing a beret, a red ascot, and black leather gloves fiddled with a camera set on a tripod.

"Keep the fat boy out of my frame for a second," the photographer said to Benny.

Benny got off the couch, took Feldman by the shoulder, and pulled him behind the photographer.

"Benny," Feldman said, looking over to Johnny, then Jerzy, then Benny, "what's going on?"

"I got another little acting job for you." Benny turned to the photographer with upturned palms.

"You say you want quality," the photographer whined, "but you rush me. You say you want it to look real, that you want it nice and stark . . . you think real and stark is easy to come by, Ru? It takes finesse."

"Yeah, well, sometimes the exigencies of life dictate function over form. So make it snappy."

"What are you, the fucking philosopher king all of a sudden?" the photographer said with his eyes focused on the upside-down image of Johnny Mann in his window box. The photographer walked out from behind his camera and swiveled Mann in his chair a few degrees so he was facing the camera in half-profile. "All right, snappy. Just remember, you get what you get and I ain't takin' no credit for this."

Benny shook his head and said to Feldman, "Fucking artists: little dictators."

"Come on, then," the photographer said. "Throw fat boy into the frame."

"Step right here," Benny said to Feldman. He pulled him over so that he was directly in the center of the camera's frame. Benny looked to the photographer.

The man made a face as he waved Feldman back a few steps.

Benny moved Feldman a few inches to the left, then looked back to the photographer.

"He so fucking big it don't really matter."

"Okay, don't move," Benny said to Feldman.

Feldman was now standing just three feet or so from both Johnny Mann and Jerzy Roth, both of whom started screaming through their gags. "What's going on?" Feldman said again.

"So, John, Jerzy," Benny said, ignoring Feldman, "this is what it's come down to between you and me. Ten years and my health you took from my life. Now you pay for that."

Johnny and Jerzy continued to mumble through their gags.

"Benny?" Feldman said. "Benny?"

Benny Rudolph turned to the photographer. The photographer raised his flash over his head.

Benny, without hesitation, handed Feldman a loaded tommy gun that was sitting on Johnny Mann's desk. Feldman reluctantly took it. "Aim the gun at Johnny," Benny said to him.

Feldman struck a pose, aiming the gun at Mann's chest. "Like this?"

"Lean your weight into it!" the photographer shouted.

Feldman leaned forward a little on his left foot and looked back for assurance.

"Wipe that sad-sack look off your face!" the photographer shouted. "Look like you mean it, for crying out loud."

Feldman flared his nostrils and scowled as much as he could with his fat cheeks. "Why am I doing this?" Feldman said through the scowl.

"That'sa boy," the photographer said.

Feldman held the pose and the face.

"Now shoot," Benny said coldly.

"What?"

"Pull the trigger."

"You're kidding, right?"

"Pull the fucking trigger, Feldman!" Benny said angrily, heatedly.

"Don't make him lose that look, Ru," the photographer shouted.

Benny pulled a gun out of a shoulder holster and held it against Feldman's temple.

"C'mon, Benny, please. Haven't I done everything you asked me to do? Everything . . ."

"Shoot the gun, Feldman," Benny said as he cocked his own gun and took a couple steps back.

"Don't make me do this, Benny. Please don't make me do this."

"Shoot the fucking gun!" Benny screamed. "Shoot the fucking gun, Benny, or I'll off you right here and now."

The tommy gun started to tremble in Feldman's fat hands. He looked back to Benny, and when he saw Benny about to take a step forward to brace himself against his gun's kick, Feldman looked into Johnny Mann's desperate watering eyes and gripped the trigger. He stepped into the kick of the gun and sprayed nearly the entire magazine of bullets over Mann's chest. Somewhere, in the middle of the rounds being fired, in the middle of Feldman's screams, the photographer flashed his bulb and snapped a picture, capturing the sparks shooting out the gun's muzzle. When Feldman saw Johnny Mann's head loll off to the side, he got so upset he panicked and dropped the gun on the floor; he watched the smoke curdle up from its barrel, and when the room quieted enough for him to hear the gurgle of blood spilling out of Johnny Mann's wounds, Feldman started cursing at Benny. "You no-good fuck!" Feldman screamed at him.

"Beautiful!" the photographer yelled. "Keep him angry, Ru! Angry as sin!"

"Pick it up, Feldman. Pick it up!" Benny knocked Feldman in the side of his head with his gun just hard enough to get his attention. The photographer loaded a new bulb into his flash and turned the camera on its tripod in the direction of Jerzy. "Don't make me pick it up for you," Benny said.

Feldman clumsily picked up the gun from the floor as he listened to Jerzy Roth's helpless muffled rantings from underneath his gag. Benny grabbed Feldman by the nape of the neck and threw him as best he could in Jerzy's direction. "Where?" Benny said to the photographer.

"With that look on his face? Right at me. Square him off and turn Jerzy toward him."

Benny did as he was told. He squared Feldman off so that if Feldman got it into his head to turn the gun on the photographer, he would make an easy mark. Benny then turned Jerzy so that he was framed in profile. "All right?"

The photographer played with his equipment a little. "Mmmm . . ."

"All right," Benny continued, "don't make me say a fucking word this time, Feldman. If I have to say another word this time when I finish this sent—" Feldman, feeling like he wanted to kill everyone else in the room except Jerzy, raised the gun and once again gripped the trigger, firing round after round into Jerzy's chest and throat. The photographer's flash lit the room, and once again Feldman dropped the gun. This time he dropped with it, to his knees, in front of Jerzy Roth's blood-soaked shoes.

"Now that . . . that was inspired," the photographer ranted. "That . . ." he said with his arms spread wide.

"Why'd you make me do it, Benny?" Feldman sobbed. "Why'd you make me do that?"

Benny placed his hand on Feldman's shoulder and patted it as if he were consoling him. "C'mon, Feldman, get up."

"Why'd you make me do it?" Feldman asked again.

"Feldman . . . get up."

The two grizzled men walked over and with all their might pulled Feldman to his feet.

"Get him out of here," Benny said to the grizzled men.

The grizzled men took hold of Feldman and dragged him out of the room with a gun to his head.

"What you gonna use these for?" the photographer asked as the door closed.

"Mementos. Throw the film in a bag and hand it here. Get your stuff packed up."

"I'll make it snappy," the photographer laughed. "Don't you worry."

Benny Rudolph lit a cigarette and stared silently at the corpses as the photographer packed up his things. When the photographer was ready to go, Benny told him he'd meet him downstairs at the car. Benny picked up the phone.

"Operator."

"Midtown six nine five."

"One moment, please."

"Department of Investigations, Chief Investigator Tines's office."

"Chief Investigator Tines, please."

Chapter 25

Faith Rapaport had sorted through about half of her father's file on Victor Ribe when a clerk pushing a mail cart wheeled past her desk. "Miss Rapaport, Mr. Volman told me to tell you, 'Ten o'clock, State Government Building.' He said you'd know what for."

"Thanks," Faith said, looking at her watch. It was a little after nine.

Faith bundled up, stuffed the Ribe file inside her alligator-skin attaché, and made her way to the elevator. When she reached the lobby of the Globe Building, she rode the escalator beside the elevator bank down to the subway station. She dropped her nickel at the stile, and with the sound of clanging signal bells and faint thunderous footsteps filling the graded wooden corridors, she walked to the Blue Line platform, where the train had just pulled into the station. Gum papers and a cloud of dust had been swept up into the air by the oncoming rush of the train. Faith leaned her slim figure through the exiting crowd of an emptying car and managed to find a seat. As the train jerked down the rails, in and out of the wide Blue Line stations, she picked up on the Ribe file where she had left off. She sorted through interviews with Ribe, with witnesses, courtroom notes, variations of stories, all of which left her wondering what it was she should be looking for. When the train pulled into the Commerce Street station seven stops down the line, a handwritten scrap of paper fell out of the folder as she was placing it back into her attaché. She picked up the piece of paper from the floor of the train and read its jottings over a few times as she made her way up to street level. She wasn't sure what its significance was, wasn't sure what to make of it, but her gut was telling her that it was something important.

> —According to BR, Lardner beats rap on peddling H in exchange for evidence against syndicate. Lardner's pharmacy—122 Hatherton Street. Supplied by Eliopoulos Mondays/noon; Crown Crackers delivery; Mann and Roth 20% cut 3rd Wed./month. Suspects ANB takes a nickel on 20. Klempt, Dubrov, Collins on the take? Shortz blind to it?

The narrow snow-blown lanes all around Commerce Street were bustling with office clerks carrying greasy brown paper bags, traders and bankers and stenographers in heavy black wool overcoats caught with thick flakes of snow. Before she headed over to the State Government Building, Faith decided to make a quick stop into the International Trust Bank to see if she could make use of the key she had found on Murray Crown's desk earlier that morning.

The bank was located on Commerce between Shrine and Grand in the shadows of the Exchange. Faith walked through a stand of Corinthian columns into the bank's lobby. A cupola ceiling ornately frescoed with winged cherubs ascending into the heavens looked down over orderly lines of patrons and pilasters. She followed the signs to the safety deposit vault in the basement and presented her key to a woman with a distant gaze and porcelain skin.

"Name," the woman said.

Faith hesitated, then decided to try her luck. "Faith Rapaport."

The clerk lazily got up from her seat and walked to a filing cabinet built into the wall. She opened a drawer, flipped through some papers, then returned to Faith with a form in hand. After glancing at the form, to Faith's surprise, the woman turned to an old husky security guard leaning against the counter, and said, "Six eighty-four."

She handed the key back to Faith and pointed her chin at the guard. "He'll take you."

With a slow lame gait, the guard led Faith into an open vault behind the clerk's station. They found box number 684. Faith inserted her key; the guard with a bit of a shaky hand inserted a master key, then removed the box and handed it to Faith. Faith waited for the guard to leave the vault before she sat down and lifted the box's lid. Inside she found a nicely printed handwritten note addressed to her and paper-clipped to the note a manila envelope. The note read:

> *Miss Rapaport,*
> *The same men who did this to Boris Lardner murdered Murray Crown and your father. There are more photographs that accompany these. If you're interested in seeing them, be at Prescot Shoe Repair in the Prescot Building at one o'clock.*
> *B. Rudolph*

Faith wasn't able to place Rudolph's name, but she couldn't help but wonder if he was the BR mentioned in the paper she had just found in the Ribe file. She set the note off to the side and opened the envelope to find two photographs, one of a man, arms flailing, careening down from the el platform. The picture seemed to be taken from the street and captured the man somewhere in the middle of his trajectory. An arrow marked in fresh, slightly smudged ink pointed to the man, and written next to the arrow was *Boris Lardner.* The other photo, taken from another point of view on the street from a good distance, was an image of Boris only inches away from crashing into the window of Schweitzer's Piano Shop. Off to the side was another man looking over his shoulder, watching as Boris was about to make his impact. *Victor Ribe*, it read next to his shoulder in the same smudged ink.

Faith hurriedly replaced the photos inside the envelope, along with the note, and slipped them into her bag. At the very least, she now knew that her father's instinct about Ribe was right. If these photos had anything to say about it, he was innocent of killing Lardner. The questions remained: What more did he know? What could he have known to have gotten him killed? What was this B. Rudolph's relationship to her father? Faith walked out of the narrow confines of the vault leaving the box on the table. The guard was waiting outside for Faith when she stepped out. He escorted her back to the clerk's desk. "You mind if I have a look at the form you've got there?" Faith asked, pointing to the piece of paper the clerk had removed from the filing cabinet.

"It's yours for the asking," the woman said as she handed the form to Faith, her distant gaze focusing on Faith's eyes for the first time.

The form showed that Samuel Rapaport and Benjamin Rudolph had rented the box jointly some years before Sam's death, and recently written in as one of the depositors—in the same hand as the note in the deposit box—was *Faith Rapaport.*

"Would you happen to know anything about this man, Benjamin Rudolph?" Faith said to the clerk, pointing at Rudolph's name on the form.

The clerk looked at the piece of paper and tilted her head. "No. But it shows here," she said, pointing to a section on the form, "that he's been the one making the payments on the box."

Faith looked over to the guard, who was staring at her and scratching his beard like he wanted to speak. Faith leaned a little in his direction as if she wanted him to speak.

"He was just in here yesterday, miss," the old guard said. "He used to come in here pretty frequent years back. He and Mr. Rapaport—the newspaperman—he and that Mr. Rudolph would sometimes come together. If memory serves right," the guard said quietly, "I remember him being a private detective."

Faith inched a little closer to the guard. "How's that?"

"I try not to listen in on what folks talk about back there, but I heard him talking to Mr. Rapaport when they come in together, and

I sometimes heard them talking bits and pieces of cases. I thought he was a policeman, but I heard talk about clients and whatnot and figured him for a gumshoe. My brother-in-law, that's his line, and well I know when I hear it."

Faith gave the guard a kind smile and a wink. "Thanks for the tip."

Chapter 26

When Faith reached the State Government Building, the snow seemed to hang suspended between the building's two pillbox towers. She hurried through the empty front entrance of the south wing and walked into the press gallery, where Harry Shortz was already taking questions. She spotted Owen James, a *Globe* photographer with whom Faith worked regularly, a scrappy-looking man with a wool suit in need of a good pressing; he was standing in the wings, jotting down notes on a steno pad. When Faith reached him, Owen shot her a wink and handed her his pad and pencil, looking happy to be rid of them. "I owe you one," Faith whispered as she read over his chicken scratch.

"I'll add it to the list of the ones you owe me."

"Give me the quick once-over, will you?"

"It's all there: they found some foul play in Crown's room—broken window, bloody straight razor. . . . Tines's taking over the investigation."

"What's this about Eliopoulos?" Faith asked, flipping a page over on the steno.

"He skipped town last night, and Mann and Roth—nowhere to be found."

Faith nodded along as she absorbed the information from Owen's notes and lips and listened with half an ear to Shortz speculate about how Crown could have been dragged out a fourteenth-floor window.

"Don't you think someone would have seen this?" asked a reporter from the *Herald.*

"As I said, no witnesses have come forward yet," Harry responded.

"The officers on duty, are they suspected of any wrongdoing?"

"No."

"Have you been questioned by Investigator Tines?"

"No, but I'm sure I'll have my turn."

"Are you considered a suspect?"

"Not to my knowledge."

"Mr. Commissioner!" someone screamed out. "The suicide note. Will you please tell us what it said?"

"The suicide note," Harry said, removing the note from his jacket pocket. He read it slowly and with little emotion as the reporters wrote it down on their pads word for word.

Faith snapped to when she heard it. . . . *I couldn't take the pressure. I couldn't take living in fear like that anymore.* . . . In her head she could see the note under the lamp in Crown's office; she could see her father staring blind with dead eyes at the ceiling of their apartment; she remembered what the commissioner had said to her about her father the other day on the ferry, on the way to Long Meadow— *He always knew how to twist the knife into the right part of the body when he had you in front of the world. He could make it hurt pretty bad when he got in there nice and good.* Was it that Sam was onto something rotten in the bureau? she wondered. The moment Harry was through reading, Faith shouted out the first question. "Who exactly was he afraid of, Mr. Commissioner?"

"I assume that he was referring to Mann and Roth."

"Do you think Mann and Roth have left town with Eliopoulos?" another reporter shouted out.

Before Harry could answer the question, Faith stepped down the aisle and walked toward the front of the gallery so she could more easily be seen. "Considering how much Mann and Roth have invested here in the city," Harry said with his eyes on Faith as she approached, "I highly doubt it. But, at this point, I'm afraid to say anything absolute about anything."

"Mr. Commissioner, if I may follow up . . ." Faith shouted out.

"Miss Rapaport."

"Is it really safe for me and my colleagues here to assume, given that Murray Crown was killed on your watch, that he wasn't afraid of you and the members of the bureau?"

The eyes of the room, the eye of a newsreel camera, turned on Faith.

"What are you trying to say?" Harry asked, the timbre of his voice deepening.

Faith crossed her arms and took her time now that she felt she had the room's attention. "No disrespect, Mr. Commissioner, but it seems that the one other time you managed to get someone to turn evidence on Mann and Roth, he ended up dead as well."

The room began to murmur.

"I'm afraid I don't know what you're referring to, Miss Rapaport."

"I'm referring to Boris Lardner, Mr. Commissioner."

Harry Shortz looked confused. "What about Boris Lardner?"

"When I heard about Murray Crown this morning," she said, "I started doing a little reading down in the *Globe*'s archives. According to notes made by Sam Rapaport, who covered the story, before Boris Lardner was killed, he was informing for you against the syndicate. Wasn't he?"

Harry was slow to answer. The hesitation was registered by all the members of the press, it was so obvious. He turned Crown's suicide note over on the podium and then turned it over again as he considered his response. "Yes," he said.

The gallery murmured again.

"The connection feels a little similar, don't you agree?"

Harry stared Faith down for a long moment as the low roar of the gallery continued. "Let me be clear, Miss Rapaport," Harry barked over the noise of the room. "Mr. Lardner ended up dead for no reason other than that he serviced dope fiends, like that Victor

Ribe who killed him. At which point, I might add, Mr. Lardner was no longer informing for us."

"Let *me* be clear, Mr. Commissioner," Faith said as she pulled from her pocket the note that had fallen out of the Ribe file. "You're not denying that Mr. Lardner was playing snitch for you."

"He was an informant."

"How did he come by that role?"

"I don't recall the specifics."

"Is it possible," Faith said as she glanced down at the note, "that Mr. Lardner was selling heroin over the counter of his pharmacy on Hatherton Street? Heroin supplied to him by American Allied Pharmaceutical, delivered by Murray Crown, overseen by Johnny Mann and Jerzy Roth?"

Harry tried not to look shaken, but his face had fallen a little. "That sounds about right. But as I said, I don't recall the specifics. It was a long time ago."

"Perhaps Mr. Dubrov and Mr. Collins would recall the specifics?"

Harry started looking around the room for another question, but the gallery was silent. "I fail to see the connection," Harry said, his eyes still shuffling about, looking for someone to save him.

"You said that Mr. Lardner had been released from his responsibility?"

"Yes."

"By whom?"

Harry hesitated again. "By me. He had served his purpose."

"If he had served his purpose, why is it that neither Mann, Roth, nor Eliopoulos was ever brought up on charges?"

"Because we had insufficient evidence to charge them."

"From what I understand, Mr. Commissioner," Faith said, "every Monday at noon Mr. Crown made a delivery to Mr. Lardner's pharmacy at one-twenty-two Hatherton Street; every third Wednesday of the month Mr. Mann and Mr. Roth collected twenty percent of Mr. Lardner's proceeds; and every Monday at one," Faith said, hearing a little quaver in her voice, "Officers Dubrov, Collins, and Klempt took five percent off the twenty. Do you deny this?"

Harry's eyes narrowed and his hands took hold of the press gallery podium as if he was going to lift it off the floor. "Miss Rapaport," he started quietly and harshly, "I have devoted my entire career to getting these guys. When I see an opportunity, I jump. As best I recall, we thought Mr. Lardner had good information, and it turned out he didn't. Boris Lardner was killed by a junkie while he was selling illegal drugs. And, I'd like to add, that same junkie went on to kill one of my officers. Victor Ribe was tried and convicted. To suggest that I had anything to do with this is obscene and outrageous—not to mention completely irrelevant to today's events."

"I don't remember mentioning anything about you, Mr. Commissioner," Faith tried to continue on. Harry turned his body away from her to the other side of the room, where he found Ralph Smith from the *Times,* an old champion of Harry's. Faith made her way back to her photographer, knowing from what she saw on the commissioner's face that she was onto something.

"Harry," Smith said as though he were greeting an old friend.

"Smitty," Harry said as he pushed up on the knot of his tie.

"How do you feel about Chief Investigator Tines investigating the Narcotics Bureau? You two aren't exactly known for seeing eye to eye."

"If there's any wrongdoing, I welcome Mr. Tines to help us unearth it."

"Are you nervous that his investigation might have a negative influence on your run for office?"

"Right now that's the least of my worries. The people know my past, know who I am, what I've done, what I stand for." He shot Faith a look when he gave this answer.

"Where does this leave your case against the syndicate?"

"To be perfectly honest, I don't know. With Mr. Crown dead and American Allied out of business, I don't know if a case will need to be made."

"But surely, if Mann and Roth are guilty of the crimes you say they are, they will find a new supplier and drop man."

"I have no doubt that would be the case."

"Then it isn't over."

"No. Nothing's over yet." The gallery started to come back to life. "Lang."

"Mr. Commissioner, this morning I heard a rumor that the Southside Docks property was sold by Mr. Eliopoulos to Noel Tersi. Can you confirm this?"

"No, first I've heard of it, but I'll certainly look into it. If Mr. Tersi has any information about Eliopoulos's whereabouts, I'm sure he'll be forthcoming."

Everyone started talking again and a few reporters quickly stood up and left the gallery.

"Mr. Commissioner."

"Ted."

"If I may—knowing your active interest—I'd like to address a question to you about the impending walkout at Fief Munitions."

Harry nodded a little reluctantly.

"Do you believe that the workers at Fief should be replaced if they follow through with their strike starting Monday?"

"No, I don't think that. I think—"

"Do you think, considering that Fief is working under hostile conditions, that Mr. Fief should be allowed out of his contract with the town of Long Meadow?"

"I'm not going to speculate about something that none of us know as fact."

"But they've called for a strike starting Monday, Mr. Commissioner."

"Which is absolutely within their rights."

"But Mr. Commissioner, isn't it likely that we'll be going to war again, and if we do, won't we need to be as prepared as possible? Isn't the smooth operation of a company like Fief's in our best interest?"

"Hard work, no matter for whom it is done, no matter what the conditions, should be rewarded fairly. That is in our best interests."

"Putting the rise of fascism and the real possibility of war aside, Mr. Commissioner, by their own admission Waters and Capp have been members of the Communist Party and have contributed columns to a Trotskyist organ."

"That's within their rights as well."

"Are you saying that you don't consider the communist apparatus a significant threat?"

"No, I don't."

"But, Mr. Commissioner, please—just as a practical matter, don't you consider the recent strikes at the steel mills across the country to be evidence enough that our national security may be threatened if we are forced into a war with Nazi Germany? If the Long Meadow Munitions Workers Union is allowed to set this precedent—"

"As it stands now," Harry interrupted, "as I've said over and over again, I've seen no evidence to make me feel that there's a group of so-called communist underground operatives working within the labor movement to bring this country to its knees. Look—I'm not here to fight against movements or causes, I'm here to fight for law-abiding citizens, for decency, for hardworking men and women who deserve a voice in a collective bargaining process. When they work hard, they should get what's coming to them. What is not within the rights of the Long Meadow Munitions Workers Unions is to sabotage their plant, endanger workers, or commit a conspiracy that would undermine the welfare of the plant. A strike for the sake of fair contract negotiations may force Julius Fief to tighten his belt a little, but it will also require the union to tighten theirs. As far as I'm concerned, before Julius Fief is ever allowed to be released from his contract with the residents of Long Meadow and the union, those people have every right to place demands on the Department of Investigations to provide indisputable proof that

Long Meadow union leaders were, in fact, *responsible* for the explosion at the plant and were *involved* in a conspiracy to undermine Fief Munitions. Chief Investigator Tines's belief that a socialist labor movement is threatening to destroy American business interests—that, and the small bit of circumstantial evidence he has against Mr. Waters and Mr. Capp—is not, in my opinion, grounds enough for him to make a case that could potentially level a grave injustice against the livelihood of an entire town—a town, I should add, that invested so much capital to provide Fief with his facility."

"Mr. Commissioner . . ."

A man dressed in a gray belted overcoat and black fedora entered the room and, ignoring the reporters, approached the podium. Harry excused himself and allowed the man to whisper in his ear. The man leaned away and then stood beside Harry and looked out into the crowd.

"Well . . ." Harry said with a small voice. "I won't pretend to have a grasp on this, but it seems that Johnny Mann and Jerzy Roth are dead." He talked over all the reporters shouting out questions at once. "They were found shot inside Johnny Mann's office at the Triple Mark. Tines's men are on the scene and . . . I'm sorry," he said, "I'm afraid I'll have to cut this short." Harry made a parting half-gesture with his hand and said, "Please, excuse me." With the narcotics officer flanking his side, Harry walked out into the crowd of reporters amid flashes and shouts, and made for the elevator. The reporters, nearly trampling one another to get out of the press gallery, flooded onto the street outside the State Government Building. Those who had cars got into their cars. Those who didn't have cars got into the cars of their colleagues, and headed to the Triple Mark, Faith and her photographer included.

Standing outside Harry's office was a young, clean-cut officer from the Department of Investigations with an envelope in hand. The door to Harry's office was open, the phones were ringing, and Zelda was standing in the threshold, staring in at several other department men who were rummaging through Harry's desk and files.

"What's the meaning of this?" Harry said to the young officer when he arrived from the press gallery.

"I tried to keep them out, sir," Zelda said. "I told them to wait until you got back, but they barged right in."

"It's all right, Zelda," Harry said, pointing her to the door leading to the hall. "Why don't you take a break."

Zelda grabbed her purse off her desk and left, shaken.

The young officer handed Harry a folded piece of paper. "We have a warrant."

"What for?"

"Corruption. Murder. Obstruction. Take your pick."

Harry glanced at the warrant. "On what evidence?"

"Chief Investigator Tines gave me this to give you. As a courtesy." The officer smiled glibly and handed Harry the envelope.

Harry opened the envelope and pulled out half a dozen blood-splattered photographs.

"We found them up at the Triple Mark, in Mann's office. Mann was keeping them warm for us when we got there."

"Who is this?"

"That there? That, I am told, is Boris Lardner."

The picture on top was the same photograph Faith had found in the safety deposit box at International Trust Bank, Boris Lardner flying down to the street from the top of the el. The picture following that was the one of Boris about to crash through the window of Schweitzer's Piano Shop. "I take it this here is . . ." Harry pointed to the man standing in front of the shop.

"That would be Victor Ribe," the officer said, deadpan.

Harry's heart felt as though it had skipped a few beats. He grimly flipped to the next image.

"These big fellas I'm told you should know."

Harry could clearly see Ira and Pally on the el platform holding

Boris Lardner by the collar of his druggist coat. Boris looked as if he had been beaten so severely he wouldn't have been able to stand on his own. Off to the side was Maurice Klempt. Harry's heart skipped a few more beats as he flipped to the next image and found his three men hoisting Boris up by the arms and the legs. In the next image, with all their might, they heaved Boris's body over the rail, down toward the street.

Harry could suddenly see in his mind the newsreel camera turning on Faith Rapaport as she brought up Boris Lardner's death just a few minutes earlier.

"There's one more you might be interested in," the officer said, making use of his glib smile again.

Harry flipped to the next photo. It was dark, taken inside a dimly lit garage, but Harry could easily make out Ira and Pally heaving Crown into the trunk of his car in his bedclothes.

"We've already picked up your men," the officer said.

Harry was speechless. Even though he already knew it was Ira and Pally who had killed Crown, the sight of the hard evidence made him feel as though he were plummeting to the earth from a great height.

"Say, Mr. Commissioner," one of the officers said from Harry's office, "you want to give us the combination to this safe, or you want that we should haul it off and open it ourselves?"

Harry now took a seat on one of the chairs in front of Zelda's desk as he remembered placing the blackmail note in the safe along with the deed to the Ten Lakes property. He felt utterly defeated. As soon as he sat down, he got up again and walked over to Zelda's desk. He wrote out the combination and handed it to the officer.

"I don't want to be here for this, if you don't mind."

"Suit yourself," the young officer said dryly. "Tines wants to talk."

"He obviously knows how to get to me." Harry walked into his dismantled office and grabbed his coat and hat, wrapped himself up, and made his way out.

Chapter 27

Arthur Brilovsky—now forty-two years old, gray around the temples, shoulders stooped, cheeks round and jowled—stood in the third-story window of his suite in the Ansonia Hotel, where he watched Elaine and their nineteen-year-old son, Joshua, walk outside into the heavy snowfall. Joshua took his mother by the arm and stepped carefully over the slippery street. They crossed the avenue and then started walking uptown; as they walked beyond the view of the window frame, a bearded man wearing a black overcoat and fur hat stepped off a streetcar; he was studying a piece of paper, looking at the building numbers. The man stuffed the paper into his coat pocket, then crossed over the avenue. He passed through the visible exhaust of an idling car and disappeared under the hotel's brocade awning.

Seeing the man spurred Arthur into action. He drew the curtains to all the windows and turned on the lights. He walked over to a cabinet, removed a bottle of vodka, and placed it on the table among two covered trays, a basket of black bread, and a small bowl of pickles. He then opened the door to the room and stood by it as the bearded man walked toward him, down the hall, past head-lit busts of robed men and garlanded women who sat on pedestals recessed into paisley walls.

"Hello, Mitya," Arthur said warily as Professor Tarkhov walked past him, entering the suite without greeting Arthur. Arthur picked up the conversation in Russian. "Were you able to get away without any trouble?"

"Yes."

Arthur shut the door. The professor walked to one of the windows, where from the side of the curtain he looked out onto the falling snow, at the people passing on the avenue, at the gray windows of the building opposite the hotel. "They're happy to accommodate me in every way."

"Good."

"Yes, good." The professor turned from the window and looked at Arthur, his eyes narrowed, his heavy chin raised, his complexion reddening.

"I trust that everything is going according to schedule?"

"Everything is as your people told me it would be."

Arthur, maintaining his indifference, approached Professor Tarkhov and offered his arm for his coat and hat. "You should step away from the window, Mitya," Arthur said mildly as he approached. "Please. There are people out there watching us."

The professor, somewhat startled, looked back out the window, and though he saw no one who seemed to be looking in on them, he did as he was told. He then slowly removed his wet garments, all the time studying Arthur's face. It looked more determined than he remembered it in Petrograd following Arthur's arrival, when the professor was taken away from his studies at the university to serve as Arthur and Elaine's translator. The man he knew then was frightened and naive, his eyes compassionate and easy to comprehend; they were the eyes of a physician, of affluence, of privilege, not those of any kind of revolutionary he had ever come across. They lacked a singular and obvious motivation, any haze of rigorous self-deception. Now, however, this was the time-worn face of a man well acquainted with the subtleties of all deceptions, his eyes recondite, his features unwaveringly noncommittal.

"Do you have the package?" Arthur asked, still holding out his arm for the professor's garments.

The professor nodded his head and handed Arthur his coat and hat and draped his ascot over his arm. Arthur hung the wet clothes in an armoire and joined the professor at the table. The professor took an envelope from his jacket pocket and pushed it over the tablecloth in Arthur's direction. Arthur opened the envelope and removed a small hand mirror.

"Will that help you see yourself more clearly?"

Arthur smiled politely at the professor, then examined the clasps holding the mirror's backing. He easily twisted one of them around, twisted it back, then returned the mirror to the envelope.

"What is it for?" Tarkhov asked as Arthur opened the bottle of vodka. "That I had to carry it all the way from Moscow."

"It's better that you don't know," Arthur said.

"Is there anything good I can look forward to knowing about this arrangement?"

"No," Arthur said. "I'm afraid not." Arthur uncovered the two plates of steak and potatoes, poured a glass of vodka for the professor and himself, then raised his glass perfunctorily. "To your safe passage," he said benignly.

Professor Tarkhov didn't say anything. He lifted the vodka and drank the shot along with Arthur, then reached for a pickle from the bowl, pressed it lengthwise against the whiskers under his nose, and inhaled a long deep breath. He placed the pickle on his plate and stared at Arthur, waiting impatiently for the next formality.

"Please eat," Arthur implored. "Eat, and say what's on your mind."

Tarkhov looked at his food, and seeing the thick piece of meat before him, he reached for his knife and fork and sliced into it. But before he could bring his fork to his mouth and bite into the steak, he shook his head and placed the utensils down. "I will say this first, Arthur. Had you come to me, had you sent me a letter warning me what was to happen, perhaps, *perhaps,* I would have understood this. But the way this happened . . . the way this happened? It is unacceptable!" The professor raised his hand and hit the table with the butt of his palm. The silverware clattered, the bottle shook, and the professor, going against his reserved nature, stood up as if he were about to lunge at Arthur. "Can you imagine?" he said, standing over the table, over Arthur. "You might say you can, but I don't think you can. They came in the middle of the night. In the middle of the night. Irina and I were in bed. The children were asleep. In the middle of the night, we hear the knock on the door. The police, knocking on the door. Irina immediately began crying and holding me and telling me how much she loved me and that she knew this would happen and what would she do and will they take her too and what will become of the children . . . should we hide? . . . should I run? No, you can't imagine. You can't imagine."

"Thankfully, it wasn't what you believed it to be," Arthur said, looking away from the professor to a crack in the edge of the table. He started rubbing his fingers over the small serration, feeling it prick at his soft skin.

"No, there is nothing to be thankful for, Arthur. Nothing was explained to me until I arrived in Moscow. Until then, no one would tell me why I was being taken from my home—and then only details, minutiae, more details, of what I am to do, and then threats, saying that if I don't do it, my family's safety was in question. This I should be thankful for? . . . And before that? The humiliation? 'Professor Mikhail Tarkhov,' this young nobody announced at the door of my apartment, 'you are required to accompany us. Please pack a suitcase of clothes.' Nothing more than that. Irina? She was beside herself. She thought I was being arrested. I thought I was being arrested. I could hear the neighbors through the walls when I was packing. *They* thought I was being arrested. Irina fell to her knees and started begging the officers to leave, to leave us alone. I had to lift my sobbing wife off the ground and put her in the children's room while I dressed and packed. And then when I left, I thought I might never see them again." Tarkhov continued to lean onto the table, bending forward, inching his nose closer to Arthur's head. "It was only after I reached *Moscow,* after *ten* hours on the train, that I found out about all this nonsense and was allowed to telegraph my wife and tell her I had a *special duty* to perform for the state."

"I apologize," Arthur said, sounding incapable of expressing his regret.

"No, no you don't. You can't even look at me."

"I sincerely apologize, Mitya," Arthur said as he continued to watch his fingers run along the edge of the table. "Please," he said, finally looking up. He lifted his hand and started gently waving it at the professor as though he were patting the head of a small restless animal. "Please, sit down and listen to me."

"How could you have done this?" the professor continued in his agitated state, now looking Arthur square in the eye.

"Please, Mitya."

Professor Tarkhov reluctantly inched back and resumed his place in his chair. "I truly did believe we were friends, Arthur."

"We are friends, Mitya. And you must believe me when I say that it was an act of friendship that brought you here."

"Having me forcibly removed from my home, from my country, with threats made on my family?" Tarkhov laughed with sarcasm. "This is an act of friendship? Please, forgive me. I must be a little thick."

"If I hadn't done what I had done, Mitya," Arthur said plainly, "if I hadn't staged this as it was staged, those knocks on the door that you mistook for the police coming to arrest you would have, in fact, been the knocks of the police coming to arrest you."

The professor raised his chin and narrowed his eyes as he had done when he first beheld Arthur's face. "What are you saying?"

"I'm saying this, Mitya—that within a week from the day that you were taken from your apartment, by my men, there was to be a purge within several departments of the university, including your own."

"How is that possible?"

"How is anything that happens in Russia these days *possible*?"

Tarkhov's eyes blinked rapidly behind his wireless spectacles as though he were trying to recall all the words that he had written over the past ten years. "But what could they possibly want with me? I lead a simple life. I write. I write boring articles and books about classical painters who matter to no one, including myself. Quietly, I do this. So quietly. Since my voice has fallen out of favor, I've done all that I can to be quiet and not draw attention to myself. How could I possibly accept this as the truth?"

"How, you ask?" Arthur stood up from his chair and went into the bedroom. He returned carrying a file, which he handed to the professor. "It's all there in your hands," he said. "According to whoever wrote this, it appears that even when writing about your benign subjects, you continue to exhibit a defiant tone. I don't claim to make any sense of it."

Professor Tarkhov opened the file and flipped through some of the pages, skimming. "I don't understand this." His anger now tempered by his confusion, he took hold of his beard and stroked it softly as he studied the documents and mumbled to himself. Professor Tarkhov shook his head as he flipped through the pages. "How do I know you didn't manufacture this?"

"How would I benefit by doing that? I could have just as easily done exactly what you thought I had done for my own selfish gain and then sent you back home. Why would I have gone to the trouble of getting that file if it weren't out of concern?" Arthur put his elbows on the table and leaned in the professor's direction. "Look, Mitya, let me start with this, so you can put it into perspective, all right? . . . Whether you want to believe it or not, the fear that you felt when they came to take you to Moscow? I do understand. I understand all too well. I have been living with that same fear for many years now. Many years. And not so quietly."

"Come, Arthur. You and I both know that you are the 'they' that we speak of when we speak of 'them' coming in the middle of the night."

"That's just not so."

"But I have seen you as such only recently," Tarkhov said, sounding more unsure of what to believe. "I have seen your picture in the papers with Party officials. You are a hero of the revolution."

Arthur laughed. "You of all people believe what you read in those papers?"

"Of course not. But if you'll recall, I spoke for you when you first arrived. I witnessed you endearing yourself to these people, working on their behalf."

"That was a long time ago, Mitya. A very long time ago."

There was a silence between the two men as they both got stuck reminiscing about the early days of the revolution.

"I failed them," Arthur said. He leaned his head forward a little more so that Tarkhov could see his face clearly when he said this, and suddenly his eyes seemed to soften a little. "Yes, I was a *great* hero of the revolution. I secured money from all over the world, made arrangements for businesses to come in and out of Russia. And, yes, it's true, I once believed that I could help make the Soviets strong and decent. But, for reasons too complicated to even consider, every business venture that I started on behalf of the Party failed miserably, Mitya. Miserably. And for each miserable failure, I was held responsible for the huge sums of money that the Party lost. Do you understand what that means?"

"I don't know how much I care to understand what it means."

"It means that I was slowly but surely becoming a candidate for *enemy of the people, enemy of Stalin.* It's a wonder that I survived the purges. But, I'll tell you, if I suddenly disappeared one day, no one on the inside would have been surprised, or cared for that matter. All anyone would care about is that it wasn't him."

"So then, if this is true, how is it you escaped?"

"I ran. And I'll continue running once these paintings are sold. Look, Mitya, what is important for you to know is that when I knew I would be returning here to the City, part of my plan consisted of selling my collection of paintings. I knew I would need money, and I believed that the Rodhinskys would potentially fetch more money if they were being presented to the world by an expert, by a man like yourself who knew Rodhinsky well, his writings, the world in which he worked. I thought if I offered you a percentage of the money earned at auction, and if I could arrange asylum for you and your family in the States—so that you could live freely, Mitya, write freely, show your face in public as the man that you are—you might be interested. . . . In any event, I made a phone call to a man I had done business with in the Cheka, to find out—if you were indeed interested—what would be involved in getting you and your family out of the country. And that's when I learned that you were to be arrested."

"Why would this official give you that kind of information?"

"Why? Because he knew I wanted you. He knew that by helping me, rubles would soon be in his pocket. That's why. And as things sometimes turn out in a corrupt world—our greed and selfishness led to a decent act."

"If that's what you want to call it."

"Yes, that's what I'd like to call it. I paid him his bribe. He made arrangements for you to leave Russia and conveniently made your arrest warrant disappear. A decent act."

"If this is true," Tarkhov said, his voice still sounding unsure, "what's to become of me?"

"It's entirely up to you."

"And what's to become of Irina and the children?"

"Again, that's entirely up to you. I've made arrangements to bring them here, if you wish it. I didn't feel comfortable doing this without talking to you first, since you were the one in immediate danger. But if this is what you want, it's already done. All I need to do is send word."

"And if I should return home?"

"If you return, I can give you no assurances. This man in the Cheka, he may find a reason for that warrant to reappear. On the other hand, he could go through life without ever thinking of you again. I couldn't possibly speculate."

"And if I stay?"

"Then you stay. Lead a normal life. Learn to love baseball."

"I don't know what to say. I don't know, Arthur. I just don't know . . ."

"Say nothing for now if that's what you want. Take some time to think about it."

Tarkhov's eyes wandered from Arthur to the bottle of vodka on the table. Thinking of Irina and his children, he reached for it and filled his glass. Without letting go of the bottle, he drank down the vodka with an image of his wife's face in his mind, and then he filled his glass again. With an image of his two children in mind, he drank this glass, filled it again, then just sat at the table with Arthur in silence. As the vodka warmed and numbed the back of Professor Tarkhov's throat, he now saw in his mind the image of Rodhinsky falling toward the pickax wedged between the floorboards of his apartment, and then he drank some more.

Arthur, this time, filled the professor's glass, and then filled his own. And then, one glass after the next, they drank their way down to the bottom of the bottle. Finally, Tarkhov started to cry. He cried at his misfortune, he cried for the misfortune of Russia, he cried to God for making his life so difficult, he cried for the hardship he would place on his wife and children, and then he stopped crying and smoked a cigar with Arthur.

"How did you get it?" Tarkhov asked, his body swaying, as Arthur unsteadily held a match out to the professor's cigar.

"I already told you."

"No no, not the file. The painting. The Rodhinsky. How in the world did you get it?"

A downturned smile came over Arthur's face and the severe mood that had been in the room just moments before lifted. "If I tell you, if I tell you, you must promise not to reveal my secret."

"I make no such promises!" the professor said ardently. "But if I feel it is a secret worthy of my discretion, I will seal my lips."

"It doesn't really matter," Arthur said. "After this, you deserve to hear it. After this, you deserve to tell the world."

"Then say it."

"I stole it," Arthur proudly announced. His eyes filled with the light cast from the fixture hung over the table.

"From where?"

"You'll never believe me."

"You may be a scoundrel, but you would never lie to me about something so meaningful to the both of us, this I'm sure of."

"All right, I'll tell you. From Rodhinsky's apartment, I stole it."

"When?"

"The very night that he killed himself."

"How in the world . . . ? You? In Rodhinsky's apartment? When he killed himself?"

"If anything in this world is destined, Mitya, this undoubtedly was."

"Every detail, please."

"There's not much to it, really. I was at the Ministry of Culture that night when I witnessed what Rodhinsky said to the minister. I wanted to talk with him. I wanted to understand why he was putting himself in such danger. . . . Well, I didn't know him well, and perhaps I didn't know what exactly he would do, but I knew him well enough to know that he was up to something. So I followed him from the party to his apartment."

"Do you mean to say that you saw him die?"

"No no, of course not. When I saw that he went home, I suddenly wasn't sure what to think. I thought maybe it was just a fit of rage and nothing more. But then, as I waited outside, wondering whether or not I wanted to be in his company while he was in that congenial rage he was so famous for, I finally decided that I wanted to see him. *Kchyortu!* I thought. So I went upstairs, knocked on his door, and when the door opened from the force of my fist hitting it, there in the room that he used for his studio he lay on the floor impaled on that pickax."

The professor's eyes looked as large as eggs, they were so large. "So it's true then that he killed himself as he depicted it in the painting?"

"Yes." Arthur shook his head slightly. "It was very gruesome."

"Was he still alive when you entered?"

"No. I placed my hand over his mouth and felt no breath, and then I saw the painting, and then *my* breath was taken away. I couldn't believe it. I fell back on my ass, I was so astonished. The only detail missing from that room at the moment was myself, knocked nearly prostrate next to Rodhinsky."

"It was then you took the painting?"

"Yes, because as I stood there, looking at it, realizing what it was, what it meant, how beautiful and important it was, I thought about what would become of it, and all I saw was some ignoramus setting it on fire. I couldn't stand the thought of it. So I found a blanket and wrapped it up and quietly left Rodhinsky to his immortality."

"But how did everyone know about the painting then?"

"Because . . ."

"Because . . ." The professor wagged his finger at Arthur. "You were the one who wrote the pamphlets, weren't you?"

Arthur wobbled his head in affirmation.

Tarkhov's voice suddenly sounded thrilled. "In the voice of the policeman!"

Arthur nodded again.

"You were the anonymous policeman. I can't believe it," Tarkhov said, scratching his head. "I can't believe it."

Arthur smiled again, and laughed almost giddily.

"I can't believe it," Professor Tarkhov kept saying. "I can't believe it. I can't believe it. . . ."

"Mitya?"

"I can't believe it. . . ." Mikhail Alekseyevich Tarkhov puffed on his cigar and started to cry again.

"Meeee-tya," Arthur said in an avuncular voice. He got up from his chair. "Come," he said tenderly. He walked around to Professor Tarkhov and took him by the shoulders. "Come come come, I'll take you downstairs and put you in a taxi."

"Arthur," Tarkhov sobbed, "Irina and the children will be all right, won't they?"

"If I wire my friends tonight, Irina and the children will be in Helsinki by the end of the weekend," Arthur said solemnly. "They'll be perfectly fine. Trust me. Trust me, my friend. Please."

"Yes, all right. All right. Please wire your friends and tell them to bring my family to me."

"Whatever you want."

"I know what needs to be done now."

"I'll wire my friends from the lobby as soon as I put you in a taxi."

"I'm sorry for being rude to you, Arthur. Under the circumstances, I'm sure you understand."

"If anyone should be sorry . . ."

"No no no . . . it is right, this. It must be."

Arthur walked Professor Tarkhov to the armoire in the foyer and dressed him in his coat, ascot, and hat. With his arm over his shoulder, he then escorted him down the paisley hall to the elevator, in the elevator down to the lobby, and onto the sidewalk, where Arthur put the professor into a taxi and sent him on his way back to the Martins' estate. Once the taxi had turned off Shrine Avenue onto Thirty-sixth Street, he casually walked into the Ansonia's restaurant, took a seat at the bar, and ordered a glass of whiskey. As the bartender poured his drink, he removed the envelope that Professor Tarkhov had given him and placed it on the bar. In the bar's mirror, he watched as a man carrying an attaché approached him from behind. The man sat next to Arthur and set the attaché on top of the package.

"Is he in a cooperative spirit?" the man asked.

"Yes."

"Are you sure?"

"Yes, I'm sure."

"Good."

The man, not saying another word, removed his bag from the bar, and along with it went the package. Arthur continued sitting at the bar for some time, nursing his drink, looking at himself in the bar's mirror. He tried to recall the last time he had done something decent, but he couldn't think of a single thing. And then he thought of Joshua, but the idea of him brought him no peace.

Chapter 28

As Arthur Brilovsky and Professor Tarkhov drank together, Victor Ribe continued to observe Elaine and Joshua Brilovsky from a near distance. He watched and listened as they strolled through the dim, empty corridors of the Natural History Museum, passing dioramas of early man and woman, taxidermied apes and lions, snakes, gazelles, wildfowl. Joshua, a tall gangly young man with a deep voice and world-weary eyes, eyes like those of a young sage, held his mother's hand as they walked over the polished granite floor. He spoke English with a Russian accent. "What will we do when Father leaves?" Joshua asked his mother.

"This is disgraceful the way they've represented these poor creatures. It can easily lead a young man like yourself to despair. They look so pathetic and hungry and tired and frightened. . . . Does no one ever relax in the wild? Recline on a bed of moss or pick at their teeth with a stick? They look so severe."

"When he leaves tomorrow," Joshua persisted, ignoring his mother as she had ignored him, "he's moving across the country. Won't you want to at least be near him?"

"I don't wish to be anywhere near him."

"Will you ever forgive him?"

Elaine shook her head. "If you want to be near him, Joshua, I won't stop you. You're a grown man now. You can do as you please."

"Mother, I don't forgive him for what he's done, either, but I would like both of us to be near him. . . . Maybe one day we will forgive him."

"You have a good heart, darling, but there's much you don't understand about your father."

"Tell me."

Elaine shook her head again as she found a pair of stuffed bonobo monkeys, face to face, hanging from a branch with their legs entwined. "Now, here, this is the way the wilderness should be." Joshua let go of his mother's hand. His mother immediately took hold of it again.

Joshua looked at the two monkeys solemnly and read the plaque. "It says here that they're very promiscuous, that they're the only other animals in the wild to procreate while looking at each other's face."

"A lot of good it does us to see the other's face when we can't see what's behind it."

"Really, Mama, is he so bad?"

"It's true he can be sweet and adorable at times," she conceded in such a way that it was obvious she didn't believe what she was saying. "No," she said, correcting herself. "He can appear sweet and adorable and deserving of love, but, Joshua, when it comes right down to it, your father is deceitful. He's unapologetically selfish and ambitious and has done things in this life I hope for always you don't know about." Elaine turned to her son and with a pained look in her eyes tucked a small dark tuft of hair behind his ear. "When your father and I first met, he was very kind to me, and at that time, I needed a gentle man to be kind to me. But over the years, I realized that just like with everyone else he's charmed, he was charming me in order to cast a shadow over his true intentions."

"Which were what?"

"I don't honestly know. . . . I'll tell you this: your father's ambitions know no shame. They never have. He is his father's son, and that's all I'll say to you. Unlike my father—who was ruined for his foolish principles and for being taken in by your grandfather—

Arthur Brilovsky is a shameless man with no true direction. He is a joke as a man representing any form of ideology other than his own narcissism. And I have seen him grow more and more ruthless as he's grown older."

"You really despise him, don't you?"

Elaine kissed the place on Joshua's head where she had just touched him. "I'm sorry, darling. I'm sorry I've said anything at all."

Joshua nodded his head. "Tell me, Mother . . . if his blood is in my body, will I eventually become like him? Into the type of man you say he is? Will you end up despising me as much as you do him?"

Elaine stopped short. She grabbed Joshua by the shoulders. "Never," she said harshly. "Never place that thought into your head! You are your own man. You have the power to shape your own future. There's not an ounce of bad character coursing through your blood. If there's anything I know for certain, it's of your goodness, Joshua, your rightness. You will always be protected by your good conscience, I promise you."

"My mother can see the future?" Joshua's mood seemed to lighten a little.

"She can see beyond the future." Elaine hugged Joshua's arm. "She can see right into the window of your soul."

Elaine and Joshua held on to each other tightly as they continued through the prehistory wing of the museum. They stopped to look at the skeleton of a pterodactyl.

"Mother," Joshua said quietly, turning to Elaine so that the two of them were looking each other in the face, "please don't look away from me when I say this. . . ."

"What is it?"

Joshua looked over his mother's shoulder and watched Victor as he stood beside the immense foot of a brontosaurus. "I think there's a man following us."

"Where?" Elaine asked. When she realized that Joshua was looking at him over her shoulder, she started to turn around.

"Mother, don't," he said.

Elaine turned around and saw Victor standing there, and when she saw him, she immediately knew it was him. Her father had called yesterday afternoon and told her that he was in the City looking for her. She had spent the last day anticipating this moment, wondering how she would feel when she saw him. And now that he was nearby, she found herself full of nostalgia for a time in her life that was much more simple; she was also intrigued by and fearful of what both she and Joshua would discover.

Elaine turned back to Joshua. "What makes you think he's following us?"

"I first noticed him in the lobby of the hotel yesterday. His face wasn't black-and-blue like that, though. . . . And now he's here. He's been walking behind us the entire time we've been in the museum."

"For all we know, he's looking after us," Elaine whispered.

"We'll have to tell Father about it."

"Yes, right when we get home, you tell him, dear."

Victor followed Elaine and Joshua through the museum, then walked with them over the fresh blanket of snow in the park. He walked with them downtown until they reached the Ansonia Hotel, where Victor watched them swing through the revolving doors. When he saw them enter the elevator, when he saw the elevator doors close, he walked inside and asked the concierge for a piece of paper and a pen. He wrote a short note to Elaine and asked the concierge to deliver it immediately. When the concierge took the note from Victor's hand, he told Victor that there were two men waiting for him at the door. Victor turned around to find at the door the two grizzled men. Without a word spoken, he walked over to them, and together they walked out of the hotel to the grizzled men's car.

Chapter 29

"Operator."

"South End three nine eight."

"One moment, please."

The phone rang once, twice.

"Hello."

"Evelyn."

"What is it, Freddy?"

"We need to talk."

"It's not a good time."

"No, you don't understand. We need to talk."

"I'm afraid I can't, Freddy. Really, you really shouldn't be calling me."

Freddy could feel the phone moving away from her ear. "I'm in trouble, Evelyn, a lot of trouble. . . . Will you please see me for just one minute? It's important that we talk."

There was silence on the other end of the line.

"What have you done?"

"Will you please see me? See me this one time and I swear to God you won't ever hear from me again."

There was more silence.

"Where are you?"

"Across the street. I'm across the street at the bakery."

"If you're coming, you'd better make it quick. William is coming home for lunch."

Freddy hung up the phone and walked out of Cuccio's Bakery.

He had already bought a pink box full of pastries, and he had had Mrs. Cuccio tie the box off with a white ribbon.

Evelyn was standing inside the door of her apartment house wrapped in a heavy coat when Freddy approached. She stood atop the stoop, her waves of chestnut hair hauntingly still in the wind, her eyes fixed coldly on Freddy's beaten face. Her eyes and mouth tightened with concern for a brief moment and then became indifferent. Whatever meaning Freddy had once held for her in her life had been dismantled, and seeing the absence of affection Freddy could feel himself dematerializing. He could feel himself turning into something vague and ghostly. He was invisible to her. All he could think of was how much he would prefer to be chiseled into a pile of dust rather than say what he had come to say.

"What did you do?" Evelyn asked when Freddy reached the middle of the stairs.

"What I did doesn't matter." Freddy tried to hand Evelyn the box, but she wouldn't take it. "What matters is that what I did do . . ."

"What is it, Freddy?"

"I'm going to make things right for you, Evelyn," he managed. "I've done everything wrong by you, I know that."

Evelyn nodded her head and looked away into the drift of the storm. "I think I should go in," Evelyn said. She started to turn away from Freddy.

"Wait," Freddy said, raising his voice. "Just wait a minute." He walked up the stoop a few more steps.

"Are you going to tell me what this is about?"

"I need you and the baby and William to go stay with your mother for a few days," Freddy said in a serious steady tone.

"What?"

"Like I said, Evey, you and the baby and William need to go stay with your mother for a few days."

"Why?"

Freddy shook his head. "Please don't ask me why. Just do as I say. Call William right now, then after you get off the phone with him, take the baby and go stay with your mother. If you have to, tell William there's something wrong with the heat in your apartment, tell him anything you think he'll believe, but please, just go. Everything will be fine by the end of the weekend. I swear it."

Evelyn looked so scared she seemed afraid to move. "What have you done, Freddy?"

Freddy took another step up the stoop. "I can't tell you that. For your own sake, for the sake of the baby, Evelyn, please do as I say."

"You have some nerve, Freddy. Coming here and scaring me like this. Are you that cross with me that you have to come here and scare me like this?"

Freddy started to shake and his voice started quavering. "Something went wrong," Freddy said desperately. "Something went very wrong. If anything happened to you . . ."

"I'm calling the police, Freddy. I'm calling the police right now. You have no right, no right at all!"

"Yeah," Freddy said, feeling the force of her voice constricting his chest. "Yeah, do that. Call the police. Tell them that you're afraid I'm going to do something to you. Tell them that I've been after you, that you're afraid for your life."

Now Evelyn looked scared and confused. "Is that what this is about?"

"Tell them to talk to Mrs. Cuccio," Freddy said, pointing behind him. "Go ask her how often I stop by and have pastries sent to you, so that I can watch you stand in the doorway."

Evelyn looked at the pink box in Freddy's hand, glanced across the street, then back at Freddy. "Do you really want to hurt me, Freddy? Is that what you want? . . . You've lost your mind. You've really gone and lost your mind once and for all."

Freddy nodded his head complacently and placed the box down on the stoop. He wedged it into the snow, took another step up the stoop, and reached out his hand. "I promise, Evelyn, I'll make it all right."

Evelyn, who had her hand on the door, quickly took a step back and slammed the door in Freddy's face. Freddy continued looking at the door and could feel his diaphragm contract as though it wanted him to cry. He turned down the stairs and started to convulse as a man does when he's incapable of crying, when he hasn't cried for such a long time that his body has forgotten how. He walked away quickly in the direction of the subway, punching at himself in the gut, slapping his face; not paying any mind to the people watching him do this, he threw himself against a stone wall of a courtyard, desperately trying to push the feeling out of the cage of his chest, as though if he didn't, the feeling itself would grip hold of his heart and lungs and squeeze them closed until they ruptured. When Freddy reached the subway entrance, hovering above the first step, he could finally feel the pressure start to release; he could feel his eyes expand in volume, the tear ducts swell with water, a force as strong as ignited gunpowder compacted within a solid metal casing expanding inside his throat, and then, all of a sudden, two men in heavy coats and gray fedoras took hold of his wrist, wrenched his arm behind his back, and threw him in the backseat of a car. Instead of crying, Freddy let out a moan and wail that instantly transformed into laughter.

"It's time to be getting back to the office, Mr. Stillman," one of the men had said severely as he stepped in front of him. "You're really starting to try our patience."

Freddy couldn't say a thing to this. He couldn't stop laughing. He was laughing hysterically now. He didn't stop laughing until the man who sat next to him in the backseat of the car took hold of his shoulder and with a pair of brass knuckles forcefully hit him with an uppercut right in the solar plexus, at which point Freddy rolled onto the car's floorboards. He wheezed out the last of his breath, then started coughing uncontrollably and gasping for air.

"Don't you dare touch her," Freddy kept saying spastically when he was able to speak. "Don't you dare touch her," he said to the man's wet shoe.

"It's all in your hands now, Mr. Stillman," the man said. "It's always been in your hands."

Freddy reached up to the seat and tried to pull himself up. But when he got to his knees the man took hold of his shoulder and dug back into his gut with the brass knuckles, sending Freddy back down to the floorboards.

When the car came to a stop, the man reached over Freddy, opened the door, and pushed Freddy out onto the sidewalk in front of the Fief Building, where his fellow dispatchers were leaving the building for lunch. They watched the car speed off, up the snowy boulevard; they watched Freddy slowly lift himself from the ground, watched him brush the snow from his clothes and his beaten face. They all stood there silently in the downpour of snow and watched Freddy, half hunched over, his breathing still labored, limp by them and enter the lobby. With his head down, Freddy pushed his way through a crowd exiting an elevator, and rode upstairs. When the doors opened on the ninth floor, he walked under the snow-covered glass ceiling of the rotunda and locked himself inside his office. As the snow fell between his window and the window of the empty apartment across the air shaft, he removed from his coat pocket the list that Feldman had given him just this time the day before, opened the drawers to his filing cabinet, removed a thick set of dispatch forms, and spent the next half hour filling them out. Thinking of Evelyn's stillness as she stood in the doorway, thinking of the delicate pliant features of Janice Gould—bruised from being bound, her larynx crushed, her voice snuffed out by a large pair of hands, by Stu Zawolsky's brutish hands—he filled out the forms as he should have done the day before. He prayed for Evelyn's safety; he prayed that she would never know what he had done. When Freddy was through, he bound the paperwork into a casing, stuffed it into the pneumatic tube beside his desk, and pushed it into the sucking current of air. As it streamed away from his fingertips en route to the armory foreman's office, he prayed some more that Evelyn wouldn't be harmed. He didn't know to whom or what he was praying, but he prayed nonetheless. This was all that Freddy cared about. This was what his life amounted to now, to Evelyn's image remaining intact, the image of her, serious and withdrawn, fearing him, there on the top of her steps, looking ready to crush his small pink package.

As soon as Freddy had filed the dispatch forms, he called the number Feldman had given him. The man on the other end of the line said in Benny Rudolph's unmistakable voice, "Who's there?"

"Stillman."

"It's done?"

"Yeah, it's done."

"You got the carbons like we wanted?"

"Yeah."

"Good. Now make yourself scarce."

"What?"

"Get out of the building. Go home. And bring the carbons with you."

"Why?"

"Go home and bring the carbons with you."

"I thought this was it? I thought you were finished with me?"

"Go home, Mr. Stillman. You know the consequences if you don't do as you're told."

The man abruptly hung up.

Freddy nervously gathered the carbon copies of the dispatch forms that he would usually send to his supervisor, neatly folded them together, and then slipped them into an envelope. He put on his coat, his scarf and gloves, and with the envelope in hand, he walked to the elevator bank.

All the way home, Freddy thought he saw pairs of men following him through the storm; he saw them reflected in the windows of his subway car, on the platform of the Eighty-fifth Street station when he exited the train. But, as far as he could tell, he was now alone, and he had never felt more alone knowing that after today, after that episode on Evelyn's stoop, he would never be able to see or speak with her again.

The storm was now the strongest it had been all day. The snow fell into the heavy gusts of wind with greater ease, in large tufts. Like cold clenched fists, the snow landed hard blows on Freddy's head and face. With his hat in his hand, he walked into the wind, into the icy snow with his chin up, his eyes up. He noticed, as he looked to the facades of Celeste Martin's buildings along West Eighty-third Street, that icicles had hardened onto the cheeks and fingers of the gargoyles leaning precariously over the sidewalks. The gargoyles were heavy with snow, the wet pack weighing down on their narrow shoulders and large heads, inside the deep hollows of their sunken eyes; their open hands reached out as if they were laying claim to the face of a small child, as if they were reaching for an invisible, unobtainable object. They reached out as if they wanted to dive and be aloft in the wind for the few moments it would take for them to crash to the ground.

As Freddy approached his building, he could see rafts of ice floating in the river's current; he could see freighters propelling the ice onto the shore; he noticed that when the ice crumbled, it didn't shatter like glass, but broke more like bone, slowly, as if there were sinew strung throughout its crystal lattice. Freddy thought for a moment that he would walk out to the dock and look more closely at the river. He wondered how long a body would take to freeze in icy water, and if it was frozen and hit by a ship if his bones would crush with the consistency of ice. He had read in a novel when he was a boy about a seaman whose boat had been capsized in northern waters, and in the description of his death, the writer made the state of hypothermia seem like a blissful end. There was part of Freddy, an automatic part of him, that wanted to walk onto the dock, to walk without stopping until he was submerged in the current of the river, where his thoughts would drift with the ice as his body slowly turned numb and uncomprehending. But then he thought of Evelyn again, of the letter he had written her early that morning, and something suddenly occurred to him, something that he knew would give him everything he wanted.

Freddy crossed the street to the home of Celeste Martin and knocked on the door. When there was no response, he knocked again. Then again. After the third round of knocks, Freddy stepped back a few feet from the window and, still facing the house, walked down a few steps on the stoop. He looked up and could see standing inside one of the third-story dormer windows Richard Martin. Richard was looking down, but not down onto Freddy. He was looking across the street.

Freddy turned around, to find entering the front door of his building two men wearing dark trench coats and fedoras.

"What is it?" the cook asked when he finally opened the door. His large cheeks and small eyes were downturned.

Freddy turned to Steven, distracted. "I need to see Miss Martin."

"She no see you now."

"I must see her," Freddy said. "It's urgent."

"She no feeling good, no good at all."

"Please, just ask her if she'll see me for a few minutes."

"No," Steven said firmly, shaking his cheeks.

Steven tried to shut the door on Freddy, and Freddy stepped into the threshold before Steven could shut it. He forced his way in, pushing Steven's thin frail body back as if it were part of the door.

"No," Steven said, "you mustn't." He frantically grabbed at Freddy's arm and tried to pull him back outside, but Freddy easily pushed by him.

"I must see her," he said calmly.

Steven threw his hands up. "No matter," he said, shaking his head. "No matter," he pattered. "You see her, but she no see you."

"Where is she?"

"There," Steven said, pointing at the sliding door that led into Benjamin Martin's study. "Suit yourself. Go. You be ashamed. No good will come of it." Steven walked away, back into the kitchen. He slammed the door shut and yelled through it some unkind-sounding words in Chinese.

Freddy stood in the foyer, stubbornly looking at the closed door to the study, wondering if, in fact, he should enter the room. He knew whose room this was and what it meant to Celeste. It was the room to which her father had gone to brood, to paint, to die. It was a room that had been blacked out from the sun as long as Freddy had lived across the street, and as long as he had come to visit Miss Martin's home, the room that had given the entire bottom floor of the house a musty, stuffy, thick odor, as if all the smells from the rest of the house for the past twenty years had gathered inside and festered.

Freddy could hear nothing on the other side of the door. All he could hear was the angry clang of pots coming from the kitchen. He took hold of the brass handle on the door and pushed. He pushed the door into the slot in the wall. A thick odor, surprisingly sweet, unlike the odor he expected to smell, wafted out of the room in a billow of smoke.

Freddy found Celeste Martin dressed in a yellowing crushed silk gown, sprawled out on a purple divan in the center of the room, her gray wig set on a mannequin head. Beside the divan was a pipe that resembled a tall, thin vase with a silver crown at its head. The pipe was freestanding; a long tube ran from the base of the crown to one of Celeste's fingers and was attached to a crooked knuckle by a silver ring. Motionless. Celeste was motionless. Her hair, her real hair, was cropped short, as gray as her wig, and her face was as gray as her hair. If she weren't so obviously haggard, there in the dim light, the way her body was splayed, the way her dress was hiked up around her thighs, she might have appeared sexual. But she *was* old and haggard and the furniture was old and dusty and the paintings of the flowers on the walls were dusty and hung with cobwebs; and haunting portraits of Celeste and Richard as teenagers hung above a desk on the opposite wall, their figures looking so frail that they seemed more like little children than young adults.

"She won't be able to help you right now, Freddy," Richard said from the stairs.

Freddy turned around and looked up. "I'm sorry," Freddy said. "I didn't realize . . ." He looked back at Celeste.

"It's all right," Richard said calmly. Richard walked down to the first floor and took hold of the door and closed it as if he were shutting Celeste away inside a mausoleum. He then took Freddy by the arm to a sitting room just opposite the study. "What was it you wanted to discuss with Celeste?"

"Money," Freddy said. He stepped close to Richard Martin's kind dignified face. "I'm sorry to be so forthright about it, but . . ."

"Yes?"

"It's just that I was going to ask Miss Martin if she would loan me some money to help me out of some trouble I'm in, you see."

"I see."

"It's just that she's been so kind to me in the past, and I don't mean to take advantage of her generosity, but I'm in a very uncomfortable position, a very bad situation, and I . . ."

"How much do you need?"

"Quite a lot, I'm afraid. More than I've ever imagined asking anyone in my entire life."

"Please, Freddy," Richard said gently, "you must calm down." Richard placed his hand on Freddy's shoulder. "Please," he said again.

"Five hundred," Freddy said. "I need five hundred to get me out of this mess. I realize it's a fortune, but, if I don't have it . . . if I don't have it, I don't know what's going to happen to me."

"When do you need it?"

"Immediately."

"I'm not sure if we have that kind of money here in the safe, Freddy."

It suddenly occurred to Freddy as Richard said this, as he nodded his head, that Richard Martin looked almost exactly as he had in that portrait hanging in the study. He was still an innocent. At the end of his life, he was still as innocent as he looked in that painting he had posed for in his youth. Richard tilted his head. "But if it's here, it's yours."

"I don't know how to thank you." Freddy gripped Richard's shoulder and held on to it tightly. Freddy could feel the bones of his arm as if he were gripping a skeleton dressed in a jacket. "I'll get it back to you as soon as I'm able, Richard. I promise."

"No," Richard said, smiling, "I don't expect you will."

"But I will. I promise."

"It's all right, Freddy. It's of no consequence."

"What do you mean?"

Richard gently patted Freddy's hand, slid it off his arm, and feebly walked away. Freddy watched him. He watched him walk out of the room and back to the study. He opened the door, then shut it. After a few minutes, he returned to the sitting room with a handful of nicely stacked bills.

"There's six hundred here," Richard said, handing the money to Freddy. "That's all there was in the safe."

Freddy took the money and held it in his hand. He had never held six hundred dollars all at once before. "I really don't think I'll need more than five hundred."

"Sometimes it's better to have more money than you thought you needed."

Freddy looked at Richard, feeling distracted by the gesture, suddenly feeling as though he had misjudged him. The way Richard was looking at Freddy, he seemed to intimately know exactly what Freddy was about to do. "Why are you doing this?"

"Because you're in trouble and I've found, personally, that the best use for money, whether it be yours or mine, is to remedy troubles. And as far as I can tell, I think, perhaps, your troubles are closer than you think."

"What do you mean?"

Richard looked over his shoulder in the direction of the window that looked onto Freddy's apartment, and then he looked back at Freddy. "I saw them go in," Richard said, suddenly not looking as innocent as he had before.

"Yeah, I noticed."

"Would you like me to call the police?"

"No," Freddy said. "That wouldn't help matters."

"Whatever you think is best," Richard said.

Thinking of the men in his apartment, Freddy wanted to say, I may not need your money after all. But he didn't say this. Instead, he let Richard continue speaking.

"Whatever you've done, whatever has happened, whatever will happen, Freddy," Richard said with some certitude, "God will forgive you."

"You're a kind man," Freddy said as he opened his coat and neatly placed the stack of bills inside his pocket, next to the envelope with the dispatch forms.

"Celeste would want you to have that money," Richard said. "She doesn't like anyone she knows to suffer if she can help it."

"Thank you for your help," Freddy said.

"Godspeed," Richard said, wiping his brow with his handkerchief.

Freddy shook Richard's hand and turned away from him. "I'll see myself out."

Freddy walked out of the Martins' townhouse and stood on its stoop again. He stood on the stoop for a long time, looking across at the windows of his ground-floor apartment, trying to see in. But all he could see was snow and ice forming around the fanciful ironwork of the gates bordering the property. As he walked down from the stoop, all he could think about was the drop from the ninth-story window of the Fief Building to the bottom of the air shaft that separated his former office from Janice Gould's window. He could see himself falling. He could see himself wanting to step out, wanting to waste no time to be with her. He wondered what it was at the origin of this desire. He wished he could explain it to himself, how it was that he needed it, how it was he needed to be used by her. His fate always seemed to be written by such hidden desires; he vanished into such desires, into their intrigues, as if they were unlikely afterlives, in order to find the basic pulse that allowed him to endure what he knew as true. As he walked across the street, he recalled the instant that he knew that he would kill the man who had murdered the woman and her little girl in the French countryside. Kill the man or die trying. And he realized that it was death that he had yearned for at that point in time; it was death, not vengeance, that he had wanted to touch, and that secretly he had wished that the man had fired at him before he had fired at the man.

Chapter 30

After getting a glimpse of Johnny Mann's and Jerzy Roth's corpses being hauled out of the Triple Mark by the medical examiner's men, Faith shared a short taxi ride across town with her photographer. When they reached the newsroom, the shades of Marty Volman's glass-encased office were drawn, the office was lit, and everyone on the floor was watching Marty's shadow pacing back and forth behind the scrim of the shades. Marty had pulled the shades of his office down only once in the past five years, when he had heard the news that his wife had died after getting hit by a car outside their West End apartment building. The time before that was fifteen years ago, when Marty found out that Sam Rapaport had shot himself.

"Someone die?" Faith asked Jonesy, Marty's old sidekick, a small bald man with a gut and a big bow tie. She sounded concerned.

"Aside from the bums you been after all day?" Jonesy flipped, trying to make light of it. "I don't think so."

Faith gave Jonesy an arched brow.

"I don't know," he said more seriously. "I tried talking to him, but he don't want nothing to do with me."

"How long's he been in there like that?"

"Couple of hours, ever since you left. . . . What you say to him?"

"Nothing that would throw him into a stupor as far as I know."

"Well, pay it no mind for now and get to work," Jonesy said, walking away from Faith. "I want to get the late afternoon out early."

"Sure, all right," Faith said, walking in the opposite direction away from Jonesy over to her desk.

Faith wrote up the story on the deaths of Crown, Mann, and Roth, about the disappearance of Elias Eliopoulos and the rumored sale of the Southside Docks to Noel Tersi. She made it a straight reportage with little color, wrote the facts as they had been revealed at Shortz's press conference. She left out the knowledge she had that someone had thrown Boris Lardner from the el platform all those years ago, and that it was most certainly not Victor Ribe. As she wrote, she would occasionally look over her shoulder to peek into Marty Volman's office. A few times when she looked, she could see from his silhouette that he was in there pouring himself drinks, and not from the bottle of seltzer he kept on his desk.

Faith finished the story in about a half hour, tapped the pages into place, and dropped them with Jonesy. Jonesy gave her a smile and wink, snatched hold of a pencil resting behind his ear, and started editing. Faith walked off with her eyes on the drawn shades of Marty's door. It was too big a day for Marty to go under, Faith decided. She needed to know what he knew about Benny Rudolph, needed his take on the photos, the notes, on Shortz, Dubrov, Collins . . . she needed his advice. She went back to her desk and grabbed hold of her attaché, and she walked over to Marty's door.

The loud rap on the glass stopped the bustle around her, and everyone looked over to see what would happen. "Marty," Faith called out into the door, "I'm coming in."

"No! Don't you dare!" Marty screamed out.

"Or what?" Faith screamed back, mocking him a little. Faith shrugged her shoulders for the benefit of those watching, opened the door, walked in, and shut the door behind her. Without an invitation from Marty, she took the same seat she had sat in that morning before she left for the bank. She found Marty sitting at his desk, his body slumped forward, a burned-out cigarette wedged between his fingers, his bottle of seltzer drained, and a bottle of bourbon nearly half empty.

"Take a seat," Marty said to Faith.

"I'm already sitting, Marty."

"Yeah, I see that." Marty sounded more sober than she thought he would from the looks of him. Faith leaned over Marty's desk and took the burned-out cigarette from his fingers and replaced it with a new one.

"So," Faith said, as she lit the cigarette for Marty, "what's brought this on?" Faith couldn't stand to see him so upset, but she wasn't going to let him know it was bothering her. She was expressing her sympathy like a cranky old woman with a soft spot for a warm cuddly animal.

"You wouldn't understand," Marty said.

"Try me."

"No," Marty said, shaking his head.

"Come on, Marty, why are you drunk at this time of the morning? It's a big day out there. You gotta pull yourself together."

"I want no part of it."

"Why not?"

"Because I got pain, cupcake. I got tragic Shakespearean pain, murderous pain, and it ain't gonna go away until I'm dead."

"Marty . . ."

"We'll take it up later. How's about that? Later, when your finger's ready to point to exactly where I'm hurting."

"You're making no sense."

"And ain't it beautiful to sometimes make no sense?" It seemed like an accusation. "What you come in here for?"

"I just got done with the pages on Shortz and the murders and—"

"Hand them over to Jonesy. I'm on holiday."

"I already handed them to Jonesy."

"Then what do you need me for?"

"I've got some questions."

Marty shook his head, his heavy hooded lids half closed. "No, right now, this here is my own desert island until the end of the day. That snow out there ain't nothing but white-hot sand and this bottle of bourbon ain't nothing but my coconut with a straw sticking out of it. And you, my dear kid, ain't nothing but a gorgeous mirage that is ready to fade away right through that magic door there," he said, pointing to the door with his crooked elbow.

"I guess we'll talk about this later when the rescue party's come with the smelling salts."

"Yeah, sure. Come back when they've finished salvaging my head for scrap."

"Have it your way."

As Faith was almost out of his office, Marty said, "I told you, Faith . . ."

Faith turned back. "What you tell me, Marty?"

"I told you you'd be alone on this one. I wasn't kidding," Marty said with a sadness in his voice that Faith had never heard before.

"Yeah, all right," Faith said straight. "I'll tough it out alone, Marty. No skin off my back."

"I wish that part were true, sweetheart."

Faith shook her head in confusion and left Marty to his stupor. She walked back out onto the floor, then walked in the direction of the elevator, wondering what had shaken Marty up so much. She rode down to the basement for the second time that day and walked into the dark corner housing her father's archive. For the second time that day, she went back to R, on the outside chance that there would be a file for Rudolph. She pulled the drawer toward her, and sure enough, a few tabs beyond RIBE, she found RUDOLPH, PI, a thick file. She started looking through the stack of papers—short profiles on gangland figures, cops, politicians, average John Q. Citizens, scams, rackets—and could tell instantly that Rudolph was one of her father's close sources. There were dozens of notes in Sam's hand like the one she had found in the Ribe file on the way to the bank: *BR says the witness is a plant; 789 47th Street, murder weapon under the bed. . . .* It was only when Faith turned to the end of the file that she found what she was looking for. Amid some sloppy notes written on cocktail napkins from the Triple Mark, she found one of Rudolph's business cards. Written on the back, scribbled in pencil, was ITB684. It was the same number as the safety deposit box Sam shared with Rudolph. And suddenly her mood lifted. She popped a Lucky into her mouth and then started sorting through the articles Sam had written on Rudolph's arrest for extortion and his alleged ties to the syndicate. The last article was filed the day before her father died; in it he questioned the credibility of the arresting officers, Dubrov and Collins, on whose testimony Rudolph was sent away. And Faith couldn't help but notice that Rudolph's sentencing had taken place the very day her father supposedly put the gun to his head.

Faith packed the Rudolph file into her attaché and rode back up to the newsroom. A young clerk holding an unmarked package was waiting for her when she reached her desk.

"Miss Rapaport?"

"Are you all right?" Faith asked. The boy's face was pale and his entire body was trembling.

"A big guy in the lobby told me that I was to deliver this to you."

"All right."

"He told me that you were to call this number and tell the person on the other line that you had received it."

"All right," Faith said again, wondering why the boy was worked up.

"He said that I should stand by your desk until you made the phone call."

"Why?"

"For peace of mind. He said that if he found out that you didn't make the call, he would be waiting for me after work. He said that I wouldn't want that to happen."

"I see," Faith said, taking the slip of paper from the boy. "I'll call right away. You can calm down now."

"Thank you, Miss Rapaport. I'll try to. I've just never been . . . I've just never had a man like that . . . He scared me good, Miss Rapaport."

Faith nodded her head and reached for the phone and dialed the number on the slip of paper. It rang a few times and then the same man with the broken-down voice who had called her early that morning answered the phone. "Yeah," he said.

"I've got your package," Faith said.

"Good. Send the clerk away."

Faith placed her hand over the mouthpiece. "Everything's all right now," Faith said.

"Are you sure?"

Faith got back on the phone. "Tell the kid everything's all right. You got him scared half to death." Faith handed the phone to the clerk. "Here, he'll tell you himself."

The clerk took the phone. "Sir? . . . Yes, sir. . . . Thank you, mister." The clerk handed the receiver back to Faith. "Thank you, Miss Rapaport," he said.

Faith waited until the clerk was halfway across the floor, on the way to the men's room, before she said, "What's this all about, Mr. Rudolph?"

"I knew you'd catch on, girlie. You got your father's blood in you, for sure."

"You knew my father well, I see."

"Well enough to know he loved you more than himself, and would have suffered a lifetime of pain before he put a gun to his head. Unless, of course, someone was threatening you."

Faith was quiet. A sadness started to swell in her chest as she thought about what Rudolph just said. "I see you tipped him off pretty often."

"You know the game by now, sister. He used me. I used him. Sam Rapaport didn't get around without putting his nose in it. That's why he was as good as he was. But you know that. You were at his knee while he was at it."

"Yeah," Faith said, not wanting to continue in this way about Sam, "so, what have I got here?"

"That there? That's what I sent your father the day before he was murdered. That there was the thing that got him killed."

"This is what he'd put in that safety deposit box you steered me to?"

"That's right."

"What is it?"

"Some notes I wrote down on behalf of a client."

"That client wouldn't happen to be Boris Lardner, would it?"

"That's right."

"So, whoever killed Pop killed him to get this back?"

"To get that back and because of what he knew."

"Who are we talking about here?"

"That's the curious question, isn't it?"

"You don't know?"

"Sure I know. The same ones who set me up and sent me away for ten years. The same ones who killed Boris Lardner."

"Who?"

"I think you probably already have an inkling."

"The two narcotics cops?"

"That's right. But the question is, if they're involved, who else?"

"All right, who else?"

"Take a look at the file, then bring it over to the Prescot. I'll see you there shortly."

Faith hung up the phone. She turned around in her chair and looked across the floor in the direction of Marty Volman's office. His shadow was in the doorway; it stood there as Faith bundled up and walked to the elevator. Faith rode down to the lobby, headed over to the coffee shop on the corner, took a table in the back, and opened the package.

. . .

As Faith left the building, Marty Volman's phone started ringing. He listened to it ring as he poured himself another shot of bourbon. He slowly drank the bourbon down, and then answered the phone and without saying anything, he listened to the coarse wheezing voice on the other end.

"Have you started packing up the office, Volman?"

"Not yet," Marty said. "I'll wait for her to come back."

"She'll know everything by then. You sure you want to wait around?"

"I'll wait for her to come back and then you'll have everything you want."

"Like I said before, Marty, if you don't run it yourself, the others will."

"It'll be run, don't you worry."

"I want it out before five."

"You'll have it."

"You starting to feel a little what it's like to put the gun to your own head, Marty?"

"Don't worry, I won't give you that much satisfaction."

"Don't get me wrong, Marty, I ain't looking for that kind of satisfaction. That's too quick for satisfaction. I want you to feel it, feel it deep in your gut, in the marrow of your bones. I want you to see it in the faces of everyone who ever had an ounce of respect for you. Now, that's satisfaction, Marty. That's satisfaction."

"Yes, I suppose it is," Marty said deliriously. He pulled the receiver away from his ear and looked at it as Benny Rudolph continued to talk. "I'll be sitting here, stewing," he told the phone.

With the voice trailing away from him like the wake of a very loud boat, Marty pushed the receiver onto its resting place, poured himself another, then splashed the bourbon into the back of his throat.

Chapter 31

After Harry Shortz gave over his office to Tines's men that morning, he decided he didn't want to be there while they turned everything upside down. To avoid the reporters lulling about in the lobby, Harry took the back way out of the State Government Building's South Tower and walked up the road to police headquarters, where he headed downstairs to the Medical Examiner's Office and the city morgue. The dissection room was closed. A few orderlies leaned against the walls in their white lab coats and smoked cigarettes. The man who had been on duty when Freddy was by was no longer there; sitting in the ME's chair was Dr. Ned Bromberg, who handled the homicides that fell into Narcotics' jurisdiction. He had a nasal voice, pink complexion, and gray stubble thickly sprouting out the bottom of his chin.

"Afternoon, Harry."

"Ned."

"What brings you into the tombs?"

"Dead girl."

"You got a name?"

"Gould. Janice Gould. She was brought in yesterday from the Beekman."

"Gould . . ." Dr. Bromberg said as he slipped on his glasses. He opened a file drawer labeled G and fingered through the folders for a minute. "There're Goulds, but no Janice." Dr. Bromberg walked back over to his desk and moved aside a half-eaten bowl of soup and looked through some files on his desk. "You sure about the name?"

"What about Lowenstein, Katrina?"

"Same girl?"

"Yeah."

Bromberg returned to the file cabinet and sorted through the L's. "No," Bromberg said. "You sure she's here?"

"No one's been brought in from the Beekman?"

"I've been here all day today and I haven't heard of anyone. Who was investigating?"

"Two men from the Third. Didn't get their names."

Dr. Bromberg screwed his face up and scratched his chin. "Sorry, Harry. Hope it wasn't anything too pressing."

"No one out of the ordinary was in here today?"

"No one other than you," Bromberg said with a wink.

Harry smiled placidly. He turned to go, then doubled back. "You mind if I use your phone?"

"Go right ahead. Here, I'll give you some privacy. I've got to check on something."

Harry watched Dr. Bromberg walk down the hall and turn the corner. When he turned the corner, Harry picked up the phone.

"Operator."

"Beekman Hotel, please."

"One moment, please."

The phone rang.

"Beekman Hotel for Women."

"The concierge, please."

"Speaking."

"Yes, hello," Harry stammered. "Is this the concierge who was on duty yesterday afternoon?"

"Yes."

"This is Commissioner Shortz calling."

"Yes, hello, Mr. Commissioner. You left in a hurry yesterday. I hope everything is all right."

"I was just wondering if you were able to find out the name of the moving company for me."

"Hold on just a moment, Mr. Commissioner."

Harry held on and looked over a bulletin board covered in photos of corpses in various states of decay and dissection. Some of the eyes on the bodies were open, staring at Harry.

"Mr. Commissioner?"

"Yes, I'm here."

"Yes, the moving company is Santini. U. Santini Moving and Storage. South End eight zero eight."

"Thank you, you've been very helpful."

"Don't mention it."

Harry hung up the phone and then lifted the receiver.

"Operator."

"South End eight zero eight."

"One moment, please."

The phone rang.

"U. Santini," a man answered. It was the confident voice of a man who moved heavy objects.

"Is this U. Santini Moving and Storage?"

"That's right."

"Tell me, were you the ones who did a pickup at the Beekman Hotel for Women yesterday for . . . ?"

"Who wants to know?"

"This is the super over at the Beekman. I was holding some things down in the basement for the resident and was wondering how I could have them sent over to you. Can you do a pickup?"

"No. The girl, she just came by not more than an hour ago and picked up her things," the man said, his voice turning chatty. "She's all paid up."

Harry was silent for a long moment.

"You there?"

"Yeah, I'm here. Just so I know . . . just so I know I got the right girl, we're talking about a redhead, good-looking, young—about twenty?"

"That's her."

"Her name was Gould?"

"No, Lowenstein's the name I've got."

"Katrina Lowenstein?"

"That's right."

"That's the one. I was looking at the wrong room. . . . She leave a forwarding address?"

"No. She came by in a truck. With her fiancé. His name he told me, if I can only remember. A writer, he said he was."

Harry reached into his jacket pocket and pulled out his small notebook. It was still turned to that page. "Greely?"

"That's right, Greely. Said he made movies, but I never heard of him."

"And they didn't give any hint as to where they were going?"

"They were heading out west, they said. The girl, she was gonna be in a picture. But I'll tell you, they had a roll of cash as big as my fist. They could have been going anywhere in hell they wanted to."

"You don't say."

"She gave me a nice tip. Nice young girl. Kind of funny, though."

"How so?"

"Just funny like young girls tend to be. She left behind a package for someone to pick up, but said I could have it if he didn't show. I asked if he knew it was here. She said no. I said how's this person gonna know it's here then? And she said she had a feeling he would find it."

"Did she say who?"

"The name's on the package."

"Would you mind telling me? Someone was by here the other day looking for her and inquired about a package."

"No, not at all. Just hang on a second."

Harry hung on. His heart was beating. Harry could feel his body pressing outward. Inflating with consternation and air. He could hear on the other end of the phone the man fumbling with the receiver. "Shortz," the man said when he got on the phone. "Just like the commissioner."

"You don't say," Harry said again like a nervous tic.

"Was that the name of the person who was by looking for the package?"

"As a matter of fact it was. I'll get in touch with him right away and send him down. You've been very helpful."

Harry took U. Santini's address and hung up.

Harry hailed a cab outside the morgue and was driven to the warehouse district in South End. As they slowly moved over the thickening pack of snow, Harry wondered when the people behind this decided to break the news to the press about his affair, about the dope they would eventually find in the cellar of the Ten Lakes house, about the real reason he had released Boris Lardner that spring.

U. Santini stood in the grated shadows of the Eastbend Bridge two blocks from the river. Harry asked the cabby to wait for him and headed inside. He found standing over a counter piled in paperwork a short husky man in overalls, a fat wet cigar clenched between mustard-yellow teeth. Leaning up against the counter was a tall thin rectangular package wrapped in brown paper and marked *Shortz.* The second the man looked at Harry he grabbed hold of the cigar with his fingers and pointed the stub at Harry.

"Hey, I was just joking with the super at the Beekman that this package had your name on it." He turned the cigar on the package. "What are the chances that the name on it actually was yours?"

Not wanting the man to recognize his voice from the phone, Harry didn't say anything; he gave the man a self-important grin, signed for his package, and made his way back to the taxi. With the package resting on top of his shoes, he gave the cabby the address of his East End townhouse.

Beverly was sitting in the living room just off the front entrance reading the afternoon edition of the *Herald* and listening to the radio when Harry walked in. The boys were at her feet on the floor playing a quiet game of checkers. When Beverly saw Harry, she got up from her chair and shut the boys into the room. "The news," she said quietly, taking hold of Harry, "it's too much to take in."

"Yeah," Harry said listlessly. The feeling of Beverly's arms hugging him underneath his coat suddenly felt more suffocating to him than anything he had experienced so far that morning.

"Father's been trying to reach you at the office for the better part of an hour. He said he hasn't been able to get through."

"I'm sure he wasn't the only one."

"Shouldn't you be back there?" Beverly let go of Harry.

Harry took off his coat and hung it on the rack beside the door. "Come with me," he said. Harry took hold of his package with one hand and took hold of Beverly with the other.

"What have you got there?"

Harry walked Beverly upstairs to his study, set her down in his desk chair, leaned the package against the wall, and shut the door.

"What is it, Harry? You have such a pained look about you."

Harry kneeled down in front of Beverly, took her hands, and looked over the fine lines that had etched their way into Beverly's face in the twenty-two years they had known each other. "There's something I need to tell you. Something I wished I never would have to tell you."

Beverly took hold of Harry's chin. "Whatever it is, you have nothing to fear from me, Harry. You look as though you've died and left me a widow."

When Beverly said this, Harry broke away from her and stood up.

"Oh, Harry, come," Beverly said in a tone obviously intended to diffuse Harry's mood. She stood up and took hold of Harry's waist again, looked up to his eyes. "I have to say—I'm always so happy I married a man from humble stock, but for Christ's sake, sometimes you carry your life about as though you had a ton of coal weighing down on your back. If you hadn't chosen to be a man of the law, you would have undoubtedly been destined for the robes of a priest. So serious."

"I hope you'll be able to laugh at what you just said in a minute."

"I'm laughing already," Beverly said, and then she craned her neck forward and laughed for Harry as though she were laughing politely at a bad joke told at a cocktail party.

"Just be a little serious for a minute."

"Please, Harry, if you and I were meant for serious conversation, there never would have been a marriage," she joked. "You married me because you knew I was frivolous, and don't deny it."

Harry could feel his mood lightening. He could feel the full effect of his wife's gall take hold of him and fought against the feeling because he knew she didn't really mean what she was saying. "Please, Beverly, just for a minute let me be grave and sullen, all right?"

"All right," she relented. "Be a bore. Go on."

Without pause, Harry blurted it out. "I was unfaithful to you, Beverly."

Beverly's face instantaneously transformed. The smile that had just radiated her face, the glint in her eyes, instantly deadened, and she let go of Harry. "When?"

"A long time ago," Harry said as Beverly sat back down in his chair.

"When?"

"Shortly after we were married."

Beverly took a moment with the news and looked down at her hands in her lap. "Were there any other times?"

"No," Harry said. "I swear. But—"

"I don't want to know details," Beverly said, cutting him off.

Harry could feel Beverly drifting from him for a moment.

"This affair you had, was it with a woman named Lowenstein?" Beverly asked.

The pit of Harry's stomach felt like a block of ice splitting apart.

Beverly stood up from her seat and gazed out the window for a moment, out onto the snowy street. "Why in the world bring it up now after all these years?"

"How did you know about it?"

"Don't be silly, Harry," she snapped. "*How did I know?* Do you really think a hard woman like that, a woman who was madly in love with you, would let you get away without first trying to wreck your life? Please. Are you really such a nincompoop? I thought you were a man of the world. You're supposed to have the mind of a detective, for crying out loud."

"How much do you know?"

"Everything."

"Everything?"

"Every-thing."

"How long have you known?"

Beverly turned on Harry. "I've been sending that woman money every month for almost twenty years."

"You've done what?"

"Why in the world do you think you haven't heard hide nor hair of her for all these years? Do you really think a sensible woman in her right mind would have let you get away with what you did . . . without wanting to at least torment you? Especially a man like yourself, with responsibility, with stature?"

Harry took the seat Beverly abandoned and looked at her with a dumb expression on his large masculine face.

"Don't get mute on me now, Harry. I want to know why now. Why now is this coming up out of your mouth?"

"Because . . ." Harry said carefully.

"Out with it."

"Because, in a matter of no time, everyone's going to know about it."

"Oh . . ." Beverly said as though the wind had been knocked out of her. She started shooing Harry with her hand, motioning that he should get up from his chair. Harry stood up and allowed Beverly to sit. When she sat, she looked mortified.

Harry maintained his respectful silence.

"Explain," Beverly said strictly.

"I'm not sure I can, fully," Harry said, now keeping his distance.

"Then explain what you know."

And Harry did just that. He told her everything that he knew.

My God," Beverly said when Harry was through. "You just may be finished," she continued, the weight of it all sinking in a little bit deeper.

Harry nodded in agreement. The room became quiet.

"Finished with you too?" Harry whispered a little pathetically after a thorough silence.

Beverly didn't answer at first, then shook her head.

"You mean that?"

"I think so."

"You're certain?"

"Pretty certain."

Harry slowly got back down on his knees. "Bev, why didn't you ever let on that you knew?"

Beverly reached out and touched Harry's face. "I just sort of wanted to let it go."

"Do you think you can do it again?"

"I think so."

"You're certain?"

"Pretty much so."

Harry paused. "There'll be rough times."

"They'll be rough times with you, Harry. I can live with that."

"I certainly hope so, because I know I couldn't live with it any other way."

"Then I guess we're stuck with each other." Beverly leaned forward and took hold of Harry's broad shoulders. "As long as you got me, you're a rock, Harry, and I'm not letting anyone take a sledgehammer to you."

"What about your father?"

"What about him?"

"How will I break it all to him? How will I look him in the eye and tell him . . ."

"About the affair?"

"Yeah."

"About that, well, he already knows."

Harry leaned back on his heels away from Beverly's arms.

"Where do you think I got the money to pay off Miss Lowenstein, Harry?"

"He knows."

"He's known from the beginning."

Harry shook his head. "Well, how will I tell him the rest? He'll be disgraced."

"He'll be more disappointed than disgraced," Beverly said, looking Harry in the eye. She took a pair of scissors from Harry's desk and reached for the package. "If you like, I'll give him the news, soften the blow."

"No," Harry said.

Beverly clipped away the twine holding the package together and removed the paper to find in a gold-leaf grand baroque frame a painting of a young man with cold eyes, a thin smile, and a crooked nose. Stuck within the corner of the frame was a note.

"It resembles you," Beverly said about the painting as she pulled the note from the corner. "Though . . ." She looked at the painting, at Harry, and back at the painting, her tone a little lighter than before. "You look a little sinister." She handed Harry the note. It was from Katrina.

"Dear Harry," Harry read aloud. *"Mom painted this a long time ago. I kept it to remind me of the bum that broke her heart. I thought you should have it to mull over. I've lived with it long enough. You now have back all that you gave her—the ring, the house—everything except me. I expect that you're in for plenty of troubles and anguish soon. I hope it does to you what it did to Mom. Good riddance, Katrina."*

"Tough girl," Beverly said.

"Yeah," Harry said. He lifted the painting from the floor and walked over to the study's closet. He opened the door and placed the painting down by his shoes and shut it in.

Beverly then went to the closet and retrieved the painting.

"What are you doing?" Harry asked.

"As a reminder," Beverly said. She placed the painting on the mantel of the fireplace. "I'll hang it later, myself."

"You've got a funny way about you, dear."

Beverly shrugged her shoulders. "Why don't we take the boys to Mom and Dad's? You can talk things over with Father and decide on a lawyer to represent you."

Harry nodded his head.

"Tomorrow, you'll hold a press conference and drop out of the race. They don't deserve the likes of you anyway."

Harry nodded some more.

"And then . . . you'll take some time off work and we'll go to Europe for a few months."

Harry continued to nod.

"Until this blows over, I'll make the decisions."

Harry followed his wife out of the study into the living room, and Harry sat with his two sons and listened to Louis Armstrong play "West Side Blues" on the radio. Beverly went into the foyer and dialed her father and told her that she, Harry, and the kids would be by for dinner.

Chapter 32

After Victor left the note for Elaine with the Ansonia's concierge, he met the two grizzled men at the hotel's entrance and walked with them to their car. Snow and ice covered the windshield so that when they settled in—Victor in the back, Sunshine and the moper up front—it was as if the three men were tucked away inside an igloo. "I see they did a nice job on you there," Sunshine said to Victor.

"Why wasn't anyone around to take care of those two?" Victor asked.

"The boss wanted you to meet the men that killed Lardner."

Victor looked confused.

"Look at him," the moper said. "He looks like one of those cartoon characters who got it in the head with a frying pan."

"But weren't those the two cops who found me in Boris's apartment after I killed Klempt?"

"So you remember them. The boss thought, being as mellow as you were, you might have forgotten. He wanted to refresh your memory, so he let them in on where you were."

"No, I remember them, more or less. Except their names."

"Dubrov and Collins. Klempt, he was their third wheel."

"How do you know it was them?"

"We got pictures."

"What?"

"Yeah, we got pictures."

"From who?"

"Mann and Roth."

"They had 'em in this big vault in the cellar of the club," the moper said. "Nice vault, too," he said, turning to Sunshine.

Sunshine nodded his head. "It's true. Nice vault."

Victor looked at the two of them with an eyebrow propped up on his forehead. "Why would they give them to you?"

"They won't be needing them anymore," the moper said squarely.

"What's that supposed to mean?"

"It means they won't be needing them anymore," the moper said again with a little levity in his voice. He nearly cracked a smile.

Sunshine could see how Victor was looking at the moper a little funny. "I can see you notice something a little different about my other half here."

"Nothing out of the ordinary."

"He had a good day with the cards."

The moper pulled the corners of his mouth back nearly to the tips of his ears and beamed at Victor.

"He beat me at one hand," Sunshine went on. "He gets like this when he wins a hand. He suddenly gets a little mouse running rampant on his go-wheel."

"It was a beautiful hand, Vic. You should have seen it. Just beautiful."

Victor nodded with his mouth a little open. "Yeah . . ." Victor said, letting a moment pass for the moper's enthusiasm. "Were Mann and Roth, were they the ones who called Boris's murder?"

"That's neither here nor there," the moper said.

"You mean you don't know, is what you mean."

"Exactly," the moper said. "Exactly."

"So who are you two in all this anyway?"

"Us?" The two grizzled men looked at each other. "We're just a couple of bums who do dirty work," Sunshine said.

"Businessmen," the moper said, pulling down on the lapels of his coat.

"In business for who?"

"Would we be in this business if you were meant to know that, Victor?" the moper said as though Victor had just sworn in front of a nun.

"I suppose not."

"Very perceptive."

"Yeah, all right. . . . So, you're saying those two cops . . ."

"That's right," the moper said. "That we know. Those two, plus the one you did away with."

"Here, I'll show you," Sunshine said.

"Allow me," the moper said.

"Go ahead, have your fun while it lasts."

The moper turned back to Victor. "I live for winning hands."

The moper had a black briefcase sitting on the front seat. He undid the clasp, slipped out a couple of pictures, and then handed them to Victor one by one.

"You at least know why they did it?" Victor asked as he looked over the photos of Dubrov, Collins, and Klempt sending Boris Lardner to his death.

The two men shook their heads again. "All in good time, Victor," Sunshine said, looking at his watch.

"When's that time coming?"

"Right now, as a matter of fact."

"Where?"

"At the Prescot Building, inside the shoe repair shop."

The moper stepped out of the car and brushed the snow off the windshield with the sleeve of his coat. When he was through and back in his seat, Sunshine turned over the engine and started driving down Central Boulevard.

Just as Sunshine turned the car's engine over, Benny Rudolph entered Sidney Lardner's shoe repair shop inside the paint-chipped lobby of the Prescot Building. It was a quarter to one.

Sidney stood behind a messy glass display case full of galoshes. The walls were covered with loafers, square-toed oxfords, and an assortment of wing tips. The shop smelled like leather and polish. A couple of young men dressed in cloth aprons and black knit yarmulkes cobbled away in the back room while Sidney and Benny faced each other at the counter.

"So, start talking," Sid said quietly.

"Not so fast." Benny, who was carrying a black attaché, placed the attaché on the display case of galoshes and removed his wet coat and hat. He looked at his watch. "We're expecting company."

"What kind of company?"

"A couple of people whose lives you helped change forever."

"What's that supposed to mean?"

With the back of his hand, Benny wiped away some cold green snot from his upper lip. "You like to pass yourself off as an upright guy, don't you, Sid?"

"I ain't done nothing wrong."

"Then why is it you and I are sitting here talking to each other today? Can you tell me that?"

"I thought that was clear. I thought you were going to help me finger Shortz for killing Boris."

"Is that really what you thought?"

"That's what we talked about yesterday, right?"

"You think that's why I wanted to come here and talk to you today? You think that's why you spent the day sweating this meeting out? Wondering whether or not you should go hide your head somewheres? Is that why you had your girlfriend follow Victor Ribe around town yesterday?"

"I don't know what you're talking about."

"Sure you do, Sid. You know exactly what I'm talking about." Benny looked at his watch again.

"Who are you expecting?"

Benny Rudolph took a deep breath that wheezed on its way in, then out. He breathed in as if the inhalation of air filling his chest would somehow clear up the rasp in his voice and help him breathe more easily. Benny Rudolph didn't know it as a scientific fact, but he knew he was dying. Slowly, as in sooner than later. He knew that there was something growing in his throat and his lungs, something that was making it harder for him to breathe, harder to talk, something that felt like a small animal lodged in his windpipe, a small animal that was stealing his air, taking a clear lively breath with each of his own. It sometimes left him gasping.

"Tell me, Sidney," Benny labored, "why is it after all these years you can't call it bygones? Why do you care what Victor Ribe does with his life?"

"What do you mean? Everything I know tells me Ribe killed Boris. It was only yesterday that you got me thinking maybe that wasn't the case."

"You're good at this, Sid, you know that? You're good at looking me right in the eye when you say things like that."

"You're crazy."

"Maybe." Benny laughed a little.

"Who are you?"

"Me? I'm the ghost of Christmas past. That's who I am."

"You are crazy."

"Your brother tell you that he hired a shamus to keep an eye out after he got taken in by Shortz all those years ago?"

"No, I didn't know."

"That's because I told him not to tell you."

"Why's that?"

"Because I was that shamus looking out for your brother, and I told him not to tell you anything about me."

"On account of what?"

"Now you're starting to look the way I expected you'd look."

"So you did some legwork for Boris. What of it?"

"Nervous, Sid. You suddenly look nervous, like I thought you might."

"You're not good at getting to the point, are you?"

Benny looked at his watch again, then leaned onto his attaché with his elbow so that his face was close enough to Sid's that Sid felt uncomfortable enough to pull away. "You and Boris were on the outs for a number of years is what I know. Didn't talk, didn't write, didn't even really love each other all that much. Isn't that so?"

Sidney, visibly angered, pressed the soft pouch of his belly against the counter and contorted his face as though he had just swallowed a spoiled piece of meat. "Who are you to say what my brother was to me?" Sidney pushed at the counter, pushed himself away from Benny, and pointed to the door. "I want you to leave."

"That ain't gonna happen, and you know it."

"Then I'm calling the cops."

"Go right ahead. I got plenty to share with cops."

"What, for instance?"

"Boris, he told me that when he didn't want you in on his business, you stopped talking to him."

"I never wanted in on Boris's dope business. I wouldn't have gotten involved in any of that nonsense."

Benny clicked open the clasps of his attaché as if he had just cracked a safe. He pulled out an old envelope and from the envelope he pulled out an old letter. "This is a pretty angry letter you wrote your brother. Says here that if he didn't let you in on his business, you were going to rat him out to the bureau. That you were going to go to Commissioner Shortz yourself and tell him everything Boris was into. Isn't that what you said in this letter?" Benny held the letter up to Sid's face. "Don't you know, Sid, you should never put things like this in writing."

"Where'd you get that?"

"From Boris, who else?" Benny Rudolph's face was solid. He stared at Sidney until Sidney couldn't take it any longer. Sidney looked over his shoulder into the back room where the boys were working. "Moishe, Aaron!" he yelled back. The two boys stopped what they were doing and looked at Sid. "That's it, you're done for the day." He walked into the workroom. "C'mon, get your coats on and get out of here. I'm closing up early." The boys looked at him a little dumbstruck, then sheepishly looked Benny over some. "I said I'm closing up. Out with the both of you already!" The boys quickly removed their aprons, removed their coats and hats from two hooks on the wall, and then started out. When they stepped out into the lobby of the building, Sidney locked the door behind them, then took his place by the counter. "Like I said yesterday, if you're looking for money, you came to the wrong place."

"I already told you, Sidney, I'm not interested in money."

"Then what are you after?" he asked, pointing his nose to Benny's attaché, into which Benny had replaced the letter.

"I told you, Sid, I'm looking to tie up loose ends. I'm looking to put everything right."

"What do you want me to say? Yeah, I wrote that letter. Yeah, I was angry with Boris for not letting me in on his business. Yeah . . ."

"Yeah," Benny said, "and you ratted your own brother out to Shortz is what you did."

"Yeah, I ratted Boris out, okay? He was an ungrateful son of a bitch, my brother. No good. No good at all."

"And the next thing you know, you got his death on your conscience. Isn't that right?"

Sidney looked at Benny with his fat eyes. He nearly looked like he was going to spit in Benny's face. "I raised that kid with no help from no one. I raised him up from nothing, and what did he give me in return? I deserved a little respect, a little compensation."

"You got him killed, Sidney."

"Yeah," Sidney said, "all right, I got him killed. But that's not what I wanted. I didn't want him dead. I just wanted him . . . I wanted him sitting in a jail cell, biding his time for a few years. That's all. Nothing more. To teach him a lesson. I never expected that he would end up dead like that."

Benny laughed at Sid again. "You're a good liar, Sidney. Real good. Look at yourself. Can you see yourself?" Benny pointed to a mirror behind the counter. "Take a look. Not a stitch of guilt on that face of yours. Lots of self-pity, but not a stitch of guilt."

Sidney wouldn't turn around. "What do you want from me?"

"What do I want from you? I want your confession. I want your picture in the paper for everyone to know that you set your own brother up for murder is what I want."

"All because you got an angry letter from one brother to another? Because I handed him over to the cops?" Sidney laughed at Benny now. "I don't think that's going to happen."

Benny stood up straight and lifted his brow. "You think that's all I got?" Benny said, breathing hard. He opened his briefcase again and took out a couple of photographs. "You know who these clowns are, don't you?" He showed Sidney a couple of pictures of Ira Dubrov, Pally Collins, and Maurice Klempt. They along with Sid were sitting at a table in the window of a deli.

"Who took those?"

"It doesn't matter where I got 'em. I got 'em."

"What of it? I already told you I ratted my brother out. So, I'm talking to those cops."

"Who do you think killed your brother, Sid?"

"I don't know. Those cops? Those cops, they sat me down and asked me about Boris's operation. About how it worked. I told them what I knew."

"That's what you think, huh?"

"That's what I know for a fact. We were sitting there talking about Boris. I clued them into what he was doing, what he told me he was doing, how he was doing it." Sidney now looked more than nervous. He was distressed.

As Sidney fidgeted with a stray tattered shoelace, both Victor Ribe and Faith Rapaport began knocking on the door of Sidney's shoe repair shop. "What's he doing here?" Sid asked.

"I asked him to come."

"Who's he with?"

"She's come to take your confession."

"She don't look like no priest to me."

"I thought you were a Hebe?"

"I am. We don't do confessions."

"We're gonna make an exception with her."

Benny Rudolph brushed aside his jacket and showed Sidney his gun. "Be a good kid and don't run out on me." Benny gestured with his head to the door. "Go let them in and draw the blinds."

Sidney did as he was told. He walked over to the door, his face stricken in a grimace, and he let them in. Victor and Faith looked at each other as they crowded into the small shop; they looked at Sidney, around the sloppy shoe repair shop, at Benny. Sidney drew the blinds on the windows facing the lobby.

"Benny Rudolph?" Faith said to Benny.

"That's me, sister."

"Benny?" Victor said, approaching Benny. He placed his hand on Benny's shoulder and said to him quietly, "How is it that you . . . ?"

Benny leaned toward Victor and whispered in his ear, "Let's save it for later, all right?"

"Whatever you say," Victor said as he took off his coat. "What's with the voice?"

"Later."

"Sure, all right," Victor said as he stepped away to a stool by the wall of shoes.

"Who's this?" Faith asked, pointing to Sid.

"That there is Boris Lardner's brother, Sidney." Benny turned to Sid. "I think you know Victor, Sid. This here, this is Faith Rapaport, your confessor."

"What's that supposed to mean?" Faith said.

"It means Sid here is gonna take up at least a couple of paragraphs for your piece in the late edition."

"All right. I'll take what I can get."

"We'll get to that right now, as a matter of fact. Sidney?" Benny waved Sid back to his spot behind the counter. "Stand right where you were so I can see you nice and clear."

"Mr. Big Shot," Sid said under his breath. "Always feel like you got the upper hand, don't you?" He walked back around the counter and stood in front of Benny with his face looking like it was going to melt onto his case full of galoshes.

"It appears," Benny said, "that Sid here was palling around with these three dopes before his brother got it." Benny handed Faith the picture he had just shown Sidney.

"These are the bureau men?"

Benny pointed them out. "Collins, Dubrov, Klempt."

"You don't say."

"I do say."

"Why would you do that?" Victor asked Sid.

"You want to let me in on what it is you think I know?" Sid said to Benny.

"Victor," Benny said.

Victor with a great deal of satisfaction removed from an envelope the pictures given to him by the two grizzled men. He walked over to Sid's counter and laid them out. Faith watched Victor's tired and broken face as he looked Sidney over. "You set up your own brother?" Victor said to Sid. "And then were calling for my head?" Victor stood there in Sid's face with his brow knit, grinding his teeth together.

"It wasn't like that," Sid said as he looked over the pictures. "It wasn't like that, I swear it. I honest to God never knew it was them."

"Then who did you think it was?" Benny asked.

"For all I knew it was this bum. It didn't matter who it was. It just was."

"Save it for the afterlife, Sid."

"There ain't no afterlife where I come from."

"Then all the more reason to shame you here and now."

"What's this all about?" Faith asked.

"He gave his brother up to Shortz is what it's about," Benny said. "I been thinking about it for all these years—it all started with him, with Sid Lardner's petty impish ambition. From inside this little man, from inside the little mind and heart of Sid Lardner," Benny said with the fingers of his right hand pinched together tight, "all this unraveled. Boris got it. Victor got sent away for his murder. I got sent away in a frame. And you, dearest, lost your pop. All because this schmuck wanted a piece of Boris's dope trade." Benny laughed. "And look at what he ended up with." Benny lifted his arms and waved at all the shoes. "Shoes. Smelly, broken shoes."

"It's a living," Sid said.

Benny opened his attaché again and handed Faith the letter Sid had written to Boris all those years ago. "Make sure you run this with all the other goodies." Faith took the letter and put it in her bag.

"My brother was no angel," Sid said as he watched Benny hand the letter to Faith.

"No, he wasn't. He was a bad character who probably deserved what he got. So it probably brought you a great deal of satisfaction to watch him go down for the fall."

"Now what is it you're going on about?"

"Don't you love it how this guy is so persistent?" Benny said to Victor and Faith as he reached back into his attaché.

"Not again," Sid said.

Benny had nothing but a big smile on his face as he produced a photo of Sid standing in the crowd on the el platform as Maurice Klempt attacked Victor with his gun. "How about that, Sid?" Benny showed the picture to Victor, then showed it to Sid.

"Yeah, all right," Sid said, sounding defeated, "you win. You got me." Sidney threw up his hands and sat down on a stool. "I give up."

"Good."

"What are you gonna do with me?"

"I'll think about it. But for now, get."

"Get where?"

"Back there. Get." Benny walked around the counter and followed Sid into the back room. "Stay in there until I tell you otherwise."

Benny shut the door to the back room and locked it. He then handed the photo of Sid on the el platform to Faith. As she looked it over, he said, "Now, as for you, girlie, you seeing this picture full and clear?"

"I think so."

"Why don't you let Victor here in on it?"

"Yeah, sure," she said, looking over to Victor, who was back in his seat by the wall. "I think he deserves that much."

Victor leaned forward and listened as Faith's eyes jumped back and forth between him and Benny.

"Sid there," Faith started hesitantly as she pulled a pad and a pen out from her bag and started writing, "he ratted out his brother to Shortz."

"That much we got figured out," Benny said to Victor.

"Shortz, in turn," she said, looking to Benny for confirmation, "had Boris hauled in for peddling narcotics."

"That's right."

"Shortz then twisted Boris into knots," Faith said to Victor, "until he turned informant. Because, for the first time since he'd become commissioner, Shortz thought he had a clear shot at getting an indictment on the syndicate. But before Boris gave anything up," she said, glancing to Benny, "Boris hired Mr. Rudolph to keep an eye on Shortz and his boys, hoping he'd be able to get himself out of his predicament with a little dirt."

Benny grunted an affirmation this time.

"It just so happened," Faith continued, "Benny here got lucky. He found out that the narcotics cops investigating the Triple Mark—Dubrov, Collins, and Klempt—were on the take, keeping the syndicate in business. Then, to top it off, he found out—from some

South End whore—that Shortz, once upon a time, had played a little hanky-panky with a Hungarian prostitute. Before the affair ended, Shortz had knocked her up, and instead of doing the gentlemanly thing, instead of leaving his loaded wife, he bought the whore and the baby a house in the country and said goodbye and good luck."

"And good riddance," Benny added.

"Right," Faith said. "It turned out the woman didn't like the arrangement one bit and that Shortz had bullied her into it. She, being so angry and bitter about the whole thing, told Benny everything he wanted to know when he found her. He let Boris in on it all, and then Boris went to Shortz and let him in on the fact that he knew. To shut Boris up, Shortz let him off the hook, no strings attached. The charges were dropped and Boris was pardoned. But . . ."

"Enter Mann and Roth," Benny said to Victor. "You heard of Mann and Roth?"

Victor nodded.

"Mann and Roth didn't buy it," Faith continued. "They didn't believe Boris was off the hook for a second. They thought it was some sort of a ruse. They thought Shortz had let him go so that he could inform on them from the inside. So, Mann and Roth, they blackmailed their bureau boys with pictures of them on the take, pictures of them having a little fun of their own, with some of the girls up at the Triple Mark. Thinking it might be the end of the good life, thinking they might get thrown in jail, Collins, Dubrov, and Klempt . . ." Faith paused for a second and turned to Benny. "It was Mann and Roth who had the pictures taken of Boris getting thrown off the el that day, wasn't it? To keep Dubrov, Collins, and Klempt in line for the future."

Benny nodded. "You got it."

"Yeah . . ." Faith turned back to Victor. "Anyway, Collins, Dubrov, and Klempt, they threw Boris off the el. But something went wrong that day. Before Boris took the dive down, he reached into Klempt's pocket and pulled out his wallet. Klempt must have figured out what happened and went down to the street . . . probably to get the wallet off Boris's body. But when he saw you working Boris over yourself, in front of that crowd, he decided to wait. When you ran out of the shop, he followed you up to the el and tried to get the wallet back, but ended up getting himself kicked onto the tracks."

"So that's how it was," Victor said, looking to Benny.

"That's how it was," Benny said.

"With Klempt dead," Faith went on, "Dubrov and Collins figured it was an easy frame job to make a dope fiend out as the killer. They supplied an eyewitness, got you convicted, and sent you upstate for their crime."

Victor just sat in his chair rubbing at the side of his face.

"Sam Rapaport's little girl, you are," Benny said with enthusiasm to Faith.

"Now, let me see if I got this part right," Faith said, turning to Benny. "That same day, the day Boris got it, when Dubrov and Collins went to Boris's apartment to arrest Victor, they found some papers that linked Boris to you, notes that you made that linked Dubrov and Collins to Mann and Roth."

"That's right."

"When they told Mann and Roth about it, Mann and Roth cooked some books to make it look like you were getting paid by them to bully druggists into taking part in their action?"

Benny nodded his head.

"And based on that fabricated evidence, Dubrov and Collins went to a judge for a search warrant and ransacked your office and your apartment, looking for your notes. But you had them locked away in a safe place."

"That's right."

"At International Trust Bank."

"That's right."

"Where you and Sam shared a safety deposit box."

"Right as rain."

"And when they caught up with you and shook you down?"

"I told them I didn't know what they were talking about. They had a good laugh and then threw the cuffs on me."

"And the only one who knew the truth at that point was Sam?"

Benny turned to Victor. "You remember Sam Rapaport, don't you, Victor?"

"Yeah, sure," Victor said to Faith. "He was the only one who took the time to print my side of things."

"What I don't get," Faith said to Benny, while nodding at Victor, "is how they knew that my father had your notes."

Benny stopped the conversation for a second while he cleared his throat. "That," he said after a moment, "I'm not sure you want to know."

"Why not?"

"Because it's going to make you feel a bitterness you probably never felt before."

"Thanks for the concern," Faith said, "but I'd like to hear it all the same if that's all right with you."

"Like I said, you ain't gonna like it, kid."

"I'm listening."

"So be it." Benny took another dramatic pause. "Dubrov and Collins, they knew that your dad and me played at it together. They knew I handed your father stories for a little extra cash in hand."

"How's that?"

"Things only I could know about he ended up knowing," Benny said as he tugged on his ear. "Sam gave me names—Bald Archibald, Billy Runyon . . . When I'd see the ANB boys around town, they'd rib me with the names Sam gave me. Anyway, Dubrov and Collins, they suspected that if I'd talked with Sam, the story would be going through Volman. And they suspected right."

"Marty?"

"Marty Volman."

That shut Faith up. All of a sudden, Marty's histrionics that afternoon made sense. That thing he'd said about pointing the finger at his pain made sense. She waited through a few moments of silence to let it sink in, but she still couldn't believe it. "You don't know that for sure, do you?"

Benny looked into Faith's eyes and slowly nodded his head. Benny opened his attaché again and reached in.

"How?"

"Because I know that your pop turned the story in to Volman. He wrote me a note saying so."

Faith paushed before she said, "You have that note?"

"No, but I got something better than the note." Benny pulled out a handwritten copy of the story itself with a note attached. He handed the note to Faith, and she recognized her father's handwriting. *Marty, Run this in the morning edition. If you need me, I'm keeping my head down at home. SR.* And then nearly everything she had just recited to Benny appeared to be there in his story.

"Sorry, kid."

"Why didn't you ever show this to anyone?"

"I just found it myself."

"Then where did you get it?"

"Where I got everything else."

"Where?"

"From Mann and Roth's vault down in the cellar of the Triple Mark."

"How'd you manage that?"

Benny just smiled.

"You didn't know they were gunned down this morning?"

"Yeah, I heard," Benny said, shaking his head. "Such a shame."

"You don't seem too broken up."

"Maybe because I somehow expect people like that to get what they're good at giving."

"I see. . . ." Faith all of a sudden looked a little disturbed by

Rudolph, but shrugged it off. "So what you're saying, then, is that Marty Volman told—"

"What I'm saying is that when Marty Volman realized that he might go the way of Boris Lardner, he killed the story. He buried the evidence that would have gotten all those bastards—Mann, Roth, Eliopoulos, Dubrov, Collins, and Shortz."

Faith took a pause. "Who did it? Who killed Sam?"

"Mann and Roth got Dubrov and Collins to do the dirty work."

"They made my father fire a gun into his own head by telling them they'd kill me if he didn't?"

"Pretty sinister, huh, Victor?"

"I'm sorry," Victor said to Faith.

Faith ignored Victor and said to Benny, "And then they did the same to Crown this morning. That's why you had me go down there."

"That's right."

"And you were there when they did it, weren't you?"

Benny shrugged his shoulders. "I was around. I was keeping an eye on those two."

"Yeah," Faith said, unnerved by it all. She didn't know what else to say. She turned her head to Victor and just stared at him.

"What?" Victor said after a moment.

"What do you think of all this?"

"Me?" Victor shook his head. "I think it's stinking rotten is what I think."

Faith smiled at Victor absently. "When did they let you out of jail?"

Victor looked to Benny.

"Tell her," Benny said.

"Yesterday."

"Yesterday."

Victor nodded.

"Kind of funny how it all happened at once, don't you think?

You get out of jail, then Crown gets it . . . Mann . . . Roth . . . Eliopoulos disappears . . . Shortz humiliated . . ."

"Kinda," Victor said.

Faith turned her head back to Benny Rudolph and looked into his eyes again. "Long Meadow explodes?"

Benny looked at Faith blankly, as if he weren't following her.

"It also happens that Victor's father got killed in that explosion." Faith looked back at Victor.

Benny continued looking at Faith the same way Sid Lardner had been looking at Benny earlier, as though wondering what she was getting to.

Faith stared into Benny's eyes, waiting for him to say something, but his eyes were a couple of brick walls. "Anyway . . ." Faith said. "What if I can't get Marty to run the story?"

"He'll run it."

"Why would he?"

"He's already been taken care of."

"By who?"

Benny shrugged.

"He already knows he's going to take a fall?"

"Yeah."

"Since when?"

"Since this afternoon when I told him."

Faith thought about it some more. Thought about poor old Marty and his ulcer and that bottle of seltzer on his desk.

"As soon as you're finished, he'll put out an extra. He's there right now waiting for you."

Faith didn't say anything. Thinking of going back to face Marty knowing what she knew, she put on her coat and hat, and felt a wave of melancholy.

"Go write your article, sweetheart," Benny said. "And one last thing . . ."

"What's that?" Faith asked, only half interested.

"Don't believe in men, Miss Rapaport. Don't believe in one

goddamn one of them. You'll keep getting your heart broke, over and over again."

"Thanks, toots," Faith said. She turned her back on Benny and Victor, stepped out into the lobby, and walked away.

When Benny and Victor couldn't see Faith anymore, Victor quietly said, "Why didn't you tell me any of this when we were locked up together all those years?"

Benny took a handkerchief from his jacket pocket and covered his mouth with it. A violent spasm took hold of his chest and he coughed it out. When he removed the handkerchief, a few specks of blood had splattered the already bloodstained cloth. He curiously looked at what had just come up. "I didn't see any point in getting your hopes up," Benny said, not trying to hide the handkerchief from Victor. "Getting my hopes up. I didn't have any evidence, nothing to work with. Doing that kind of time with hope in your thoughts? That wasn't for me."

"Maybe so," Victor said, recalling the way time had weighed down on him when he was locked up.

"Besides," Benny continued, "I always knew when I got out five years ago I'd find a way to have my say about things."

"And that would be today, I take it?"

"That's right. I wanted to take my shot before it got too late." Benny raised his brow and pinched his eyes narrow as he said this. He folded up the handkerchief and shoved it back into his pocket. "If you haven't noticed, Victor, I ain't sounding too good."

"You ain't looking too good either."

"Yeah, thanks. . . . Funny how vengeance creeps up on a man when he feels the lights about to go out. There ain't nothing worse than thinking that men a lot worse than you get to keep on breathing after they've stolen time from you."

"Is that why you're doing this?"

"In part." Benny looked to the door of the back room, where Sid had been sitting quietly all this time.

"You going to tell me how you got my father mixed up in this?"

Benny pulled on his ear a couple of times and scratched at his head a little. "Unlike you or me, your father was a man of principles."

"And how'd he end up in that shop a couple days before I got released from Farnsworth, Benny?"

"I convinced him it was the right time to act on his principles."

"Meaning?"

"Meaning I had a client who would benefit from what he wanted to do in the first place."

"Stop talking in puzzles, Benny. I don't have time now to work through your puzzles."

Benny pinched at his nose with his fingers, shook his head, repeating under his breath in mock disbelief, "You don't have time . . ."

"Who was this client?" Victor pressed.

"If I tell you that . . ."

"If you tell me, Benny, you'll give me some peace of mind, the first peace of mind I've had in many years."

Benny looked at Victor hard. "If I tell you, your peace of mind is only good so long as you keep your trap shut, understood?"

"I won't talk. You know that."

"So I do." Benny paused, hesitating again, then jumped in matter-of-factly. "Your father actually thought he was starting an uprising. He thought that his actions would drive Fief out of Long Meadow and the union would then be able to take over the plant."

"Why would he think that?"

"That's what he believed. What can I say?"

"Why, Benny? Why would he believe that?" Victor persisted.

"To show everyone how belligerent the union is, that's why."

"There's more to it than this, Benny, and you know there is. Be straight with me."

Benny looked Victor square in the eye. "I told him that if he did it, I'd get you out of jail. Somehow, it made good sense to him—to get what he wanted on both ends. Like I said, he was a man of principles. It was just the push he needed to do what he'd been dreaming of doing to begin with."

Victor hadn't expected that. He loved his father for doing it for him, but lost respect for the "man of principles" Benny had been describing.

"Once he understood the truth about your situation, he suddenly felt all those fifteen years of your life, suffering in that cell. He couldn't stand it that he hadn't thought better of you when you told him that you were innocent. He couldn't stand himself for having cut you off."

Victor's jaw clenched shut and started grinding his teeth.

"He wasn't supposed to get killed, Victor. And not to be callous, but it's not the worst thing I've ever done for this client. I'm not a naïf like you, a man of principles like your father. Never have been."

"You just finished saying this was different, that you're trying to set things right, and then you tell me that you're on the inside of something dirty like this. I don't get it."

"I didn't get it at first, either, to be honest."

"So what are you doing all this for? Fief can't be paying for all this." Victor gestured grandly around the room, but quickly realized that he was just showcasing a small room full of old shoes. He put his arms down and just looked at Benny, who looked up from the floor and met his gaze.

"What can I say?" Benny said, tugging on his ear again. "It was an exchange. I got what I wanted, they got what they wanted: fair deal. I wouldn't've found any peace otherwise. You understand? It's the only thing that's been keeping me going, living with this . . ." Benny pounded on his chest a little.

"It ain't right, Benny."

"I know." Benny started laughing and then coughing. This time the blood splattered onto Sidney's display case of galoshes before he could get his handkerchief out. Benny looked at the blood, bemused.

"What about the other men at the plant?" Victor asked. "What's going to happen to them?"

"To be honest, your guess is as good as mine," Benny said as he stood up. "Buy yourself a paper tomorrow afternoon."

Victor stood up with Benny and put on his coat. "So is this it, Benny? Are we done for good?"

"I never really needed you to begin with, Victor." Benny smiled again. "I just wanted to get you out."

"Yeah, well, I do appreciate that," Victor said to Benny in a soft voice. "I do appreciate that."

"I put some more money into that account of yours."

Victor didn't say anything.

"And you should also know that your father, he willed his house in Long Meadow to you. He gave this to me in case something happened." Benny took an envelope out of his attaché and handed it to Victor. "It's the will and the deed to the property."

Victor stuffed the envelope into one of his coat pockets and looked back at the door of the workroom. "What are you going to do with him back there?"

"I think I'll let him sit in there and stew for a while," Benny said. He walked behind the counter and quietly unlocked the door. "He's got what's coming to him."

"I'll see you around, Benny." Victor started out.

"Probably not."

"Yeah," Victor said, and stepped out into the lobby of the Prescot Building. He walked through the long corridor and started for uptown when he reached the street.

Chapter 33

When Freddy walked into his apartment, the two men who he had seen enter his building from the Martins' stoop were now standing inside his living room. They looked to Freddy to be too clean-cut to be gangsters; they were a far throw from a man like Stu Zawolsky, or Feldman for that matter. Their suits were conservatively cut; they wore solid ties, black shoes, white shirts; one of them wore glasses that a librarian might have worn and carried an attaché; the other had a camera dangling from his shoulder. They didn't introduce themselves to Freddy. All they did was look around at the quaint grandmotherly decoration of his apartment.

"What can I do for you?" Freddy asked, hearing the nervousness in his own voice as he looked to each of the men. Benign as this pair looked, he had no idea what he was in for.

"You have the carbons from the dispatch?" the man wearing the glasses asked.

"Yeah," Freddy said. Freddy pulled out the copies of the dispatch forms from his jacket pocket, and handed them to the man. The man looked them over some, placed them in his attaché, then nodded to the man carrying the camera. "All right, let's go, Mr. Stillman."

"Where?" Freddy asked.

"For a little ride."

"Where?" Freddy asked again.

The two men didn't answer. They turned Freddy around and escorted him outside to a black sedan and put him in the backseat.

They sludged and skated uptown through the half foot of snow that had fallen. They drove up to Ninety-fifth Street, where they boarded the Barkley ferry bound for Long Meadow. The men remained businesslike with Freddy, speaking to him only long enough to give him orders. With all the snow and barges of ice, the current of the river appeared on the surface to be slow, but Freddy could feel its force working on the ferry's starboard underbelly as they crossed the river's girth westward. Freddy remained seated in the back of the car and tried to get a glimpse of the Long Meadow Palisades over the ferry's nose as the boat dipped and dodged over the wakes of cargo ships, but through the heavy snow, the opposite shore was whitewashed; until they were a few hundred feet from shore, all Freddy could make out was the bright lights of the tugs illuminating the heavy gray daylight.

The landscape of the Palisades came into view as the ferry landed. The man who had been carrying the camera revved up the car's engine as the porter lifted the gate and slipped out the gangplank. The few cars that had ridden the ferry over to Long Meadow rumbled up the winding road leading away from the ferry landing, and the two men and Freddy followed. When they reached the top of the road at the edge of the town, the car veered right onto Palisades Parkway and the man behind the wheel slowly drove into the thickening storm with his head nearly pressed against the windshield. Every half mile the snow-and-ice-encrusted billboards covered in paintings of the birds marked the road for him. They passed the well-marked Promontory Peak and then continued on past long stands of birch and maple, oak and pine, passed small roads that seemed to lead nowhere. When they had traveled a few miles, they turned onto a narrow stretch cut through a stand of trees that led back in the direction of the river, and the driver traversed and dodged ruts and heavy tree roots hidden by the soft pack of snow. They finally reached a shack at the end of the road, just a hundred yards from the riverbank. A car was parked outside the shack and a lantern burned in the window.

"All right, let's go, Mr. Stillman," the man with the glasses said to Freddy when the driver parked the car.

"What are we doing here?" Freddy asked. A portly man in a heavy red hunting coat opened the door of the shack and stood half lit in the yellow light of the lantern.

"We need a few snapshots for our photo album," the driver said as he grabbed his camera and a flash from the front seat.

The two men swung their doors open and climbed out into the snow. Freddy slowly opened the back door and stepped out along with them, then trudged behind them to the man waiting at the shack's entrance.

When the man with the glasses reached the shack, he reached into his attaché and removed a small hand mirror. As he undid the clasps of the mirror and slipped out a piece of paper from the mirror's backing, Freddy could hear the man with the glasses say quietly, "All right, Mr. Sendak, these are the coordinates. As we discussed before, the ship will dock at midnight. You check over the plant, make sure no one is around. Open the armory at a quarter to midnight, then make your way down to the docks and wait out of sight. Got it?"

The portly man nodded his head and looked over to Freddy. "What do I do with him?"

"I just want you to stand right here so we can document the exchange of this document. . . . Mr. Stillman," the man said, turning to Freddy, "stand right here." The man took Freddy by the shoulders and set him in front of the door so his body was sufficiently facing out toward the man with the camera. The man with the glasses then handed Freddy the list. "You just stand here and hold this out so the print is facing the camera."

Freddy held up the list in front of Sendak's face.

"A little lower . . . just like that. Perfect. Don't move." The man fell back a few yards behind the man with the camera.

As Freddy stood there with his arm outstretched, presenting the document to Mr. Sendak, the flash from the man's camera burst into Freddy's eyes, turning the falling snow into shining glitter. When he was through, the man with the glasses approached Freddy again and took the paper from him, and handed it to his partner, who immediately started copying the information onto a pad. "Now, are you certain the order will be packed before the end of the day?" the man with the glasses asked Mr. Sendak.

"Yeah," Sendak said nervously. "It's a pretty tremendous order, but I'll keep men over to finish it up and have them out in time. They've filled bigger in less time."

"Good. We'll be in touch."

"You're gonna be watching my back, I hope."

"You have nothing to worry about, Mr. Sendak."

"You just keep up your end. You tell that to Rudolph. I ain't as stupid as he makes me out to be."

The man with the glasses ignored Sendak and walked away from the shack with Freddy in tow.

"Rudolph?" Freddy said to the man.

The man ignored Freddy as well and escorted him back to his seat in the car. "You keep your mind on what's important, Mr. Stillman," he cautioned him when he shut the door. "Let's go," he said to the man with the camera.

The cameraman put the finishing touches on his notes, handed the paper to Sendak, then returned to the car. He turned the engine over and pulled out away from the shack back in the direction of the ferry landing.

Chapter 34

The shades of Marty Volman's office were still drawn when Faith returned to the *Globe* offices. Faith knew that he was in there waiting for her, drunk stiff; he'd probably been drinking since she left for the meeting and by now had finished off his bottle of bourbon. She decided to let him wait. She knew that if she didn't sit down and write her story, that if she went in there to talk with Marty, if she saw his eyes, if she started remembering what he'd been to her, she might not go through with the story. She gathered together the notes on her desk, the Ribe and Rudolph files, the pieces of the story she had collected just a short while ago in Sid's shoe repair shop, and piled them up beside her typewriter. She then removed the story her father had written all those years ago, the story that had never made it into print on account of Marty, and nearly word for word copied it out, updating as she went along to tell the part of the story that involved her father's murder, Crown's murder, Sid Lardner's role in setting up his brother, the miscarriage of justice weighed down on Benny Rudolph and Victor Ribe, how it was that her father's closest friend, the man that she thought of as her own father, suppressed Sam Rapaport's story to save his own neck.

In less than an hour, after Faith had smoked herself through half a pack of Lucky's, all the connected stories were complete; the photos, the letters, the text from Rudolph's notes, were all in order; all the questions and speculations about Harry Shortz's involvement raised and thought through; all the details about how Faith received a call early this morning and how she found herself in the company of Murray Crown's corpse. She recounted how it was she discovered her father in a similar state fifteen years earlier. She wondered what exactly it all amounted to, how it was all connected, or if it was simply Benny Rudolph trying to make just an unjust past.

Faith then gathered everything together and walked to Marty's office. Without looking at any of her colleagues, without knocking, she opened the door, walked in, and closed the door behind her. She found Marty passed out, snoring, with his head resting precariously on the edge of his desk. Faith tried to shake him awake. She tried pinching his flared nostrils closed. And when she realized nothing else would work, she reached over Marty's desk, took hold of a fresh seltzer bottle, and sprayed him right between the eyes until his eyelashes started fluttering and he started hacking a dry cough. When he was alert enough to understand what was going on, he reeled back in his chair and wiped his face with the sleeve of his jacket. "Faith," he said in a weak voice. "You're back."

"I'm back," Faith said.

"I dozed off."

"I see," Faith said, looking at the empty bottle of bourbon in the trash and a fresh quarter-empty fifth on his desk.

"You got your story," Marty continued, still waking.

"Yeah."

"Yeah," Marty said. He pointed to the hip pocket of Faith's pants and made a crooked V with his fingers. Faith removed a cigarette from her pocket, lit it for Marty, and then placed it in his hand. "Thanks."

Faith took the same seat she had sat in earlier in the day and lit a cigarette for herself.

"So . . ." Marty said, looking at the smoke clouding around Faith's head.

"It's all right, Marty," Faith said. "You can look at me."

"I really can't, Faith. I'm afraid everything's a blur."

"Look at me, Marty."

Marty tried to focus his eyes on Faith. His eyes weren't shining as they had that morning, when he'd put on his charade for her. His eyes were bloodshot and drunk and full of shame. "I don't know what to say."

"Don't say anything. Just read the story and get it to the typesetter."

"Give it to Jonesy."

"I ain't giving it to Jonesy. You're taking care of this one, Marty."

"Don't make me do that, Faith."

"If I give it to Jonesy, he'll run it as it is. If I give it to you, you can edit those parts out about yourself. I don't feel the need for you to be in there, Marty."

Marty shook his head. "I can't do that, cupcake."

"Yes, you can. You're the editor."

"No," Marty said. "You don't understand. I can't."

"Marty," Faith said, "I got a brain up here, remember? I know what they would have done to you. They would have knocked you off, plain and simple."

"You don't understand."

"Sure I do."

"If I'd just picked up the phone to call the police . . ."

"Then they definitely would have killed you."

"At least Sam would have been around and all this would have come out the right way."

"I don't buy it, Marty."

"It doesn't matter, sweetheart. It's all been arranged."

"Then rearrange it."

"I can't."

"Why not?"

"Because if we don't do it this way, it'll come out in the *Tribune* or the *Herald* or the *Times* or the *Observer,* tomorrow, or in a couple of days. That's just the way it is."

"Is that what Rudolph told you?"

Marty nodded his head. "So, you see, like he said, at least I get a little feeling as to what it's like to pull the trigger myself. And you know what, sugar? He's right that it should be me who does it."

"You'll lose your pension."

"Don't worry about that. I'll make do."

"If you haven't noticed, Marty, it's hard times out there."

Marty's eyes turned misty. "The important thing is, Faith, that no matter what this says here, you gotta believe that I love you like you're my own. I loved your father like a brother. You understand that? You understand why I looked out for you all these years? Why it was I couldn't bring myself to say anything about it, right?"

Faith nodded.

"I didn't want you losing that much more hope for this rotten world."

"I get it, Marty."

"And if you feel like hating me for what I've done . . ."

"I wouldn't know how."

"You should, Faith. Because of me, they took away all you had left. Because of me . . ."

Faith could feel the idea of it biting at her for the first time. She started to feel the nature of Marty's deception run through her limbs. It didn't occur to her until just then that Marty had known what was going to happen to Sam before it happened. Her entire body started to feel as though her bones had been warped by a bitter chill on her way uptown from the Prescot Building. "They would have eventually taken him," Faith reasoned. "You knew him best. You knew he would have given them grief until it was too late."

"You got a good heart, kid. But, listen, it's okay when you wake up tomorrow hating me that you keep on doing it. Okay?"

"Whatever you say, Marty."

"But just remember when you're hating me like that, that I'll be loving you until I take my last breath."

Faith started to get a little misty now.

"Just so we're clear."

"We're clear, Marty."

"Good. Now take a powder. I'll send this downstairs and get the presses rolling."

"I'm going to go home, if that's all right with you."

"Anything you do, Faith, is all right by me."

"I'll see you around, Marty."

"Yeah, Faith, I'll see you around."

When Faith reached the door to Marty's office, she took hold of the knob and held it in her hands for a moment too long. "Marty?"

"What is it?"

"Just for the sake of it, will you hear me out about one last thing?"

"Sure, anything."

Faith turned around and sat back down on the edge of the chair opposite Marty's desk. "There's something bigger here. You know that, don't you?"

"What are you talking about?"

"C'mon, Marty, I know it's been a rough day, but try to think. Think about all that's happened in the last few days. Think about it."

Marty shook his head drunkenly. "If you want me to see beyond this," Marty said, patting Faith's story with his hand, "you're going to have to do some thinking for me."

"Look at it," Faith said. "All in a few days, what have we got? We got an explosion in a machinist shop in Long Meadow. Six men get killed. At about the same time, Victor Ribe gets sprung from jail, and it just so happens that one of those machinists killed in the explosion was his father. Crown turns up dead, then Mann and Roth, American Allied goes out of business, and Eliopoulos disappears, all in the same day. What's the connection, Marty?"

Marty drunkenly shook his head again.

"It's gotta be right in front of our faces for chrissakes."

"I wish I could tell you, Faith."

"I wish you could, too, Marty. Because I feel it in my gut."

Marty looked down to his desk in such a way Faith thought he was going to be sick, but she saw that Marty was reading though the article she had written in the afternoon edition.

"The Southside Docks," Marty read slowly from a paragraph in the middle of the story. "Tersi bought the Southside Docks from Eliopoulos. Why?"

"Don't know."

"You ask me, you should find out."

"Why?"

"A hunch."

Faith looked at Marty lovingly. "Won't you think it over?" she said, pointing with her nose to the article she had just written.

Marty shook his head.

Faith stood up and walked behind Marty's desk. She bent down, gave him a kiss on the bald crown of his head, and looked down on him. "You know, Marty, you played it up good this morning. Real good."

"Thanks, sweetheart."

"You've been good to me all these years."

"I tried. I really did try to be."

Faith gave Marty another kiss. "I'll see you around."

"I certainly hope so, cupcake."

Faith let go of Marty and walked out of his office. She gathered her things from her desk, put on her coat and hat, and rode the elevator to the lobby.

Chapter 35

When Victor left Benny Rudolph at the Prescot Building, he rode the subway to midtown and took a booth inside the coffee shop opposite the Ansonia Hotel. For the better part of an hour, he drank coffee and stared through a small hole he had rubbed away in the restaurant's steamy plate-glass window. As it came to the end of the hour, he saw Elaine Brilovsky crossing the avenue in his direction out from the downpour of snow. He watched her step over the curb and pull open the door. When she walked inside the coffee shop, Victor slowly stood up and anxiously waited for her to recognize him. To his surprise, she saw him immediately and, without hesitation, made her way over to his table. As she approached, he could feel his eyes open and close, as though each blink of the eye were the still frame of a motion picture. When she was standing before him, looking cautiously at his beaten face, he could now see that she was no longer the woman that he kept in his thoughts. The skin around her eyes and mouth had started to wrinkle; her face had become more full; thick, unruly silver wisps of hair hung like floating electric charges, as though they had grown directly from the core of her youthful intensity. She now appeared to have grown calm—and resigned—and, perhaps, more kind-looking. "Are you all right, Victor?" she asked. The ambient sounds of the restaurant fell away from Victor when she spoke, and Victor realized at that moment that he had forgotten what her voice had sounded like; he had forgotten how much solace he felt whenever she spoke his name. "Victor?" Elaine said. "Haven't you anything to say?"

"Yes, of course," Victor said. "I'm sorry. I just . . ."

"Yes?"

"I just can't find the right words."

Elaine tilted her head slightly. "Your face, Victor. I was trying to ask about your face."

Victor touched his face. "Part of my past caught up with me," he said plainly.

"Seems to be happening a lot lately." Victor watched Elaine as she pulled off her gloves with the same air of self-possession that he had remembered for all these years. With the gloves off, she reached up to his face with her right hand and gently held it there, then pulled him down so that she could kiss his cheek. "Why don't we sit," she said as she released him.

"Please," Victor said.

Elaine removed her coat and hat and hung them on the hook of the booth. The waitress walked over. As Elaine ordered a coffee, Victor reached into the pocket of his jacket and removed the picture that he had carried with him for so many years. He set it down on the table when the waitress left and pushed it to Elaine's side of the table. As delicately as she had greeted him, she touched the corner of the picture and drew it close to her. "I've carried it with me everywhere," Victor said quietly.

Elaine rubbed her fingers over the most worn parts of the paper. She remembered the day clearly. She remembered Victor easing her off the boardwalk of the seaside into the photographer's studio. She remembered when they were children growing up in Long Meadow how carefreely she and Victor spent time together in the fields that ran along the Palisades. She remembered how as they walked through tall spring grass and wildflowers, his long fingers would unknowingly and harmlessly brush the new blooms as they swayed in the breeze. She remembered that when she first knew him she thought she would love him unconditionally for the rest of her life.

She recalled her father's disdain for Victor's lack of direction. "Now I don't know what to say," she said.

"You don't need to say anything." Victor shook his head. "I know it might sound odd, but I just wanted to thank you for keeping me company."

Elaine continued looking at the picture, at the flags atop the carousel, at the way Victor's hand so nicely fit inside the gulf of her young waist.

"I needed to remind myself that it was all once real."

Elaine was struck by how remarkably her son resembled Victor in this picture, and then by how remarkably similar their temperaments were, and she began to wonder what her life would have been had that part of her been absent. "It's never stopped being real for me," Elaine said as she ran her fingers over the image of Victor's face.

The waitress returned to the table and left Elaine's coffee. Elaine took a sip from the mug, then turned to the fogged window and looked in the direction of the hotel. After a moment, she said, "Did you know that Joshua noticed you following us these past few days?"

"I can explain that."

"No," Elaine said with a kind smile. "You don't need to. Father, he told me that you were here and . . ." She continued to smile. "I know this may seem cruel, but when I saw you myself in the museum earlier today, I was relieved that your face was so bruised as it is."

"Why?"

"Because I was afraid that Joshua would recognize himself if he saw you. I thought it might startle him."

"Then he doesn't know about me."

"No."

Victor extended his jaw as if he were about to say something, but nothing came out. The dark crevices that meandered through his face were suddenly attenuated; they stretched into a map of taut creases that made apparent to Evelyn the long quiet suffering Victor had been through in the years she hadn't see him.

"I tried to find you," Elaine said. "Did you know that?"

"No."

"I'm not surprised Father didn't tell you."

"No, I'm not either."

"Well, when I found out that you were gone, that you had been sent overseas, I was devastated. I . . ."

Victor reached out and touched her hand to silence her, and then withdrew it. "I'm glad you found someone to take care of you."

"Arthur was very kind to me."

Victor was quiet for a moment. "When I got back from the war," Victor managed, "after your father told me what happened, I thought I would travel to Russia and try to find all of you."

"Why didn't you?"

"My nerves," Victor said. "I was pretty broken up. I always intended to go, but the more time that passed, the more I convinced myself that if we were going to see each other again, if I was ever going to see my son—Joshua—fate would eventually draw us together."

"Fate."

Victor nodded.

Elaine smiled. "Is that really what you believed?"

"I don't know." Victor smiled now. "You have to understand, Elaine, when I returned from the war, after seeing the things that I saw and doing the things that I did to stay alive, what we had together all those years? It was this wonderful, beautiful dream. I couldn't take it if I did anything to ruin it."

"But I treated you so horribly."

"You were the most decent thing that happened to me in my entire life." Victor started running his finger up and down the edge of a knife sitting on the table. "When I was in prison? Every morning when I'd wake up in my cell, I would dream of you, of us." Victor suddenly felt so moved, as if the knife he was playing with had split open a vein.

"Victor, please say what you were going to say."

Victor remained silent.

"Please, Victor."

"They were just dreams."

"Tell me about them."

Victor set the knife aside and took hold of his empty coffee mug. "I didn't know what Russia looked like," he started, and he looked renewed to Elaine as he talked, like an entirely different man. "I didn't know what your husband looked like, or Joshua, but I dreamed of you all sitting inside a cozy dining room by a small kitchen, eating your breakfast and drinking your coffee. After morning roll call, when I went to work in the quarry, I dreamed of peasants breaking their backs in the fields, and I would see you and Joshua pass by, wrapped in warm coats, carrying bags of bread and cheese. When I had to walk in endless circles in the prison yard, following the other inmates in a line, I dreamed of you and the boy running through some grand park with big oak trees and ponds with small boats floating across the water. When the lights went out in my cell at night? I was there by the boy's bedside with you, just sitting there, watching him sleep."

Elaine reached across the table and took one of Victor's hands.

"Will you promise me something, Victor?"

"Yes."

"In the spring, when the snow's cleared and the trees have come back, will you take me and Joshua walking along the bluffs in Long Meadow?"

Victor lost his voice again.

"We'll pack a picnic, just the three of us."

Victor's lips began to quiver.

"And we'll walk among the cherry blossoms where we used to meet?"

In Victor's mind, he could feel Elaine's hand in his as they walked along the stream beside the cherry blossom orchard.

"And we'll wait for dark and we'll tell Joshua how we would sit by the stream and wait for the birds to fill the branches of the trees?"

Victor nodded his head. He nodded it violently. An incredible pressure was now filling the walls of his chest. It was building inside his head. "I need to go now, Elaine," he said, letting go of her hand.

"But we've only just started talking."

"I know," he said. "I'll call for you tomorrow, if that's all right with you, but right now, I've got to go. I've really got to go."

"In the morning. Arthur, he'll be leaving early tomorrow morning. Come by then."

"I'll be by as early as I can."

Victor left Elaine at the table and rushed out into the snow, bumping diners and upsetting coffee cups on his way out. Once outside, he just walked in the snow with no one looking over him. He walked feeling the pain from the blows he had received the night before; he walked feeling the loss of his father, feeling the lost time taken from his youth, and the tears that he had held back at the table with Elaine, held back while locked inside his prison cell for fifteen years, broke from their ducts like a river bursting forth through the concrete seams of a faltering dam, and as the water flowed through the deep crevices of Victor's face, he let out a horrible moan that bellowed through the storm and into the canyon of buildings. As he walked, he remembered feeling the warmth of Elaine's lips on his cheek, and the moan grew deeper in pitch, and then Victor Ribe quietly sat down on a bus stop bench and quietly began to sob.

Chapter 36

Shortly before five o'clock on this snowy Friday, the *Globe* extra hit the streets. The newspaper boys, emanating from smoky truck exhaust filling the loading docks, trudged out of the *Globe*'s distribution center weighed down by heavy canvas bags, screaming, "Globe *extra, special edition! Narcotics Bureau caught in corruption scandal! Read all about it! Commissioner Harry Shortz murder suspect! Read all about it!*" On the front page was the photograph of Dubrov, Collins, and Klempt heaving Boris Lardner off the el tracks. Inset was the photo of Klempt attacking Victor with his gun, Sidney Lardner in the background. Inside were photographs of the blackmail letter from Sid to Boris, and an excerpt from Benny Rudolph's case file on Harry Shortz's affair. Also printed was the original story written by Sam Rapaport on all that was discovered by him those days before his murder; his story ran parallel to Faith's more current account. And there was a formal resignation letter from Marty Volman.

Before the paper had gone to press, Marty Volman, in his drunken state, somehow managed to find the clarity of mind to write an honest and dignified *mea culpa* to his readers and his colleagues, neither pitiful nor self-justifying. When he finished the note, for the first time since Sam Rapaport's death, Marty went down to the basement to Sam's famous file drawers and pulled out a photo of Sam taken outside a mayoral inauguration. Sam was dressed in his signature overcoat and a strangely positioned top hat as he blew cigar smoke up the mayor-elect's nose. Marty returned to the newsroom and dropped the photo with Jonesy. Told him to make sure it ran opposite Sam's story. *Thought this image of your father would please you,* Marty wrote to Faith in a note when the first papers rolled off the presses. *It pleases me no end.* He clipped the note to the page that ran the photo, then left the Globe Building. He walked uptown in the storm and hand-delivered the paper to Faith's doorman, knowing full well she would be pleased.

As the newsboys screamed his name on the sidewalks, Harry Shortz sat in his father-in-law's study explaining to him the full extent to which he was involved in this scandal. Man to man the two went over everything that had happened in the past few days and eventually got around to discussing Harry's lapse of judgment with regard to Edward Kelly's daughter. Harry swore to his father-in-law that it was the only time in his marriage that he had strayed. He swore that though he had improperly exonerated Boris Lardner, he had taken part in no plot to kill him. He swore that the promise he had made to Boris Lardner he had kept, and that he had no knowledge of his men's deceits.

"I should have seen it coming," Edward Kelly said with some regret. "I can't help but feel a little responsible."

"Why do you say that?" Harry asked.

"Why?" Edward Kelly said, his elbows on his desk, the palms of his hands resting against his cheeks. He sat across from Harry in front of a wall lined with photographs of Harry, Beverly, and his grandchildren. He was an aging man in good health and good spirits, with a headful of graying brown hair, distinguished in every regard. "I was warned."

"I don't understand."

"Before your nomination was announced," Kelly said, leaning back in his desk chair, "Tines came to see me and tried to tell us to back away from the election."

"How exactly?"

"He wasn't specific in any way. He just said that he thought it was a mistake for your career, my reputation. . . . He intimated that it would be a grave misstep for the party to try to push you through to the fall. I honestly thought it was all a bunch of nonsense and bluster, and took it as an assault on our confidence in you."

"Why didn't you ever tell me this?"

"I didn't take him seriously. Yes, I knew about the affair and the girl, Harry—and I remain disappointed in you for that—but, that aside, I never saw it amounting to anything like this," Kelly said with his clear blue eyes trained on Harry. "I honestly didn't think Tines was clever enough to make something like this wash."

Harry just looked back at his father-in-law. "It wasn't all him."

"What have you left out?"

"Claude Fielding paid me a visit last night."

"What did he have to say?"

"It's nothing that we can repeat."

"All right."

"The State Department is behind Tines. They gave him full authority to do whatever he had to do in order to get rid of me."

"Why's the Department of State concerned about you?"

"They were afraid that if I won the election, that because of my politics, if I got wind of the Feds trying to discredit the Munitions Workers Union, I would obstruct Fief's effort to relocate his plant."

"That's ludicrous."

"Maybe so, but not ludicrous enough not to unleash Tines."

"Is Claude willing to come out and say anything? Is there any way to make a case against the Department of State, against Tines?"

"There would be if I had any evidence. But as it is, Claude said he'd deny everything if I came forward."

"Is there anything you can think of doing before we take the step of withdrawing your name from the race?"

"I hardly think so, Ed. At this point, with my men behind Lardner's and Crown's murders, me with motive to have ordered the hit . . . with the narcotics up in the Ten Lakes house connecting me to the syndicate, I don't think there'd be much of a race."

"You think Tines intends to use all this, or do you think he'll hold back and want to use you?"

"I think I'm pretty well ruined, Ed, if not worse."

Edward Kelly took a long hard breath. "I think it might be time to get you a lawyer."

"Yeah," Harry said, "I think that's a decent idea."

Edward Kelly reached for the phone on his desk and made a call. As he was waiting for the answer he said to Harry, "We'll arrange a time for you to withdraw your name from the race tomorrow morning."

"Yeah," Harry said.

As the snow fell and packed the streets nearly a complete foot, as shades of indigo darkened the westward-facing windows across the street from her apartment, Faith Rapaport swallowed three sleeping pills chased by a large glass of whiskey. She closed her phone away inside a bureau drawer and placed a pillow over it for good measure. When the doorman delivered her newspaper from Marty, she looked it over briefly and then propped the photo of her father up on her nightstand. When she shut her eyes, the image of the smoke billowing out of her father's mouth wouldn't leave her head; it drifted into the hole she had seen in the back of Crown's head that morning; the smoke drifted around the black gluey blood pooled around his body; it drifted through her father's dead mouth, into her own, and once the sleeping pills took effect she dreamed of smoke sifting out of every pore of her body, until she was nothing more than mist and stillness.

Victor Ribe was nearly frostbitten when he returned to Fuller House. For more than two hours he walked the streets. For the first time since he was arrested, his mind could no longer contain his anguish, and he now wished it were he and not Benny Rudolph who exacted revenge against the forces that had put him behind bars for all those years. He now wished that when Ira and Pally had pulled him onto the street the day before, he had resisted and beaten them down and made them pay for what they had done to him. In the short time that he sat across from Elaine in the coffee shop, he understood from her tone of voice that the love they had felt for each other in their childhood was a true lasting love and that in his haste to run away from her after that day he escorted her to the abortionist's office, he had abandoned that love as much as Elaine had. If he had only stayed behind, if he had only challenged Elaine and her father, if he could only have been as strong as the two of them combined, if he could have inherited his father's stubbornness at that moment, his life would have been his own. Instead, he wandered haplessly into his manhood and inextricably joined himself with the worst horrors of humanity. He hated himself most of all for it. He hated his listless nature. He hated the man that he had allowed himself to become because of it.

For the first time in a very long time, a yearning so complete with a life of its own took hold of Victor, and he wanted more than anything else to find some dope.

By five o'clock, a deep calm had come over Freddy Stillman. Time for Freddy now slowed to an even slower increment of slower time. He spent the better part of an hour in a steamy bath. He anointed himself with bath oils. He shampooed his hair several times, until it was squeaky clean. He clipped his fingernails and nostril hairs and trimmed his pubes. He shaved his face and the uneven hair on the back of his neck, the hair growing like a vine up from his chest to his throat; he tweezed the middle-aged roots at the end of his earlobes. He pushed back his cuticles with a butter knife and brushed his hair with his fingers. He pressed his nicest suit and shirt and tie and brushed the lint off his hat and his coat, polished his shoes and his cufflinks, folded a handkerchief, and when all dressed, Freddy Stillman, though a little beaten and bruised around the eyes, looked as good as Freddy Stillman could possibly look. Six hundred dollars lining his inner pocket like a soft brick.

Freddy locked up his apartment and ventured back out into the storm. He rode the train downtown to the coffee shop next door to the Castaway movie theater, where Gloria Lime was already waiting for him, looking as becoming as Freddy hoped she would look, the soft flesh of her bosom exposed in the grim light of the restaurant. Freddy lightly tapped on the window and smiled at Gloria and looked onto her plunging neckline, at the line of its cleavage, as if it were a third party at the table, smiling knowingly at Freddy. And Freddy sighed. He sighed and he sighed again.

"Freddy," Gloria said with concern when Freddy walked up to her table, "what happened to your face?"

"It doesn't matter, Glory."

"If you weren't bruised up like that . . . what I mean is, you look handsome in that suit, Freddy." Gloria took hold of Freddy's hand and pulled him down next to her. "You look too good to be eating in a joint like this."

"What do you say we move on, then? Over to the Biloxi?"

"Get outta here, Freddy. Since when are you loaded?"

Freddy stood up and offered Gloria his hand. "I've been saving for a special occasion."

"You mean it?"

"Yeah, I mean it. I've been thinking about you a lot today, Glory, an awful lot. How it is you and I found each other the way we did at exactly the right time."

Gloria stood up from her seat and reached up to touch Freddy's forehead. "You sure you're okay? You sure no one knocked you silly?"

"If anyone knocked me anywhere, they knocked some sense into me." Freddy reached over to a hook on the wall near Gloria's table and removed her coat. He wrapped it around Gloria's shoulders and buttoned it for her, the entire time looking into her eyes, onto her painted face. He felt as though he could see every detail that went into making her and all he could think of was how he wanted to examine her more closely. If Freddy was going to be excommunicated from the living, he wanted to do as he pleased one last time.

Freddy held Gloria by the waist as she bundled herself into her hat and scarf and gloves, and then, arm in arm, Freddy and Gloria Lime walked into the stormy night. With the wind and the snow to their backs, they walked over to the Biloxi Hotel three blocks away, where instead of going to the restaurant, they took a room and ordered room service.

Sidney Lardner wasn't much of a drinker, but after Benny Rudolph did his number on him that afternoon, after the unwanted company left his shoe repair shop, a gulping thirst for liquor came over him. He spent his last hours of anonymity at the bar inside the Prescot Building surrounded by life insurance claimsmen going over actuarial numbers. Oblivious to the men glibly bandying these numbers about, Sid quietly drank drink after drink, preoccupied not nearly so much with what he had done to his brother, not with the possibility that he might be brought up on charges for being an accomplice to his own brother's murder, but more with the fact that Gloria Lime, the only person he genuinely cared for on this earth, the woman he loved obsessively, would soon learn what he had done. He was suffering more guilt for this deception than he had ever suffered for telling the bureau investigators where to find Boris the day they killed him. In fact, for interfering with his life at present, he hated Boris that much more on this day and wished he could watch him murdered all over again. Such was the nature of Sid Lardner, Sid thought to himself—lonely, pathetic, bitter, and full of anger for the world.

Such was the reason no one all throughout Sid Lardner's life cared for him.

Sidney got so drunk that afternoon, when he tried to make his way to the door, the insurance claimsmen—all of them customers of Sid's—had to take hold of him and escort him back to his shoe repair shop. When they saw that he was alone with no one to care for him, they held him over the dirty toilet behind his workroom and tried to get him to purge himself of the liquor. Sid slurred incomprehensible curses at them until his big bovine eyes rolled up into his head, at which point one of the men found a shoehorn and, with his shirtsleeves rolled to his elbow, heroically stuck it down Sid's throat until he gagged and vomited into the bowl what amounted to an entire bottle of whiskey. The men, feeling they had been sufficiently humane, left Sid, who was now awake, on the bathroom floor, hugging the toilet. He sat there in a fetal position for the better part of an hour, throwing up and nodding off.

When his head cleared and his body stopped convulsing, Sid, smelling of puke and sweat, wandered out onto the street. It was already dark, and he could hear in the distance, echoing up from the canyons of the financial district, paperboys screaming, "Globe *extra, special edition!*" He had no interest in seeing his picture in the paper, but cared less than anything else if those reading the paper saw him wandering the snowy streets, sodden and disheveled. On his way uptown, he walked into the throng of the rush-hour streets believing that men and women recognized him for what he was. He walked defiantly, he and his stink, staring anyone in the eye who bothered to take notice of him. He rode a crowded subway car and felt a surge of bitter power as people avoided him, buried their noses in their scarves, gave him space for his body to breathe. He rode all the way uptown to Gloria's apartment, hoping he would be able to tell her in his own words what had been done to him this afternoon, hoping vaguely that she wouldn't believe a word of it. He believed that if he could talk with her for just a few minutes, he could make her believe that the whole story, the pictures, were fabricated to discredit him, for accusing the government in the first place of killing Boris.

His anxiety became all but unbearable when he found Gloria was out. Then he remembered that she and Freddy Stillman had a date down at the Castaway. Sid stumbled into a corner liquor store and bought himself a pint of scotch and made his way downtown through the snow, walking with his coat and jacket open, his gut hanging over his belt, his hat tipping back on the crown of his head, cursing himself for nothing in particular—*"You stupid fuck,"* he said, *"you stupid fuck."* He *fucked* at Freddy Stillman as much as he *fucked* at himself. He babbled away into the storm, stopping occasionally to dramatically crane his neck back as he tipped his bottle for a drink. When he finally felt the cold on his already numb skin, he descended back into the subway, and with rush hour coming to a close, he found a small spot on the back of the train and rode downtown relatively unnoticed.

The Castaway was so brightly lit Sidney had to look away from the marquee. *A Marriage to Forget* was playing, with Carl Gantry, Kate Horn, and Jimmy Swain. Sid placed the bottle under his coat, straightened his hat and coffee-stained tie, and bought a ticket. He went upstairs to an empty balcony and entered the film somewhere toward the end, as Jimmy Swain and Kate Horn were drunk and off for a swim. Sidney leaned over the balcony's railing and tried to search the crowd; when a moon over a gazebo lit up the theater, he could see that Gloria and Freddy weren't there. He flopped back into his seat and took a long drink, a very long drink, so that when he removed the bottle from his lips, the inside of his throat felt like someone had put out a whole carton of burning cigarettes inside his body. He *stupid fucked* himself some more and *fucked* Freddy Stillman an equal amount. When the house lights came on between shows, Sid's fat pathetic eyes were once again rolled up into the back of his head and his bottle had dropped to the sticky balcony floor.

. . .

At around nine o'clock, Freddy woke up from a deep sleep. He woke up screaming deep from within his chest. When he opened his eyes, he found Gloria shaking him, her beautiful breasts shaking along with him. Freddy's first instinct was to calm Gloria's breasts. They were distraught, moving in ways beautiful breasts shouldn't move, herky-jerky-like, so that they suddenly were no longer beautifully curved objects to be admired, but two inconsolable weapons. Freddy cupped Gloria's breasts in his hands and defused them. Gloria tried to push Freddy away and screamed at him to cut it out. He wrestled her around so that he lay over her, so that her breasts lay still on either side of her chest, like two poached eggs.

"It's all right," Freddy insisted. He could feel the sweat dripping from his face, and although Gloria was no longer thrashing him about, he could still feel his body shaking, like an aftershock, but he couldn't remember for the life of him why he was so upset.

"What's happening, Freddy?" Gloria looked and sounded alarmed. "The things you were screaming . . . I've heard you scream some horrible things in your sleep, but nothing like this." When she said the word "this" she looked scared.

"What did I say?"

"Please let me up, Freddy."

"What did I say?"

"Who is Janice? What did you do to Janice?"

"What do you mean?" Freddy suddenly felt a shiver of fear.

"You were confessing something. You were swearing that it wasn't you who killed Janice."

"What did I say?" Freddy insisted, his mood turning. "What?" He started to shake Gloria.

"Stop it!" she screamed.

"What?" Freddy screamed back at her. "What did I say?"

Gloria's face cringed and her body tensed up all over. "You're hurting me, Freddy."

"No," Freddy said, letting go of Gloria, "I would never." Freddy lifted his weight off of Gloria. He slid over to the opposite end of the bed and held his hands up so both he and Gloria could see them. "No," he said again, "I would never."

"Who is Janice?" Gloria asked as she pulled away from Freddy even farther and pushed herself off the bed. She opened a bureau drawer and took out a white hotel robe. She put it on and lit a cigarette.

Freddy sadly watched Gloria retreat to the window, looking out the deluxe suite they had taken. All he could think of was that Gloria's breasts, her thighs, her delectable rump, were covered by the bathrobe. He wasn't through with her yet. He had an overwhelming irrational need for her.

"You're really scaring me, Freddy," she said, looking back at Freddy, her voice shaking. Her hand with the cigarette looked as though it were having a seizure.

"It's not what you think," Freddy said calmly. "It was just a dream."

"No," Gloria said. "You didn't hear yourself. You spoke so clearly."

"It was just a dream, Glory. I swear it."

"Tell me what's going on with you, Freddy, or I'm walking out of here right now."

"No," Freddy said desperately, "you can't." Freddy got up out of bed and stood next to Gloria, his penis erect and pointing at her. "You don't understand," he said. Freddy reached for the sash of Gloria's robe. "You can't leave me," he said. "Not tonight. I need to have you here with me."

"Don't!" Gloria said, pushing herself away from Freddy.

Freddy looked down at his hand as if it were a foreign object. The sash of the robe was in his hand. "Please, Glory," Freddy said. He walked toward her with the robe's sash dragging across the floor.

"Don't come near me, Freddy," Gloria warned as she retreated along the length of the wall. Her robe had come undone. Her breasts were exposed, her belly button staring at him like a third eye, and all Freddy could think of was to take hold of her.

"Try to understand," Freddy kept saying quickly, frantically, as he walked toward her, "I . . . I . . . Just this last time . . . just this one last time so that I know that it was worth the . . ." He couldn't finish the thought. He could only feel whatever the thing was inside him that was broken. The unidentifiable thing. The thing that he couldn't locate in himself for as long as he could remember. He could feel this piece of himself missing that should have been there to tell him that what he wanted to do was wrong, was horrible. But all he could answer to at the moment was his desire. Freddy took hold of Gloria's shoulders and threw her onto the bed. He gripped her throat, his thumbs pressing down onto her windpipe; his torso crushed down on her chest, his hard cock rubbed up against her inner thigh. Gloria struggled and writhed, swung her head from side to side, and then acquiesced when she noticed that the burning cigarette she had been smoking was smoldering on the sheet beside her. As Freddy let go of her throat and lifted himself over her, she grabbed the cigarette and with all her strength dug it into Freddy's cheek.

"You fucking bastard!" Gloria screamed at Freddy when he fell away from her. She hit Freddy across the face, right where she had burned him with the cigarette. She swatted at him with her fingernails, and then she hit him again and again with an open hand, and Freddy, with a beaming deadness to his eyes, let her hit him. He didn't move.

"I'm sorry, Glory," he said each time she hit him. "I don't know what came over me. I really don't," he said, when Gloria tired herself out and Freddy's face was red and gouged.

"What did I do to deserve that?" she cried, the tears running down her face. "All I've ever done is love you, the idiot I am."

Freddy now retreated to the corner of the room and in the darkness felt the heat generating around his face. He fingered the cigarette burn on his cheek. Gloria just sobbed. "Why couldn't you just love me back? Why couldn't you? I would have loved you a hundred times more than Evelyn ever did."

Freddy shook his head. "I don't know I don't . . . feel," he tried to explain. "I just don't feel anything anymore. I'm ironclad, Glory."

"You need your head examined."

"I don't think an examination is going to help. Think it needs more than that." Freddy lifted his naked body from the corner of the room and turned on the lights. He walked back to the bed and slowly sat himself down beside Gloria. She started to move away from him, then stopped when she saw the pained look on Freddy's face and the damage she had just done to it. Freddy noticed that his hands had left thin blue marks on the delicate skin of Gloria's throat. The sight of it scared him so much he wanted to throw himself out the window. He reached out to Gloria's wet cheek and brushed away some of her tears. "I'm so sorry. I'm truly sorry."

"I think you should leave now," Gloria said with some resolve. She shook her head and looked at Freddy crossly. "No one does that to me, not even you."

Freddy stood up and started getting dressed.

"I don't want to see you again," Gloria said. "Not never."

"I don't think it'll be a problem."

Gloria started sobbing.

Once Freddy had his coat and hat on, he removed a hundred dollars from his pocket and placed it on the hotel's bureau.

"I don't want your goddamn money," Gloria said. "I ain't your goddamn whore."

"It isn't like that," Freddy said. "Just . . . just buy yourself something nice, something to remember me by."

"What, like some brass knuckles?"

"Something like that, sure," Freddy said. "Something nice, something to remember the good times before tonight."

Freddy didn't look at Gloria again and Gloria didn't say anything more. Freddy walked out of the room and headed for the elevator. When he reached the lobby of the Biloxi, he covered his face up in his scarf and walked out onto the street, and as though he were walking toward the gallows, he started uptown.

The hulking disheveled figure of Stu Zawolsky stood outside the darkened entry of the Triple Mark when Freddy arrived at ten o'clock. The club was closed, but Freddy could smell the liquor on Stu from twenty feet away. The snow had stopped falling, and through the bright lights all around him Freddy could see patches of darkness opening in the sky as he looked up into Stu Zawolsky's rosy pancake face. "Follow me," Stu slurred to Freddy. Freddy followed the drunk Stu Zawolsky across town over the trodden path of sidewalk in the direction of the theater district, keeping his distance from the big man's drunken bob and weave. Even with the storm, the burlesque houses and nightclubs were full; people were standing out on the street behind red velvet ropes waiting to make their way in. Freddy followed Zawolsky for two blocks to the entrance of the Revolver, a nightclub that advertised a floor show. Stu mightily pushed his way through the crowd inside the ropes, provoking a string of berating curses from men and women alike. Freddy followed him in his wake to the front entrance, where the man at the door nervously parted the ropes for Stu and stood aside. "He's with me," Zawolsky said without looking back, and the two of them made their way in. The Tiny Braggs Orchestra was swinging jungle music as the hostess led Stu and Freddy to one of the reserved tables by the stage. A chorus line of black dancers dressed in feathered bikinis three rows deep were coming to the end of a gyrating stomp onstage. When the number finished, when the trumpet players pulled their shiny gold homburgs away from their coronets for the last wa-wa, the women ran from the stage to be immediately replaced by a female dwarf dressed in a pink negligee: Binky the Ballerina, performing a striptease in toe shoes, dressed in belly dancing veils. She was skinny in all the right places and heavy in all the other right places, tall enough that she could extend and kick and leap, and graceful enough that it wasn't a downright joke, even though it most certainly was. Stu Zawolsky got it. He got it well enough that he loudly guffawed and waved a few dollars at the dwarf to come sit on his lap. Stu Zawolsky, Freddy realized, wasn't just drunk, he was plastered. With the dwarf on his lap, Zawolsky started squeezing one of the dwarf's breasts with one hand and tweaking her nose with the other. Binky, in turn, gripped Stu Zawolsky's cock tight through his pants, and the harder she squeezed, the harder Stu Zawolsky laughed. From the back of the room, Freddy could see the tuxedo-clad nightclub manager signal to the band to play it up. The band turned in Stu's direction and played a heavy bass line, top hat, and whomped cat calls. Instantaneously, the dwarf was being manhandled by every man in the joint save Freddy; all who could get a grip on her were stuffing her negligee full of cash until she looked like a diminutive scarecrow.

"Is this a bad time?" Freddy asked as Stu let Binky go. Stu stood up to lord over Freddy; it was hard for Freddy not to notice that Stu's cock was still erect in his pants. Both men looked down at it and then looked back at each other. Stu shrugged his shoulders as if to say, "Heh," and then with a drunken grin on his cauliflowered face, he adjusted his pants and fell back into his chair, snickering.

Freddy, thinking this might be the opportune time to act, slipped his hand into his jacket pocket and removed the money he owed Zawolsky. He reached across the table and stuffed the bills into Stu's hand. Stu seemed sober for a second when he caught sight of the cash. He tilted a little to one side, licked his oversized fingers, and counted. When he was through—with a drunken eye trained on Freddy—he folded the bills in half and tucked them into a bulging money clip. "Nice doin' business with you," Stu slurred over the raucousness. "Now scram."

Freddy, who wasn't through with Stu yet, leaned over the table and placed his hand on Stu's bowling-ball-sized shoulder. "I got another job for you," he shouted into Stu's ear.

"Better pay well," Stu stammered, the stubble of his cheek scratching at Freddy's freshly shaven face. "Because business is booming since Mann's and Roth's tickets got punched."

"Tomorrow morning at eleven a.m., at three-nineteen West Eighty-third Street, bottom floor. . . . I want you to kill the guy that lives there."

Stu pulled his head away from Freddy's. He gave Freddy a lopsided grin. "I know that address," Stu shouted, his head now rocking from side to side. "What are you trying to pull?"

"No one will be in the building other than me."

Stu puffed up his cheeks and blew some sweet whiskey breath up Freddy's nose.

"I want you to use a gun," Freddy continued.

"You mean to tell me you're hitting *yourself*?"

"If you take me down into the cellar, no one will hear a thing."

"Go on," Stu laughed, shrugging his shoulders.

"I want you to shoot six rounds into my face."

Stu grimaced. "Why?"

"I got my reasons," Freddy said.

Stu paused for effect. "Suit yourself." His eyes rolled around in their sockets for a while. "Three hundred," he said when they stopped and fixed on Freddy.

"Deal," Freddy said.

"All the money up front this time."

"Yeah," Freddy said as he started reaching into his pocket, "sure."

While Freddy's hand was lodged in his pocket, Stu took hold of the back of Freddy's head and pulled him close. "Now, this is how it goes: the second you hand me that money you're reaching for, the deal is done and there's no turning back. You're a dead man. Understood?"

"Understood," Freddy said nervously.

"There will be no last words. Last words annoy the hell out of me. If you've got something to say, put it in writing."

"Yeah, sure," Freddy said.

As he had done this morning while giving orders, Stu looked into Freddy's face, into his eyes, and took a moment. "You're a brokenhearted son of a bitch, aren't you?"

Freddy could feel tears coming on as the room erupted into pandemonium around him. "Yeah," he said pathetically. "I just ain't right anymore."

Stu nodded his head solemnly.

Freddy felt strangely calmed by Stu's observation. He reached into his pocket and stuffed the remainder of his cash into Stu's oversized hand. "You're a dead man," Stu said coldly. "Try to find some peace." Stu Zawolsky got up out of his seat and started across the room in the direction of Binky the Ballerina, who had taken up fifth position on top of a cocktail table.

Freddy continued to sit where he was. He thought of brushing away the tears on Gloria's face just a short while ago. He saw her eyes weeping and he suddenly could feel the tears well up in his own eyes as he thought of this. And then he could feel the water run down his face. He realized at that moment how much he loved womankind, how he loved it so much, but that he didn't know how to love it in a way that it would love him back. He felt so cold and vacant. He knew without this knowledge he was nothing, not even vapor.

An usher woke Sidney when the house lights came on, and he could hardly remember how he got there. He went to the bathroom and cleaned himself up as much as he could. It was coming on midnight. He had slept through the film twice. Still feeling Gloria on his mind, unable to get her off his mind, off his splitting head, he rode the train back uptown. The light in her window was lit and he was about to ring for her, but to his surprise, he found the door jarred open a little. He quietly walked upstairs and placed his ear to the wood and listened. He could hear himself breathing at first and then he could hear Gloria inside, sobbing, sobbing as if she were crying into a pillow. He could hear long painful sobs and groans, as if she were in so much pain her body was tight all over, her teeth clenched, her hands needing to grip something. The loud private groans made Sidney feel scared to move, made it so he was afraid she would hear him out there and feel the intrusion. Listening to these muffled noises, a swelling rose from his chest, into his throat. And then all of a sudden, Gloria cried out. The swelling he felt in his throat turned into a panic. He started to step away from the door, then stepped back, and knocked loudly.

"Glory?" He knocked some more. "Gloria? It's Sidney. Open up."

The crying stopped abruptly. "Sid?" she said, with an unsure voice. She nearly sounded pleased he was there. But then something changed. "Go away," she said. "Not tonight, Sid."

"Please, Glory," Sid followed. "I hear you in there. I heard you in there."

Gloria didn't say anything. Sidney couldn't hear her move or breathe. As he was about to say something more, she said, "It's open."

Sidney opened the door slowly and peeked his head in. Gloria was dressed in her robe, the collar turned up, and she was clutching it with her hand so obviously that she looked like she was hiding something. Her eyes were red and swollen and the hand that was holding her cigarette was shaking. He could tell from the way that she looked at him that she hadn't seen the paper that evening. "Glory," Sid said carefully, "what are you doing with your door open like this?" Sid walked in and shut the door behind him. Locked it. And he noticed that on the coffee table on which Gloria set out the chocolate-covered cherries for him when he came by there was a revolver and a box of ammunition. Gloria just looked at

Sidney, and after looking at him with those swollen red eyes, those pathetic eyes, she let her hand fall from her robe, walked over to Sidney, and hugged him. The second she got her arms around him, she started crying again. Sidney could feel the warmth of her wet cheek against his ear, and he had an image in his mind of marks on her neck. Sidney walked Gloria over to the couch and sat her down, then, not wanting to let go of her, not ever wanting to let go of her, he gently pushed her away and again saw the blue-red marks on her neck and throat.

Gloria stopped crying and looked at the gun. "I was hoping he'd come by to talk," she said.

"That's why you left the doors open." Sid could feel his sadness for Gloria turning into rage. She didn't need to explain what he'd done to her. It was obvious. But Gloria told Sidney what had happened. She told him everything, and after listening, Sid walked to Gloria's icebox and from the top of it grabbed the bottle of gin she kept there and started drinking again.

"Why is it you look so bad?" Gloria asked.

"Never mind that."

Sid poured both of them a drink. They drank one drink together, and then Sid put Gloria into bed. He sat beside her until she fell asleep. When she fell asleep he brought the bottle into her room and spent the night in the chair, drinking from the bottle slowly until he fell asleep.

Chapter 37

Just before eleven o'clock, Benny Rudolph was sitting in his black sedan on the Ninety-fifth Street Barkley ferry landing. A sign was posted on a guardrail: *Closed Due to Weather Conditions.* A snow-heavy ferry was nevertheless idling at port, chugging steam. As Benny waited, a few cars pulled up, read the sign, and turned back. On the seat beside him was a copy of the *Globe*'s extra. He couldn't take his eyes off it, he was so pleased to see the photographs of Dubrov, Collins, Klempt, and Sid Lardner, all damned as the villains in Boris Lardner's murder; he was pleased to see Victor cleared of the crime, Sam Rapaport given his due, Shortz implicated; he was especially pleased to see himself cast as a hero in the shadows, as a man unjustly convicted getting even with those who had done him wrong.

However, as he sat there waiting to take care of his last order of business, he started to feel his conscience working on him. He was haunted by thoughts of Victor's father and the other men who had died in Long Meadow, thoughts of Waters and Capp unjustly accused of crimes they hadn't committed. He had wanted his revenge so bad, he had convinced himself that setting Katrina Lowenstein and Shlomo Feldman on Freddy Stillman, that planting the dynamite inside Waters and Capp's shack, that turning Paulie Sendak and Walter Ribe against their union, were acceptable costs of his vengeance. Only now that he had what he wanted, he wanted just as much to reverse the course of events; he wanted to even the odds for those whose lives didn't deserve to be destroyed. The only problem was that like so many of these people, he himself had been taking part in a plot he couldn't see clearly in his mind.

When Benny saw a taxi appear at the ferry landing, he grabbed his revolver, got out of his car, and started waving his free hand at the driver. He dragged his feet through the snow with the car's headlights shining in his eyes, and walked around to the passenger door. He wiped away some frost and looked into the dark compartment. The passenger was screaming at the cabby with his arms gesturing fury. Benny pulled open the door and pointed his gun at the man in the backseat. "Come with me, Mr. Brilovsky," Benny ordered.

"Who are you?" Arthur Brilovsky insisted, turning to the driver. "What's the meaning of this?"

"I'll take it from here," Benny said to the cabby.

The cabby didn't say anything. His face was in shadow, his eyes staring back cold from the rearview mirror.

"Let's go, Mr. Brilovsky," Benny said as he reached into the car. He took Brilovsky by the arm and pulled him and a black briefcase out into the snow.

"Who are you?" Brilovsky insisted again as the cab turned around and headed away from the docks.

"Don't worry, we'll get to that," Benny said as he pushed Brilovsky between the shoulder blades. "Just walk and take a breather beside the car." When Brilovsky was up against Benny's car, Benny patted down Brilovsky's coat, reached underneath, and patted him down again. He opened the briefcase and found thick stacks of hundred-dollar bills. "Get behind the wheel," Benny said.

Benny watched Brilovsky step into the car, then lifted the ferry's guardrail with the briefcase. With the guardrail open, he walked over to the passenger door and took a seat with his gun aimed at Brilovsky's head. "Drive on," Benny said, handing Brilovsky the keys.

Given the circumstances, after his initial outburst, Arthur Brilovsky was unusually calm. He turned the engine over with a steady hand and drove onto the ferry. His lack of emotion, his cool resignation, interested Benny.

When Brilovsky had parked the car, Benny reached over and removed the key from the ignition. The ferryman appeared from a stairwell, closed the guardrail, and walked back up to the helm.

"What's this all about?" Brilovsky asked Benny in a collected tone of voice.

"That's what I want to know from you."

Brilovsky turned in his seat and looked at Benny. "I don't understand."

"You see, Mr. Brilovsky, I been running a lot of bloody errands around town on behalf of a lot of people, and I want to know why exactly."

"Who are you?"

"The name's Rudolph. Benny Rudolph."

Brilovsky shook his head as though he were at a loss.

"No, I don't expect you would know who I am." Benny pressed his lips together and pinched his heavy brow so that it folded around the upper part of his thick nose. He handed Brilovsky the *Globe* extra, turned to the page with the part of the story about Benny.

Brilovsky took the paper and started reading in the dim light. "What do you want from me?" he asked with his eyes on the paper.

"What I want is to know what you know. Everything you know. Everything about you that's important to know. See, I got part of this picture in my head about the fall of a union, dead gangsters, disgraced politicians . . . but I'd like the rest of it, and quick."

"May I ask why?"

"No." Benny pointed out to the water in the direction of Long Meadow as the boat pulled away from the dock. "I know, for instance, that on the other side of the Westbend something's about to happen, but I don't know exactly what. Somehow I think you know, Mr. Brilovsky," Benny said as he patted the briefcase sitting in his lap. "Somehow, I think whatever's happening on that shore over there is the reason for why I been doing everything I've been doing. You understand?"

Brilovsky looked away from Benny and back out onto patches of clearing night sky.

"Obviously, you do understand," Benny said when Brilovsky didn't talk. "Why don't I let you in on a little of what I been up to. After all, it's only fair that before you let me in on what you know I tell you a little of what I been up to, of what I'm up to right now, in fact." Benny leaned over to Brilovsky a little so that Brilovsky could smell the rotten breath coming out of Benny's dying lungs. "For starters," Benny went on casually, "this morning I had Johnny Mann and Jerzy Roth machine-gunned to death. You know who I'm talking about, right?"

"Yes," Brilovsky said reluctantly.

"You heard about the hit?"

Brilovsky nodded.

"Last night, two men taking orders from me forced Mann and Roth to call the hit on Murray Crown. You know that name too, right?"

"I heard about it," Brilovsky said through his teeth.

"This afternoon, Mr. Brilovsky, I got rid of a man named Shlomo Feldman. He I don't think you would have heard of."

Brilovsky didn't move for a moment, then shook his head. His eyes were still as rocks, but Benny could see Brilovsky was thinking hard about where this was leading.

"Feldman, he was a syndicate man who double-crossed me and my boss. You know of the syndicate?" Benny asked as he scratched his temple with the muzzle of his gun.

Brilovsky nodded.

"You heard about Crown, you heard about Mann and Roth. . . . What about the disappearance of Elias Eliopoulos and American Allied Pharmaceutical?"

"Yes."

"I took care of that, too," Benny said as he trained his gun back on Brilovsky's head.

Brilovsky's eyes turned on Benny now.

"In the past month," Benny said, "I helped influence a group of communists inside the Long Meadow Munitions Union to sabotage the plant, framed some of the union's leaders for the job, bullied a Fief dispatcher into arranging a shipment of munitions," Benny said, pointing back out to the water in the direction of Long Meadow. "Any of this ringing a bell behind that leaden look you got on your face, Mr. Brilovsky?"

Brilovsky didn't respond.

"Would it surprise you to learn that to finish things off, I'm now supposed to get rid of you?"

Brilovsky didn't flinch, but the recognition of his dilemma was apparent when he blinked his eyes a couple of times and let out some heavy breaths.

"That's right," Benny said, nodding his head, his broken voice trying to keep up with his thoughts. "There are two cold-hearted men waiting for you. Out there in a cemetery on the edge of the Palisades."

"Tines, he gave the order to kill me?" Brilovsky asked as though he had just snapped to.

"Did I say anything about Tines?"

"I should have known," Brilovsky grumbled.

"What kind of arrangement have you got with Tines?"

Brilovsky didn't say anything.

"Well, you must have made some sort of arrangement with him, seeing that he sent you to me, and I'm taking you over to two of his most lethal goons . . . and despite these boys' numbskull appearance, as you'll soon see for yourself, they're very clever, industrious men. Would you like to know what they're working on up there?"

Benny waited a second to continue.

"They've dug up the grave of one of the union men that died and plan to bury you at the bottom of that hole. They then plan to lay on top of you the casket that was in the ground previous to your arrival."

Brilovsky's hand started fidgeting with a loose thread on the cuff of his coat. "What can I tell you to keep you from taking me out there?"

"You'll tell me everything I want to know. You'll tell me everything you know. You'll leave nothing out. Not one piece of yourself. If I smell the smallest fib, there's nothing stopping me from dragging you out there," Benny said, pointing toward Long Meadow with his gun. "Understood?"

"What do you want to know?"

"You understand me, right?"

"Yes," Brilovsky said clearly, "I understand."

"Good." Benny paused. "Why don't you start by telling me why Tines wants you dead . . . and why don't you tell me what you've got to do with all this while you're at it."

Brilovsky looked reluctant to start talking.

"Suit yourself," Benny said with indifference.

The drone of the ferry's engine filled the compartment of the car for a while.

"He wants me dead because he can't imprison me," Brilovsky said, turning to Benny so Benny could see his face clearly.

"Why's that?"

"I've got immunity."

"Immunity from what?"

"Fraud, money laundering . . . there's a long list."

"And who gave you this immunity?"

"The Department of State."

"Why don't you spell it out for me."

"It's complicated."

"In a nutshell then."

Brilovsky's eyes turned on the gun pointing at him.

"Like I said, you don't leave anything out," Benny said.

"It goes something like this," Brilovsky said after a moment. "I spent the last twenty years defrauding a lot of American businesses for the benefit of the Soviet Union. But Tines's grudge against me and my family goes back a lot farther than that."

"To when?"

"To when I worked alongside my father, when he was the head of the Brigade. You know about the Brigade?"

"Yeah, what of it?"

"The Brigade used to run American Allied on the Southside Docks before Eliopoulos took it over. Before the syndicate you talked about was known as the syndicate, American Allied—run by the Brigade—was its supplier."

"Before Eliopoulos, you supplied the syndicate?"

Brilovsky nodded. "The money we made we sent abroad to help fund the Russian Revolution. Tines knew it. And as I'm sure you're aware by now, he's quite vigilant when it comes to dealing with communists. Especially ones who manage to circumvent his authority."

"What do you mean?"

"He wasn't able to get an indictment against us for either the political activities or the narcotics. However, he did manage to get my father thrown in jail for something else, and with my father out of the way, he broke up the Brigade. When that happened, my father chose Eliopoulos to take over the business."

"Why?"

"Because it made good sense. Eliopoulos had supplied Allied with its opium, from the Far East. My father and Eliopoulos had became good friends—they were sort of cut from a similar cloth, both radical in their own way. When my father bought up the Southside Docks in the teens, Eliopoulos agreed to let my father place the title in his name."

"Why would your father want to do that?"

"For insurance. To keep the government from finding a reason to seize the property. At the time, Eliopoulos was clean."

"And your father trusted this Eliopoulos character?"

"Yeah. He was a little unusual, sure, but as I said, he and my father had an understanding. When my father went to jail, I went to Russia to work for Lenin, and Eliopoulos, he took over the business. Which is when the REM syndicate became the REM syndicate."

"What did you and your father get out of it?"

"Eli sent money to my father to keep my family afloat and sent a percentage of the proceeds to me to reinvest in the Soviet Union. Look, it was never about the money for Eliopoulos. He was already very wealthy. It was an intrigue for him. He liked the danger of the life. He found the underworld glamorous."

"He's a fruit, you know that?"

"Sure, everyone knows it."

Benny lifted the side of his face, then dropped it into a look of disgust. "So, if your father's the true owner of the Southside Docks, what's this I hear about Noel Tersi taking it over?"

"Eliopoulos sold the property to Tersi. Not sold, exactly. Gave."

"Eliopoulos *gave* that property to Tersi."

"That's right. On my father's wishes."

"Come again."

"It was part of the bargain," Brilovsky said.

"With Tines?"

"With the Department of State."

"I don't get it."

"Tines is working with the Department of State."

"I still don't get it."

"He's working with them to kill the labor movement in Long Meadow and get Fief onto the Southside Docks. Why do you think Tines hired a rogue like you to bust up the syndicate and help discredit the union, Mr. Rudolph?"

"To disgrace Shortz. To keep him from making trouble for Fief."

"Sure, okay. But of equal importance is so the government could free up the Southside Docks for Fief. To help get him out of Long Meadow for good. In case we go to war, the Southside Docks would be all his. No syndicate, no retribution. No union, no questions of propriety or strikes. No government men seen, no union martyrs made. But in the end, it's a land grab where there's a shortage of land. Plain and simple."

"But Tersi's got the docks."

"It's a sham. For the same reason Tines set you up as a fall guy, they did it that way to make it look like Fief and the government wasn't involved in acquiring the property. Tersi's a real estate developer. They made him the front man for the transaction."

"What do you mean, set me up as a fall guy?"

"Why in the world would Tines get you to do what he could have done himself?" Brilovsky said with a little vindictiveness.

Benny ignored him. He had thought of it himself, but he didn't like Brilovsky thinking it for him. "What's Tersi get out of the deal?"

"Nothing from the real estate as far as I know. But he's getting paid off in another way."

"With what?"

"When I left Moscow I had a collection of art worth a small fortune. The Department of State kindly suggested that I offer it as payment to help me get back into the country. The deal was that I could take a quarter of its face value." Brilovsky pointed to the briefcase in Benny's lap. "Tersi had the work appraised yesterday and gave me that tonight, just before the cab driver took his detour in your direction. Tomorrow Tersi's going to hold an auction and get five times as much for the collection."

"How can you be so sure?"

"The appraisal wasn't exactly on the level, but I had no room to argue."

"All right, so now I know how Tersi gets his, but how's Fief get from Long Meadow to the Southside Docks?"

"As I was suggesting—with this so-called communist revolt you helped start over in Long Meadow when you got those men to blow up the machinist shop."

Benny looked up in the direction of Long Meadow. "Yeah, but who's that shipment of munitions going to? What exactly did you do for the Department of State to earn your immunity?"

Brilovsky reached into his inside jacket pocket and pulled out a cigarette case and lighter. "I promised a few Soviet officials a shipment of American munitions," he said as he slipped out a cigarette and lit it. "To be delivered by a Russian smuggler we both trusted."

"You're saying that shipment is going to Communist Russia?"

Brilovsky lifted the side of his mouth ever so slightly.

"You're saying that Tines took part in a plot that had a shipment of American munitions falling into the hands of communists?"

"Who better to take Fief's arms if you're intent on proving that there's a communist underground infiltrating the American labor movement?"

Benny grunted, then coughed up the sweet taste of blood in his mouth.

"What's more interesting," Brilovsky volunteered, "is how the Department of State went about it. While I was still in Moscow, they supplied me with the coordinates to find an abandoned American merchant marine vessel. The smuggler I spoke of, he took the ship a few months ago . . . and as we speak," Brilovsky said, looking at his watch, "he is on his way through the Narrows."

"I don't get it."

"It's a setup, Mr. Rudolph. The shipment's not supposed to make it. Tines is supposed to catch him and come out the hero, see."

"What's going to stop this smuggler once he's got the munitions?"

"He's supposed to rendezvous with a Soviet military transport waiting for him once he reaches international waters. But I managed to get the coordinates and handed them over to Tines. So when the ship is about to reach the rendezvous point, it'll be seized by the U.S. Navy."

Benny was quiet as he mulled all this over in his head.

"And what happens to you in all this if I let you live?"

"Me? I've got immunity. I leave the City. Go someplace where I can't be found for a while."

"Who will you be hiding from?"

"Why do you think I left Moscow, Mr. Rudolph?"

"To avoid this very situation you're in right now?"

"Precisely."

When the two men came to this, the ferry landed. As the boat settled into its dock, Benny turned to Brilovsky and looked at him for a long time.

"What is it?" Brilovsky asked after a while.

"How badly do you want to live?"

Benny Rudolph and Arthur Brilovsky got out of Benny's car and walked upstairs to the observation platform and watched as the American merchant marine cargo ship Brilovsky had spoken of drifted into an icy slip on the Fief Munitions dock. Paulie Sendak was there as planned. He caught the ship's moorings and tied them down. Once the ship was properly harnessed, the captain of the large vessel disembarked. Limping along behind him was a man with a clubbed foot. Behind him was a ruthless-looking lot of mariners armed with carbines. Paulie Sendak escorted these men dressed in worn hooded coats and dark knit caps to the pier manager's shack at the foot of the docks. There, Paulie, the captain, two armed men, and the man with the clubbed foot squeezed inside the station while the mariners waited outside in the snow.

Captain Chubayev, a thick man with a strong jaw and an inward-gazing countenance, spoke first. "Where are munitions?" he asked in a slow baritone that purred like a lion at rest.

Sendak turned his round, pockmarked face to the shack's back window and pointed to the service road that led to the armory's loading dock. "You send a dozen men up that road. Quietly."

"They will be quiet," Chubayev said, biting into each word as if it were a cigar. "What of guards?"

"There's no one up there."

"Good," Chubayev said.

"The munitions are all crated, the trucks are loaded. All you need to do is go get them and put 'em on board. Like you're putting a baby into a cradle."

"Do not worry. We are family men," Chubayev laughed.

Sendak looked around the shack, at the dire whiskered faces. "Okay then."

"What of your men?"

"It's just me."

In the most manly expression Paulie Sendak had ever seen, the Russian curled the left side of his lip up, the right side of his lip down, and winced his eyes at the man with the clubbed foot. The man produced a bottle of vodka from inside his coat and handed it to Chubayev. Chubayev placed the bottle on the table, then quietly purred out a long string of Russian to this same man. When he was through speaking, Chubayev pointed to the door with his chin. The lame man relayed the orders to the mariners outside, and the men with the carbines stood outside the shack's entrance.

Chubayev undid the top of the bottle and handed it to Sendak, and Sendak nodded to Chubayev and took a healthy taste of the liquor. As the two men sat watching and drinking, the Russians started marching up the service road, six at a time, up through the back of the town, along the Palisades to the thick steel gates and doors of the armory entrance, where a dozen large trucks were loaded full with mortars and bombs, projectiles and grenades. The two men watched the hulking figures of the sailors as their black coats were swallowed by the darkness.

"May I ask," Chubayev said, "why you do this for Soviet Union?"

"I'm not," Paulie Sendak said. "I'm doing it for myself."

Chubayev frowned and took a drink and handed the bottle to Sendak.

"The men I work with are fools," Sendak said. He took a long drink, wiped his mouth with the sleeve of his coat, then handed the bottle back to Chubayev. "They don't know how to get what they want."

"Sometimes a man needs to rise up for himself before his people rise up for him, eh?" Chubayev said.

Paulie was silent to this.

"I prefer to remain at sea," Chubayev said with the bottle to his lips. "I prefer to rise up on the back of the ocean. It is rough, unpredictable, but much more safe than on land. Because, when at sea, I am the law." Chubayev drank again. "Have you been on ocean in boat?" Chubayev asked Sendak through the corner of his mouth.

Paulie shook his head.

"Not for everyone," Chubayev seemed to agree.

Paulie took the bottle from Chubayev and drank.

A few silent minutes later, the caravan of trucks was on its way down. The men drove the trucks onto the docks, and Chubayev's crew, forming a fire line from the bottom of the gangplank to the cargo hold, started to unload.

When the last of the munitions were being loaded, Benny Rudolph, holding his gun on Arthur Brilovsky, disembarked from the ferry. The two men walked along the docks in the direction of the shack in which Chubayev and Paulie Sendak were holed up.

"He speak English?" Benny asked Brilovsky.

"Yes."

"Speak English so I know what's being said."

Brilovsky nodded. "But the men with the guns won't understand me unless I speak to them in Russian."

"Just keep in mind, I've got this gun aimed right at your back."

"I understand."

When the two armed men waiting outside the shack saw Benny and Brilovsky walking toward them, one of them knocked on the door to alert Chubayev, while the other placed himself between the men and the shack. Brilovsky raised his hands. "We're here to see Chubayev. Tell him it's Brilovsky."

The man at the door leaned his head into the shack for a moment. When he pulled his head out, he told the other man to stand away, and both men moved aside. Benny and Brilovsky walked in, followed by the armed men.

"Arthur," Chubayev said in Russian. "This is unexpected."

"What's going on?" Paulie Sendak asked. He looked startled and angered. His pockmarked face started to glow red.

Benny leaned over to Sendak. "Keep your mouth shut if you don't want to get yourself shot," Benny whispered. He then turned to Chubayev's hardened face. "There's been a change in plans."

Chubayev looked Benny over some, then, disregarding him, turned to Brilovsky. "What's happened?"

"In English," Benny said to Chubayev with a thin smile. "So I understand you."

Chubayev didn't avert his gaze from Brilovsky.

"They know where the transport ship is," Arthur said in English. "You mustn't go near it."

"They know I am here?"

Arthur nodded his head.

"How do they know this, Arthur?"

"I don't know how. We came to warn you."

Chubayev sucked on his teeth a little. "Who is this man you're with?" Chubayev asked in Russian.

"An old contact," Arthur responded in English. "He's all right. He was the one who came to me with this."

"And how did he come by this information?"

Arthur looked to Benny as though he were seeking his approval. Benny nodded a little, realizing he was meant to play along.

"He's inside the government," Brilovsky said.

"If they know I'm here," Chubayev continued in Russian, "they are out there, waiting for me."

"What did he say?" Benny asked.

Arthur ignored Benny and responded to Chubayev in Russian, "I don't know if they're out there, but it's very possible."

"In English," Benny said to Brilovsky.

"Why is this man so eager to understand everything I say?" Chubayev asked Arthur in Russian. "He doesn't trust you?"

Arthur looked at Benny, then back at Chubayev. "If he's seen here it could mean his life," Arthur responded in English. "He's nervous."

Chubayev looked at Benny and laughed at him. "But I am one in trouble. If you nervous, go," Chubayev said, pointing to the door. "You say what you have to say. Go."

Benny didn't move.

"What will you do?" Arthur asked Chubayev, trying to get his attention off Benny.

"We will go," Chubayev went on in English. "We will go. If need be," he said to Benny, "we fight. We have much to fight with, no?" He snickered at his men, then chewed on his tongue a little. Chubayev's men smiled with their captain, even though they didn't understand what he was saying.

"Nu, davai, tovarishchi," Chubayev said to his men as he walked to the door of the shack.

"Good luck, Grigori," Arthur said to Chubayev.

"Same to you, Arthur," Chubayev said in parting. He brushed against Benny's shoulder and walked out the door, his men trailing behind him. The cargo by now had been fully secured and the ship was ready to depart.

Benny, Arthur Brilovsky, and Paulie Sendak watched the men board the ship, and when Benny saw Chubayev and his men were safely away, he pulled out his gun and pointed it at Paulie. "Get moving," Benny said. "To the ferry landing."

"What's this all about?"

"Get moving," Benny said again. "You too," he said to Arthur as he waved the gun at him. "A government official?" he said to Brilovsky.

"He bought it, didn't he?"

"Jesus Christ."

"You mean, you ain't with the government?" Sendak said.

"Walk," Benny said.

Brilovsky and Sendak walked a few steps ahead of Benny in silence. When they reached the ferry, the ferryman was waiting beside the boat, drinking a cup of coffee. Benny told him to take them back to the city. He then marched Brilovsky and Sendak to the car, put them both up front, and took a seat in the back.

"What's next?" Arthur asked passively, his eyes looking at Benny in the rearview mirror.

"I'm thinking about it," Benny said.

"Will one of you tell me what's going on?" Paulie said again.

Benny turned his gun around in his hand and clocked Paulie in the back of the head.

"Just shut the fuck up," Benny said pensively. "Just shut the fuck up. Both of you, keep your traps shut until we get where we're going."

When Rudolph, Brilovsky, and Sendak reached the City, Benny ordered Brilovsky to drive across town through the park. Brilovsky drove them through a stone-walled passage that wound through the park's upper woods and dropped them onto Grand Avenue in the East End. They continued on to Shrine, then Halifax, then drove down Halifax to Seventy-eighth Street. Benny ordered Brilovsky to park the car off the corner of Seventy-eighth and Halifax and then ordered the two men out of the car.

"What are we doing here?" Brilovsky asked.

Benny didn't answer him. He opened the back door of the car

and stepped out onto the empty street, his gun at his side. He opened Brilovsky's door and stuck the gun in Brilovsky's ribs. "Let's go." He took hold of the collar of Brilovsky's coat and held on to it as Brilovsky slowly got out of the car. He kicked both doors closed and then walked to the other side of the car. "Open up," he said to Sendak.

Paulie Sendak pushed the door open and looked up to Benny pathetically. "Come on, already," Benny said when Paulie didn't move. He turned the gun from Brilovsky to Sendak. With his red pockmarked cheeks nearly dragging off his face, Sendak pushed his rotund body out of the car and stepped out onto a small embankment of snow that had been shoveled onto the walk. Benny let go of Brilovsky and placed Sendak alongside Brilovsky. "Through those doors."

An elderly doorman sat on a chair asleep in the lobby of the apartment building they entered. He came to in a sleep haze when Benny nudged his leg with his shoe. "Let's go," he said to the doorman, waving his gun in his direction. Once seeing the gun, the doorman's eyes were alert.

"Where to, mister?"

"Miss Rapaport's apartment."

"What business have you got with her?" the doorman asked the gun.

"Get the keys," Benny rasped.

Brilovsky turned his head over his shoulder slightly. "Rapaport?"

Benny didn't say anything.

"The reporter that wrote that bit about you in the paper this afternoon?"

"I didn't think you were paying attention," Benny said.

"I won't talk," Brilovsky said.

"You'll talk."

"If I talk, I'm as good as dead."

"If you don't talk, you're as good as dead."

"If you talk," Brilovsky countered, "you're as good as dead."

"I'm already dead, Mr. Brilovsky, if you haven't noticed."

"I ain't talking neither," Paulie Sendak said over his shoulder. "You got no right. I want a lawyer."

"I'll give you a lawyer," Benny said as he turned and angrily and forcefully knocked Sendak over the head with the butt of his gun again. To Benny's surprise, Sendak's legs fell out from under him and the man dropped to the floor. "Aw, shit," Benny said just as the doorman stepped up to Sendak's head with a clanging ring of keys. The doorman looked up to Benny with drooping bloodshot eyes. "All right," Benny barked, "the two of you, get him into the elevator."

Brilovsky bent down and took Sendak by the shoulders, the doorman took his legs, and together they dragged him into an open elevator. Benny shut the gate and the door and the doorman pressed number 6. Sendak started to groan a little when the elevator moved and had his hands on the back of his head by the time the elevator reached the sixth floor. Brilovsky and the doorman struggled the stout man onto his feet and wrapped his thick arms around their shoulders.

"Which door?" Benny asked.

"Right there, six oh three."

Benny knocked hard on the door. "Faith!" He waited a moment and knocked again. Benny ran through the key ring and found the key for Faith's door. He slipped it into the lock. "Get the light," he said to the doorman when he opened the door. Benny moved out of the way and the doorman and Brilovsky swung Sendak around and the doorman flipped a switch that lit a fixture in the corner of a simply decorated living room—worn couch and chair, lamp, bookcase, coffee table with nothing but ashtrays and a stack of newspapers. Benny marched the men through the small apartment, back through to the bedroom, where the doorman flipped on the light and all the men huddled around Faith's bed, where she was dead asleep. Benny found the half-filled glass of whiskey and the bottle of sleeping pills. He bent down and patted Faith's face. "Hey, kid," he said, "wake up. Faith, wake up. Come on, girlie, I got a big scoop for you. It's gonna knock your socks off."

Chapter 38

Before first light, Nicol and Byron Sands attached a plow to a tractor and plowed the Martins' private road that led to the country estate. They plowed a smooth flat path two miles long that ran to and from the train station. Celeste, Richard, Noel, and Steven rode the first train of the morning and were picked up by Byron in a school bus his father had hired from the nearby boarding school. Riding on the same train was an auctioneer hired from Leslie's; also from Leslie's were four art handlers; in the same car with the auctioneer and the art handlers rode the musicians, a string quartet, and the caterers from the Tea Room, seventeen men in total, eight waiters, three bartenders, two chefs, three line cooks, and a florist. They brought with them, from the finest markets in the City, crates full of oysters and cheeses, cured meats, wines and liquor, barrels full of hothouse lilies and orchids. When they all arrived at the estate, Dr. Gamburg and Professor Tarkhov were already awake and dressed; they were going over Dr. Gamburg's opening remarks. All the paintings had been hung in the gallery and were being watched over by Aleksandr and his son, Slava. A stage and chairs were set at the head of the gallery's partition, and on the stage was a lectern for the scholars and the auctioneer. Behind the lectern was a hand-carved rococo easel on which the art handlers would display each painting. Nicol's and Aleksandr's wives had already laid out on the mahogany banquet tables the silver and the china, the serving trays, all set before the windows that looked onto the sculpture garden. At public events such as this, Steven no longer played the function of cook, but rather took on the role of Celeste's keeper. At events such as this, he wore a fine hand-tailored suit, a boutonniere, and a monocle, and over his shoulder would hang a black leather purse that contained Celeste's pipe, her smoking opium, and massage oils. In the afternoon after the affair, Celeste and Steven would retire to her room, where Steven would undress her, rub her down, and then draw her a bath. As she bathed and smoked a pipe, he would sit by her side and, in his thick accent, read short passages from Proust's *Remembrance of Things Past,* until Celeste nodded off in the tub, at which time Steven would carry her off to bed, pat her dry with a pink towel, then dress her in her gown. He then cumbersomely laid her out on the couch, in front of a window that looked out onto the sculpture garden, and he would sit by her side. Together, the two of them would doze in and out of consciousness until the middle of the night. Sometime around one in the morning, he would carry her to her bed, at which point he would retire to his room.

No one who knew Celeste well expected anything more from her in her old age. She was notorious in her circle for abusing her fortune and all the freedoms that had come with it. Many said that both she and Richard were far too naive to be responsible for the amount of money they had inherited. Many speculated that Noel Tersi had taken control of her money from her many years ago and that if he hadn't come along when he had, she and her brother would have been destitute after the crash. Others, who didn't know Celeste, conjectured that she was more savvy than people gave her credit for being, and that Noel Tersi, who had been made the man he was by her charity and influence, was her instrument in the world of finance. The truth, of course, was that Celeste cared very little for money and power. All she cared about was living her life as she pleased. As long as she was allowed to behave as impulsively as she liked, she wasn't concerned about who was controlling her wealth. To both her and Richard, exercising power was a frivolous activity when more temporal and sensual activities could be had. As long as Richard had time to think and dwell in his moods, in his books, in his thoughts, he was happy to allow the responsibility of his position to fall onto the shoulders of someone who did care for that responsibility. He preferred that someone else be morally compromised by such behavior. He had always been too sensitive to dirty his hands with the harsh paradoxes of doing business. Even when he was out in the world, traveling from culture to culture, he always did his best to seek out tranquillity in nature, away from man, away from bazaars, away from war, away from any kind of commotion or upheaval that might require him to act. If he had had his life to live over, he would have spent it in a monastery, in a silent tomb.

The guests seemed to arrive all at once on the noon train. Byron made four trips with the bus to the station. Those who had to wait were accommodated with hot cider and crab cakes. When everyone reached the house, they ate and drank and chatted for the better part of an hour. Everyone seemed to know everyone. The crowd consisted of the moneyed, who came to bid, the hangers-on, who came to gawk and be part of the event, and the artists, writers, politicos, intelligentsia who came to see, in particular, Rodhinsky's long-hidden masterpiece. A dozen journalists, including a cameraman, were also in attendance. Arthur Brilovsky, to Professor Tarkhov's surprise, was curiously absent from the event. The professor was very anxious to receive word from Arthur about his wife and children. He had been calling the Ansonia all morning, but was told by the operator that Mr. Brilovsky had left his room early that morning with his bags, and that his wife and child had already gone out for breakfast. Dr. Gamburg had no knowledge of Arthur Brilovsky when the professor casually asked him if Arthur would be attending the event, and Noel Tersi, when asked if Mr. Brilovsky would be attending, said to Professor Tarkhov that perhaps he had been delayed, and with that said, Mr. Tersi, who appeared unusually anxious in Professor Tarkhov's company, conveniently excused himself to attend to his guests. The professor began to perspire, reliving the last moments he had spent with his family, and then started torturing himself with thoughts of them clandestinely crossing the Finnish border in the back of some freezing truck, wrapped in blankets with nothing more than the very things on their backs. As the lavish gallery became more and more full, the dread and loneliness and guilt that the professor felt were indescribable. He forced himself to be polite to a couple of elderly Russian exiles from noble families who had come to the city by way of Paris shortly after the revolution. Though they were pleasant and full of enthusiasm for the lecture the professor would give, he felt the great divide between himself and their former nobility. They had many questions for him about life in Leningrad these days, and then unabashedly reminisced about the former St. Petersburg, how they missed its beauty and grandeur, the canals and cathedrals, the concert halls and palatial gardens, and of course their homes. They envied the professor so for being able to walk along Nevsky Prospect, over the Neva, to the Admiralty, on his way to the university every morning. By the end of the conversation, the professor surprisingly felt disdain and contempt for these people and found himself sadistically wishing that these two, as pleasant as they were, hadn't escaped and had been forced to watch their home subdivided and their property usurped, to spend their lives in the company of peasants. Here they wore jewels and finery and attended parties at estates, maybe not in the style to which they were once accustomed, but, still, here, even without their wealth, they were able to pretend that their status was somehow equal to what it once had been, as if by their breeding alone they were worthy of being admired and celebrated. In Leningrad, the professor thought, they would be relics relegated to the propaganda machine, despised anachronisms in the mouths of young schoolchildren.

At one o'clock in the afternoon the guests were asked to take their seats, at which point Professor Tarkhov walked onto the stage with Dr. Gamburg and sat next to the veiled easel holding Evgeny Rodhinsky's *The Disappearing Body.* When everyone was seated, Dr. Gamburg approached the lectern and, on behalf of the Martins and Mr. Tersi, welcomed everyone. "This afternoon," Dr. Gamburg said to the audience, "it is my great pleasure to introduce you to one of the Soviet Union's foremost scholars of contemporary art, a man who has not only chronicled the history of painting over the past twenty years, but has witnessed it as it came to fruition. Professor Mikhail Tarkhov has traveled from Leningrad this past week to bring to you one painting in particular that has never been seen before in either the West nor the East—Evgeny Rodhinsky's *The Disappearing Body.*" Dr. Gamburg stepped back from the lectern and unveiled the painting. "*The Disappearing Body,*" the doctor continued as the guests craned their necks forward for a good look, "has been in the hands of an anonymous private collector, who, for reasons unknown to us, has entrusted this painting to Professor Tarkhov to be sold today at auction. As Professor Tarkhov will attest, it is a small miracle that this painting of Rodhinsky's has survived—because of its controversial content and because of the controversial figure that painted it. That we have the distinct privilege to look at it here today, and to hear the story of its making, makes this event a truly historic occasion. Without a doubt, whoever purchases this painting today will be acquiring nothing less than both an artistic and a historic treasure."

As Dr. Gamburg went on to cite Professor Tarkhov's credentials and list the articles he had written, Professor Tarkhov tried again to find Arthur Brilovsky in the crowd, but there was no sign of him. The professor's mind began to cloud with panic now, but when called to the lectern by Dr. Gamburg and the applause of the audience, he managed to clear his head enough to begin his lecture. He carefully tapped some crisp sheets of paper before him and smiled at the audience as best he could, looking over their distinguished-looking faces as he did so. "Evgeny Nikolayevich Rodhinsky," he began, "was born in 1888 to a bourgeois family in the town of

Tsarskoye Selo, not very far from the Summer Palace. His mother was a minor poet and his father was a political philosopher and schoolteacher." Professor Tarkhov went on to chronicle the rather unextraordinary childhood of Evgeny Rodhinsky and described the tenuous relationship he had to his rather conservative father, whose political philosophy supported the rule of the czars. "Rodhinsky, who took pains in his youth to travel the countryside to discover the real Russia, despised his father for his lack of understanding and for conceiving social philosophies based on knowledge no more extensive than his immediate surroundings and books and articles he had read. In his passion to find truth and understanding, in his attempt to connect with his people," Professor Tarkhov went on to explain, "Rodhinsky, who was an accomplished student of science in the gymnasium, ceased his studies and took up painting. He continued traveling the countryside, and while on the road, he painted the peasants at work. There are several sketches here from that early period," the professor noted to the guests. "You can see from these sketches that Rodhinsky was a natural. His lines are impeccable and his eye for detail is nothing less than that of a genius. Rodhinsky drew and painted what he saw," the professor continued, "in the style of the Renaissance masters. He was mostly concerned with the shape of the bodies he observed as they worked in the fields. In these early drawings and later the paintings made from these studies, you will always notice men and women bent and stooped, while at work and at rest; their skin is always baked from the sun; the young look nearly as old as the old. The landscapes are lyrical in their overall composition, but you will also notice, if you look closely, the rather benign-looking fields in all their earthen colors are jagged in shape, almost as though you are meant to look upon fields of broken glass. I believe it is in the shapes of the harvested crops, the crooked, bent shapes of the human figures working the fields, that we first see Rodhinsky, in a very naive and innocent state, move away from direct representation of the figures and the landscape before him and turn to more abstract geometric forms of representation. However, it isn't until the war, when Rodhinsky visits the front in uniform, that we see the most dramatic shift in his technique. While on the open battlefield all along the snowy tundra of the western border of Russia, Rodhinsky was stifled by what he saw—the broken, shattered, dismembered bodies of his comrades, the bins of discarded limbs in the field hospitals, meatless bones and splayed entrails of human beings—scattered about in the snow and ice. It has been said by his comrades that Rodhinsky, so fascinated and disturbed by the horror of the landscape, would wander off in the middle of heavy fighting and go in search of the worst carnage on the battlefield, and while under fire he would sketch what he saw. These sketches, a few of which also survive in this room, show the dramatic break that Rodhinsky makes from the strict realistic representation of his earlier works to a decidedly abstract form of representation. We see snow-white backdrops and dismembered human shapes verging on strict geometric forms. He would come to give these paintings very mundane titles, such as *Grenade Blast, Sniper Fire, Land Mine.* As Rodhinsky developed these themes, his earlier work was discovered by the new official artists of revolutionary Russia. When he returned from the war to an overturned St. Petersburg, he and his peasant paintings were already well known and in the cities instantly became emblematic of the struggle for emancipation. Rodhinsky had never been politically minded as much as he was reactionary. He was a revolutionary in the strictest sense, in that he believed in what he saw, and that if he could make others moved by what he saw, then he would inevitably alter the course of history. When the Communist Party first began using his paintings and the style of his paintings as weapons of propaganda, he was delighted to see the images he had struggled to create magnified. He soon gained popularity and fame, and for a time his face was one of the great faces of the revolution. He became known by everyone and was soon a folk hero in his own right, and with this status, he flowered as a man and was irrepressible in the company of Soviet leaders. Rodhinsky, however, true to his pursuit of truth in art, grew tired of 'the revolution' as agitprop, and over the course of several years after the civil wars and collectivization, he found himself reacting once again to the flaws he found in humanity. He was yearning for an all-encompassing sense of spirituality. He started researching ancient forms of mysticism, and inspired by religious and philosophical texts banned by the government, his painting became more abstract than ever, relying purely on line and form, color and texture. The cosmos and its vastness was his preoccupation now. This, of course, ran counter to what was expected by the state. Socialist realism had already become the primary function for art in the Soviet Union. Rodhinsky, by painting and showing his work publicly, by continuing to run against the accepted aesthetic of this time, was running perilously close to being arrested for, more than anything, his sheer arrogance. Rodhinsky knew this. He knew this, and this was the point of this work as far as he was concerned. His intent was to create a work so free that it couldn't possibly be undermined by propaganda. However, a very clever man running the Ministry of Culture, Sergei Varvarin, managed to find a way to incorporate the new style of Rodhinsky in such a way that it disparaged the form. He belittled it in posters for schoolchildren, denouncing Rodhinsky's freethinking as a provocative social disease whose inevitable outcome was to promote bourgeois individualism. The posters fashioned after Rodhinsky's designs, using the colors and textures of his paintings, were transformed into bacteria leaching away the life of healthy organisms represented as groups of cells in the body. This assault on his sensibility sent Rodhinsky into an inconsolable rage and in my estimation turned him insane. There is no saying what exactly was in Rodhinsky's mind, for no one that I know would risk talking with him at this point, but it seems evident from this painting that sits before you today what happened next. It is safe to say that he was spiritually defeated, that the image he had of a just society, the belief he had that revolution and radicalism would transform the world into a more enlightened, transcendent realm, was obliterated. Over the period of a few months, Rodhinsky shut himself away in his studio absolutely intent on creating a final work that would resonate with whoever beheld it. When traveling extensively in his youth, he spent some time on the Dalmatian Coast, where he apprenticed for a brief time in a small cathedral with a master builder, to learn about masonry. When his short apprenticeship was over, the builder gave him as a gift a pickax like that you see in the painting. According to one man who claims to have visited Rodhinsky one afternoon to drop off some books, Rodhinsky took the pickax and wedged it between two floorboards, and while painting, would stand before it, painting his studio. For two months or so, he meditated over this ax, its point always up, waiting for him. He painted himself into the image as you see here, and, as you can see, Rodhinsky has now returned to painting as he once did, in the style of the Renaissance masters, with clarity of detail so real and so precise you would think he had been painting this way all his life. Yet, if you look carefully at the windows, in the shadows of the windows, you will notice that there, in the windows' darkened stained glass, you will find the remnants of his entire career, dwarfed by the realism, the attention to corporeal form, the attention to perfect representation that he himself had inspired in the painters that started the socialist realism movement. And in the shadows of the windows, you can see, again in abstract form, the police outside the open windows coming for him. The night Evgeny Rodhinsky killed himself, he attended a party at the Ministry of Culture uninvited. He famously approached Sergei Varvarin and yelled at him, 'Form without meaning is not a hand, but an empty glove filled with air!' He admonished Varvarin for being a fool and a dimwit and condemned him and Stalin for the hands of tyranny they were using to suffocate the people's minds. He then stormed out of the party. He returned home and locked himself in with the finished painting, and then, as you see in this painting, with all his might, he threw himself down on the ax. Evgeny Nikolayevich Rodhinsky was forty-four years old. His body was discovered by the secret police who had come to arrest him. According to some accounts, the painting was already missing when the police arrived; according to other accounts, the painting was there, and one of the policemen was so moved by the painting he hid it and then spread rumors of Rodhinsky's death and what was found when the police arrived. Until now, the painting and Evgeny Rodhinsky's suicide were the stuff of legend, but now, I am moved when I say that the legend has come back to life to haunt us."

When Professor Tarkhov had thanked the audience for listening, he stepped back from the lectern to resounding applause. Dr. Gamburg returned to the lectern and thanked the professor for such an eloquent speech, and then started to introduce the auctioneer from Leslie's. *The Disappearing Body,* which would be the last painting auctioned that afternoon, was taken from the stage by two art handlers. A less important work was put in its place and the auctioneer, reading from Professor Tarkhov's notes, gave a brief description of the painting, which was already described in the catalog. Professor Tarkhov once again perused the audience for a sign of Arthur Brilovsky, but again, he was nowhere to be seen. It was then, as the professor's eyes roamed the room, that he noticed at the back doors of the gallery a group of men dressed in dark suits. The men entered the room and walked toward the stage. There were six of them in total. One announced, "Ladies and gentlemen, Department of Investigations. Please don't be alarmed. Please remain in your seats and don't interfere with our business." Two of the officers walked along the partition in the gallery, past the paintings, toward the stage. Professor Tarkhov remained seated. He was unable to move; his heart was beating so fast and his head was feeling so light he couldn't possibly lift himself from his seat.

"Professor Michael Tarkhov," one of the officers announced to the professor.

"Yes," the professor responded weakly.

"You are under arrest for espionage."

The professor looked puzzled. He couldn't say anything in response to this. The guests at the auction let out a collective gasp, and several started asking what the meaning of this was and how dared they treat a man of distinction this way.

"I don't understand," the professor said.

"Please come with us. All will be explained to you."

The professor willingly gave himself up. He rose to his feet and extended his hands. The officers took him by the arms and led him out of the gallery as the room erupted in boisterous discussion. As the professor walked with these men toward their cars, all he could think about was his wife and children. He wondered if his wife had ever received the telegram he had sent from Moscow. He wondered if she hadn't simply been told that he had been arrested as they initially thought. He suddenly had an image of his wife believing forever afterward that her husband was somewhere in a gulag. He hated himself for having embraced Arthur Brilovsky the day before. He couldn't for the life of him understand why he deserved this fate. He was a good man. He was a kind, sweet, gentle man. The thought of this alone, that this could happen to him, brought him such a great deal of misery.

Chapter 39

After Benny Rudolph bullied Arthur Brilovsky and Paulie Sendak into telling their stories to Faith early Saturday morning, he left them to the fates on the corner of Seventy-eighth and Halifax. Benny knew there was no one to whom he could hand them over without their ending up back in Tines's hands, so he just let them loose. The sun was rising as he drove home to the Belvedere Arms to collect the records he had kept of his relationship with Tines. He planned on picking up the small bundle of notes and dropping it in the safety deposit box at International Trust Bank. Because he hadn't slept, his lungs were tired and heavy, and when he reached his room, he started spitting up heavy clots of blood. He worked quickly to gather the scattered papers that lay around the room. He folded them neatly into a nice package, jotted a short note to Faith telling her where she could find him if she needed him, and then stuffed all into an envelope. He placed the thick envelope inside his coat pocket and, leaving everything else behind, made his way out to the street. When he stepped out of the building's lobby, it came as no surprise to him that from his left and his right converged the two grizzled men, who took him by the arms before he saw them coming.

In many ways, Benny was grateful when his two colleagues took hold of him. Their grasp was reassuring. "Relax," Sunshine said to him congenially. Benny, taking his advice, relaxed. And in this relaxed state, the three men, arm in arm, took a pleasant walk. The sky was clear and the air was crisp, and Benny had always wanted to die out of doors. Securely fixed in the grizzled men's arms, he found that the lives of the men in Long Meadow, the truth, principles of justice and injustice, mattered very little. He wasn't so arrogant as to think knowledge of his deeds would help or hinder the state of the world or the state of his eternal soul. He was at peace with himself now and understood that had he not exacted his revenge, no matter what the cost, he wouldn't have been able to die feeling so at ease. He had successfully purged himself of his rage, and it was worth all the wrongdoing. For better or worse, his spirit had been cleansed.

The boys were kind enough to ask Benny where he would like to go. Benny wanted to sit by the river and watch the current of the water pass before him. He wanted to see the ships drifting toward the sea. He wanted to sense the open space before him and have his back to the City. He hated the idea of dying in the City. He hated the grid of its streets, the way the tall buildings dampened the sunlight; he hated the way the wind channeled through its canyons. He hated the obstructions. If he had had his choice, he would have hired a boat and sailed out the Narrows to the open waters and he would have waited until there was nothing but water surrounding him.

But Benny Rudolph would have to settle for the riverside, for a view of it through a chain-link fence behind some kid's pigeon coop. The two grizzled men sat him down on a wooden crate covered in snow, so he could enjoy watching the passing tugs and freighters. Sunshine asked Benny if he would put up a fight, and Benny said he wouldn't. So Sunshine walked behind Benny, and, holding the knife he kept sheathed on his leg, Sunshine held Benny's forehead with his hand and pressed the back of Benny's greasy pomaded hair against his coat, and with one precise cut he slit the artery in Benny's neck.

As the black liquid ran down Benny's chest and pumped out onto his feet and onto the snow, Sunshine held Benny's head up as a mother would hold the head of a newborn babe. Benny and the two grizzled men watched the boats. They watched the boats and they watched the river adrift with ice. Benny watched the frozen river and he dreamed of the sea. He dreamed of the sea, and no sooner did he dream of the swirling sea than he was dead. And when he was dead, each of the grizzled men gave Benny a sympathetic pat on the chin. They then opened the kid's pigeon coop and threw Benny inside.

Chapter 40

The night before, Freddy spent a long time walking around the park after leaving Stu Zawolsky at the Revolver. He walked along the edge of the lake, over the hills, through the wooded paths. As the storm pushed out over the ocean, heavy gusts of wind blew snow crystals from the branches of the trees. They drifted through the air, lit up like fireflies as they passed under the park's lamps. Freddy crossed the great lawn, feeling the invisible contours of the ground on his feet. He tried to imagine what the park would look like in the spring bloom, the daffodils, the tulips, the cherry blossoms, the dogwood, the magnolia, how when the trees' leaves sprouted from their buds, they looked like burgeoning heads of cabbage. But as he saw this in his mind, the trenches and the battlefields appeared as well, the bodies piled one on top of the other as far as the eye could see, arms and heads and legs and chests, decomposing in piles of flesh and bone on top of clusters of dirt and rock, amid shovels and barbed wire and unexploded mortars and unexpressed screams on the stiff faces of the dead. However much time passed, the bodies would always be visible silhouettes in the most beautiful things in Freddy Stillman's mind. They would always shadow his most pleasurable thoughts and fill them with dread and fear; they would inhabit the very concept of love and fill it full of suspicion.

As time slowed, slower than Freddy's heartbeat, slower than the most instant flash of thought, Freddy could feel the most internal part of himself shutting down like a turbine with nothing to make it flow. It was early in the morning when Freddy returned home. The dark sky over the river faded with shafts of sunlight. At the top of his stoop, he removed from his coat the envelope containing the letter to Evelyn and his insurance policy, and he dropped the envelope in the mailbox. Freddy then went inside. He hung his coat on the rack beside the door, went to the bathroom, and, as best as he could, washed away the scabs of blood left by Gloria Lime's hands. He then sat at his kitchen table and tried to find the image in his mind of Evelyn. He tried to see Evelyn and her child walking through the park in the spring.

Freddy died at eight-thirty in the morning, not at eleven as he had planned. For several hours, he sat at his table, looking at his hands, looking at the contours of his thumbs, at the hair on his knuckles, the bulges in his palms. He knew nothing of palmistry, but he wondered if anyone were to read his palm it could be seen that what he had planned for himself was inevitable. He wasn't much of a believer in God, but as he sat at his kitchen table he wanted to be comforted by some sort of faith. All he could find in his mind was Evelyn, she and her boy walking hand in hand through the park.

Freddy began teetering on the edge of himself. The violence that he knew would soon be done to him started to inhabit his mind, and all he could think of was the faceless German soldier he had killed so many years ago and the exultation he had felt when he unloaded his gun into his face. He felt joy when he released the rounds from his pistol into the man's face, an ecstasy so complete that it had shadowed his entire sense of himself for all his life after that moment. As he sat there, meditating on his death, Freddy felt that God was present that day in the French countryside, inside the chamber of his gun, his love, God's love, inside every granule of gunpowder igniting his rage.

Freddy Stillman, this inert object of a man, this vacuum of a human being, this sad mess of emotions, knew more than ever that he wanted to die, so badly he was unwilling to wait until eleven o'clock. So he stood up from the kitchen table. He went into his bedroom and started to fashion a noose out of sheets.

Before Freddy could finish his noose, however, at eight-thirty in the morning, there was a soft knock on his door. Freddy listened to the knock. He listened to the knock, trying to decide if he should answer it. Dragging his sheets across the floor like a child dragging its favorite blanket, he inched his way to the knock, closer and closer, until his cheek was pressed up against the door. "I hear you in there," a voice said calmly. "I hear you as plain as day." When Freddy heard the voice, as though it were the voice of God himself, he slowly undid the lock and pulled the door open to find standing before him the disheveled figure of Sidney Lardner pointing a gun at Freddy's chest. Freddy stood there with a quizzical look on his face and watched with curiosity as Sidney angrily and lovingly unloaded a chamber of the gun into Freddy's gut. Freddy felt the bullet puncture his body like a hot fist of steel. The pain was unimaginable at first, but then it quietly eased and Freddy realized that the blast had thrown him down to the floor. Without really knowing why, Freddy struggled to lift himself up to his feet. Sidney's face had been thrown into a spasm from the first shot, and he shot at Freddy again. In his herky-jerky rage, he only grazed Freddy's shoulder this time. Freddy opened his arms and leaned forward in Sid's direction as the third shot sounded. This bullet entered Freddy's chest; it ricocheted about his ribs and planted itself directly in his heart. Freddy now found himself lying on his side, staring into one of the muddy pastel watercolors of Celeste Martin's country property. He could feel his injured heart trying to beat, to pass blood around the wedge of metal. But Freddy could no longer breathe. His body struggled, but his mind was focused on the painting, on the pastel clouds billowing in the sunlight.

. . .

Sidney turned cold from the absurd reality of murder as Freddy, who after being jolted by the shot in the chest fell forward and, for a brief moment, took hold of Sidney's body in a bear hug. The two men awkwardly danced a few steps into the living room. When Freddy fell to the floor, when Sidney realized that his clothes were wet and sticky from Freddy's black sludge, Sidney, feeling a surge of panic, anxiously fired two more shots into Freddy, one in his leg, the other in his neck. The shock of what he had done started to become real to Sid. For an instant, in this drunk rage of his, he could see through the eyes of Victor Ribe standing over his brother's body, and with that image in his mind, Sidney, drenched in blood, grabbed Freddy's coat, and with a hysterical gait ran out of Freddy's apartment, down Eighty-third Street toward the water, where he ripped off his blood-drenched clothes and threw them into the river.

When Stu Zawolsky arrived at eleven o'clock, he was a little confused. He didn't know exactly what to do. But then something came over Stu Zawolsky: a feeling that he owed something to Freddy. So, according to Freddy's wishes, Stu stood over Freddy's dead face and emptied six rounds into it. Stu Zawolsky then casually walked out onto the street and headed in the direction of the park.

Moments before Chief Investigator Tines went down to the Civic Center's press gallery to deliver his statement, Freddy's body was discovered by the two grizzled men, who, after murdering Benny Rudolph, arrived at Freddy's apartment to kill him. They phoned the chief from Freddy's kitchen, and Lawrence Tines, upon hearing the news, sent two officers to arrest Freddy. The two officers, of course, found Freddy dead and called the Medical Examiner's Office. When the medical examiner's men arrived, they laid

Freddy out on a stretcher and drove him to the morgue downtown and set him inside the drawer next to Benny Rudolph's body, which had been discovered in the pigeon coop by a twelve-year-old boy. The boy, whose family was destitute, and whose poverty was so severe he had no fear of Benny's corpse, looted Benny clean. He took from his wrist his watch, from his pants a small roll of bills and his sterling-silver money clip, and from his jacket the notes Benny had intended for Faith Rapaport. He then called the police.

Chapter 41

Faith Rapaport woke from a deep sleep as she felt someone gently patting her face and calling her name. When she opened her eyes, she found Marty Volman standing over her. She had fallen asleep on the sofa in what was now his former office after she had stayed up all night taking down Brilovsky's, Sendak's, and Rudolph's stories.

"Tired?" Marty asked.

"I had some late-night visitors. Found them huddled around my bed like lost children."

"Jonesy gave me a call and told me all about it."

"They spent the night. Spilled their guts with Rudolph's gun to their heads."

"You didn't mention that in your story."

"No."

"Why not?"

"Because I believed Rudolph had the truth behind him is why not, and I don't like being manipulated. Especially by the likes of Tines. . . . Has the paper gone out yet?"

"It's on its way."

"Good. What time is it?"

"Just after noon."

"Why didn't Jonesy wake me?" she said, getting to her feet.

Marty took her by the shoulders and sat her back down. "He tried. He couldn't get you up."

"I missed Tines's press conference."

"Don't worry, I covered it for you."

"No kidding—you went in there all on your own?"

"I got a few cold shoulders, a few evil eyes . . ." Marty twisted his face and looked away from Faith for a second.

"What you find out?"

"The munitions got away."

"For certain?"

"According to Tines."

"And who's getting the blame?"

"Waters and Capp, and some other union men. About a dozen of them were arrested this morning, all of whom were apparently in the company of Paulie Sendak last night on the docks when the armory was cleaned out. Waters and Capp between them supposedly had a small fortune on them when they were taken in."

"And where's Sendak?"

"In protective custody."

"I'm surprised Rudolph let him go before he could turn him in."

"A regular hero Sendak is for coming forward and agreeing to snitch out the fellow travelers, Tines said. . . . Who would Rudolph have turned Sendak and Brilovsky in to if he'd had the chance? Why do you think he went to you?"

Faith nodded her head a little.

Marty took a pad out from his jacket pocket and flipped it open. "Freddy Stillman, a Fief dispatcher who acquisitioned the order," he went on, "was assassinated in his apartment by, I quote, 'communist operatives'; when Tines's men showed up to arrest him his body was riddled with bullets. A Professor Mikhail Tarkhov, who apparently came under the cover of art historian to help sell a collection of valuable Soviet paintings for Tersi, was arrested on charges of espionage, and was made out to be the primary Soviet operative who masterminded the plot."

"What else?"

"According to Tines, Noel Tersi, having arranged for Tarkhov's visa into the country, felt responsible for what had happened, and so, in turn, offered Fief his newly acquired Southside Docks to work from."

"Just as Brilovsky said it would be." Faith groped for a pack of cigarettes she had left on the arm of the sofa, knocked one out, and lit it. "Tines is going to regret bringing this out into the open," she said, jabbing the lit cigarette at Marty's pad.

"I'm not so sure, Faith," Marty said.

"What do you mean?"

"What I mean is that Tines, on top of briefing everyone on Long Meadow, also briefed everyone on the progress he was making with the syndicate investigation he took over from Shortz."

"Yeah, and . . ."

"Not that I can say how this will affect what's about to hit the streets, cupcake, but . . ."

"What is it, Marty?"

"Benny Rudolph is lying dead down in the morgue."

"When did that happen?"

"Early this morning."

"He left my apartment early this morning."

"According to Tines, it was a gangland revenge killing for Rudolph's arranging Mann and Roth's murder."

"Where was he found?"

"Down by the docks in a pigeon coop with his throat cut. Some kid found him."

"At least he managed to wound Fief before he got it." Faith was quiet for a moment. "What about Brilovsky?"

"No mention of him."

"Did you ask?"

"He didn't take any questions."

"So he's got everything covered then."

"Not everything. There's still you, your story. A lot of people are going to believe it, Faith."

"Yeah, but without the sources around it just doesn't come off, does it?"

Marty shrugged his shoulders. "It may make it blow over for now, but as you and I both know, you can't cover your tracks forever."

Faith looked deeply into Marty's sagging eyes. "I just hope it happens before we kick over."

"Have a little faith," Marty said with a grin.

Faith grinned back superficially, then made her exit.

Faith grabbed a copy of the afternoon edition at the newsstand in the lobby of the Globe Building, then headed down into the subway. She rode an uptown train into East End and headed over to Harry Shortz's home. She stood outside for a long while, wondering what she was doing there. She removed a pen from her pocketbook and wrote above the masthead of the paper, *Don't give up on the race. I'll write your side of things. Front page. Let's talk. —Faith Rapaport.* She walked up to the Shortzes' stoop, slipped the paper through the mail slot of the front door, and walked into the shadows in the direction of the park.

Chapter 42

When Victor Ribe woke up that Saturday morning inside Fuller House, the dark mood that had consumed him the night before had waned. The early-morning sun broke through the dirty narrow window of his room and dappled his body in a warm yellow light. The bruises on his face had started to fade and the swelling around his nose was hardly perceptible anymore. He lay in bed, watching haze and dust envelop his arms and legs, and he could see through the window a gray seagull perched on an ivy-entwined cross above the stone chapel of the old mariners' cemetery. He watched as the bird opened its wings into the wind. Without the slightest effort, it was lifted from its perch, where it hovered motionless in midair, looking as though it were staring down upon Victor. With a short twist of its neck it was raised into the sky and spiraled above the rooftop. Victor sat up on the edge of the bed and watched the gull gracefully fly in his direction with the sun to its back; its white belly flew upward at a steep angle and drifted out of sight.

The city was waking up as Victor left Fuller House for the last time. The streets were whitewashed in snow. The wind was frigid, but the air was warming to the point that by noon the snow would start melting. Merchants shoveled storefronts and streets, making way for customers and pushcarts. Trucks silently motored by, their heavy tires cutting ruts in the serene white blanket. Small children, who had been out with the first light, were building snow forts in alleyways, stockpiling snowballs. Victor walked in the street in the shin-deep snow, able to smell the furnace fires burning out the chimneys. The tinctured smell of burning coal singed the inside of his nose in the crisp air. He carried with him the deed to his father's home in Long Meadow, a set of house keys, and a bank book marked for one thousand dollars. He walked to the river with his hands in his pockets and followed the line of freighters and tugs northward, uptown. He watched the large ships offset the snow-heavy ice and for a long while he watched the spectacle of a boat being launched out of the naval yard on Conscript Island. He was just in time to see the immense battleship roll off its planks and its bow splash into the river. He could hear the roar of a crowd assembled and could sense the pride and glory that it held for them.

When he reached midtown, he worked his way back into the shade of the streets and boulevards, and as he had done every day since he was set free, he sat in the lobby of the Ansonia Hotel, where he kept to himself, watching the people come and go. Sometime between eight-thirty and nine, Joshua and someone who Victor could only assume was Arthur Brilovsky exited the elevator with a bellhop. Joshua, his eyes misting with tears, walked alongside Arthur to the hotel's entrance, where Joshua embraced his father and appeared to have a difficult time letting go. Victor watched as the bellhop loaded Arthur's bags into a limousine carrying a blond woman wearing an expensive-looking blue hat. Arthur kissed his son on the cheek, looked into his eyes for some time, and then stepped into the car, giving the woman a long kiss on the mouth. Joshua, his head bent low, his eyes now wet, returned to the lobby and went back upstairs.

Victor wanted to follow Joshua into the elevator; instead he went to the concierge's desk and phoned Elaine. When Elaine answered the call, Victor could sense that she too had been crying.

"Should I come at another time?" Victor asked.

"No," Elaine said. "I think Joshua and I could use some company this morning. We'll be down in a little while," she said. "Please, wait for us."

Victor wanted to say that he had been waiting nearly half his life for this. "I'll be right here," Victor said.

An hour later, Elaine, holding Joshua by the arm, walked out of the elevator. Holding on to his mother as he did, Joshua no longer looked as fragile as he had just moments ago. He now appeared self-possessed, with a look of self-assurance Victor had never known within himself. Aside from Elaine's dark eyes, he was undoubtedly the physical likeness of Victor in his youth; but Joshua's confidence, his obvious intelligence, gave Victor pause as to how he should try to relate to his son. In that brief walk from the elevator to Victor, Victor wanted more than anything to prove to Joshua that he was worthy of his mother's company and deserving of Joshua's respect.

"This is Victor Ribe," Elaine said to Joshua.

Victor stood up as straight as he could and extended his hand as he searched Joshua's face for some sign of recognition.

Joshua took Victor's hand and keenly studied his bruised face. "Mother's told me a great deal about you," he said.

"We read about you in the paper last night," Elaine added as she greeted Victor with a warm kiss on the cheek.

Victor didn't know what to say. He couldn't imagine what Elaine could have said to him.

"I was thinking," Elaine said, taking hold of Victor's arm now, "that we could ride the ferry to Long Meadow this morning. To show Joshua where we grew up."

"I'm afraid the town has changed since you were last there."

"I was thinking we could take a picnic to the Palisades, take a walk in the snow. I understand the Palisades have gone untouched."

"They're as beautiful as ever," Victor said.

"Good. It's decided then."

"We have a car in a garage down the block," Joshua said.

"I haven't driven a car in a long time," Victor said. "I'm not sure if I should try on a day like today."